PRAISE FOR **DAVID J. SCHOW**

"By virtue of being smart, scathing, and verbally inventive to an astonishing degree, David J. Schow distinguished himself early on as one of the most interesting writers of his generation."

— Peter Straub

"[David J.] Schow is so fine a writer, so imaginative a storyteller, that he deserves a place in all contemporary fiction collections."

— *Library Journal*

"Take-no-prisoners fiction that rarely pulls away from the grisly heart of the matter, Schow's prose is extremely cinematic, filled with pungent dialogue, sharp, memorable characters, and a sense of macabre irony worthy of Alfred Hitchcock."

— *San Francisco Chronicle*

© BRIAN DOUGLAS

about the author

DAVID J. SCHOW

is a multimedia writer whose work includes the script for the dark cult classic, *The Crow*. His award-winning short stories are featured in dozens of anthologies and collected in the volumes *Seeing Red*, *Lost Angels*, *Black Leather Required*, *Crypt Orchids*, *Eye*, *Zombie Jam* and the forthcoming *Havoc Swims Jaded*. He is also the author of *The Outer Limits Companion* (on the classic TV series) and a critically acclaimed book of essays on modern media, *Wild Hairs*. He lives in Los Angeles, California.

To receive notice of author events and new books by David J. Schow, sign up at www.authortracker.com.

● ● ● also by DAVID J. SCHOW

novels

THE KILL RIFF

THE SHAFT

ROCK BREAKS SCISSORS CUT

story collections

SEEING RED

LOST ANGELS

BLACK LEATHER REQUIRED

CRYPT ORCHIDS

EYE

ZOMBIE JAM

HAVOC SWIMS JADED (forthcoming)

as editor

SILVER SCREAM

THE LOST BLOCH, Vols. I–III

ELVISLAND by John Farris

nonfiction

THE OUTER LIMITS COMPANION

WILD HAIRS (essays and columns)

DAVID J. SCHOW

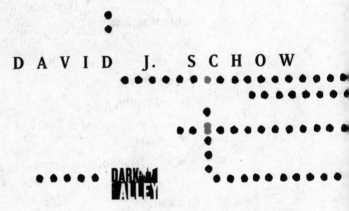

An Imprint of HarperCollins*Publishers*

bullets of rain

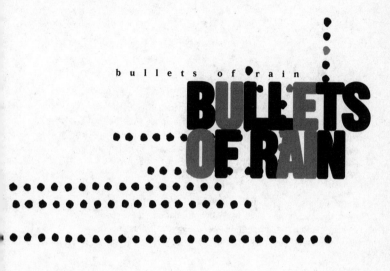

BULLETS
OF RAIN

HarperCollins books may be purchased for educational, business, or sales promotional use. For information please write: Special Markets Department, HarperCollins Publishers Inc., 10 East 53rd Street, New York, NY 10022.

FIRST EDITION

Designed by Shubhani Sarkar

Library of Congress Cataloging-in-Publication Data

Schow, David J.
    Bullets of rain / David Schow.—1st ed.
        p.   cm.
    ISBN 0-06-053667-5
        1. California—Fiction.   2. Recluses—Fiction.
    3. Storms—Fiction.   I. Title.

PS3569.C5284B85 2003
813'.54—dc21

2003048875

03 04 05 06 07 WBC/RRD 10 9 8 7 6 5 4 3 2 1

for everyone who complained
that I'd never do the novel thing
again. thanks for reading.

BULLETS
OF RAIN. . .

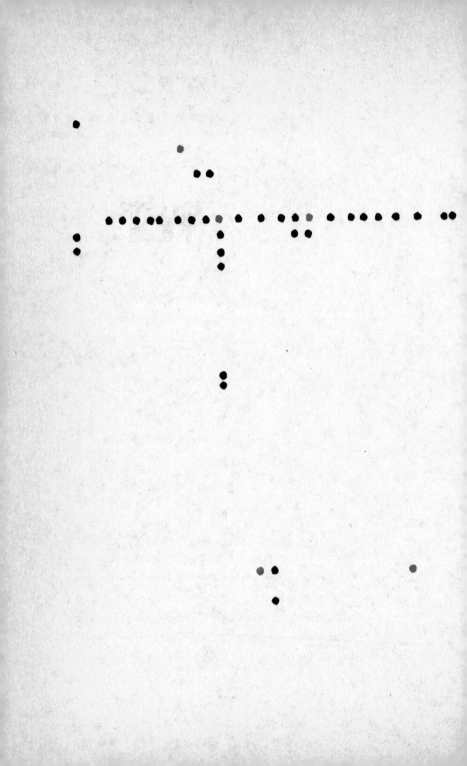

THURSDAY

Art did not care exactly which day it was. Dawn had sneaked up behind his home, vermilion and gorgeous, but he missed it. Specific dates, and chronological time itself, were demoted in importance; irrelevant. Time passed in terms of work, meals, diversions, stacked-up phone messages (mostly unreturned), sunrise, sunset, and airing out Blitz for exercise. Days blurred together, except for that little extra bit on Thursdays, of course.

He polished off his usual double-sized mug of cappuccino, double strength, as the sun climbed and fought to penetrate the overcast. Then he installed into his metabolism a pint of juice laden with a zillion times the minimum adult daily requirement of vitamin C. This invested him with the will to face his daily assessment in the mirror; shower or not? He gave it a miss. Blitz intruded, sniffed him, and made Art reconsider.

Blitz was an Alsatian-Dobie mix who had essentially flunked out of police dog school and wandered into Art's stewardship two doggie steps shy of German Shepherd Rescue. His lines were straight and level and fortunately free of the potential for hip dysplasia that often plagued purebreds. He had been taught to respond to a few commands spoken in German, a conceit Art rather enjoyed, since it was colloquial, not the sharp-edged K-9 monosyllables favored by

1

the canine gladiator academies. Blitz decided which commands were obeyed, or ignored, with an endearing sort of canine resolve that probably made perfect sense in dog-logic.

"Komm her!" Art shouted, down-beach. Blitz duly galloped forth in a scatter of sea-spray and salty sand.

Thursday's extra adventure was the mail.

Art's mail was delivered to a Mail Boxes Etc. branch in San Jose. Once a week, the manager, an energetic power cell of a woman named Keiko Nakamura, bundled the catch and next-dayed it to the rural box near the turnoff from the highway to Art's home. The red, white, and blue tearproof package generally arrived heavy with catalogs and junk. Art enjoyed riffling his mail, a week's worth at a time, seeking the small, interesting exceptions like treasure: Mom sometimes sent cards from Louisiana, always expressing the same concern and never forgetting to mention the weather—another anachronistic holdover from a time when people who had nothing to talk about still engaged in written correspondence. It struck Art as quaint; he did not wish to change the way his mother did anything. Sometimes birthday greetings arrived, and they always shocked him, because he had stopped keeping track of his birthdays. As years passed, those annual howdy-doos had dwindled to about five dogged friends and two ex-lovers. He had not received (or solicited) an actual gift in over a decade. Bills, or anything with a cellophane window, went into a separate pile to ignore until Art's once-per-month check-writing sessions. He refused to permit creditors to dominate any more of his time. Trying to stay ahead of the streamlined, mechanized assault of bills was like treading water with a cinderblock tied to each leg, a loser's game. Art tamed his bills by allowing them one evening per month, no more, no matter how urgent they claimed to be. It was a small gesture of defiance, and a pointless one, but it appealed to his sense of control. He

2

occasionally purchased odd or obscure books, trinkets, or toys from online auctions, and when these arrived he always saved them till last, savoring their tiny revelations as though he had not expected to receive them. They did not count as gifts.

The mailbox was at a five-minute walk from the house. It was fifteen inches tall, all metal, and not mailbox-shaped. Two keys; Art had one; his mail carrier, a civil yet befuddled fellow named Mr. LeBow, was caretaker of the other. There was no flag on the box, and no giveaway nameplate. Art preferred the small delight of opening the hatch, every Thursday, and "discovering" the packet there.

The bundle was thin and weightless this week, bound with consumer flotsam by a fat USPO rubber band. A sheet of white paper had been deformed into the back of the mailbox—most likely shoved in through the narrow top slot by some passerby prior to the mail delivery. Art drew it out and flattened it. PARTY, it proclaimed in huge block letters.

There was a hand-drawn map of the coast road. If the page had been legal-sized, he thought, there would have been enough room to depict the distance to his own home, to scale, and he thought contemptuously that most people needed to learn what a ruler was. The directions indicated the residence a half mile to the south of his own. There was a handwritten notation in the lower left: HOWDY NEIGHBOR! DON'T BE A STRANGER! DROP BY AND SAY HELLO! It was signed *Michelle*. Some sort of celebration was due to commence at 6 P.M. tonight, and last until ?????

"Blitz, get your ass back here." It was one of the few English phrasings Blitz had doped out; otherwise it was *beweg' deinen Arsch hier rüber*. The dog tore himself away from whatever fascinating dead thing he had found to smell, and delivered his dog buns hence, to await the next diversion.

Art decided to make the short hike to the Spilsbury house, which he knew to be storm-girded, therefore currently tenantless. He could barely see it. A persistent, thick roll of ocean mist was clogging the air. Up above, somewhere, was the sun. The house beyond Spilsbury's, the one pinpointed by the flyer, was not visible, already lost in a ghostly limbo of drifting mist banks. Art was curious as to whether there was also a flyer lodged in Spilsbury's box, even though nobody would be home there until next May.

If he found one, he intended to crumple it up, too.

● ● ● Arthur Latimer had originally constructed his Point Pitt house for his wife, Lorelle. Panoramic ocean frontage based on a design of slanted aluminum beams incorporating a forward-thinking stormwatch durability. Teak decks blended into shatterproof polymer windows, the architecture anticipating a hellacious Pacific blow. The curvature and wind-deflection schema were derived from geodesic domes used in the Arctic, to protect radar and microwave dishes in high winds at more than a hundred degrees below zero Fahrenheit. It had cost Art a bunch of glass to rethink the windows into their current pyramidal layout, but once he'd nailed it, he won a feature spread in *Architectural Digest,* plus a couple of trophies.

His specialty was rethinking space in terms other than square feet. His designs had replaced everything from the Mondrian glass boxes of the 1960s to the forsaken strip malls of the 1980s, and always in an unpredictable way, sometimes incorporating bits and pieces of a place's original layout into its retrofit, the way rich Victorians used to pay to have "ruins" constructed on their manicured grounds. Backers became enthusiastic, and began to dole out, big-time.

Another conquered beast on his trophy wall was a new attack

4

on residential solar power systems. He configured an overlapping disk network that followed the natural arc of the sun phototropically, like a flower, having gotten the inspiration after staring abstractedly at a pile of CDs near his stereo. The idea was nothing new, but his containment frame attracted immediate notice—he blueprinted an innovative way to conceal the array so that it didn't resemble most solar panels, which usually looked like a collapsed dinosaur skeleton on the roof of a house. An energy corporation named Daystar had picked up the R&D tab, and, as a cookie, comped him the hardware for bug testing. The inset steel frame featured eight inches of insulation through which water could be cycled for "smart" heating or cooling, based on a computer-generated weather map of the region. So far the system had outperformed Art's usual specs, which he always biased toward the conservative. He had not yet stress-tested the network's reserve power capacity because he was still awaiting delivery of the storage cells—the "battery" part of the active system. Big enameled gray racks built into the south wall of the garage waited empty, thanks to the usual urban delays and excuses. Art relished the idea of independence from electricity monopolies, which were becoming top-heavy and cost-prohibitive in California with the virulence of a plague. Once the cells were installed, he'd be a tiny bit freer. Soon, but not today.

Art's latest challenge was to create a commercial "dining complex" for high-end restaurants that looked like something other than a jumped-up food court, which is what it essentially was. The target clientele was people who wanted the same round-robin selection in eateries that they were accustomed to from multiplex theaters—if you're five minutes late for one show, pick another. Round-shouldered from malls, this imaginary demographic nonetheless insisted on completely secure shopping, entertainment, and eating "experiences." They feared crime and sought hermetic enclosure . . . but without feeling trapped. Their illusion of free will had been shaved down to a choice they could handle—usually which credit card would pay for the meal, since one must always be seen conspicuously advantaging a respectable piece of plastic. Gimmicky Vegas-style and amusement park restaurants had had their day. Consumers were hip to the hollow con of it all, and that meant a new con was required, and the promise of upscale respectability was the best con of all.

Art had been vetted onto the gig at the urging of Alex Street, a former partner in his old design firm who had talked Art up to the financiers. Another favor owed into the to-do file, Art thought. He scooped up the assignment for an outrageous advance, set his own schedule, and was now holed up in his secluded eyrie, awaiting the coming of miracles, and deploying every conceivable excuse to dodge actually devoting any hard pencil time to the damned thing. The sun rose and set while the army-ant march of checkup phone calls dwindled. Art walked his dog. Blitz loved any excuse for extra dog-fun. The work continued to confound him. What had seemed effortless before became forced and impenetrable, like the abrupt discovery that you have forgotten or misplaced the ability to speak a foreign language you thought you knew. Somehow, an essential capacity had evaporated, erecting a wall between Art and his life's work; lost while he slept, perhaps, or diminished in the demarcation between his married life and the life he had now.

Lorelle, for anybody who wanted to know, was three years dead. Therefore, the story went, she'd never gotten to see the complete retrofit of the house. Her death had been ugly, pointless, and pro-longed—the heartbreaking kind, the kind that disallowed detail to outsiders or prying minds. Art managed his grief but was still fright-eningly susceptible to being throttled by it at the weirdest times. Perhaps it would be better for him to swallow the feelings, bury the

6

past, break the connections, and sell the house . . . but he never made it to that fourth step. It meant picking up the phone and initiating a long and eroding sequence of business events. So far he'd kept from making the first call and setting that engine in motion.

Two hundred yards to the north was a stone jetty composed of shattered granite, delivered to the location several times a year by a stonemason in San Jose. The guy's truck proclaimed him to be one of the Sons of Chispa Verdugo Villa, the company specialty being grave monuments. Leftovers, bad cuttings, and failed tombstones made up the jetty, which curved far out into deep water, a crooked, pointing finger of rock. At its terminus was a gigantic military microwave dish, its convex ear usually targeted straight up, like a birdbath stopover for Roc-sized mythological predators. At different times, Art thought it resembled a huge sundial, which is what he generally called it. It was engirded by hurricane fence, razor wire, posted warnings. He'd never seen any staff or service guys, if there were any. Local scoop had it that a lighthouse had once occupied the spot. That was irresistibly romantic, and Art had sketched it more than once. He loved the idea of its beam circling far above his home, cutting some storm.

His nearest neighbor was the Spilsbury place, built on the adjacent property sometime in the 1970s, a more classic sort of timbered beach house on stilts and pilings. It sat closer to the highway; Art had given his own place a long and nonlinear driveway on purpose—an S-shaped double switchback that permitted distance and foliage to obscure the road over there . . . somewhere. The Spilsbury place was boarded up for the winter.

Past that was the party house, half a mile downbeach, give or take. Half a mile was approximately 2,640 feet, or almost nine football fields; half a klick and change, or 160 rods, if you wanted to get totally ridiculous about it. Art didn't know much about the place

7

except that it was slightly more modern that Spilsbury's, with a big show-off glass turret pointed toward the sea. It was usually a shadow in the mist, indistinct even when he peeked, using his telescope, from his own west deck. Lights had recently become visible at night. Somebody was there, right now, broadcasting occasional life signs without detail. No strays had yet wandered as far as the jetty.

High tide brought the Pacific Ocean swells to within eighty yards of where Art's house was dug in; safe distance, even for stormy times.

East, behind the house, sufficiently obscured by dunes and brush, was the coast road. San Francisco was an hour to the north. Once per week he could hear the distress siren that still sounded from the fire station in Half Moon Bay, as though air raids by the forces of Hirohito were still imminent. It was an evocative and mournful noise; it put Art in mind of blackouts, and vigilance, and staying prepared.

The nearest convenience mart, if you could call it that, was a Toot 'N Moo fifteen miles down the highway. It had begun life as a truckstop and featured enough rest rooms for ten people, with showers. The shitty coffee shop had shut down within one fiscal year and Art only stopped there for gas, once he'd quit smoking. The counter was usually manned by a former skate punk named Rocko (according to his handwritten name tag), who mopped up, played a lot of speed metal too loudly, and fed the slushie machine from a large, vile-looking bucket whenever he wasn't zipping around the parking lot on his board. Rocko had been known to shut the store down whenever he had band practice, so operative business hours were a hazy concept at best. There was a sort of small-town market in Half Moon Bay, but it was only open from nine in the morning till three in the afternoon, administered by a couple who otherwise qualified as retirees. Instead of repairing to some bedroom community to play shuffleboard and watch cable, they invested their market with the sort of attention your grandma would devote to vegetable gardens, or quilt making. The market would die as soon as they did. Small, friendly groceries with creaky wooden floors were a last-gasp anachronism from the twentieth century, not destined to persevere.

Art drew a deep nasal hit of the salt air and felt his sinuses sluice. It was better than gulping heart-accelerating decongestants like M&M's from wake-up till sleeptime. A decade back he'd had his septum corrected, and polyps excised. A week following the minor surgery, a blood vessel high up in his skull decided to let go like a burst fire hydrant, liberating blood in fat, metronomic drops that obstinately refused to slow down, or dam up. This nasal apocalypse lost its comic value after about five minutes. What didn't drip out went down his throat in an unstoppable, inexorable, slow-motion torrent—now; *that* was funny, the thought that he could die from a nosebleed that didn't even hurt. All his blood would run out of his skull and he would die. Laugh riot. Just imagine the funeral for a guy who had croaked from a terminal runny nose.

He was vaguely ill and in the first stages of woozy shock by the time Lorelle drove him to the Half Moon Bay fire station and they caught an ambulance ride into the city, where a triage nurse estimated he had swallowed more than a pint of his own blood. A patient physician named Dr. Bloch had tried packing his nostrils with eight feet of some nonabsorbent material that looked like pasta. No good. Then, in one of those moments straight out of a 1950s sci-fi film—*it's crazy, but it just might work!*—Dr. Bloch fed a catheter into Art's nose and inflated it with a hypodermic full of water, which applied the needed pressure to the unreachable rupture. The whole event was so comedic that it sharpened Art's appreciation of the fact that he could die abruptly, by ridiculous means. Death by absurdity, without hidden meaning or footnote.

Not so with Lorelle. Cancer wasn't as funny. He still said her name aloud, to himself, several times a day. Even now.

Art's sinuses mended and he was 100 percent okay. His cholesterol was negligible. Heart, lungs, blood, all fine. He was thirty-eight and could conceivably live to ninety; he just had no idea how he was going to get that far or last that long, for reasons having nothing to do with aging or his physical state. He was a fit, average man, hiding out in a sanctuary of his own making, logging work with little joy, mourning the loss of a revised director's cut of his own life—the version in which Lorelle had lived.

What he wanted now was a storm. A violent, freezing sky show, to inspire him. Thunder and fury. His stocks were good, and if catastrophe struck, his own garage was outfitted better than a bomb shelter. He wanted to bear witness while some black bitch of a hurricane cleaved around the battlements of his stormproof fortress, this product of his will. Then maybe he could return to the stoop labor of telling restaurant technology which way to swing.

Three mornings running, now, the sky had come up dour crimson. Old sailor sayings were apparently claptrap.

"Blitz! *Beweg' deinen Arsch hier rüber!*" he shouted on the return trek from Spilsbury's. The dog, having enjoyed a longer morning jaunt than usual, snapped to and obeyed. Art assumed his dog-voice: "You're a good boy, aren't you? *Guter Hund. Du bist halt mein Bester!*" Blitz loved the sound of the word *good*. He hung his tongue to the wind like a fluttering slice of ham, agreeing that he was, in fact, a good boy. Gulls winged about, buffeted mercilessly by gusts in their unending scavenge for refuse and dead things. Blitz wanted to jump high enough to snag them. Art saw the birds reflected in the dog's rich, coffee-colored eyes.

A quick scan of the websites on his Favorites file yielded no new consumer temptations, merely an endless avalanche of pop-up windows, click-now hot links, and animated come-ons. The World Wide Web had boiled down to three basic constants: porn, advertising, and a smorgasbord of humans declaring themselves and their likes to a world they could not see, in a frantic attempt to leave a visual benchmark amid the digital waterfall of data; perhaps lend some humanity to all those invisible ones and zeros. He was aware he had not yet turned on the halogens over his drafting table; that would be too much like an acknowledgment of work. With a soft, rubberized Number Two he sketched a wandering maze, like a sky view of a rat's tubular exercise run. The pencil came from a galvanized container of twenty identical ones, all identically sharpened on a matte black device that emitted a coffee grinder noise and was guaranteed for life by its Swiss makers. Springboarding from the idea of his bullet-proof acrylic windows, he wondered how the entire restaurant complex would "present" if its accoutrements were totally composed of transparent material. To walk on a world of glass would be precarious and disorienting; it made him crack a grin that only involved half his mouth. He thought of Carlsbad Caverns, of Indian pueblos, of making the search for one's favored watering holes into some kind of urban exploratory expedition, all beneath a ceiling of skylights.

For those people who didn't do all their shopping on the internet, anyway.

It was a game try, but Art knew he was in a rut, forcing half-baked inspiration to service a contractual obligation. It was grim, akin to a gravedigger filling a hole, instead of a landscaper sculpting a garden. He had begun to wonder whether anyone actually *looked* at his designs anymore. So long as they came in on time, filled space, and were attached to the cachet of his name, did anyone really notice, or care?

The mailbag offered Citibank, telephones, gas, power, insurance, and the usual hustles from strangers. He resented the way printouts could be programmed for a nakedly obvious faux-personalization, then "signed" with a patently bogus printed signature. It was deceptive and meant to entrap, like the tony ad campaigns for most of the restaurants slated for Art's reinterpretation. Places to eat needed to be inviting, not demanding. Customers needed the humanity the internet rarely offered. They plodded into mall shops like convicts walking the last mile. Buyers should *want* to enter, not be forced by some grim need. They always slapped down cash or plastic as though making a sacrifice to the gods of materialism. The phenomenon was most pronounced come Christmastime—which was to say, the "holiday" period extending from the day after Labor Day until ten days into January. There was not much left that was enticing about a holiday that lasted four straight months, though merchants saw it the other way around. Art had given up Christmas a long time ago.

A postcard dropped out of the stack. The Golden Gate Bridge, real tourist shit. Written on the back, in marker, Art read: YOU CAN RUN BUT YOU CAN'T HIDE. HAVE A BEER, YOU FUCK. Followed by the initial D with a flourish.

That would be Derek . . . whom Art had not seen or communicated with for several years. There was no return address and the card was postmarked more than a week ago.

Derek—Darius Centurion Hill—had dropped out of Art's life shortly after Lorelle died. He had gone from being a once-per-week dinner guest to an invisible man. He had shot pool and drunk beer and hung out during a time when Art kept virtually no male friends. Buddy structures often collapsed as a casualty of marriage, but Derek had remained steadfast. When Art had blown sour blood-alcohol for a state trooper, Derek posted bail, picked him up, and

12

warp-speeded him home, violating the posted limits all the way. When Lorelle had first been hospitalized, Derek was the first outsider to visit, lying to the duty nurse that he was a family member. He could be counted on to hoist the opposite end when something needed moving. The day he came into his inheritance, he promptly quit his job at Lockheed, where he had specialized in aerodynamic design. He had collided with Art at some tech conference and they stuck to each other, opting out of the dry roll call of seminars to seek adventure in Tucson, which, at the time, had been a new city to both of them. Instead of titty bars and sleaze, they found an air museum of antique warplanes, a science-fiction triple bill of vintage black-and-whites at the New Loft Theatre, and an excursion on rented Harleys into the high desert, deep enough that they encountered real Lawrence of Arabia–style dunes, no litter, and saw a live rattlesnake just crawling around out in the open. They watched it prowl with a mesmerized, almost benevolent interest; then they left it alone. The snake never acknowledged their intrusion in any way, which pleased Art enormously.

Lorelle had always read books voraciously; Art did not try to keep up with her and excused himself as selective. Derek could pace her, talking obscure classics and current bestsellers, always with both of them swapping recommendations. Then he could digress onto the mean worth of the work of artists Art had never heard of or remembered, without missing a breath. He loved finding conversational links, and Art appreciated his way of thinking around corners. Derek entertained a succession of youngish girlfriends, mostly brown-over-brown fitness fanatics, and Art rarely bothered to try telling them apart, depending on Derek to clue him in if it was important. He lingered over one such partner—Art recalled her name as Erica—and the two of them had blazed off to Hawaii in search of volcanoes. That was it. Until today, two years later, or was it three?

The card was not from Hawaii. It had been postmarked in San Francisco. Art propped it on his desk—not his drafting table, but the wraparound workstation where the computer monitor dominated a third of the space. He wondered if Derek had any idea how to find him, then smiled to himself again.

"Hey," he said in English to Blitz. "Remember Uncle Derek? From when you were still a puppy?" Blitz cocked his head, trying to figure out if the question had anything to do with anything edible. Art hit a key command to let the computer slide to sleep mode. The monitor made a strange little *boink* sound that always caused Blitz to bark, exactly once. Art was perpetually amused by this, and never chided him.

The house clicked and popped from a sudden strong gust of wind. Art knew all the sounds of the house intimately. Sometimes he dreamed Lorelle was walking through their front door—now refaced in stainless steel, another task yet undone while she was alive.

She returns from some errand and he hears the locks crank, and the jangle of keys. Every person's keybunch has a sound as characteristic as a fingerprint. He hears the thud of her leather shoulder bag on the glass-topped entryway table. She calls into the house to determine whether it's empty, and he hears her voice ring. The acoustics are different because the house is a wreck and most of the seaward windows are boarded up with plywood, prior to reinstallation. They can't keep the plaster dust out of the kitchen and are forever stepping on stray screws or nails or sharp curls of cut metal. Most of the furniture is sheeted in plastic, or not yet bought. Plans and the detritus of reconstruction are everywhere. Art hears Lorelle call his name into this wasteland, this work in progress . . .

. . . then he always bolted awake, panic about burglars popping a quick sweat on his skin, the silence broken only by his own breathing. He could always smell the emotions he dragged back from the dream state and they always embarrassed him. There was nobody to be embarrassed before, until Blitz intruded with his own menu of needs. Dogs are tolerant and forgiving. No matter how you screw up, they look at you with an expression that says they still love you.

It had always been difficult or impossible for Art to get back to sleep after these Lorelle interludes, which did not actually classify as dreams. Every tiny noise sprang him back to queasy wakefulness, and as a result he suffered a maldistribution of REM sleep similar to that experienced by alcoholics.

Art was what is known in idiomatic parlance as a "morning bear." It was generally not a good idea to speak to him or otherwise distract him, or list demands, until about two hours after he'd opened his eyes, had coffee, gotten oriented to the day. He often thought of the rattler he and Derek had seen in the desert—its aggressive patterning, its never-blinking slit-eyed gaze, the warnings inherent in the devilish design of its weaponlike head. *No molestarme.* Don't mess with me. Art often fancied that the snake was coiled inside his own chest, its blunt length separating his lungs, its ballistic skull resting atop his heart, absorbing body heat. Once it warmed up, it could pursue its own meditations, and safely be ignored. Lorelle, a talker, had never fully comprehended Art's need for quiet upon waking and his disinclination toward breakfast chitchat, but she accommodated it, accepting the trait as Art's wall against distraction. She usually rose before he did and left him fresh coffee on the nightstand, retreating to putter. She maintained an intriguing work habit, which was to install herself before her own computer immediately upon waking, before caffeine and the real world could fully kick in. In this half-asleep, half-awake Zen state, she said, things flowed around the logic roadblocks in her brain,

15

directly to her fingers, and her keyboard, making her good for a thousand words, minimum, before she had to think about getting dressed for real or what obligations the day mandated. She had been halfway into the bones of a novel when she died.

Art would wonder forever how that story was supposed to end.

When you live with another person for a significant length of time, your body sensors become attuned to the sounds of your partner, elsewhere in the house. Art missed waking to the smell of fresh-ground brew and hearing the fluting sound of his wife's half tunes. Lorelle sang to herself, and hummed a lot, never complete songs. Hence, Art now kept his stereo hot, and the big-screen TV on most of the time, just to experience voices or a presence other than himself that could aid in defining spaces and the acoustic weight of rooms in which he was the sole occupant. He preferred cinema channels with no commercials and no "original series"—just movies—but Blitz actually seemed to pay attention to the nature channels, especially the ones that featured graphic veterinary surgery and looked, at a glance, like shows about the warp and woof of torture. Art was also held victim to a bizarre fascination for the History Channel, or as he called it, the Hitler Channel, since every other program seemed to focus on World War II. "That logo, that little *H* in the box? It stands for Hitler." That never failed to crack Lorelle up. It was part of their secret language. The Hitler Channel was about the past; you could see it was the past because of the black-and-white footage, the film scratches, the view through a time-keyhole refreshingly free of digital perfection.

Art fired up all systems and settled for CNN, to see if anything in the world had really changed. Nothing had. He got more coffee, bisected a bagel, and continued doodling.

Before the semicircle of black leather sofas grouped around the electronic fireplace of the TV screen was a low glass table the size of a child's inflatable swimming pool. Art perched his athletic shoes on it. Once a week he rigorously cleaned and dusted all the surfaces in the house. You had to anyway, with a dog in residence. Shortly after Lorelle had died, he'd disengaged their housekeeper, Mrs. Ives, a top-heavy, gray-bunned Welsh lady with a gait like a pouter pigeon. He'd discovered that he could fill time with basic maintenance. Keeping track of seven principal rooms with two and half baths could become a job instead of a chore. Every time he vacuumed rugs or polished countertops, he thought that no matter how thoroughly he cleaned, there would always be pieces of Lorelle in the house— microscopic motes of shed skin cells, fading scents on still-hanging clothes, a baseboard scuff where she'd once kicked a door shut in anger. Last week he'd found one of her auburn hairs behind an antique armoire, and he'd slid slowly down the wall to a sitting position, legs out like a kid in a sandbox, and wept for twenty minutes. The memory, even dulled by time, could flood back that quickly, blindside him that unexpectedly, and cut past all his calculated defense mechanisms, draining hope from his heart and disturbing the rattlesnake, who held fast within his chest, coiled around Art's emotions, its slanted, evil-looking mouth seeming to grin.

The corridor to the south wing, bedroom and library, was crowded with framed photographs that also haunted him. Wedding shots, excursions, parties, adventures on foreign soil. Pictures of both her late parents still hung there. Lorelle had been born a month before Neil Armstrong had stepped onto the surface of the moon. Her mom and dad had been college students trying to fathom the Summer of Love. They had died within a year of each other, in 1992. Dad had acquired ALS—amyotrophic lateral sclerosis, more popularly known as Lou Gehrig's disease—and had hung on long enough to see his daughter marry; it was almost as though he could let go once Lorelle had found Art. Mom went totally unexpectedly, after a bus jumped a yellow light verging on red and broadsided her Acura. She arrived at the hospital comatose and never woke up. Lorelle and Art had been there for all of it, the deathwatch, the sorrow, the funeral, and the discomfiting silence and emotional flatline that polluted their next few months.

Doctors discovered Lorelle's tumor in March 2000, and by mid-April Art found himself back on the deathwatch chair. As time ran out, Lorelle's hospital stay seemed both excruciatingly protracted (in terms of her pain) and too fast, too soon for Art. Morose hindsight taught him that one either winds up dying, or watching someone else die. Do this long enough, and all too quickly your points of reference for the world are systematically erased. Events grow distant, celebrities die, your friends and family precede you, and suddenly nobody knows what you're talking about. That was when time itself had begun to blur for Art. The next thing he remembered was trying to answer questions from strangers as to how his wife should be buried. They never decided definitively what *kind* of cancer it was, exactly, and everyone apologized a lot. It did not require a medical education for Art to realize the doctors were out of their depth. Tumors morphed into new and frightening forms; that was enough information to forestall keener inquiry from strangers who didn't care anyway. People apologized. And the globe spun on.

Most of the subsequent nine months—give or take—vanished into Art's recycling bin in the form of empty bottles, or up his reconstructed nose in the form of cocaine. It took another year to resurrect his career, and these days he stuck to occasional beer and wine. He let his hair grow out again and tied it back, not minding the gray threads that appeared and gradually got longer, seemingly because he was looking right at them.

He had incorporated as Lattitude, Ltd., punning on his own

name. Latimer plus attitude. *I don't know about "Art," but I know what I like.* His business cards were arrogantly stark—two geometric lines resembling open boundaries embossed in show-off metallic ink, the company name, and a row of reps and contact numbers, one of which was for Charlie Brill, an agent who had actually sold some of Art's designs as framed collectibles. Art always signed *Latt* in the appropriate box on the blueprints.

Blitz mooched a bite of bagel that vanished down his gullet with no chewing whatsoever. CNN advised that the government was vaporlocked as usual and Wall Street was caterwauling over a single-percentage-point drop in something or other. Children were starving to death in India and 70 percent of the people in Africa, it appeared, were HIV positive. A hot-air balloonist had crashed and drowned somewhere between Art's home and Hawaii. In Los Angeles, the heat was on to make random weapon sweeps of private homes legal; Art thought of the Hitler Channel. San Franciscans were advised to button up for a big, wet storm over the weekend. Art's porch barometer was dropping steadily.

The satellite dish feed offered five hundred channels of nothing. Art picked up the novel he had begun . . . what, weeks, months ago? Yesterday? He was only fifty pages in.

Lorelle's bailiwick had been fiction, for which Art had little time among the temptations of research and tech journals. Occasionally he made a stab at reading for entertainment and was usually disappointed, feeling he had to process too much to gain not enough. Make-believe just did not grab him, although he presently made sorties into the novels Lorelle had left behind, as if preserving one of her favorite pastimes would help her endure in memory.

His habit was to read at night, before dozing off, but he sensed oncoming defeat, and . . . sure enough. He lasted through a few more chapters of the overwrought bestseller about a made-up serial killer, and knew he would read no further. There; a decision had been made and it was still early in the day. Art found invented fiends far less interesting than genuine killers, although he could argue persuasively that Jack the Ripper was probably the most infamous "invented" serial murderer in all history. Few candidates held a candle to H. H. Holmes, the guy who had constructed his "Murder Castle" in Chicago just in time to prey upon the throngs that came to experience the World's Columbian Exposition of 1893. Far fewer tomes had been written about Holmes than saucy Jack. Art had accumulated a respectable short shelf of true crime, and had done a great deal more reading since Lorelle's death.

The telling of stories was fundamental to human nature, an expression of the anthropological need for the species to constantly arrange things into cogent groupings, which trait was supposedly its most salient distinction from the lower orders. Humankind organized thoughts, wants, needs, and dreams into a coding called language, expressed via spoken words, then put that conveniently opposable thumb to the task of ordering that language into graphic symbols. All human interaction was based on storytelling, one individual or group relating a story to another. You got together with your friends and swapped stories, or voiced opinion on topical events called news. Everybody decided what political or religious stories spoke to their condition, and new stories were fomented much in the manner of a spreading virus. Art, already a compulsive arranger, was aware that he had begun absorbing stories from pages and screens and displays as an alternate form of human contact. Not many actual humans were loitering around his life, at the moment, to listen while he told his own story, which he felt was dunningly one-note . . . right now, anyway.

In the bathroom he spoke to himself again in the mirror. "Your ballroom days are over, baby."

By noon it was time to "do shots." Blitz understood what that meant in purely selfish dog-terms; it meant he would be permitted to sortie downbeach a certain distance and then return, since he did not care for the loud noises made by his Person.

In the back of Art's master bedroom closet was a fireproof Corsair gun safe, half-stocked with maximal security lockboxes that guarded certificates, a few bits of jewelry, and petty cash. These were stacked atop a disused shortwave radio with its own power supply. The rest of the space stored his gun collection, including several collector's items that could technically be defined as illegal. He drew down an overpriced Benelli shotgun with a pistol grip and a pair of handguns, both hanging on pegs in shoulder holsters—a Beretta 92F nine-millimeter and a big-cock Desert Eagle .45. All the weapons were loaded. (Art's father had taught him this was the best way to prevent an "accidental" shooting with a rig presumed to be "unloaded.")

Art's improvised, bare-bones range was on the north side of the house, where what he laughingly called his "yard" hung on for dear chlorophyllic life. He had provided for this lawn area in the basic plan of the house and had thrown a board fence around it with a future eye toward cactus, or some hearty gardening—indistinct plans for amateur horticulture that became extinct once Lorelle had been removed from the equation. Now the lawn was more like one of those welcome mats woven of tough brown fiber, the beds for flowers or plants gone to weedy dirt. Salt air had killed the grass to the point where every footstep raised chaff. Hardier grasses sprouted from the dunes separating the house from the highway, but Art had nothing to do with that.

He cut Blitz loose to roam and arranged a lineup of two-liter plastic beverage jugs scrounged from the big recycling bin. Filled with water, they took hits most impressively. Art knew bowling pins to be the target of choice for gun geeks because a bowling pin was an "anatomically correct" sketch of the hit zone on a human being, from narrow chin to fatter sternum, but he enjoyed the way the plastic bottles responded. A nine-millimeter hollow-point round would punch a hole the size of a Bic pen and blast an exit path as big as a dessert plate, causing the bottles to somersault, pinwheeling jets of tap water. The .45 cut them in half like a scythe, and the shotgun caused them to simply disintegrate.

Behind the rickety post rail of bottles at waist height, Art hung regulation paper targets on a nylon clothesline, for the usual plinking. The sky was a dirty dustmop hue, and more than once Art felt speckles of moisture on his bare forearms as he set up.

He destroyed a few of the bottles with the Beretta, alternating to the paper targets for double- and triple-tap shots. Each round blew a sonic cocoon of air toward his face. Blowback was an oddly pleasing sensation, but the targets were already dancing in the wind, unstable, some barely tethered. No good for skill.

Concentrate, raise, sight, fire. The motion had to be fluid, more natural, making the gun an extension of his reach. Not plinking, now. As he tried to focus, he knew that he was in danger of retrofitting Lorelle into some kind of no-fault goddess. The conundrum of death was that it sometimes made the dear departed perfect, an icon against whom the still living could never compete. He and Lorelle had navigated through many fights and conflicts; that was just part of getting accustomed to someone who fit you like one hand into another, even though they were inside different skins.

They'd once had a terrific argument about guns, for example.

● ● ● Lorelle is wearing astonishingly brief cutoffs and no underwear, which gives her a low-blow advantage as she assumes what Art has come to know as her defensive posture. She's on the sofa,

● ● ● DAVID J. SCHOW

knees drawn up to her chin, ankles crossed, arms hugging legs, eyes set in infinity focus. It is summer and sea aerates the house, blasting through open windows and doors to rinse out the ambient staleness. Most of the reconstruction of the house is complete, or relegated to buffer zones in need of tweaking. Whenever Lorelle speaks and does not look at him, he knows they have spread their picnic blanket in a minefield.

"If it's for self-defense, why do you need a dozen of them?"

"I like the hardware. Call it a boy thing."

"You're talking about them as if they're toys. Look at a handgun. It exists for only one purpose—to kill people."

"And a lot of people act irresponsibly when it comes to their basic rights or freedoms, and I'm not any of them."

"God, you're starting to sound like an ad for the NRA. All that Second Amendment garbage made sense during the Revolutionary War, but not now. Now you've got gun nuts hiding behind the Constitution, the same way censors hide behind children."

I love you, Art thinks. Anyone else would button their lip, be less honest, let it ride. Nevertheless, this was an argument, and they had both sailed through debate at the collegiate level, which made them ruthless.

"You're what those 'gun nuts' call a 'limping bunny in the meadow.'"

That gets a rise out of her. "What the *fuck* is that supposed to mean?" Now she is looking directly at him, but he is ready for the double-barreled blast of her gaze.

"Think it over: If you're a hungry predator, what do you dream about? A limping bunny in the meadow. Bunnies are tasty and can't hurt you when you kill them. Limping bunnies can't bounce away and make you waste energy by chasing them. A meadow is a wide-open space with no place to hide; the grass betrays the bunny's every move."

"What if the bunny is limping because it has gangrene?" she says. "What if the bunny is faking it so the predator will step into a bear trap hidden by the grass?" She waggles her eyebrows.

"Limping bunnies are people who don't consider the reality of their own vulnerability. Like people who expect the police to protect them from burglars in the house. Like drunks who act out in public with strangers because they never think those strangers might kick them in the face until they die while they scream for help."

"So you're saying that the muffin in the leather mini and fuck-me pumps, who's staggering around a bar parking lot at two-thirty in the morning, deserves to be attacked, right?"

"No. But she is a limping bunny."

"That is still the stupidest thing I've ever heard," she says, wincing from its truth. "What does that have to do with all that 'We the People' stuff people use as an excuse to arm up for their own personal world war?"

"Every time the word *people* appears in the Constitution, it refers to an individual right, not a collective one. The mechanism of change is inherent in the document. If the country doesn't like it anymore, then we'll have a sort of Prohibition on firearms, and we all saw how that eradicated alcohol, right?"

"So as a result of that kind of thinking—which is called paralogia, by the way—everybody now packs a zillion guns."

"No, they don't. The issues are so polarized that it's a hot-button topic just by existing. There's nobody who doesn't have a furiously extreme position on guns; there are no gun moderates. Everyone is passionate. What most normal citizens don't know is that most times a gun is used for self-defense, it is *not* fired. All the times they're not fired are never included in the statistics . . . but suicides are. No fair."

"You know as well as I do that statistics mean nothing. Zero. Either side can use the same damned statistics to support whatever position they favor, because it's all selective vision."

"Okay, then look at it this way: Most normal citizens have never actually had the experience of feeling like prey. Of being helpless, and having a predator grinning at them."

He is accessing a thorny memory, and he knows it. Lorelle had been date-raped in college by a charming footballer whose draft prospects went swirling because he felt he was owed sex. Of the two, Lorelle had recovered more admirably.

"Low blow, Arthur." She makes a little hissing noise of disgust, because he is breaking the rule about making the conflict personal. "Even if I'd had a gun, I wouldn't have shot him. I don't think it's right to take another human life."

"Guy wasn't a human in any sense of the word. Chances are, if you'd had a gun, you would never have had to fire it. He would've backed off. No rape, no hospital, no therapy, no screening for AIDS, no self-loathing."

"You're really being a prick about this," she says, pointed and sullen, now determined to sting him in return. "What if things didn't go as conveniently as you say and I did have to fire it? Then I'd be a murderer. Think of the self-loathing then."

"Point. But abstract the idea: If you have handguns, then women don't have to depend on men for defense. That's why they were called equalizers. If everybody's armed, everybody else gets a lot more polite."

"I don't depend on men for defense."

"Sexist."

"Nothing personal," she lies. "That's one of the more bloated male fantasies."

"Is it? If there was trouble, wouldn't you call a cop?"

"What if it was a lady cop?" She cracks a tiny smile at that; it's better because they both know they shouldn't be sniping at each other.

"Police do not magically show up to make things better. That's one of the mass delusions of our age. That's bunny thinking. I wouldn't depend on the police for anything, I mean, christ, look where we live. Think of the response time."

"Oh, now we're on the wild frontier all of a sudden."

"It's a state of mind, that lawless wilderness. It occurs in the flash of a synapse. All it takes is some nitwit on PCP seeing the lights on and deciding to knock over the house. Zap—you're lost in the woods with no light, and no ability to defend yourself."

"You can hide. Run away. The impulse is fight *or* flight."

"Not if the guy after you can run faster and jump higher, or sniff out your hiding place."

"Now you're getting into this whole caveman macho thing: *Me crushums all enemies*. That's not me. The fact of the matter is that there are too friggin many mental deficients out there toting guns already."

"They're the predators. I say arm the prey."

"There's like two firearms for every man, woman, and child in the country now. Too many; it's already overkill. Nobody asks all those gun nuts to take a psych test, or even demonstrate the barest competence or responsibility. You just go in, sign a paper, wait a couple of weeks, and you're loaded for bear. You can walk right out of the store with a rifle and ammo, same day."

"So let's say that in order to own a firearm, you have to prove to an instructor that you know how to handle a weapon. I'm all for that. Any imbecile with an opposable thumb can get a driver's license, and cars kill more people than handguns. So let's ban cars."

"Now you're being ridiculous."

"Not really. What I'm saying is that given a choice between a sweeping sort of police state versus sensible rules, I know what ought to play in a democracy. Let politicians pass laws that allow cops to bust into your house with no prior cause, just rooting around for weapons? No thanks. But pass a test that proves you can responsibly use a gun? What the hell—throw the politicians their bone, because they'll always need an issue to chew on, and if that calms them down, I'd rather submit to a test of my own ability as opposed to mob rule."

"Mob rule *is* a democracy," she says. "The greater good for the majority equals the lowest common denominator for everybody."

"I love you when you talk like that."

"I don't need a gun, anyway. I have a police dog." Blitz cues directly to the word *dog*, and plops down close enough for Lorelle to wrap her legs around him, ruffling fur with her bare toes. She has beautiful, gracile feet and Art feels a wanton surge.

"We have an *almost* police dog who is goofy and undependable. And who won't fit in your purse."

Blitz regards Art with his tongue hanging out, a full serving of idiotic love, making Art's argument for him.

"I am not going to become a pistol-packin mama."

"I'm saying just a little personal tool, to carry around, so light you won't even feel it, but you'll know it's there if ever you get boxed in. Better to have it and not need it than need it and not have it. Like a little Baby Eagle you can carry cocked and locked. Or a—"

"Oh please, don't start fetishizing the damned things. 'Baby' Eagle; jesus h. christ."

"I'm not fetishizing them."

"No? Ever take a close look at those gun magazines? The photo spreads are more lewd than *Hustler*."

"When were you ever looking at gun magazines?" Art gives her his penetrating-inquisitor look. *I just found out something about you.* "I know *I* don't subscribe to any of them."

"Are all your guns legit? Registered? Accounted for?"

"Not all of them, no. I've got a couple of unpapered ones."

"Why?"

"Because it's a collection, not an arsenal. Because I'm an enthusiast, not a gun nut. And because if Confiscation Day ever rolls around in the great state of California, I want backup."

"Listen to yourself. You're rationalizing all this with jargon, and sprouting a big ole woody just thinking about all your firepower. That's so teenaged. If you're just an 'enthusiast,' then why don't you wear those headphones when you shoot outside?"

"So I'll know what my gear sounds like in a combat situation, so there are no surprises, so I won't flinch, so I can keep my attention on the target without distractions. Which is also why I shoot at night sometimes—so I'll know what the muzzle flash is like, what the conditions look like; so I'll be prepared to do it for real."

Lorelle liberates a huge sigh. "You're still doing it—rhapsodizing over your guns. It's compulsive. Are you paranoid, or do you just feel vulnerable and weak, not able to face the world without a shootin iron?"

"They're *just guns,* Lorelle." Art resents the trap into which she has led him.

"Don't you dare use my name like my mom, dressing me down. I hate that."

Gladly, his back is turned when she cuts that one loose. He has moved to the fridge to find a drink. "Sorry," he calls from the kitchen, making it more an acknowledgment and less an apology.

"And if they're just guns, why do you have a dozen of them? Plus a shotgun."

Lorelle had adjudged the shotgun particularly ugly, and as a killing device, its sleek lines and matte finish lent it the paradoxical, hideous beauty of a black mamba. It was a Benelli M3 Super 90 Tactical with a polymer pistol grip, a consumer version of the Entry Gun available only to the police and military. It was also one of Art's unpapered weapons, so Art thought it best not to linger on the biggest gun in his collection.

"They're all *loaded*, all the time. Who's going to lay siege to us? Do you know something I don't?"

"I don't have a dozen." Art stands right in front of her as he says this, hands on hips. "I only have five."

"Oh," she says, broadly. "Never mind, then. Five loaded guns is certainly no cause for alarm." After a beat for timing, she adds, "Did you know there's a law in Arizona that makes it illegal to own more than six dildos?"

"Loaded or unloaded?" Art does the math. "You know, if you had six, you could hold one between all of your fingers and still have your thumbs free."

"Fat chance." She gives him a comic little frown. "You wouldn't be able to get it up from jerking off over all your big guns, so you'd need 'em. I bet you a dollar." She brazenly grabs his balls, right through his sweatpants. "Oops. Guess I owe you a buck."

Art is convinced his wife uses these little debates as foreplay, sort of mental aerobicism to tune the sensory nodes and turn up all the nerve endings, to resharpen the keen edge of physical perception. Within fifteen minutes they are naked and delirious on the carpet. Blitz snorts his disapproval and seeks other adventure while his masters make friction.

"Hold me tight," she says as their breath runs rapid and healthy perspiration breaks. "Hold me down."

Art knows this is so she can rock back and raise her legs on thigh muscles that thrum like bass strings. When she orgasms, those legs will scissor him crushingly as she momentarily forgets all about him. He is getting a cramp in his right foot when she climaxes the first time, so he eases back and brings her legs together to hug them against his chest, still hard inside her but not wanting to spoil her aftershocks by continuing to ram around like a clockwork machine.

Her expression says a car battery has been hardwired to the pleasure centers of her brain. "Whoo, first stage separation," she says breathlessly, meaning her first climax, always the toughest. From here on they'll go off like champagne bubbles, or spinners in a fireworks show. She grabs Art's ass with both hands and *pulls*. He slides in to the hilt through molten quicksilver; where she was wet before, she is now hotter, slicker, more insistent.

Art begins thrusting deep and firm, full-length strokes that cause her breasts to jar in an enticing way special to him, and private, because Lorelle has wonderful, natural breasts that only move that way when he is making love to her. He thinks—fragmentedly—that it's all wrong in movie sex, in porn sex, where it's always two lusty predators tearing the shit out of each other in a contest having nothing to do with affection or personal regard. There is no *respect* in movie sex; the best it can depict is a kind of gladiatorial combat. This isn't that, even though Lorelle is now openmouthed and rollicking like she wants him to bifurcate her.

She husks in a raw breath, which causes her to cough. When she coughs, her muscles tighten unexpectedly around his cock and he is suddenly shoved into the freefall of orgasm. It shudders through him and he grabs her upper arms so tightly they'll leave bruises by nightfall. He is shaken by the scruff and tries, tries, *tries* not to make a stupid face when he comes.

"You made the Wile E. Coyote face again," she says, meaning the expression Wile makes when he expects to get blown up or crushed, then doesn't, then does. "Baby, don't go." She feels his penis easing out of her, stunned for the moment, slipping.

"I gotta get off my knees." He collapses into a sitting position, back against one of the sofas. "Dammit."

She sees he has rug burns on both knees and rolls to show him a dorsal view. "I did it again, too." She has sustained a nearly identical scuff on the bone ridge below the small of her back.

"Great, now our war wounds match."

"It's a mating mark," she says. "Live with it. But I can't stay on the floor. Bed?"

"Bed, definitely."

"Good thing we didn't make it up, then. Because you're far from done." She crawls into his arms and he wraps her up.

"I'm so glad you didn't say I was *spent*."

"Sooo . . . how much *does* one of those lady guns cost?" she says, with the fakest contrition in the world, and they both start laughing, because they are deeply in love.

That was the gun story.

● ● ● Remembering the gun story reminded Art of the danger inherent in idealizing his dead wife into someone perfect, a glossy memory that could never be competed with, or equaled. They had blazed through fights, lots of them, none a dealbreaker that could derail their relationship. The fights had been spice, or speedbumps, or one day's ill mood inflicted on a partner. Now Art could blast them all away, *boom-boom-boom*.

He racked the huge, underslung action of the Desert Eagle and concentrated on single shots. The kick from the triangular slide was as feisty as that from the high-power ammo. The gun itself was so huge and formidable looking that it turned up in movies a lot as a badguy weapon. Art knew the Desert Eagle could be chambered for .50-caliber rounds—great for home defense if you wanted to destroy an intruder by blasting both halves of his sundered body through a cinderblock wall, and maybe tear a hole in the space-time continuum.

The tang of gunsmoke hung in the air only long enough to be instantly blown away. Too damn windy. Art gave the shotgun a raincheck. He had planned to make a ham and cheese sandwich and mountaineer out onto the jetty, about halfway to the dish—the Sundial, sunless today—but the ocean had other plans. Spume from incoming waves whitecapped and shot straight up when they crashed against the rock, indicating the violence and speed of their delivery. Art stowed his artillery and looked for Blitz, closer to the beachline, which was sizzling with foam. Blitz disliked the aural shock of gunfire; another reason for his low grades in police dog school.

Art thought ruefully about the gun story—the *rest* of the gun story. The punchline. The winning gambit.

"Okay," says Lorelle, incapable of detouring from topic despite the good sex. She extends her fist as though holding an invisible microphone. "Why don't you tell our studio audience what they really want to know, apropos your sick gun fixation?"

"Which is what?"

"Have you ever actually shot anybody? Like, pointed a gun at another human being and made him or her, ahem, eat lead?"

"No." Art knows that to hesitate is to raise suspicions. "I have never shot anybody."

"Aha. So all this you were saying, about defense and logic and realistic options—it's all theoretical, then, since you don't have any experience with what you're talking about?"

"I don't ever want to have to." Pause. "But I want to be **able** to, if I **have** to."

Their discourse had shriveled and died with that. Bottom line: Art had yet to apply practical experience to his lofty justifications. Easy to become a dead shot when your enemy is a paper target or plastic bottle. He had not lied to cover some past transgression—he was a virgin when it came to shooting people. He had never been burglarized, or assaulted or held up or simply mugged, not once in his entire life.

And he intended to keep that record as spotless as he could manage, striving *not* to become the guy who never leaves his house for fear of getting mowed down by a bus, or perhaps struck by a wayward meteorite.

There was a bottle jutting out of the wet sand near where Art caught up with Blitz. It was not truant garbage of Art's. It was glass, which flared his temper quick and hot as a strike-anywhere match. Whoever had left this goddamn litter hadn't thought about it breaking, or slicing up his dog's feet.

It looked like an Old Crow whiskey bottle. There was a message inside. The sea had scoured the exterior of the bottle free of all labels and paste, and it was as blunted and lapidary as driftglass, which meant it had been rafting around in the water for some time. The screw-on cap was edged with rust.

Art opened the bottle and extracted the single page, vainly trying to get it to uncurl from the stubborn tube into which it had formed. He saw neat handwriting in blue ink on mellow linen paper. The wind made his effort to read useless, nearly comic.

It might have been a runaway page from a forlorn diary, but it had a legible beginning and end. Moisture blotted out some of the words. It might have been a circumlocutiony confession of suicide. It was a pocket mystery that deserved later thought. Blitz came capering back from his latest thrilling excursion, clearly ready to retreat to the house for the day. He had what looked like a human bone in his mouth.

"*Was ist das denn?*" he asked the dog. What have you brought me?

● ● ● . . . *are confused and hurt and angry and lost* (the note read), *and it pains me to witness your own pain when I feel torn between the things I feel I should do versus the things I know I must do. I don't want sympathy or pity: no one to mourn me. If I were a poet, I'd say beware of all the ways in which love can become a lie. I truly believe love is the single most difficult human endeavor, and almost no one is prepared to deal with all of its ramifications. We are all amateurs, and I failed.*

If you are reading this, and ever see the face of love, try your best not to fall short of its demanding mark. It is very important that you understand . . .

The note appeared to be the middle page of a multipage tract, since there was no salutation and no signature. The page began and terminated in midsentence. The blocky handwriting could have belonged to a woman, or a man. To Art it was particularly confounding. If it was one of a million gag notes thrown into the sea every year by pranksters, why wasn't it better rehearsed, more definitive? If it was for real, had its author really wanted to leave the earth with so few words, whoever he or she had been?

Epitaphs were always concise.

Maybe the tombstone pieces of the jetty had depressed him or her, and she'd decided to end it in a grand, spasmodic gesture of self-murder. For some reason, people who killed themselves in the ocean always felt compelled to go in naked. Had she pitched her bottle, divested herself of clothing, and dived in? Had there been more than one note? Was that the reason for its brevity—she'd had to write it ten times, or a hundred?

It'd be easier to Xerox, in that case, thought Art. *I want to make sure everybody reads this little haiku I wrote to my life, not that they'll be able to figure it out, and I'd like two hundred on goldenrod and two hundred on astral blue, please.*

The page had inevitably gotten damp during the homeward jaunt, and the ink had blotted. This was handwritten, probably this one time, by someone who very possibly was dead now. A jagged shiver wriggled up the back of his neck and nested in his scalp . . . not from that conclusion, but from Art's sudden realization that he had already assigned the mystery scribe a default identity as female in his imagination.

His inner caveman advised he merely needed to get laid. The serpent around his heart sighed, softly and with self-satisfaction, and resumed grinning its evil snaky grin.

The bone Blitz had salvaged was slender and tapered, less than a foot long, picked clean and bleached by the sea. It looked like one of the two forearm bones, the ones that crisscrossed every time you turned your wrist. Art was not certain; he'd have to look it up. It had arrived on the scene simultaneously with his disinterment of the bottle. Were they related?

35

His lunch plans aborted, Art decided to check on the local storm conditions and saw the word *hurricane* a lot.

Hurricanes. What did he know about them? He knew that typhoons and cyclones were both hurricane types that preferred the Pacific Northwest to the California coast. They rarely manifested around here with the severity dealt to tropical islands, the Gulf of Mexico, or most sodden Southern states. He knew they were basically caused by air movements—upward spirals that gathered heat and energy through contact with warm ocean water; the more sea surface water that evaporated, the stronger the storm got. He had a radio in the garage that would pick up the watches and warnings broadcast by the National Oceanographic and Atmospheric Administration, and assumed that if things grew serious, he would listen for tone alerts and await advice, which usually meant evacuation—in which Art was not interested. His outer walls were sixteen inches thick and his shatterproof windows featured louvered metal shutters that dropped down at the touch of a button . . . or via hand crank, if the power took a dump. He knew one of the United States's most catastrophic hurricanes killed over six thousand people in Galveston, Texas, in 1900, most of the casualties due to what was called "storm surge" coupled with "storm tide" (a wind-and-storm-powered adrenalation of the natural tide) that inundated the town in breakers nearly nine feet taller than the highest elevation on the island. That, plus the 140 mph winds, basically kicked Galveston's butt. The storm was still a record holder, a century later.

On the internet, Art found out about something called the Saffir-Simpson scale, a severity chart for hurricanes that reminded him of a preview card for a motion picture, with five categories: Minimal, Moderate, Extensive, Extreme, and Catastrophic. Category Five included Hurricane Camille, which had destroyed substantial portions of Louisiana and Missouri in 1969 with "sustained winds" over

155 miles per hour. That was long before Art's mother had moved to New Orleans. There was no category listing Galveston; Art thought "Apocalyptic" might make a good Number Six.

The National Weather Service had just upgraded their short-term watch for the Bay Area and environs south, warning of possible flooding in terms of rainfall inches and throwing up a red flag for high winds. Storm watches specified the possibilities within a thirty-six-hour window. In the time it took Art to check, the report bumped from "watch" to "warning." That reduced the window to twenty-four hours, and advised that hurricane conditions were to be expected, a general batten-down was nearly mandatory, and the less prepared should start thinking about evacuation.

This was the condition Art had been waiting for, to stress-test the design of his beach house. If it reacted as blueprinted, the winds would shear away, deflected by the structure. If a ten-foot wave crashed straight down on it from the heavens, the aluminum braces would act as shock absorbers and slough off the impact in a sort of lightning rod effect—most of the force would be detoured straight into the ground. If the polymer windows bowed under pressure, the metal shutters could be dropped. If the "display areas" of the house succumbed, the garage was as secure as a bank vault in a subma-rine, with backup CB and NOAA radios, gas, fuel, supplies, even waste management and a power generator. Art thought of that con-crete bunker as his own little Mars outpost, but it was a fallback, necessary only if his house design did not respond defensively, like a martial arts master who never hits you, yet never lets you land a blow: At its best, the effect would seem to be a confluence of physics and magic, the secret ingredient that pushed all the best designs into the spotlight.

Dish reception on the big Proton monitor was disrupted by occasional digital frazzing, but nothing critical. The phones were still live and the cable lifeline to the internet displayed no ominous quirks. The power was on; there was still "fire in the wire," as electricians say. Computers did what satellites told them and subtly rearranged the disk network on the roof to snare more power. The barometer was dropping steadily but slowly, like a pearl descending through molasses. Art ran a power supply check on the shutter system and pronounced it sassy. His home was his castle, his literal Bastille.

Derek's postcard was an excuse for him to lay in some guest stock before the weather worsened. He whistled Blitz to the kitchen. Their mission: Drop the drawbridge and sally forth into the enchanted faerie wood to procure supplies. The Jaguar XLS had been garaged for so long that its last wash-and-polish was membraned in a perfectly even layer of undisturbed dust. He really should have spread the car cover over it. For a steed, Art chose the Jeep—a muscular indulgence fully armed with padded roll bars and high-intensity lights, more equal to inclement turns of nature. Blitz assumed his accustomed sprawl in the suicide seat and Art remote-keyed the garage door shut. It seemed to crush the light from inside, cutting them off life support, leaving them in a world of blue-gray thunderheads.

They took the coast road, a serpentine limited-access two-lane that fed inland to Highway One via intermittent tentacles. Art quickly gained on a laggard Volkswagen bug—one of the new ones—puttering determinedly south, pinballing in search of the center stripe, which was nearly invisible in the rain now sheeting off the slurry-sealed tarmac. Art flashed, signaled, and blew around it impatiently. There were several hunched silhouettes inside, but the fellow travelers gave no indication of acknowledgment. They dwindled in the rearview and were swallowed by the elements.

Art passed the turnoff for the party house, spying only a quick impression of lights, parked cars, a little cluster of humanity. Perhaps the bold adventurers in the VW were bound for that good time. If they were headed anywhere else, they'd probably be in trouble before long.

As he made the turn onto the highway, a big Peterbilt rig monstered past in the northbound lane, road spume billowing from its wheel wells; another Dexedrine-happy road jockey fighting to make San Francisco before the storm cornered him.

Rocko's primer-gray Charger lurked at the far end of the Toot 'N Moo lot like a cannonless panzer tank waiting in ambush. Four hundred and twenty-seven cubes, glass-packed twin Cherry Bomb mufflers, no trim, and dark blue tinted windows like wraparound sunglasses. It had a leather-sleeved doughnut steering wheel that Rocko had once joked was "in case I have to drive with handcuffs on." Art appreciated the jacked Seventies gas guzzler in a sidelong way, as though it was the only aspect of Rocko's odd personality he, as an older guy, was permitted to comprehend.

The brightly lit interior of the stop mart was awash in some bass-heavy hip-hop that sounded, basically, like a factory stamping out metal folding chairs. It was sampled and snarly, white boys grunging out nursery-rhymed despair in cinderblock time, throttling their instruments like gator wrestlers. Rocko grinned at Art's entrance, interrupting his jammy little air dance to mouth, *Hey, good-lookin!* Art could only hear the vowels. From the jewel case atop Rocko's boombox, he gathered that this new musical horizon was the work of a person or assembly called NegrAlien, with the *N* turned around backward, no umlauts.

". . . fuckin *blows*, huh?" Rocko said as he cut the volume.

"Say again?"

"This fuckin weather. Sucks. I was just about to close up and say fuck it, right?" He blew a huge pink bubble from the wad of gum in his jaw.

"Doesn't look like it wants to give us a break, does it?"

"I fuckin heard *that*." Rocko popped his neck bones and ran a worn black comb through his pomp.

Art prowled the aisles and accumulated whatever junk snacks struck his fancy, gradually building a small pile on the counter. "Got any Dixie Double Hex?"

"How many cases?"

"Just one." Art added, "for company," too quickly, smarting at his own memory of how he used to destroy a case and a half a day, not so long ago. The bad part was that Rocko remembered this, too. Art pulled down a thick plastic packet of beef jerky, mostly because Blitz was a slave to it, and at the last minute decided to toss in two packs of cigarettes, just so he could be the compleat host, should Derek actually show up. *Not for me. For company.*

"You staying or going?" Rocko hefted the case of longneck bottles on one shoulder. Art raised his eyebrows. "The storm. They say it's gonna punch in. You staying or going?"

"Staying. I have to see if my house is up to it." Another excuse, basically.

"Well, don't forget to wear your fuckin rubbers. They say the waves will be intense. If I was a better surfer I'd take my board out. They say waves like this only come along during hurricanes in Australia. Fuckin extreme." About once every fifteen seconds, Rocko would slide his palms against the dark thighs of his gas-station-issue trousers. A big chromium chain for a biker's wallet hung down nearly to his knee on the right side.

"Where do you live, Rocko?"

"Half Moon Bay. I got a studio. I was living with this chick but she took off to follow some fuckin band up to Seattle, and that was six months ago. Love's a fuckin bitch, y'know?"

Art suddenly felt ridiculous, maundering on in his head about his dead wife. This crap befell everyone, sure as spoiling fruit; all you had to do was live long enough, and getting your heart broken was basic field issue. "She never calls, she never writes—right?"

Rocko snorted around his gum. "I don't think she knows *how* to write. You start smokin again?"

Art felt a defensive flush creep up his neck. "I've got company that might. Just in case."

"I tried to quit. Fuck that action. I quit for my girlfriend and she dumped me, so now . . ." He shrugged, bobbing his head side to side. Rocko was essentially a lot like Blitz.

New rain started pelleting in, changing directions every minute. Rocko helped Art load the Jeep and they both got instantly soaked. "Stay dry, furhead," he said, grabbing Blitz's ears and ruffling his head. Blitz dealt out one of his single enthusiastic barks.

"You're my last customer of the day," Rocko said. "I'm bagging this shit and taking to higher ground. Good luck!"

"You, too," said Art.

Rocko had killed the outside lights to the stop mart before Art was out of the lot. It was time to batten down.

● ● ● Technically, the entire day classified as twilight; Derek showed up with the drop of actual nighttime, forgoing the bell, banging on the door as though the Eaters of the Dead were chasing him on horseback.

"I don't believe it," was the first thing Art said.

It was Derek, sure enough and against the odds, which was his custom. Neon-blue eyes, shaggy black hair (he was bareheaded and

41

his hair was damp), wrapped up in a shearling bomber jacket and bulky merchant marine sweater and still standing two inches above Art's own five foot eleven. "I brought flesh," he said with a satanic grin. "You'd better have a fucking grill in this showoff dump."

"Any dead bodies in your car?"

His visitor's brow puzzled. "No. Oh, wait, well . . . there might be a—"

"Shut up, Derek." They used their firm handshake to yank each other into a bearish combat hug. Art knew his long-lost friend would slap him on the back exactly three times, back off, and repeat the process again, starting with the handclasp. It was way too manly.

"All the right parts in all the right places. You astonish me," Derek said, his smile big enough to cleave his face. "Invite me in before I moisturize to death."

"I forgot—you've got to invite the monsters over the threshold."

Derek stomped droplets from his canvas-sided military boots. His jeans were snugged inside the uppers. In one arm he slung a big, wet bag of groceries. He looked rakish and windblown, as though he'd just stepped from the cockpit of a Sopwith Camel after a good run against those blasted Jerries.

Blitz caught a whiff of Derek and went berserk, drowning them both out with a fusillade of barks until Art himself barked, "*Sitz, du blödes Vieh!*" The dog shut his trap and sat down immediately.

"Damn," said Derek, marveling.

"He's sort of trained." Art shrugged; no biggie. "Actually, he's just showing off." He shut the door firmly to make sure it seated, since the door's weight was gradually skewing the hinges, and got down to the most crucial introductions.

"Derek, meet Blitz. Blitz is a dog. Blitz, meet Derek. Don't eat him, just yet."

42

Derek squatted down slowly, careful not to move fast. "Hey, guy." He held out his hand, palm up, empty. No threat. They worked their way toward each other and after about thirty seconds were best friends. Blitz was peculiar that way. Art suspected it had to do with scent tracking; Blitz could smell whether Art thought somebody was okay or not. If it wasn't true, it should have been.

Custody of the bag—the next thing to interest Blitz—was remanded to Art while his pet and his guest checked each other out.

"That's T-bones, four of 'em, plus spuds, plus your basic salad shit. You get to do dressing, beverages, and dessert."

"Done deal," said Art. He looked in the bag and saw each steak was the size of a Frisbee. "*Four* steaks?"

"Y'know, in case we just want to eat the good bits, and give the rest to . . . *I don't know who.*" He said this last right in the dog's face and Blitz was overcome with rapture.

"Remove your spacesuit and grab a beer, why doncha?"

Derek shucked his rain-speckled leather. "Dos Equis still your poison?"

"I made sure I had a case of Dixie Double Hex when I saw the postcard. It's like a porter, but you'll live. Be adventurous and try something besides your usual watery swill."

"Only one case? You sure you don't have me confused with, like, a lightweight?" Derek was looking at the living room like someone unsure of the correct address. "This *is* your house?"

"Every square foot. Try not to gape."

Art led the way to the kitchen and church-keyed a pair of Hexes. "Never trust a beer that unscrews." They clinked longnecks and Derek commenced to wander. Despite his weakness for snack-bribery, Blitz kept track of every step. The dog would behave this way until he ultimately decided on his own that Derek was approved.

Art marinated the steaks in red wine and garlic while the pota-toes baked, then seared the cuts over a quarter-inch flame for exactly eleven minutes. The salad was in no way a beacon of nutri-tion, and the potatoes were burdened with real butter and sour cream, on top of too much salt and pepper. Both Art and Derek agreed, numerous times, that their repast was sufficiently unhealthy to commemorate their reunion. In the gaps between, Derek got caught up on the Lorelle story, and did his best to ease his friend past the awkwardness it imposed as a duty.

"It sucks," said Derek. "I could say I'm sorry for you a million times over, and it wouldn't change a thing."

"No, it's an obligation." Art picked up a scrap from his plate and instantly had the full attention of Blitz. "I can't see you after all this time, then string you along with chitchat all night, then, suddenly, when I'm drunk enough, go, *oh, by the way . . .*"

"Sounds like you did a little serious drinking, after."

"Heroic. I once drank an entire fifth of Jack Daniel's in three hours and shit myself. I did most of a quart of pepper vodka and woke up eighteen hours later, facedown in the sand, outside, in the middle of the night. Blitz licking my face finally woke me up, and I puked on him." Art flung the fatty bit of steak and Blitz intercepted it in midair, chomp, gulp, and gone. "I backed off to beer, rationing it out. For a while there I was extremely popular at the Toot 'N Moo, because I'd just load up my Jeep. *Gimme eight cases of beer and a pack of mints.* That was my idea of provisions."

"And some beef jerky."

"Right. You've been through the rest."

"You mean when you realize hugging the toilet and choking back your small intestine should not be part of your daily regimen? Yep. On the other hand, I don't think I could ever fully trust someone who never spent at least some time humbling himself before the throne."

"Jesus, how masculine is that? Tough guy poets, that's us. Complete romantics. *Urrrrrppp.*" Art mimed vomiting.

"Seductive, ain't it?" Derek swigged his beer.

"If Lorelle were here she'd reality-check us on how full of shit we are."

"Point. She was a lovely lady, and I miss her." Derek held out his bottle and Art clinked it. "You start getting morose on me and I'll give you a head noogie."

Art knew his purpose was not to hold a wake, not tonight. "I'm stuffed full of meat and fat and alcohol and all this blood and protein is shoving a fist up my brain's ass." He chortled. "Ignore me, please. We've still got dessert—chocolate ice cream with cookie dough and stuff in it."

"Uh, maybe later," Derek said, patting his stomach. "We could take the beer and make floats. Let's repair to the War Room for cigars and brandy . . . if your delicate sensibilities can take it."

"How about more beer and a monster movie instead?"

"Good answer." Derek gave a thumbs-up. "But first I need to tell you what the beginning of the twenty-first century wreaked on my sorry tail."

"Yeah, what happened to you, man?"

"I was in prison in Hawaii," Derek said, fully knowing what he was starting. "I was doing time for murder."

● ● ● "I met this Chinese guy named Ang, who was doing a nickel tour for smuggling. His real name was too goddamn long to keep track of and nobody could ever get it in the right order. We got into some half-assed discussion of comparative religion, and he said something that always stuck with me: 'It doesn't really matter what people believe in, although it causes some of them to do strange things in the names of gods,' he told me. 'What matters is whether *I* believe in people.' Well, Arthur old chap, I believe in you. You're a friend, and I owe you the story, and I'll tell it once if you comp me another beer."

"Get it yourself," said Art, grinning.

Derek's gait was loose and cowboy-ish, although it seemed to Art that cell time had pulled his friend's shoulders inward a bit. He returned with two fresh-cracked Dixie Double Hexes.

"That aluminum thing in there is the biggest goddamn refrigerator I've ever seen for a single person," he said.

"The kitchen was all Lorelle's doing." It was mostly true; she had specified the dark granite countertops, the area-specific fluorescents that delivered optically pure whites, and the stainless steel jazz that always impressed as a kind of operating theater for food. All the cutting boards were bleached-blond wood and the breakfast bar stools were some Swede's idea of ergonomic perfection in rolled, enameled metal and black leather. Sitting on them would not fatigue the back, so went the hard sell. One look at Art's kitchen would immediately leave the impression that it was a place where germs feared to tread.

"Here's to it," said Derek, and they clinked bottles again.

"Okay. How does Derek wind up in the Gray Bar Hotel?"

"I shot a guy in the lung." Derek tossed off a little eyebrow shrug that suggested he, too, still thought of it as minor and ridiculous. "You'll want to know what kind of gun. A brand-spankin'-new Sig Sauer .357 chambered for forty-caliber slugs, loaded with hardball rounds. No serial number. That got me in more shit, too, later."

"Self-defense?"

"He was banging my lady. Which the court is less interested in once they hear *'unregistered handgun'* and *'concealed loaded weapon'* and *'no serial number.'* It'd be a felony even if the fucker hadn't've died."

Lorelle's voice drifted back to haunt Art: *Have you ever actually shot anybody?* In some ways he wished he could be more like Derek—a doer, instead of a talker.

"So, murder. The M-word."

"I didn't shoot to kill him, Art. I could have. You know. I had a fifteen-round magazine and I know how to aim a gun. I fired exactly once. They didn't care. He bled to death in the hospital, and I dearly hope he died in excruciating pain, or at least was conscious for some of the fall. See, when Erica and I—"

"Erica was the woman you originally took off for Hawaii with?" Art knew, but felt like checking.

"The same. Brown hair, brown agate eyes, body like a panther—you know, the type you always teased me about."

"Sorry." Art grinned anyway. Sarcasm as a trait of male bonding.

"We got a place on Kaunakakai, away from a lot of the tourist bullshit. A lot like this place"—his arm indicated the sweep and scope of Art's overdone house—"but with, you know, no money involved. We were together for a year until one morning she rolled over and said, 'I think we need to see other people.' Point-blank, like that, while I'm still thinking about not waking up. She hung around most of the day, but it was clear all she wanted to do was run. We saved the first real argument for when she got back, and I swear I could already smell the new guy on her. Now picture me: I'm burned out from Lockheed, all that corporate crap, all that *political* crap, and she's the only one who understands or gives a damn, and we'd even mentioned getting married once or twice, and now she's out the door like I have the plague."

"You talked about getting married?" Art let his disbelief register on his face, mostly to prompt an explanation. "You weren't on speedballs or anything?"

"Afraid not, amigo. I know—alert the media." He killed half the beer in a swig, just tipped it down his throat without swallowing, the way Blitz would do it if he had a taste. "I'd come around to thinking about human relationships, the patterns people stick to. You've seen most of my girlfriends."

"They tend to blend at the edges. I remember Brady, that vice-president of something or other from the company in the Transamerica Tower."

"She worked in publishing—that outfit that did the series of books on how normal people were supposed to figure out what were then called 'home computers.' Why do you remember her?"

"Because she had fabulous legs, knew how to walk in heels, looked like Gene Tierney in mint condition, I thought her glasses were cute, and she came right over and talked to me without looking toward you for permission, which is something a lot of the others did, like puppies waiting for a command they don't understand anyway. We had this very memorable conversation about modern hard-boiled novelists, and it turns out we held a lot of the same tastes. After Crumley, Westlake, and Willeford . . . forget it, everybody else was just a pretender or a recycler. I'll admit I got most of that line from Lorelle, but Brady liked it."

"She did read a lot of books. Fiction books."

"She was slightly older than you, too, as I recall."

"One of the few. Erica was a decade younger, and that was no strain until she decided it was high time she had a midlife crisis, mostly to find out what it was like. Her whole life had been smash-and-grab, chase-and-run, trade on her looks, slip through the cracks, and as soon as she stabilized and got a tiny bit of security, of permanence, I think it scared the shit out of her."

"She was thinking, *Great, I'm old, I'm over already?*"

"Or words to that effect. So, how do you countermand this feel-. ing? You run as fast as you can back to what you knew worked when you were in your twenties."

"A lot of people do that. Chase it, hoping to recapture it."

"Meanwhile, I'm sitting around with this not-bad life, thinking that most people do the same thing, which is why the range of human relationships runs on a scale from one to ten—one is the ini- tial attraction, and ten is growing older together, and I knew far too many people who had concentrated on becoming world-class experts on one through three. As soon as 'four' threatened—let's call 'four' a longer-term relationship than normal—they freak out, self-destruct the current relationship, and reset to one. It's not liv- ing, but it's a life, if you know what I mean. You get the allure of unwrapping a fresh body as opposed to the normalcy of sleeping with the same person for a year. Get out of the house before the home makes you feel stagnant, and you accumulate too many mementos. Stay below the tax radar, move at will, and pick who you want to fuck on a disposable basis. All that's left is paying the bills."

"It's easier to get into new relationships than it is to get out of old ones," said Art. Blitz crawled into his hideout, the space between the supports for the big oval coffee table, and sprawled on one side. He seemed to think he was safe in there, despite the fact he could plainly be seen right through the glass tabletop.

"Erica's 'new relationship' was a dipshit named Tommi, with an *i* at the end. Big Italian fucker, a club rocker edging up on forty and still trying to cut some lame demo with his lame band. A ladykiller with a motorcycle and a microphone case and very few strings attached. Kind of guy who dyes out the gray in his hair so he can still pretend to be twenty-five in the clubs, and shaves clean so he doesn't get salt and pepper on his muzzle."

"A free spirit," said Art, meaning *an irresponsible buttwipe locked into the box of his own teenage past.* "I bet he moved from girlfriend's apartment to girlfriend's apartment."

"Yeah, Tommi was a dog with no papers, all right. He had a bungalow to himself near the beach—everything in Kaunakakai is 'near the beach'—all to himself because his previous chick just moved out on him, emptied the closets and vanished. Which left him with six weeks free rent and free cable, but without a fuck bunny for the weekend, which is where Erica comes in."

"And Erica, who has a level head up until this moment, gets swept off her feet?"

"No, she got swept onto her back," said Derek. The sting of memory still held residual venom, and the power to hurt him. "You ever read that fairy tale, *The Girl Who Loved the Wind*?"

"Is it a classic?"

"No, it's a modern one, written in the Seventies. I checked it out. A girl has this overprotective father who keeps her inside this fabulous garden, to shield her from the wickedness of the world. It's a gilded cage that also protects her from anything real, and finally the Wind, which whispers of the world's promise and endless possibilities, blows over the wall and woos her away. It's a loss-of-innocence parable; you can read it as anything from gaining maturity to loss of virginity."

"And you're the evil, imprisoning father figure."

"Sort of. Erica saw our relationship as a box, and I thought it was a safe house; I mean, everyone's got to deal with the world. Instead of us progressing to four or five on the relationship scale, which is scary and intimidating, she decided to go 'back to one,' as the movie people say."

"With some rock 'n' roll dood with no attachments, no obligations, and no worries."

"Yeah, he was the Wind, and he blew her." Derek snickered at his own crassness. "You know what it feels like to *lose* to a loser like that? Anything I could say was too reasoned, too rational, not spontaneous, and all just a trick to get her back in the box. She just lock-stock-and-barreled out the door to something less predictable and more familiar to the rest of her life. How do you argue with that? You don't. It's a choice, and you eat the fallout, which is why people advise other people never to fall in love."

"It couldn't last, though," said Art. "It's not designed to."

"But once it tarnishes, see, she's recaptured the mind-set and can just breeze onto the next thing, like a skipping stone."

"What yuppies call *grazing* instead of *cocooning*."

"And never get in too deep on anything you can't bail from at a moment's notice, because there's always another branch to light on. So, she's making no immediate noises that she's anything but deliriously happy and free and sampling life's rich cornucopia . . . with Tommi-with-an-*i*, who is a world-class meatball. This causes Derek—that's me—to brood a lot, because I wanted to invest my life in this person, and it's like she's saying that's swell and all, but has no value. He's the Wind, and I'm the Cinderblock. She gains the world and I feel like I've lost everything, and I start to ask myself, gee, does she have to figure some things out, or is she really that shallow?"

"Scared, maybe." Art thought it was sad. Did two people ever run in parallel, or was it all just lies partners imposed on each other, a shadow play of life as it was supposed to be, not how it was?

"I couldn't do anything useful, so I gradually worked my way around to the idea of scaring Tommi off. Maybe, I thought, she left me so easily because I didn't fight for her."

"Mmm." Art rolled his eyes and stuck out his lower jaw into a ridiculous gorilla expression. *"Ug do battle for woman. Crush enemies."*

Derek leaned forward, elbows on knees. They'd started an actual, real blaze of actual, real wood in the fireplace, and burning cedar had filled the room with a rich, smoky tang. An occasional knot fizzed and exploded against the spark grate. They were savanna hunter-gatherers, swapping sagas by firelight.

"I find out where Tommi lives and stealth over there, thinking I'll keep the clip in my pocket and shove my gun in his mouth and scare him into I don't know what. But her car's already there and through the side window I can see them fucking in the bedroom. She's being really loud, really vocal, which is funny because she rarely did that with me. Her new personality. I guess I just saw red; I thought if I could just see them fucking, then *click,* my brain would know that it was over and done. Wrong. I burglared in—just add breaking and entering to my tab, thanks—and pushed the door open with my foot and shot him. She was on top of him, bucking away like somebody was filming them, flailing and hooting, and the round went right between her left arm and armpit and hit him in the tit as he was trying to sit up. He flopped with a little grunt—I think that was when he blew his load—and when Erica looked down she saw a bullet hole with a red air bubble of blood already growing out of it. She saw me and I said something really moronic, like 'Remember me,' and I turned and walked out."

"Jesus."

"Then I did the only thing dumber than what I've just told you."

"You went to a bar with a thatched frond canopy and drank yourself idiotic until a cop tapped on your shoulder."

Derek tipped his bottle toward Truth and finished it off. "Detective, actually. When I got arraigned it came out that I hadn't paid any income taxes since Lockheed, which was another rather shortsighted life decision. The list of charges ran over two typed pages by a single line, and when judges see that staple holding more than a page, they tend to get a bit irritable. I got a pit bull of a lawyer who sacrificed my one-time accountant to the tax beef, and played the crime-of-passion angle for all it was worth, which is to say, all I could be billed for."

"That doesn't explain why you're here, what, a couple of years after a murder charge. How does *that* work?"

"Three years and change. It happened right when the second-degree murder charge got changed to 'voluntary manslaughter.' Hawaii has no death penalty, but even second degree carries a life sentence."

"*With* possibility of parole, I take it."

"It was the state versus me, and they concluded no premeditation."

"Crime of passion?"

"Better." Derek allowed himself a private grin. "Third degree. They concluded that unpapered gun of mine actually belonged to Tommi, and they believed it when Erica showed up in court and said it was so. My lame hit hung a corner into self-defense. Nobody was more boggled than I was. That was the last time I saw her, and god knows why she did it, because I never got to ask."

Art knew his old amigo better than that. "What's the part you're leaving out?"

Derek chuckled. "The attorney part. The bribery part. The money part. The parole-board-payoff part. The showy-good-behavior part. The under-the-table—"

"Stop, stop, or I'll drown."

"I am, in fact, a murderer, if you want to get picky about it. Personally, I'd rather believe the story than the reality. It's bad enough that I'll have that dumb fuck Tommi's face in my brain for the rest of my life." Derek knotted his hands between his knees, risking a reverie.

"And how does the parole thing work, and give you the latitude to show up on my doorstep in another state?" Art was still skeptical.

"I was technically in violation of my release the minute I stepped onto a plane for San Francisco. Lawyer's there, a grizzled fella by the name of Thurston Cutler Junior. You ever need first-class rep, he's your man and you can tell him I sent you."

"What'd all this cost you, if you don't mind my asking?"

"What is costs, Arthur, is you have to stop calling me Derek. My name's Jacob Hume now; Jake to my pals."

This time Art brought the refills. "Here you go, eh, Jake. Would you like to hear about our specials for this evening?"

"Comedian. A lot of those in the ole big house. You'll do well."

"What happened to—?"

"Erica?"

"Yeah, Erica. Sorry."

"What'd the masochist say when asked what he liked about his lover?"

"*Beats me,*" they both said simultaneously. It was an old, retarded joke, the kind your dad might tell for forty years running. *If it was funny during the Second World War, it's funny now, goddammit,* Art's father used to cackle.

"I used to think that Erica actually got what she wanted, in a perverse sort of way. A big tragedy to add drama to her new life story.

You can get a lot of mileage out of the old murdered-lover anecdote. But where is she now?" Derek—"Jake"—shrugged. "Now ask me what it was like in prison."

"How come you didn't tell me when it happened?"

"Like you needed that grief. There was nothing to do, unless you were going to send cookies, and the guards eat all the good ones, anyway. My choice. I'm telling you now. Don't get all hurt and shit."

Art thought about what he could have done, realistically, practically, and saw his friend's point. He still felt that small pang of exclusion, though.

In order to share, match story for story, Art told Derek about the human bone and the note in the bottle found on the beach earlier in the day. Derek, abristle with the freshly picked memory scabs of Erica, snorted at the floridly vague declaration on the waterlogged paper.

"It's gotta be a chick, no offense. It's got that manipulative, self-centered, me-me-me stench. You recognize junkie behavior faster if you're inundated in it. Little Miss No-Name probably got all teary and jumped into the ocean, and if that's a piece of her you're keeping on the mantel, throw it back and make sure Blitzy doesn't fetch it."

"Junkie behavior?" said Art.

"You know—evasion, denial, refusal to address whatever's relevant? 'How're things?' 'Things're fine' . . . when they're not, when they are, in fact, all fucked up, but nobody discusses it because that would violate the gentle fib that everything's okay and everybody's getting along swell. Under all that, the hunger holds illimitable dominion over all. The hunger for drugs, or freedom, or whatever goofy perfect picture has been cooked up by the delusional. Junkie behavior."

"Hell, in that case, *I* could've written the note," said Art, and they both laughed.

"Next question," Derek said with forced brightness, as though eager to get past it. *"Did you get fucked in the ass in the slammer?"*

"I wasn't going to say that."

"Everybody says it. Everybody thinks it. And the answer is, yes, when I was fresh fish, I got held down and raped by some very big guys with shaved heads and a lot of scar tissue. By the time newer fish rolled in, I was old news, and the population had figured me out, at least as much as they cared to, because I could draw. Pictures."

Art cocked his head. It was a quizzical expression, like Blitz would make.

"Remember it," Derek said. "If you're doing time, and you can draw, then you can tattoo, and if you can tattoo, you can survive in prison. Although you'd have to get a little artier than blueprints." He coughed. *"Blue prints*—hey, that's funny."

"Yeah, but jail ink is usually shit—dragons and gang tags and naked women done by somebody with a hot nail and no style."

"That was my target. I could actually draw, that is, illustrate. I got a lot of attention for the right reasons, instead of for the rape-ability of my asshole, or my superfine, sensuous mouth. Once you cycle into the population and learn where the goods come from, you can score practically anything. I spent a shitload of dough on an electric toothbrush, and made it into a tattoo gun. You rubber-band a bunch of needles around the wiggly bit. It worked pretty fair."

"I was going to ask about the eyeball on the back of your hand," said Art. "Kind of a bit of a problem in the 'identifying marks' category, isn't it?"

Derek examined the eye, languidly half-open, on the back of his left hand. The eye looked back at him as if wondering how interesting the answer would be. "It's one thing if you've got a shitload of Maori jazz crawling up your neck onto your face. This, I can hide. Cost of doing business. Call it a learning experience."

"Still . . ."

"I read you. I designed the eye so I could cover it up with a driving glove. Then those fingerless motorcycle gloves fell out of style and the joke was on me, right?"

"You could wear a snappy single glove, like that inspector in that Frankenstein movie."

Derek's brow furrowed. "Hey. Bust your dog's balls, okay? I have to be careful; I have a new identity to protect. I thought of finding some guy who knows which end of a laser not to stare into, but you know what? I don't want to lose it. It looks out for me, spiritually. Keeps an eye peeled while I'm asleep, in the astral, I don't know. What can I say? It grounds me. I think it's going to stay." Derek stood up and pulled his heavy merchant marine sweater over his head. "If the eye bugs you, then you're going to hate this."

Art was going to say, *Just don't take your pants off,* but the spit dried up in his mouth. Derek's left arm was end-to-end dermagraphs. The wrist was clean but most of the forearm was gauntleted in a Celtic weave of knots. At the elbow on both sides was inked an anatomically correct bone joint. Wrapped around the biceps was an armor-patterned snake, flicking its forked tongue toward the rattles on the tip of its own tail. Above that, near the ball of shoulder, was a sun or star that looked to be going supernova. Derek moved closer and sat cross-legged on the floor so Art could observe the tour of the gallery.

"Problem is, most guys bring photos they want to immortalize. Girlfriends and pets, RIPs. Sword and sorcery hokum, biker chic, broken hearts. Mom. Shit from some dog-eared girlie magazine. Anybody who bothers to go to the library usually requests an Egyptian symbol or classical image."

"I was going to ask if that was the Eye of Ra."

"Sort of. My interpretation. But you've got the inspiration right.

57

Another biggie is astrological signs. Flags of all nations. One guy whose bro died in prison came to me to duplicate his friend's tat, as a remembrance."

"What was it?" Art was fascinated.

"Just a purple sort of flower, like an iris. At least it wasn't a hula girl, or Hot Stuff." He indicated the sleeve. "Celtic patterns are always good. The barbed wire thing was popular, but I always thought it was kind of pussy—you know, *wooo*, you've got a *picture* of razor wire on you. That's like wearing an empty cartridge belt as a fashion accessory."

"That bone thing looks gruesome, like the inside of your arm seen through X-ray Spex."

"Hurts more to do the back of your hand, or fingers, or your knee, or the top of your foot. That's where the bones are closest to the surface. Once I did this baby, guys started asking for all sorts of bone overlays. A lot of skeleton hands, and never mind the fucking pain, they'd say. If I'd stayed in longer I would've gotten to try a full-on skull on this skinhead guy named Turk, no lie. I'd put spiders on the backs of heads, with the legs curling around the ears. Cobweb patterns. Inevitably some clown wanted me to tattoo a bone on his dick—'yuh know, the bones that *grows*, haw haw—but I was spared the delight."

"That serpent looks familiar."

"You got it. That's our snake, immortalized."

Art was surprised by the speed with which he'd gone from initial distaste to considering an identical snake for himself. The thing on Derek's arm was Art's exact idea of the imaginary rattler inside his vitals. He wondered what Lorelle might have requested, and came up with nothing obvious.

"Why just the left arm?"

"Because I'm right-handed. So it's long sleeves; I don't really mind. It's not that weird anymore. Twelve-year-olds are getting inked and pierced at the mall; they can buy niobium safety pins at any drugstore. I know this guy, a studio guy down in L.A., who has a great big curlicued FUCK YOU tattooed right across the center of his chest. Says he loves to sit in bullshit meetings, just knowing it's there, just thinking about the day he quits and unveils it at the correct moment."

"Speaking of Hollywood, I think I've got just the movie for your mood."

"Thrill me."

They sat through *I Married a Monster from Outer Space*, a Fifties classic about aliens taking over human bodies in order to mate with Earth women. It was better than its hysterical title, it was in glorious black-and-white, and best of all, it featured monster-fighting dogs, a pair of German shepherds, one of whom gives his dog-life to repel the invaders.

Blitz was not moved by the selfless sacrifice of his brethren.

"Ever notice that?" said Art. "Dogs are always the first line of defense against extraterrestrial bad guys. Purebred Monster Fighters." He thumped Blitz. "Would you take on a slimy alien for us? At least let us know one's around?"

"Not if the alien brings a steak," said Derek. "I think ole Blitz would turn traitor on us, for a steak. Say *steak*."

Blitz woofed, exactly once.

"When your dog betrays you, that's the worst. You're not listening, are you?" Blitz put his head back down on the carpet with a capacious nasal sigh, and remained encamped under the table.

"How's this for a transition?" said Derek. "One of the reasons I'm bound for L.A. is a fella named Joseph Clawfoot, Joe to his friends."

"That's one way to avoid being made," said Art. "Hang out with people who have inconspicuous names."

"Joe's in construction, and they've got him slaving away on this refitting of the Cinerama Dome Theatre down there. They're restoring it so it can show actual Cinerama movies—the screen is curved, and it'll be ninety feet wide. Only other place that can show true Cinerama is in Seattle."

"How many movies are there in Cinerama, anyway?"

"Fewer than ten. Most people know *How the West Was Won*. Anyhow, Joe asks if I know anyone who'd be interested in his next project, and I thought of you."

"I don't build 'em, I just draw 'em."

"You make my point for me. What he needs is a new design for a very special kind of movie theater. See, the multiplex is dead as a concept. That big ole screen you've got in your living room is proof. People don't want to pay, what, nine—ten bucks to see essentially the same thing with no focus and some guy spitting popcorn in their hair. So Joe wants to tear the guts out of an existing multiplex, and plug in a single theater with one-third the seats. Nice recliners. Beverage service, including champagne. No kids allowed. Legroom. Big screen. Ushers. One projectionist. It's like bumping the ante on a Hollywood screening room, the kind you have to have special invites to go on studio lots to see, only better."

"Any movie house where they serve you champagne is a step up. Most multiplexes look like giant porcelain restrooms."

"Here's the most outrageous part: It costs fifteen bucks to get in."

"I'd pay twenty bucks, for that."

"Joe thinks a lot of people would, because you can have all the movies in the world in your house, but there's still this atavistic need to go *out* to see a new movie. Or an old movie. As long as it's the right movie."

"Okay . . . so?"

"So, if the flagship floats, he wants to tear out the rest of the multiplex boxes and retheme the whole place, and he needs some-one to come up with a design that's new, because just tearing out seats and tossing in a bigger screen won't excite the backers."

"Derek, this is dangerously close to a passion of mine."

"I know.. Why do you think I told Joe? Think of it, man—valet parking and appetizers. No more drug dealers with switchblades. Hollywood massacres its own history faster than any other city in the country. They're trying to tear down the Hollywood Bowl right now, and build a venue three times bigger on the same spot, for rock shows, because the L.A. Philharmonic's contract eats shit and dies in 2005. The Bowl is only one of the three most recognizable buildings in Hollywood. I bet cash money you know the other two."

Art thought about it. "Obvious: Grauman's Chinese Theatre and the Capitol Records Building."

"They can reinforce the existing structure of the Bowl, but the guys who made billions off the subway project down there are hun-gry to tear down and throw up. The Chinese wasn't even Grau-man's, for more than two decades, and now they're crowing 'anniversary' and not counting the lost years it was called Mann's Chinese. The main house has been rechristened Grauman's now that they added another rat-maze multi. It's happening to all the showoff theaters. The time is ripe for you to strike. You're inter-ested, right?"

"In the theater thing? Sure. But my interest equals exactly zero."

"I just need an excuse to put you two together, and you'll achieve critical mass all on your own. Can you knock out some time to come to L.A.?"

"Right *now?*"

"Shit yeah, right now. Let's jump in the car and haul ass. It's a rental; it won't matter if we wreck it. We'll be there in seven hours." Probably less, if Derek still drove the way Art remembered.

61

Adventure beckoned. It frequently did within moments of any appearance by Derek.

"You mean take off with a known felon on a road trip to chase a movie theater?"

"Basically, you got it. If the cops pull us over, just call me *Jake* and all shall be cool. Pretend I'm somebody else. Crank up the stereo. Catch a little highway air."

"Half the coast road'll be out. There's already flooding, south of here. There's a storm coming."

"We can outrun it." Derek's eyes were bright now, full up with mischief. "That's what that pedal on the right is for."

"Neither of us is in what you might call driving trim."

"Fuck that, I'll be sober in an hour. Good to go. Come on, man, get out of this cage. I just got out of mine. Check out something completely mysterious. Who knows? Lots of eligibles in L.A."

"I'd love to—"

"*But,*" Derek interposed. "You're gonna *but* me, aren't you?"

"Shut up. Listen. This storm coming in is a big deal for this house, the one you're sitting in right now."

"So lock up, drop your shutters, and fly. We'll take the dog with us. You wanna go to L.A., Blitz?"

Blitz stretched and aired out his tongue. Yes, adventure was fine with him, too.

"No, you don't understand. This house is a design that some people have called revolutionary. If there's a big blow coming down, I need to monitor it. See how the structure weathers it. Because if I'm right, then rich people up and down the entire coast will be calling, and I won't have to design a goddamn futuristic food court."

Derek blew out an exasperated breath. "All right. If you're gonna puss on me, then here's what I'll do: I will call you from L.A. with the skinny from Joe. By then the storm'll be done. I will then come back up here and drag your sorry ass back down there, because I want this excursion with you."

"I can drive down . . ."

"You're missing the point of the whole trip. We have to stay awake all night, drink road beers, get so punchy that everything we see turns viciously funny. I need it, I want it. But you had to go do what you always do, which is logic me out of it. You didn't give me a bullshit excuse, you gave me a real one, so just say yes to the second part and I'll forgive you for the first. And for being such an anus."

"Am I that much of an anus?"

Blitz barked. *Yes.* Both humans dissolved into laughter.

"Well, stay the night," said Art. "Take off in the morning."

"Nah," said Derek. "I was listening to the radio, too—what there was of FM. That storm will fuck up the roads soon enough, and I want to get inland."

"Right this instant?"

He rubbed the two-day stubble on his cheeks. "Not if you've got another monster movie. And maybe one more beer."

"Deal." It wasn't until Art stood up again that he realized he was quite drunk already.

● ● ● Art opened his eyes to a vista of blank blue on the big Proton TV screen and a wasteland of beer bottles, congregated on the glass table like innocent bystanders at an accident scene. Pain stabbed up and over from his occipital, like a muscle tension headache. His first impulse was to douse some of the overbearing lights; his second, to gulp a fistful of Excedrin . . .

. . . just like the bad old period that followed Lorelle's death, when he'd been doing that bottomless-pit drinking that frequently brought blackouts, and lost him entire calendar days.

Panicked and unbalanced, he looked for the nearest clock and saw that it was eleven-thirty; the darkness outside would make that P.M. But was it eleven-thirty on the night Derek showed up, or some further date? Art stumbled to his computer, holding his head as though he'd been mugged.

Eleven thirty-two P.M., it advised. Same day.

So you're by yourself, he thought, walled up in your own fortress, minimizing human contact, and what happens? A flamboyant character from your past shows up practically unannounced to regale you with catch-up stories. He does most of the talking while you bask in nostalgia.

Art's lungs suddenly felt hot and tender, as if the rattlesnake's maraca tail segments were tickling his chest with dread. He did not like the possibility that was racing toward his conscious mind like an ominous, dark juggernaut.

Derek shows up and is the very embodiment of hearty macho camaraderie. He spins a fanciful story of how he took charge when his lady was cheating on him in some exotic foreign port, blew away her paramour as smooth as a country-and-western song lyric, and wound up in the Gray Bar Hotel. Yet he's a free man scant years later thanks to a Houdini of a lawyer, or a loophole in the law, or . . . something. Was there a chance in hell of these cards playing in a shooting death? Art didn't know, and the very seductive convenience of Derek's story began to gnaw at his logic.

They had talked the follies of love, drunk beer, and watched monster movies, strictly according to Art's idealized template of their past, when Lorelle was alive. Derek even had "their" rattler tattooed on his arm—how likely was that, in the real world?

His asshole buddy from the bygone had manifested right on his doorstep, and Blitz had accepted him instantly. He unspooled edgy stories of his exciting, tightrope life, and his coming attractions included some dream gig in Hollywood. He had been ruthless and logical about shooting Erica's supposed lover, yet went to a bar and got drunk instead of submerging into a backup identity he had tucked away all along.

Derek's story was beginning to submerge due to its own leaks. It had all the brio of a braggart's tale, made up on the fly to impress distant friends. That was not Art's worry at the moment.

Art's fingertips had grown frigid. Now he was scared. He could smell alcohol metabolizing through his skin; the whole living room was clogged with the reek of beer and cigarettes.

Art was scared that he had imagined the entire evening with Derek. That he had fabricated his friend's visit as an excuse to get drunk. That he was so lonely and disconnected that he was beginning to hallucinate old buddies, full of piss and vinaigrette. That he had sat and watched a monster movie by himself, talking to dead air and confusing his dog.

Nothing in Derek's backstory held a drop of plausibility. It was like something Art himself would confect, given what he knew about prisons and statutes and what kind of laws swung in *Hawaii*, for god's sake.

Art's heartbeat had doubled. He looked around for evidence of Derek's passage, and the primal fear quadrants of his primitive hindbrain freaked even more when he couldn't find any.

The bottles—Art could have killed all those soldiers himself. The smokes, ditto. His throat felt raw and shitty. His metabolism flashed back to his smoking days.

In the kitchen—remnants of dinner for two, but Art could recall no particular about the meal that would confirm he had not eaten it himself. There was a sodden paper grocery bag in the garbage bearing a receipt for the stuff Derek had brought. Seemingly brought. The receipt was local; Art could have scored it all himself, then blocked it out. One of his own business cards sat on the glass with a beer-bottle ring soaking it.

Blitz offered no clues or advice.

Wet footprints on the threshold—dry now, but still visible on the carefully laid flagstone. One set. Art's shoes.

The bathroom—nothing. Either Derek had been fastidious, or he hadn't actually been here at all.

Art looked for a stray hair on the couch. Apparently Derek didn't shed the way normal humans did.

Derek had sung the praises of an attorney too good to be true . . . because he probably did not exist at all.

The postcard was still at Art's workstation. HAVE A BEER, YOU FUCK. It now seemed like a telegram from a madhouse, addressed to Art personally, inviting him to an alumni reunion.

Christ, he thought. Did I even write the card myself? Mail it to myself?

If Derek's surreal job offer had anything to do with the actual world, Art would be getting a phone call, not quickly enough to allay his new fears, but soon. Hang on to that.

This little ember of hope stabilized him a bit. Then Art's reality vertigo took an even deeper plunge, so hard it forced him to sit down with a heavy woof of breath.

If the story about Derek wasn't true . . .

. . . how true was the story about Lorelle?

Had he done something bad to his own wife?

The words of the castaway note in the sea bottle might almost have been from Lorelle, chiding him about whatever bad, unaccept-

66

able thing he had done, before his swan dive into some psychotic fugue of a far-too-ordered, imaginary life of grief.

It pains me to witness your own pain . . .

Gentle castigation from the dead.

I don't want sympathy or pity; no one to mourn me.

In that context, the bone Blitz had retrieved was too gruesome to consider.

Was it possible Art had harmed her?

Pain divided his brain like a cadmium shaft. He leaned forward, pinching the bridge of his nose. One gasp escaped him, then he vomited on the living-room floor. The puke punched out of him all liquid and beery.

Blitz was looking at him as though Art had just morphed into a tentacled alien. Getting ready to be a Monster Fighter.

Art looked up into the poisonously rich blue of the TV screen. It made his skull throb even worse. The satellite dish was out; no signal. If he'd fallen asleep watching the system, he should have awakened to a scrolling menu.

"Sit down!" he yelled at the dog, who was making motions that suggested he wanted to trot over to lap up the puke on the floor. Blitz flinched and sat, his tail unmoving.

Art's muscles screamed. It felt like a randy soccer team had used him for fuck practice and left him ass-up in a Dumpster. His head swarmed with toxic fog. His vision jarred in and out of focus as he lumbered for the front door like a drunk. When he jerked the door open, the house's alarm system went off, another napalm attack on his senses.

If Derek had really been here, would the alarm have been set? That didn't make any sense, either.

Art punched in the key code and the shrill air-horn noise ceased. Wind lashed rain over the threshold and stung his face with cold. He tilted against the blow and fought his way to the highway turnoff. The five-minute stroll became a ten-minute slog. En route he saw that there were no fresh tire tracks. The wind had already erased them . . . if they had ever been there.

At the concrete corral for the trash, he checked the recycling bin with a flashlight, fearful that he would find it brimmed with empty bottles. There was nothing. Thursday was also garbage collection day for the outlands.

The rain agonized in like sleet, raking his arms and face. He was suddenly afraid his own door would lock him out. It swung toward the jamb, moved by the wind, as he approached—just subtly enough to panic him and break him into a run for the house. Nothing definitive. The universe seemed organized toward disorienting him, not actually smashing him down. Not yet.

Had he finally cracked, shattered, lost his mind? Blitz was still sitting exactly where he had been told, and somehow that frightened Art even more. Dogs could sense madness. When the TV news crews showed up, the first thing upon which they would fixate would be Art's modest library of serial killer books.

He mopped up his own vomit and used lime spray to kill the acidic stench. He had to wash, to sleep, to restart his entire day and maybe his whole life.

He wished Derek had left Joe Clawfoot's number . . . if either of them really existed.

That was when his attention was snapped around to the sliding glass doors on the seaward side of the living room. A woman was outside on the deck, banging the slanted door with the flat of her hand, her voice strident. Blitz charged forward and began barking.

Art inadvertently grasped his chest. *This is what a heart attack feels like*, he thought.

FRIDAY

Suzanne was about five-five, short and rounded, with hair chopped off straight at the chin line. Its tint varied, favoring amber, with a stark dyed violet streak arcing back from the left temple. She looked to be bravely weathering her midtwenties. Beneath her inadequate Victorian sweater she came clad in a bewildering array of black undergarments that ganged to form an outfit; a lot of thin straps vied for space on each shoulder. Her clothing was completely sodden from the brutality of the rain. She entered Art's house goose-bumped and shivering, barefoot, her toes white as milk.

Art had shaken off his bizarrerie long enough to tell Blitz to shut the hell up, and unlock the sliding doors. A blast wave of frigid ocean air practically pushed Suzanne inside. The abrupt quiet, once the doors were shut again, was precarious with pocket drama.

"God!" she said. "*Fuck,* it's *freezing* out there!" Her eyes were a vague gray and seemed slightly hunted. They darted around to catalog Art's living room as if she'd just blundered into a police station or a church by accident. "Thank you, thank you, and thank you. I'm Suzanne." She did not stick out a hand. "Thank you."

Opening lines were everything, but Art still had demons poking his brain matter with fondue forks. "What are you doing outside," he said, "in *that?*"

69

"Sure looks like rain, don't it?" The fireplace caught her gaze and held it. "You don't mind—?"

"Please." Art swept a hand toward the hearth as though holding open an invisible door. You had to invite people in. "How about a towel?"

"That would be heaven. Hi, doggie."

As soon as she moved, Blitz started barking again, bracing on his forelegs like a bucking motorcycle about to kick into gear. Art snapped, "*Halt's Maul!*"—shut up—and exiled him to the "dog den" off the kitchen pantry room: "*Verschwinde in deine Hütte!*" Blitz needed to chill, to occupy himself with his favorite hunk of blanket and masticate his chew toys while Art sorted things out.

Suzanne was shucking her sweater with an *ugghh* sound as Art brought two huge towels of Egyptian cotton. The sweater clung like a jellyfish until it was bested. It hit the hearth with a moist slap.

"I've got some clean sweats if you want to throw that stuff in the dryer."

"You're trying to get me naked and I don't even know your name yet."

Her breasts caught him looking but her eyes missed his flash of embarrassment. "Call me Art, and so far I think I'm pleased to meet you, but what the hell were you doing out there?"

"You're supposed to say, What are you doing out *there at this time of night, or don't you have enough sense to stay out of the rain?*"

"Well, that, too. *Wait till your father gets home!*"

"Now you got it. Looks like there's a hell of a party going on here, too." All the beer bottles were still crowding the table space. "Smells like somebody puked."

Art's flush of color was not too noticeable thanks to the light he had dimmed just minutes before. "Uh . . . I had company."

"Did the dog barf?"

"Something like that."

Art was already walking on glass and eggshells, playing host again too soon, still wondering if he was making all this up inside his mad cauliflower brain. It threw his composure and rendered his speech halting and hair-triggered. If he had invented Derek's entire visit, who was to say that Suzanne wasn't just another fantasy he'd conjured up?

A really obvious fantasy, too, he chided himself.

Suzanne unknowingly fought back the unreal with sheer presence. "You're *not sure* whether your dog barfed. O-kayyy . . ." She toweled her hair vigorously and came up frizzy. "You want me to take my clothes off now?"

Art nearly spluttered. Good thing he didn't have a drink in his mouth.

"Sorry." She grinned evilly. "I mean, which way to the bathroom? You serious about those sweats?"

It took Art another idiotic beat to reset. "Oh. Yeah, of course. Let me collect things. Two minutes."

"I can't wait two minutes."

"Two moments, then."

"Moments, I can handle. You got any more beer or did you drink it all?"

It wasn't an accusation, although it shrieked in and detonated inside Art's head like one. "In the fridge," he called from the guest bathroom.

When he came out she was sauntering down the hall, a low-slung walk that rolled her hips naturally and was nearly impossible not to look at. She held a bottle of Dixie Double Hex and two of her many straps had drooped off her left shoulder. "Thank you, stranger," she said with a brilliant smile. "I'll be out in a bit." When she shut the bathroom door, Art heard her lock it.

Battened on guilt, Art quickly eliminated the beer bottles from the table and cleaned up. Suzanne had left damp footprints on the carpet near the hearth. He picked up her saturated sweater. So far this seemed real-world enough. This visitor left traces of her passage. Blitz had instantly flipped out into intruder mode, another proof. But no circumstance had ever before delivered strangers to Art's door, and he was in danger of getting lost in trying to figure out what every little clue meant, like the guy who can't hear the music over all the noise made by the orchestra.

He had bolted Excedrin and hydrocodone; the caffeine in the first was abetted by the buffering wave of the latter, and his skull began to relax its grip on his brain. Suzanne was oval-faced and attractive, with an almost Asian aspect to the set of her eyes. A bright intelligence danced in that gaze. His desktop schedule/planner was agreeably blank, his dance card clean, and he had no overwhelming desire to puzzle out his latest assignment or dip into another doorstop-thick, beach-read paperback. What else did he have to do tonight?

The utility cubby did double duty as a dog den. The home of the washer/dryer setup, it was equipped with a drop-down ironing board and a clothesline beyond Blitz's reach. Upper shelves were laden with canned goods overstock from the pantry. The main power panels for the house were found here, upgraded for better amperage, along with indoor meters for utilities. Some basic gardening tools were also kept here; Art disliked leaving such stuff outside, where it might reclassify as potential hardware for a break-and-enter. When it was cold like this, Blitz enjoyed lazing about the room when the dryer was running. Right now the dog sourly regarded his master from the far end of the room. *I was just doing my dog job. What if she had been a monster?*

"You can come out if you promise not to be an asshole."

Blitz livened up and sniffed the wet sweater in Art's hands. Some kind of aroma clung remotely to it. Perfume or body oil, more like a spice than a commercial scent. It helped add salacious thoughts to the shopping list already self-compiling in Art's imagination. Stop it, he remonstrated with himself. Be nice.

He heard the shower running in the guest bath. That made sense. Pound the chill out with hot water. Suzanne knew how to avoid catching cold even if she couldn't stay out of the rain.

Evidence of Derek's passage was so scarce that Art remained unnerved and off balance. The stack of dinnerware they'd used—for two—counted for nothing if he was delusional. He could have watched the movie by himself.

Or he could, more simply, have been so lonely that he was using any human contact as an excuse to doubt his equilibrium. The haughty Suzanne certainly classified as a surprise shock.

Blitz had heard that remark about the vomit smell. Sure, some-body farts, somebody pukes, blame it on the dog. It's what we're *for*, you smug biped.

"That's a great shower," Suzanne said. Her return was fanfared by a roll of steam from the half-cracked bathroom door. Art could hear the heat lamp and exhaust fans running. "You've got one of those rainfall showerheads." She peeked out, a face amid a burly cocoon of towels. "Clothes?"

"Oh." Art kept a whole row of variously logoed sweatshirts on the top rack of the linen closet. He pulled down a set in navy blue and added a T-shirt and thick socks. Suzanne was pink and radiantly warm from a brisk scrub with a back brush.

"I don't suppose you can spare some underwear?" It did not seem like such an oddball request.

"I think I can scare something up. *Momentito*." As he turned he saw her in the partially fogged bathroom mirror, towel drooping, nothing X- or even R-rated, just . . . interesting.

Art's waist had acquired several inches since age thirty-five, but nothing that rendered his belt line grotesque. He rummaged up some size-thirty shorts worn almost as soft as flannel, so old the tags had faded to complete blankness. They smelled not soiled, but old, unused. Dusty, like antique clothing. When Suzanne reached out for them, the towel tucked across her breasts unfurled, and Art snatched his gaze away so quickly and automatically that now he felt like a genuine fool.

He hadn't seen a thing, anyway.

He wondered where he'd left the party flyer he'd discovered in the mailbox yesterday morning. That made him recall Derek's cryptic postcard, which also proved that Derek had merely mailed a card, not shown up for an evening of hail-fellow-well-met drinking, dining, drinking, man talk, and drinking. Which led, inexorably, to the message in a bottle, with all its unnerving portent and signposts hinting at Art's potential for "diminished capacity." The day, the vague madness, had begun when he found the bottle. It was empty now, perched on the mantel, having spent a month in the sand and a year in the surf, or more, only to find its way here.

"You know Price?" Suzanne had selected a spot close to the fire, and drifted directly to it, the sweats too big on her, but therefore warmer. She resembled a kid in jammies, feet and all.

"Price." Information scrolled in Art's head. No matches found.

"Price. I forget his last name. That's his house, down the beach from yours, past the place that looks haunted."

"The party house," said Art. "Does he know somebody named Michelle?"

"They're supposed to be married but I don't think they really are," said Suzanne. "God, Michelle is like . . . *gorgeous*. She's perfect. She's smart. She deserves better." Suzanne bugged her eyes slightly whenever referencing Michelle's bottomless list of attributes, every single one of which, apparently, was designed to make lesser beings give up in humiliation.

"She some kind of actress or model?"

"I don't think so." Suzanne genuinely did not know. "I think she's the sort of chick who *turns down* movies and modeling." She assumed a lotus position on the couch and planted the beer bottle between her heels. "Michelle is that rare and scary woman who always wins, and Price is the guy everybody wants to know. He's this big guy, used to be a biker, used to be a bodyguard, knows all the right numbers—who to call for the best drugs, who to call if you need a bullet pulled out of you with no hospital, that kind of borderline underworld shit."

"Friend of yours?"

"Not really. I mean, he was never like my boyfriend or anything. I went to his party because Dina went. Dina's my bud; I think she's sweet on Price, but fuck that, it's like: Get in line."

"What's the party for?"

"Bastille Day? Full moon? Cinco de Mayo? Who knows. Enough time passes, Price throws a party."

"Not around here."

"No, it's usually in a different place every time, and it's usually a lot closer to the city. I think he did this one to test who would actually make the drive. Weed out the hangers-on." She disappeared into introspection, just for a second, then ruefully added, "Yeah, that worked out like a dog turd in the champagne. Not *you* sweetie."

Blitz approached, head low, willing to sniff, probably doomed to make friends with dismaying speed.

The only—virtually sole—party Art had hosted in this house had been long ago. He and Lorelle had finagled nearly thirty-five friends into "making the drive" on Halloween, a workweek night, or "school night," as Lorelle liked to call them. Most had shown up in costume; fully half had lingered until dawn. They'd organized a huge *Big Chill* breakfast outside on the deck and turned the kitchen into a free-for-all. One guy (either Grant Chastain or Ernie Lawlor, from Art's old design firm) drove halfway back to the city just to score more beverages from a friend of his who ran a liquor store. The friend even came back with him, bigheartedly playing the Santa of liquid refreshment. He was greeted with applause. He'd had an impressive, basso laugh, an opera singer's laugh, but Art could never remember his name. There had been life in this house once, and an excellent time had been had by all. Now it seemed like someone else's old story.

"So I get there with Dina and it's barely sundown yet and there's like twelve guys all over her, and she only has eyes for Price, and Price is . . . polite. Almost like she's a kid or something, I mean, not a minor, but a kid, a little kid. She disappears. There's this whole row of rooms on the second floor, and most of them have beds, because at Price's parties . . . you know." She shrugged.

"A lot of mating going on upstairs?"

"What are parties really for? You meet people, you drink too much, you fool around, and then the next day you talk about what you wouldn't have done if you hadn't been *soooo* drunk."

That urged a laugh out of Art. It was true. Between All Hallows toasts and dawn, there'd been a bit of mating going on between his guests at his long-ago soiree, in whatever rooms became available on a rotating basis. Stacey McMullen and Bernard Whitt had booted Blitz out of the dog den so they could hump on top of the dryer.

"So I find Dina in one of these rooms, alone, thank god, except for the cheeseball trying to shove coke up his ass in the bathroom, but he closes the door and we don't see him again for the rest of the night. Dina's crying her face off. Her makeup has run down into her lap. She's crying over Price, and I go, what the fuck is this bull-shit, I mean, it's not like you guys had a thing or he's your lover or something."

"Did something happen?"

"That's the whole thing. Nothing happened. And she's acting like she wants to commit suicide all of a sudden. Fucking weird. Too weird. So weird it's kinda scary."

"Was she wasted?"

"Well, everybody was pretty jolly already. Lot of booze, lot of coke, some old-timers still into 'ludes. Price generally doesn't like junkies, so there was only a couple. But the weird thing is Dina, the way she's acting. She's normally tough as nails. She's a city kid, she has pavement smarts, and even though she shows up dressed to kill, she never has any problem keeping the dogs from slobbering on her. Not *you*, sweetie." She began scratching Blitz's ruff, the one way guaranteed to immobilize canines. She took a long draw off her Dixie Double Hex. "Dina's pretty tall and she's got super-long legs, and great eyes, and she wore these really soft leather pants. All her jewelry is really sharp, and she's got this choker thing with an amethyst in it, and she's even got one of those belt buckles that has a little knife in it? Totally superior hair. And she's just *crying* and *crying*, like somebody died."

"Did something happen?" Art was at sea.

Suzanne began scratching Blitz's nose with her index finger, playing dodgem while he tried to catch a sniff. "That's it. Nothing happened. We said hi to Price at the door, and an hour later she's ready to leap off a building. So I hugged her and got her a tissue, and finally she swallows hard a couple of times in a row and asks to be by herself, for just a moment—you know, kind of letting me off the hook.

"So I go back downstairs, and lo and behold, the Asshole is slapping Price on the back like they did Vietnam together or something."

"Which asshole?"

"Bryan. Bryan Simonsen. The Bry-Guy. Used to be my boyfriend. Occupation: *total* phallus." Suzanne rolled her eyes and Art could see this was not the first time she had recounted this particular life mistake. "He's this rich computer guy, but it's all Daddy's money, y'know? He's got a Porsche and a stock portfolio and no human feelings whatsoever. Testosterone to burn; he's always spoiling for a fight, always ready to hear something the wrong way."

"You mean he's reactive. Which most people call 'intense.' A big, blustery kind of guy? Thinks being turned up too high is some kind of virtue?"

"Sometimes being turned up too high just means you're loud," said Suzanne. "Loud enough, for long enough, gets—"

"Strident?"

"Irritating. And Dina, my bud, is always giving me shit about my asshole boyfriends, but she's always around when they dump me, which is why I got worried about her. But now I've been dismissed, and what do you know, Bry-Guy the Asshole has arrived to par-*tay*."

"Is he that hostile? I mean, do you definitely *not* want to be in the room with him?"

"I definitely don't want to share the *planet* with him. He's like my five worst boyfriends of all time, rolled into one humongous Asshole. He liked to start hitting when he didn't get his way; he

78

broke my nose once." She indicated the imperfection in her profile, offhandedly, almost as though it had been a bargain price for her escape from him. "Any ex-girlfriend of his automatically joins a secret club called Those Bitches. If he lives past thirty, I wouldn't put a murder or two past him. I know he'll start shit the minute he sees me, so I snuck out onto the deck. It's raining and crappy, and I forgot my shoes, but I've had just enough drinks to be mad, and not care. But it's not particularly cold."

That would be the storm front, switching channels every five minutes and playing hob with the barometer. First warm and moist, then chilly; now blowy, now not.

"I get ahold of somebody's umbrella and start walking on the beach, pretty far up because the tide line starts looking nasty in the dark. About the time I get to the haunted house, down there—"

"That's the Spilsbury house. Private property."

"Whatever. About the time I got there, it starts pissing down rain like a motherfucker, and the wind kicks up to like fifty miles an hour, and all I can think is, *I am not going back in there. Not yet.* It's like being angry was keeping me warm. So I march on and march on, and see this place, and the lights are on, and about then the rain starts *blowing* off the ocean, like knives or razors with salt on the edges? Ow, ow, ow. The umbrella flips inside out and becomes completely useless. I threw it toward the ocean and it blew back, like twenty feet over my head. What a joke. I realized how far away I was from Price's because I couldn't see it. I didn't even know which direction it was, y'know, like those guys in the Arctic who get lost ten feet away from their door in a blizzard?"

"I can drive you back if you need it."

"Nah, not yet. It's nicer right here. All that techno dance shit Price likes starts to rattle your teeth, and I kinda wanted to give the Asshole time to get really wasted, or get knifed in a fight, or maybe drown. I was thinking maybe I could call Price's, from here, I mean, to make sure Dina's okay . . . if she hasn't split without me already. That's another reason I went outside; she was my ride, so it wasn't like I could just get in the car and run away." She looked around the living room as though it was just coming into focus. "So, do you live here all by yourself?"

"Yeah. For now." Art could not bear the thought of recounting the Lorelle narrative one more time in the same twenty-four-hour span, so he let it go.

"No significant other, no spouse, no kids, no live-in relatives?"

"Just me and that critter over there."

"You're not, like, one of those hermits who makes belts out of human nipples and lamp shades of skin, while sinking ever deeper into his delusional architecture?"

She knew psychological terms, and had even heard of serial killers like Ed Gein. Her use of *architecture* threw him. He had to laugh. "I'm afraid it's a lot more mundane than that. I just live alone now; my significant other—" he took care to repeat the words she'd just said "—my spouse died a few years ago."

"Were you in love?" It was obviously a goal of hers.

"Yes."

"That sucks," Suzanne said, nodding with what, for her, passed for sympathy. "So many fuckheads are walking around in the world, breathing air, and the people you love die. It's so unfair."

Yes, it was. Art resisted the riptide pull toward his own past history recap, though. "Listen," he said. "If you want to call down to the other house, that's okay, too. I got an invitation to that party, sort of. It was signed by Michelle."

"Yeah, Michelle's like that. I figured I could call for her and she'd take care of the whole situation. But I'm liking this for right now, Art, if you don't mind. I mean, I don't want to use up a lot of time, or—"

"Please," said Art with a deferential wave of his hand.

"You got a nice house and a nice dog—*aren't* you?—and I promise I'm not a lunatic on crack, and I'm not gonna steal anything." Blitz had already more or less cast his vote in the YES column.

"Tell him he's a *guter Hund*." said Art. She did and Blitz brightened up. "I wasn't worried about you."

"Well, you should be, letting strangers in like that. I would be."

"It's a little different out here in the middle of nowhere."

"That's for sure. Are you some kind of artist?" She was looking at the framed, signed prints hung here and there.

"I'm a specific kind of artist—the kind no one thinks of as an artist, in the way some people think painting is art, but photography isn't." He was aware of trying too hard to be glib. "I'm an architect; I'm sort of holed up here working on a project I don't like very much."

"Did it for the money, huh?"

Art shrugged helplessly, a prisoner of commerce.

"It's a great house." She knew when it was politic to change the subject.

"Hard line's in the kitchen when you want it," he said. "Forget trying to use a cell in this weather."

"I still want to wait a little bit. I mean, do you mind?" She was too comfy where she was, and Art was a safe distance away on the facing couch. He was not circling her, ravenous and predatory, and he sensed she kind of enjoyed that, as though it was rare. "The fire's way too nice. You can just sit and watch it and it calms you down; it's better than TV."

Art decided to jump directly to what he was already thinking, without camouflaging preamble. "Crash here. There's a guest room and you already know where the fridge is."

Of many potential reactions to such a solicitation, which some

81

BULLETS OF RAIN● ●●

might consider forward, he never expected her to flash livid and slam both fists uselessly into the cushions.

"Oh, goddammit all to *fucking hell . . . !*"

That's it, he thought. You blew it. She thinks you're coming on to her already, a total stranger, and it's grossing her out.

"Fuck!" Blitz scrambled to an alert stance at the strident sound of an angry human voice.

Suzanne looked at Art, her eyes now quite white in the dim light, almost as if he had walked into his own living room and caught her relaxing inside his workout clothes, taking advantage of his fireplace, petting his dog, all without permission.

"No, no, you don't understand," she said hastily. "I just realized I probably left my bag at Price's. God-dammit-*dammit!* Do I have my bag? No. Did I stomp out of Price's without it? Yes. Am I a fucking moron? Absolutely. Shit!" She blew off a huge wave of frustrated epinephrine, knowing how limited were her options.

Art wanted to talk her down. "Was it important, as in the usual stuff, or as in serious?"

She wiped a hand down her face as if trying to squeeze it into a different expression, something less nakedly emotional. "You must know what it's like to lose your bag; it's like, your identity."

Art considered how often he might have lost a purse, then stayed kind and did not say anything. He did not even make a funny face; *oh, these women and their foibles.*

"It's just a bag; I don't want the Asshole to trip over it. He'll be looking at my checkbook for my bank balance and then he'll swipe my credit card and sell it to some hacker. He'll take all my numbers. There's a single twenty-dollar bill in my wallet that'll probably wind up in some stripper's crotch up in the Mission. Where did I put it down? I had it when I was talking to Dina, because I got her a Kleenex out of it, because that cocaine cowboy was locked up in the bathroom. If Dina got the bag, it'll be fine. The Asshole never slept with Dina, so he'll treat her decent if he spots her."

"She'd look out for it, for you, wouldn't she?"

"If she doesn't get so plowed that she loses hers *and* mine. Oh, well . . . put it down to paying the party toll, I guess." She smacked her forehead with the palm of her hand. "Stupid." Blitz was gawping at her, uncertain how to proceed, and she gathered his coffin-shaped head in both hands. "It's okay, sweetie, it's not your fault. It's just another one of life's little shit sandwiches."

Blitz, being a dog, didn't think a shit sandwich was such a bad notion. Those cat turds he sometimes found were pretty tasty.

"Maybe you should just call"—Art had to summon the name from memory—"Michelle, at the house."

"Yeah, before anybody gets any more wasted. Good idea."

"Landline's in the kitchen. You know the number?"

"It's written down in my bag. But it's easy to remember: OK-o-HOLYMAN. The numbers make a word. The second *O* in OK-o is a zero. I probably don't need the area code, right?"

"No, just HOLYMAN by himself is good."

She smiled as she disengaged from the sofa—reluctantly. "You're never sure how to do things out here in the sticks."

Art was completely disarmed by his visitor. Part of him figured out that Price's number was 465-9626, while another part was content to watch Suzanne's breasts shift around beneath one of his own sweatshirts. The garment would come away fragrant with her. Even in sweats her waist was pinched; she possessed a classic hourglass shape that had fallen out of fashion in this week's version of youth culture, which was still grimly prejudiced toward models that resembled anorexic jailbait or androgynous junkies who looked like glassy-eyed greyhounds, living heartbeat to heartbeat until discarded or fully consumed. Suzanne did not strike him as callow. She was the difference between "Art" and "normal," which struck him with the distance he had managed to stray from the walking world in general.

He rubbed his eyes. He was spacing out. Too long, too much, too weird, no sleep. Suzanne's voice echoed in the kitchen, rising and falling tones indicating the presence of someone else in his house. Art did not eavesdrop.

"It's pretty okay," Suzanne reported. "Dina's got my bag and she's not leaving anytime soon. She found my shoes and spent some time looking for the rest of me."

"Kind of comic."

"Yeah. Michelle teased me about finding something better than the Asshole, and wandering off to seduce total strangers. I can go back whenever. But, you know, that guest room sounds awfully tempting. You mind if I just take you up on it, to decompress?"

Art ran her through the protocols. Where stuff was. Extra pillow. Warned her not to open any exterior door due to the alarm. The guest bathroom featured extras like single-serving toothbrushes and toiletries, mostly appropriated from various airlines. Soaps, little flossers, mints.

"I'll zip you over there when we wake up," he said. "You need anything, just tap on the last door in the hall."

"I'll do that." She disappeared into the bathroom again, giving him a last-minute peek-out. "Thanks. Really."

"My pleasure, no problem." He waved vaguely and felt if he didn't get horizontal within the next few moments, something very dire would happen to his whole body. Lack of sleep and a liberal overdose of alcohol had started his self-destruct countdown ticking. *We now end our broadcast day.*

Blitz padded into the bedroom and assumed his sleep post at the foot of the bed. His habit was to circle, then drop. After a few moments he roused and went into the hall. There was a visitor, a new scent here, and he had to keep track of everybody.

Stretching his neck back over wadded pillows felt heavenly, and Art managed to pop a few vertebrae when he twisted left to right. Darkness eased the pain in his temples. Suzanne was a total stranger, but what was the worst she could do—take the silverware? Steal his dog? He possessed few items a common thief would find tempting; most of the things he valued were not obvious. There was an ivory Eskimo carving, a drum-dancer *tupilak* made from whale tusk, that looked like a piece of plastic Halloween kitsch. There was a genuine Ming bronze on the mantel, but if you didn't know that, you'd think it was a roughcast, knockoff sort of flower vase. His petty-cash stash was locked up in the gun-room safe, accessible only through the bedroom. Suzanne did not seem the type to snatch up kitchen cutlery and disembowel him for no reason, a spree psycho. She was accountable, had given him names and numbers freely. It wasn't watertight—nothing was, if you worried enough— but it would serve, so Art had no real roadblocks to the downtime his body craved. She had certainly livened up his evening, made him feel part of the world again, a social being instead of a soul so tortured it might have invented the whole Derek scenario, just to have busywork.

For her to sleep here, she had to trust him, too. A minimum, entry-level kind of trust.

Thoughts of her body flickered around the outlands of his mind as unconsciousness quickly claimed him.

● ● ● He bolted awake in the dark, hand grabbing for a pistol that wasn't there. No dreams. The wind was really getting serious, making a lowering sound like a wounded predator, then a keening, high-

85

pitched noise Art had only heard before as a cheesy haunted-house sound effect. He marveled briefly that real wind could sound that way.

The silhouette of Suzanne's head was peering through the partially open bedroom door.

"Hey. You asleep?"

Blitz sat up. Art drew in a long breath. He was wrung out, drowsy and fatigued. Was he asleep? "Sort of."

She invited herself farther into the dimness. "I'm all fired up. I should be nodding off but I can't. Can I lay down with you?"

Whatever he said—it might have been "uh"—was adequate. She was across the room and out of her sweat clothes in an instant. The next, she was sliding under his sheets, her calf brushing his as she settled in. "A little human contact is a good thing," she said. "Especially on a night like this."

"Whoa, wait," he said. "Suzanne, wait—I—" He fizzled out. "We just met each other." Some parts of him were waking up faster than other parts, and began to pester him with demands.

Her eyes luminesced in the near dark. She was on her left side with the comforter pulled up to her collarbones. "I can't think of a quicker way for two people to get acquainted, can you?"

"But we—"

"But nothing." She slid a leg over his body and straddled him, keeping the blankets over her shoulders. "Don't lose the heat shield yet," she said. "Not until I warm up."

Art felt crisp pubic hair abrade his stomach. He saw her breasts move in shadow, rounded and gravid, achingly sexy. Her expression was obscured by the tilt of her clean-smelling hair. It was in his mind to say something else useless, to try to make this collision conform to a method he understood. She put a finger to his lips.

"Shh. I want you to kiss me." She leaned forward, nipples skirting his chest, followed by the full press of her tits, and formed an exacting seal on his lips with hers. He felt a surge of heat. His cock would be curving up between her buttocks, prodding her, but it felt as if the tactile information was getting garbled in transit. She made a little noise of pleasure—*mmmm*—as though she'd just eaten a chocolate.

She worked his mouth tenderly and teasingly, brushing his lips, seeking his likes and dislikes with flicks of the tongue, then coming on so strongly they both had to breathe nasally, then backing off for more affectionate ministrations. She kissed his closed eyelids. He wanted to chew on her shoulders, on the back of her neck as her hands got lost in his hair, tugging and pulling and bringing his mouth back into range. His hand found her breast and felt her heartbeat, which was amped up and hammering as she stroked him with her entire body in a slow, easy rhythm. She was totally excited, and completely available to him, already generating moisture against his leg. She was urgent and hungry, and it was easy to let himself be pulled along by her magnetism.

It was as though he was being towed under by the whirlpool of a sinking ship, and he had to remind himself to grope for the bedside drawer, and condoms that were five years old. His hand blundered into assorted dusty toys, including a grotesque strap-on phallus that Lorelle had gotten as a gag gift, and kept mostly to tease him. Suzanne divined what was going on and beat him into the drawer. He heard the strand of foil packets crackle.

"You don't mind, I'm sorta on my period," she said. "I took a shower and everything, but don't be grossed out."

"It's okay."

"I mean, your sheets—"

"The sheets are black. Don't worry about it."

"I just find that, sometimes, if I can do a little vigorous fucking, it actually makes the cramps better, did you know that?"

"So this has actual therapeutic value."

"You got it." She popped the condom in her mouth and installed it on him orally. He could feel the slight grating of her teeth on his prick and it was excruciatingly good.

She placed her hands on his shoulders, arched her back in a luxuriant stretch, and like magic he was sunk inside of her all the way to the latex roll around the base of his penis. She made a sound like someone who has just heard the best news of her life. He grabbed her hips, unwilling to let her go even for thrusting. He wanted to stay inside her as she rose up high enough to lose him on each stroke, only to feel her lips part anew for each reentry into the warm center of her.

He orgasmed almost immediately. He couldn't help it. His senses were overloaded. She made another little sound; the sound of someone pleased with getting what they ordered. She slid down, disposed of the condom, and took him into her mouth. He was rigid again in no time.

The covers were flung away now, unneeded as she turned to give him a full view of her sumptuous ass as she planted herself onto his cock, commencing a quick, scooping motion while holding on to his ankles. His entire lower body felt feverish and hypersensitized. She settled into a frantic pace that started her huffing softly and going *yeah* between husky breaths. When she came it sounded like something was literally tearing its way out of her, and as Art listened and reciprocated and gorged himself on passion, he felt himself ejaculate again. He could feel her entire system declaring itself through the vibrations and contractions in her cunt.

"Oh, god, that's better," she whispered, still starving for air. She grabbed a pillow and slammed down next to him like a felled tree. "What is this mattress? A futon?"

"Yeah."

"I love futons. Rock solid, no bouncing, no squeaking. Good for your back."

"Not a water-bed person, hm?"

He expected some ribald comment about a burst water bed when she said, quietly, almost shyly, "Do you . . . mind if I sleep here with you for a bit?"

He dragged sheets and blankets and comforters back from where the floor had claimed them. The air in the bedroom was still turbid with sex. "Are you kidding? You're joking, right? Of course you can sleep right here. You don't even have to move."

That brightened her, as if she had expected to be booted out. Probably had, by some of her past caveboys. *Bitch get out.* "I refuse to sleep without moving," she said. "I think sleep without moving is when you're dead. I'm gonna hit the bathroom."

Watching her walk across the room naked was like some kind of reward Art did not know what he had done to merit.

"How about something to drink? I'm dry as a sandbox."

"Got any seltzer? Club soda? Something fizzy with no caffeine?"

It was a good idea. Booze was a terrible idea. Half the soft drinks in the fridge would merely add more stimulants, more depressants to the poisonous stew already in his bloodstream. Fruit juice would leave a flat, tacky taste if he drank it before sleeping. Club soda was, in fact, a thoughtful idea.

How many times has she done this? he thought. Had this same conversation, done the same things in the same order, then breezily requested a club soda? It seemed as though she was really good at it. Seasoned.

She was lingering by the door to the bathroom. "Do you have any, um—?"

"Look in that upper cabinet. I've got all the girl supplies you could imagine."

Suzanne made a face. "How often do you restock?" she said with a sly expression that really asked, *Just how many women come trooping through this sex den, pal?*

"Most of it was my wife's." Meaning that it was as old as his quaint little tote of rubbers.

He brought two tumblers of seltzer, which they drained. Suzanne burped in the darkness, a racketing, window-rattling report, then giggled. "That's almost as much fun as coming. You feel like if you don't do it, you'll explode, and then you sort of explode anyway. You don't have to, like, wake up at the crack of your ass, do you?"

"Crack?" was all he could utter.

"Early in the morning," she translated.

"No. Especially not after this."

"Outstanding. Be right back." And heigh-ho, she was off to the loo again.

He bent his neck back over the pillows and felt it unlock. Someone had gassed these pillows with sedative. The toilet flushed but the sound seemed to come from the next county.

He wasn't aware of her return from the bathroom. Sleep battered him down. He felt her thigh push up past his knees and nestle right below his testicles. Her hand closed around his penis, not a grip, just holding it in a way that was oddly intimate and protective, as he swooned toward slumber.

The calm fire of his muscles mellowed in relaxation and he dreamed of Lorelle, who had returned to make a strange visit to the bed they had once shared. She said nothing, but put her head down next to his. She behaved as though they still had a lifetime ahead. She touched him gently, not in a hurry. He inhaled her breath, which brought back everything he had lost into a moment of limbo where he felt he was forgiven for whatever he had done wrong, however he had mishandled their lives.

Lorelle worked her way, a kiss at a time, from chest to belly to his cock, which Art felt gloved in heat as her lips collected it. She wanted him. Her tongue and teeth moved in familiar ways, up, down, generously slow.

Art's eyes fluttered open. It might have been an hour later, or five minutes. His clock was not visible. It was still dark and the wind outside was howling. Drifts of harsh rain pelted the roof and windows. Suzanne was sucking his penis, lubricating him with her saliva, and he was as hard as a railroad spike.

The transposition hit him in an opiate wave. Suzanne had obviously sampled Lorelle's perfume, still in the bathroom cabinet, unopened for years. Objet d'Art, just a drop in the hollow of the throat, enough to bring Lorelle back to bed with her. The sheet made a silken whipping noise as she swung one leg over and embedded him deep within her. He felt himself bump against the little knob of uterus. She held his shoulders down and began chopping toward an orgasm she had to find, a prize she had to win, buried treasure she was absolutely compelled to excavate. It was all Art could manage to hang on to the sides of the bed, to press down with his heels to stabilize her sudden and almost scary determination. When she came, the sensation lifted her thunderously into crescendo. She stopped her rearward fall with arms spread, in a pose that made her look like sculpture in the bluish night-glow.

Art continued the motion and dumped her on her back, her head hanging off the edge of the bed, his own need shoving everything else aside and culminating as he began to piston, fast, hard, and mechanically, an endurance motion intended to destroy all obstacles to climax. Suzanne held on, her throat whitely exposed, her mouth open as she felt blood rushing to her brain, her view of the room upside down and distorted, as she let the pounding precipi-

91

tate another orgasm, a bone-shaker that caused her to grab his ass in both hands and bite into his shoulder.

Their bodies were attempting to fuse into a single being. She was fucking herself with him, pulling him home, ramming her pubic bone against his, and when he came he thought he could see sparks of lightning inside his eyelids. His balls were contracted, drawstrung, and the spasms had their way with him, but he could not have possibly delivered anything more into her. She had hoarded the drops, the fumes, and his tank was dry.

She made a noise, a low, drawn-out hum. "That's . . . better," she said between breaths, with a tiny chuckle because she knew it was what she had said the first time. She crawled as though blind back to a right-side-up position on the bed, and managed to crawl several baby paces, hands and knees, before she collapsed like a canvas bag of rice, head hitting the pillow mostly by lucky accident. She curled on one side and was asleep before Art could start another conversation.

He knew his crotch would feel scoured in the morning. He did not care. His senses were delicately beaten into general radiant numbness edged with a rawed sensitivity, and that's how he wanted it. The biggest turn-on for him had been Suzanne's sudden, unheralded, and almost desperate need, right out of nowhere.

Lead filings began to sift into his brain. His throat was arid. He padded out to the kitchen naked, gooseflesh prickling his skin as thin drifts of chilly air eddied through his house, bullied by the blowing wind. He gulped club soda and remembered to retrieve the rest of Suzanne's rain-soaked clothing from the guest bathroom. While he urinated he noticed a fat packet of toilet paper in the trash, indicating a disposed tampon or napkin, very thoughtfully not flushed. Women tended to use a lot of toilet paper for every damned thing. Beside the small wastebasket a capsule rested on the grout between floor tiles. Before Art picked it up he washed and dried his hands, so it would not dissolve to shapeless gel in his grasp. It was like an allergy capsule, half-black, half-white. Some kind of speed? There were no batch numbers or fabrication symbols on it.

Blitz sniffed him uncertainly as Art hung up Suzanne's sweater and gave the rest of her gear to the dryer. Art was apparently very interesting to smell, right now. He could not remember whether a condom had even been involved during that last bout, which had hit him, abruptly and powerfully, in much the same manner as the storm outside.

Art left the capsule on his nightstand for future reference and Suzanne rolled, snuggling into his armpit. He couldn't inhale enough of her. Her hand found his cock almost tropistically, and they both plummeted in search of quality REM sleep.

They had achieved a state from which the storm could not rouse them, though it tried mightily. The rain got worse.

● ● ● Art woke up at ten after one P.M., to the sound of heavy oceanic rainfall splatting in fat drops across the bedroom windows. He was alone in the bed and the old panic surged back right on cue. There was no Suzanne, only a particularly appealing dream, one of the few from which he could recall key details. He was so alone that most of his life had lapsed into an hallucinatory fugue state.

"Hey," said Suzanne, tilting in through the hallway door. "I tried to make coffee on that big grindy machine; I think I got it right." She entered with two of Art's cappuccino mugs, the kind that could hold nearly a pint of liquid. "You tell me."

Or, there was another possibility—Art had died and gone to Valhalla, or Paradise. The coffee was as rich and brown as the eyes of an Indian goddess. When Suzanne put the mug down, she noticed the black-and-white capsule on Art's nightstand.

"Hey, where'd you get that?"

He sat up, groggy, and oriented himself. "I think you dropped it. I found it in the bathroom. What is it?"

"One of Price's party favors. Some kind of upper, I think." She seemed disinterested in pharmacology.

"Want to find out, or do you want to keep it?"

"Nah. I took one to wake up, basically. You should try it."

"I'll save it for later." He dropped it into a leatherette box with a snap closure. The lid was filigreed with Egyptian glyphs in gold foil. The box had belonged to Lorelle.

Why did he keep that box around, when all it did was cause him a minuscule pain every time he saw it again? Wouldn't it be better to get rid of it? He had always feared the answer, that it would be like consigning another piece of his life to the trash, and he knew he hated getting rid of anything. The box had been stationed in the same place on the nightstand when Lorelle had been taken. It endured.

The "cold gray dawn" of cheap fiction did not penetrate the bedroom. Already Suzanne was lazily pulling on his penis, priming his pump for another round. He gulped half his coffee—she'd succeeded in making it pretty strong—and they were all over each other in another couple of minutes.

For the duration of his marriage, Art had been faithful to Lorelle. Before her, he had juggled multiple lovers, keeping each at a safe distance with a menu of logical-sounding buffers. They all waxed and waned, came and went, each leaving something special while Art revealed precious little of his own heart. Then Lorelle had stormed into his life and swept him off his bearings. Her history had gone much the same way, so they sympathized, seeding on first contact their semitelepathic way of communicating; their secret language. They engaged each other on all the best levels and for the first time Art comprehended how valuable it was to have a soul mate who could be that mythological "one"—friend, lover, best buddy, partner. The myth was dashed by the naked reality of her. Their relationship held the peaks and valleys inherent in all human intercourse, but the special thing about Lorelle was that she scampered these outcrops with no thought that the fundamental bedrock of her-plus-him was ever in jeopardy. Nothing mattered more than the fact they had found each other; each was the reward at the end of the other's long desert quest. It never occurred to Lorelle that anything could threaten the core truth that they were together . . . not even when she had embarked on a brief, hasty, and ill-advised affair with someone up in the city. Art remembered the first time they had fought over this infidelity. Even then, blinded by rage, trodden by disappointment, and sinking down into sorrow, even then, when the words that confirmed the truth came from her painfully, measured in tears, he knew that for her it was not a matter of finding another, or giving up their life together. It was so simple it was outrageous. She missed the city.

If that rift never closed, at least they had built a sturdy bridge over it. Ultimately, he never got the chance to propose to her, because she beat him to it. She asked him with amazement, as if she was channeling a phantom; she was as surprised as he was. She was a woman with sour views on marriage, conditioned by a lifetime of rotten, content-free, inadequate relationships, and all of a sudden this opinionated free spirit had found someone she deeply wanted to wed. Permanence had never been important before.

In all the time Art had been with her, it had not occurred to him to be attracted away. It had never been an issue. He knew this feeling by its function, and the fact—easy to admit—that she was the

95

person for him, rendered especially appropriate by time and circumstances no one could predict. But this was the first time he held the realization in front of him, examined it, and put words to the feelings. It had never occurred to him to be attracted away from her. No exceptions.

Which meant that when Lorelle passed, Art had been sliced in half and cut adrift, with no backups, no old phone numbers, none of the fail-safes he had traditionally emplaced when dealing with lovers who were less important. It had been a long, lonely time since her death, and it had never occurred to Art to start shopping for replacements, since no one could fill that gap.

Now, years later, Suzanne had materialized out of nowhere, and was busily trying to resurrect his gnarly carcass. She pounced and kissed him; he could taste his own ejaculate. Art's usual "morning bear" failed to put in a grouchy appearance.

After some additional fooling around in the master bath's capacious shower, he loaned her an old steerhide motorcycle jacket to give her an extra layer against the cold outside. He donned a thick cable-knit sweater and threw a shearling coat over that, providing vinyl ponchos to waterproof themselves. They took the Jeep, thankful for the weight, the safeguards, the big knobby tires.

In less than a day the coast road had become every bit the disaster area Art had anticipated, and progress was so slow it made the half mile to Price's house seem like a long-haul hour. Trees were down. Severed cable whipped from tilting light poles like deadly stingers; soon the poles themselves would topple. The road surface was completely treacherous. The storm was bumping the edge of emergency.

Price's place, from what Art could make out in the buffeting rain and dicey light, was a modernist white two-story deal with two wings that married in a central, lighthouselike turret, which faced the ocean from the apex of the V-shape. Two outbuildings extended the courtyard area to accommodate a liver-shaped swimming pool. Art always wondered about the brand of people who needed a pool, with the ocean a stroll away.

Suzanne pointed at the southernmost outbuilding, raggedly cordoned by about fifteen parked vehicles. "That's the garage, and there's a guesthouse over that. The other one is a cabana thing, sunroom, hobby room, whatever you want to call it." Art visualized rattan mats and a wet bar constructed of bamboo, a surfer's hang.

When Art parked, the downpour formed a curtain on the Jeep's windshield that flooded out all view. "Do you want me to just drop you, or—?"

"No way. Come on in, by all means." She opened her own door. "Woo, get ready to get soaked again."

As they dashed around the garage and through a wooden gate to a narrow walkway, Art could hear bass tones buzzing the walls. Suzanne led the way through an unlocked kitchen door as the music declared itself to be Asian techno-pop—drum machines hammering a high-speed beat against samples and a voice shrieking in Cantonese, with the occasional *fuck you!* in tilted English. They shed the rain slickers and hung them outmost on hooks near the door, with other garments, some dripping, some humid and mildewy, some beyond help.

Through the corridor of kitchen, Art could perceive the ebb and flow of a crowd, like goldfish in a pet-store display tank. An inversion layer of smoke hung above them as they shouted party talk over the music. They appeared monied and trendy, and summarized the world outside Art's secure cocoon.

Suzanne dragged him by one hand into the melee.

Art's eyes watched the walls. The place had probably been tacked together in the mid Eighties, if the long rectangular windows were any clue. The fixtures were mostly brass. Carpet everywhere. He could see the seams in the drywall, plastered over to imitate stucco. The picture-window moldings were plastic strips patterned after wood veneer, the tinted all-weather glass held in place mostly by its own weight. Bad news, if the storm got worse. Art would have replaced these with his own special polymer. He could see an exterior deck hemmed by tubular aluminum rails. Definitely a rental party place, not a residence.

It was pretty clear which one was Price. He held court in one corner and had just smoked a cigarette down to the filter, his attention on his immediate circle, his eyes sweeping the whole room. He was ectomorphic and sinewy, tall but not thin, wearing a skintight T-shirt under a zippered leather vest and worn jeans cuffed above low-heeled engineer boots, all black. As Suzanne maneuvered Art closer, Art could see the guy had the sort of head that clearly indicated the contours of the skull beneath. Price's features were totally symmetrical, and his slightly receding hairline had been buzzed into a military crop that fit him like a skullcap. His ears were pierced, but he wore no jewelry, not even a wristwatch. Long, pianist fingers with nails bitten or trimmed to nothing. He'd suffered bad acne as a teenager, but the rough complexion somehow fit him, as though his visage had been hammered from pitted pewter. His eyes tracked Art all the way across the room.

"This would be our Good Samaritan," Price said.

"Price, this is Art." Impressing him seemed important to Suzanne.

"Art, as in *the* Art?" Price tilted his head sideways, as if he had just been introduced to an inflatable toy as someone's beloved date. "You sure it's not Artemis or something spelled weird?"

"Just Art, I'm afraid."

"Fear nothing, neighbor." Price shook Art's hand—not crushingly, not blandly, just right. "Here you can be whoever you wish to be. We all need to thank you for rescuing our little lost Suzanne." He kissed Suzanne on the cheek and then forgot about her. "This is what you call your basic party. We got food, booze, drugs, boys and girls—help yourself." Price had mastered the art of making his voice heard above the music.

Art had to lean forward, like someone getting the feel of a recording booth. "You've probably heard there's a hell of a storm coming in."

"We're not going to talk about the *weather,* are we?" Price shot his eyes sidelong, as though awaiting a knowing, on-cue laugh from his cabaret audience.

"It might be a good idea to put all these people to work boarding up your windows."

"On the other hand," said Price, "it might be cool to see what they do." This gave Art pause, because it was essentially the same reason he had chosen to stick around his own house. "Look at these people, Art. What kind of quality job do you think I'd get out of them if I gave them all hammers and nails and plywood?" An Asian woman with an incredible fall of glossy black hair laughed at this. Price squeezed her into a one-armed embrace and kissed the top of her head. "This is Shinya. Call her a whore and she'll roll both eyes and think it's funny."

"You're such a dick," she said, smiling and socking Price in the arm with no force.

"This is Shinya's date, Tobias." Price indicated the man leaning against the wall opposite. Price was between them.

"Hey." Tobias pulled a hand out of his pocket and shook Art's, damply. He was wearing a huge, untucked work shirt buttoned all the way to the neck, and his eyes were hidden by blocky spectacles with lozenge-shaped tinted lenses.

"I probably won't be able to remember everyone's name," Art said, thinking he already sounded like a dope.

"Tobias and I have a bet that Shinya will be on her ripe little knees and blowing him by midnight," said Price.

Shinya hit him again, giggling. "You do *not!* God, you're *such* a dick!" To Art, she added, "He's just fantasizing about what he can't have."

Art was not sure what the response to this should be.

"Come on, Art, let's you and me talk like grownups." Price cut Art away and began touring him. Suzanne tagged along behind them, uncertain whether she'd been invited.

"What's the party for?" said Art.

"For nothing," said Price. "Because I can." He grinned. "Actually, you're correct—I did hear about the storm, that it might even be a hurricane, and that decided me. See all these people? I get them together in rooms, like ingredients in a recipe. I like to watch what happens when you mix spice with sweet, or salt, and let the crockpot bubble. So, that architectural wonder up near the radar-dish thing, that's yours?"

"Yes, I designed and built it."

"A being of accomplishment." Over his shoulder, Price told Suzanne: "Thanks for bringing this breath of fresh air; I was beginning to wonder whether I'd ever be able to have a conversation above fifth-grade level. Now stop heeling like a dog and go find your friend Dina. She needs to know you're okay so she can get back to her own emotional difficulties."

Suzanne retreated, but grasped Art's hand, enough to turn him. "Don't leave without finding me, okay?" Then she headed for the stairs.

Price had one eyebrow raised. "Why, Art . . . did she fuck you already?" Art was mustering a properly outraged response when

Price clapped him on the shoulder and interposed: "Never mind. Unfair question. Rude, even. Presumptuous. I apologize; I don't even fuckin know you, right?"

"Something like that," said Art, not sure if he'd just been headed off, shut down.

"Normally, Suzanne is the world's biggest child twatling. Stuck-up, whiny, always bitching about how no man in the world can live up to her needs, which equals your basic daddy fantasy. She hooks up with these muscle-bound losers she thinks will protect her, and it always goes wrong. You want a Dr Pepper?"

Art expected the offer of a beer, or something stronger. It was almost as if Price was reading his mind.

"I mean, you look like somebody who did their drinking yesterday, and you need to spell yourself. Pace is the key. Have a fizzy brown caffeinated beverage."

Art accepted while Price popped not a beer for himself, but a ginseng soda. "If you don't like Suzanne, why did you invite her to come here?"

Price's expression was open and placating. "Don't get me wrong, I love Suzanne. I knew she'd come with Dina—her pal—and I needed all these ingredients for the current recipe."

"She was pretty upset, last night."

"She'd have to be, to get lost on the beach in a storm. Why'd you let her in? Scratch that; another dumb question. It must have been weird for you."

Art was not sure to which aspect Price was referring.

"You know, a stranger out of nowhere? A castaway delivered to you by the storm, who just happens to have a lush little body? It's like a letter to *Penthouse*."

"I couldn't very well tell her to go away, not in her state."

Price laughed out loud, heartily. "I'll bet! She didn't even have any shoes!" He drained most of his ginseng soda in a single robust pull and pitched the empty toward an overflowing bin. Two points.

The music—which seemed up until now to consist of a single tune an hour long, unvarying in tone—paused off for a moment during which Art could hear several people go *awww*. Then it recommenced with a vengeance.

"You know most of these people have been conditioned to hear music only in four/four time, at a hundred and twenty beats per measure? It's not that they can't listen to anything else; it's that they literally will not hear it as 'music.' "

"It's kind of loud." Art winced as he said it.

"Next you're gonna say, *That's not music, that's just noise.* Are you feeling old all of a sudden, Art?"

Spoken in another way, by another person, it might have been an insult, but Art was beginning to feel Price said nothing by accident, and divulged nothing unintended. He looked up right into Price's gaze. His eyes were the color of . . . air. He seemed to have a membrane around him that insulated him from distractions, loud music, annoyances, anything that would disrupt the focus of his attention or interest, which was always direct and penetrative.

"I've had older," said a voice behind them. A hand lit on Art's shoulder to turn him. As he faced the woman who had intruded, she kept talking to Price. "First off, Price, that Japanese club shit, or whatever it is, sounds like having a locust stuck in each ear." She nailed Art directly with wide, viridescent eyes.

"That's my house mix," said Price. "For my dance fever crowd."

"That's also Price's idea of a little joke," said the woman. "Do you see anybody dancing? Then don't call it dance music."

"Well, some of them are sort of . . . spasming," said Art, with an expression still leery of offending his hosts.

The woman laughed in a full-bodied but controlled way, a talk-show response that could not be permitted to last for more than so-many air seconds. It was husky and from the diaphragm, not a girl-ish laugh, which Art could otherwise hear all around him. This woman, with her heavy mane of chestnut hair and thoroughbred length of neck, with her elegant, small teeth and heat static lighting her eyes, had to be the legendary Michelle, She Who Signed the Invitation. She wore a satin dress with a mandarin collar, slit to the hip on both sides. Her heels made her taller than Art; without them he estimated she would be at eye level, exactly.

"Michelle?" said Art.

She automatically shook his hand. "Travers. Price rarely assigns surnames at these things. No point."

"How'd you know her name?" said Price.

"Because—"

Michelle cut Art off, overriding him. "Because he got the party invite in his mailbox, and that little muffin Suzanne probably bab-bled all about us." She looked back to Art. "Close to true?"

"Close enough. Listen, Price, I didn't mean to come off like I was bitching about your music. Your house, your music."

Price smiled a big alpha-wolf smile. "Shit, most of these dimwits wouldn't have the balls to complain if they hated it."

Michelle flinked a Zippo lighter one-handed and fired up a long European cigarette about the diameter of a nightclub drinking straw. "Did Price give you the tour?"

"We made it from the living room to the kitchen." Art sipped his Dr Pepper, feeling strangely like a child standing in the midst of drinking, smoking parents. He had already deduced that Price and Michelle had this intimidating effect on most people who encoun-tered them. It was calculated, intentional.

"Well, there's probably an orgy in the cabana house by now," Price said with a slight drawl that made him sound like a judge reluctantly pronouncing sentence. "I'll bet I can guess who: Jory and Darian, Lex and Marisa, and whoever they could get drunk enough not to care. There's five bedrooms upstairs, not counting mine, which is locked. If you were to butt into the others you'd find a variety of people sleeping last night, getting high, waking up with strangers, or huddled into an assortment of self-pitying minor nervous breakdowns."

Art thought of Suzanne's friend Dina, hiding in a spare room, trying to navigate her obscure life crisis. Suzanne was probably with her right now, apprehensive about running into her own apparently terrifying ex-boyfriend. He abstracted his gaze past Michelle long enough to verify that he did, in fact, see a woman naked from the waist down sitting on top of one of the large concert PA speakers in the living room, bobbing and weaving her head to the thumping bass.

"That's Estelle-Leigh," said Price. "She thinks my system is some sort of big vibrator."

"Excuse me," Art said. "I don't mean this to sound the wrong way . . . but is this some sort of swingers thing, you should pardon the use of the archaic term?"

The glint popped again in Michelle's gaze. It reminded Art of undersea creatures who could flash lurid colors for defense. "Ooh, Art. You mean like *wife swapping?*" She said it mischievously, like a dirty secret or the punchline to a ribald joke.

"It's just a party, Art. Friends and acquaintances. Remote location, plenty of mood-altering substances, plus lots of time. Sex happens."

What did Art think he was looking at? Actors, ingenues, parvenus, people who sought the edge because they had read it was cool. People who wanted to be like the people they saw in commercials, driving cars faster than legal. No live band. Assorted goofy shave jobs, tats, and nobelium bars. A knot of New York, clad in black, disdaining beach culture. A couple of older, shamanesque attendees who could still remember hippies. A lot of people who were just wasted and trying to figure out what came next. A couple of geeks, the kind who would comp you computer favors as payback for getting them next to actual women. A couple more who probably had a little expert white-collar crime in their legal jackets. An executive domme cast a pointed amber glance Art's way, appraising his value, then looked away with a priceless half smile of dismissal.

"Don't be so uncomfortable," said Michelle, linking arms with him. "This isn't one of those 'play party' things, because I have no patience for sensation junkies so deadened they have to wallow in one anothers' trifling little extremes, digging around in their skin with razors, trying to find nerves that still fire. No bondage rodeo—tacky."

"That would be out in the cabana," Price interjected.

Michelle put a finger to Price's lips and soldiered on. "This isn't a Tantric grope-fest or a cable documentary about the turn-ons of the shallow, and we're not Scientologists. So relax and tell me a little about yourself."

"Architect," said Price. "Built that house up near the radar thing. Lives alone, except for this German-shepherd kind of dog. Sometimes engages in shooting practice in his backyard. Y'know, there's a guy here you ought to meet, if you're seriously into firearms."

"How did you know all that?" Art felt naked, his cover blown.

"Suzanne said as much. Plus, I've seen the house up there. Some of it's fairly obvious."

"I've never seen you that far up the beach, before."

Price shrugged. "Anyhow, this young man, Luther, might be able to procure you a couple of unpapered collector's items, if you happened to be of a mind. Look for the black dude with the silver dangly earring—it's an Eye of Ra."

Art knew the symbol from his reference books, and the leatherette box on his nightstand, formerly Lorelle's. It was the image prompted by Derek's odd hand tattoo. Michelle strolled Art into the dining room, which was doing duty as a huge buffet area. "We've got two waiter-bartender people who are here for the duration. They're not scheduled to restock until three or so, and if they're smart, they're just waking up downstairs."

If this place had a downstairs, from what Art had seen, then perhaps its foundation was sufficiently anchored to keep the whole building from taking wing if the winds kicked up into triple digits. He pictured the sink plan in his mind and imagined the grade of concrete used.

"He's probably banging her," said Price. "He's one of those sexually vague, LA-actor wannabes, and she's one of those pneumatic Latina chicks. She couldn't keep her eyes off him, and I bet she finally got the best of him. I thought he was gay."

"Maybe he's up there with Stefan, and she's up there with Libia," said Michelle, smirking.

Price indicated the spread in the dining room. "Snacks? Party favors? No needle shit, is all I ask. You a coke person?"

Art shook his head. "Long ago and far away, and never again." He crossed his heart. Between a serving dish of cheeses and a bowl dusted with potato-chip crumbs he spotted a silver treasure chest, about seven inches wide, lined with purple velvet. Inside were a scatter of black-and-white capsules like the one Suzanne had lost in his bathroom. "What are those?"

"Private stock. House mix."

"Like the music?"

"A very mild accelerator. Keeps the party going. Like a second and third wind, in capsule form. If you don't like who you are, it'll help make you into someone else, for a while."

Art recognized most of the other ambient drugs. He examined a capsule. "Not acid? Ecstasy?"

Price's ready grin was prepared. "Nothing so crude."

Art replaced the capsule in the box. "Maybe later."

A woman with platinum-blond bangs, wearing a ghostly white lace dress that tracked her every movement in a wisp of veils, leaned in to tap Michelle on the shoulder. She had very pale skin and brilliantly blue eyes, her lipstick red and glossy as fresh blood. "Bryan's locked in the bathroom and won't come out," she said.

"Price," Michelle said, wearily. "Please?"

"If I catch that hunk of gymsteak shooting up, he'll never get the fucking needle out of his esophagus." Price's expression had not changed; only his eyes darkened with possibilities. He clapped both hands down on Art's shoulders. It was almost a hug. "*Attendez.* You'll want to know where the downstairs can is, anyway."

Before Price could tear him free, Michelle put her hand alongside Art's face, almost tenderly, "It's nice to get a look at you at last, strange as that may sound. Stick around; you might find something interesting, yes?" When she passed behind him, he felt her high breasts brush his shoulder blades.

The coquettish Estelle-Leigh was still gyrating on top of the speaker; Art caught a whiff of honeydust as he and Price passed. A couple of people tried to waylay Price, who sloughed them off with a terse, "Not now." As they stepped over a couple on the hallway floor sharing a monstrous Jamaican spliff, Price extracted a privacy key from a ring on a chromium chain at his belt. He knocked three times on the bathroom door. "You better not be taking a dump in my sink, Bryan, 'cos I'm coming in." He jacked the door in one smooth motion.

Their objective was sitting on the lip of the claw-footed tub, fully clothed, alone, hair lank and damp. He jerked his head up when they entered. His face was crimson and puffy; his eyes rubbed bloodshot. Tears glistened. He held a wad of paper towel in one fist.

"Okay, what's the crisis?" said Price, indicating that Art should shut the door.

The man on the tub was bare-chested inside a leather dress jacket, obviously an iron pumper who worried about things like water weight or percentage of body fat. The veins on his neck were corded to pencil thickness and he looked distantly Indian. There were tears on his pecs, his washboard abs, his thighs, as though his head had sprung a serious leak. He made groping motions in the air before Price, incapable of direct explanation. He husked a breath or two and tried really hard.

"Price, man, it's all so . . . *sad*," he said. "I feel like I wanna kill myself; it's the only decent . . . the only way I can . . ."

"Calm it down a notch, cowboy. What's sad?" Price squatted in front of him, hands on his legs, almost paternal. That's it, thought Art: He's acting like a dad, a father confessor.

"I—I just . . . hurt so many fuckin' people." The man sucked a sobbing gasp of air. "I mean, I don't mean to, but I hurt every-body . . . the world doesn't fuckin *need* me, y'know? The world has got enough fuckin problems."

"Who did you hurt?" said Price.

"Nobody, tonight . . . I mean my whole life, I just use people up, I hurt them, and I don't care that I hurt them, I don't even know I'm doing it, and when I do know, I don't ever care . . . oh, christ, I feel like shit, man." He slammed the heel of his hand into the bridge of his nose and pressed hard; more tears flowed. For this man, it was like acid rivuleting out of his soul, to distill. "I hurt . . . I hurt Cheri-lyn, I mean, the day I dumped her I took all the money out of her wallet, and she called and I never bothered with her, because I had used her up. I totally dissed her; all done. I hurt Suze, fuck, man, I can't believe that I'm such a blackened fuck that I actually hit her, but I *have* to believe it, because I know I did it on purpose."

Art was almost startled into recoiling. He was looking at Suzanne's dreaded ex, the Asshole, the Bry-Guy, crying his eyes out with remorse, definitely not playing the role of callous abuser and taker of advantages. This guy was nearly prostrate with sorrow.

"I have nothing in my life, man," said Bryan, his respiration hitching. "I take all this shit and never give anything back. Just have a good time, have fun, and wait to die. All I do for other people is make their lives worse; do you know how much that fuckin *hurts?*"

"I hear you," said Price, softly, his tone confidential and succoring. "But who's in control of all that? You are. Who's responsible? You are. You need to apologize or make amends, do it. If you can't, then cauterize it and try to do better next time. But you're not worthless, man. I wouldn't've invited you here if you were worthless; I don't know any worthless people."

Bryan sounded like a lost child. "What do I do?" It was hopeless, a rhetorical question.

"What you do is nothing, right now. What you do is relax, because you're all atwist, right now."

Art recognized Price's careful build and repetition, his voice level as a salt flat, eye contact rock hard, all the mannerisms used by someone into hostage negotiation. He was boring right into Bryan's psyche, with the sure aim of a surgeon, and talking him down.

"You listening?" Price used his knuckle to bring Bryan's chin up so Bryan could not avoid his gaze. "It's good that you're actually listening, paying attention to me, because I wouldn't want to feel like you were blowing me off, or ignoring me, because that would be what you hate the most about yourself, am I right?"

Bryan nodded.

"Let's work together on this, Bryan. Open."

Bryan dutifully opened his mouth. Price inserted one of the black-and-white capsules.

"Swallow," Price said, and Bryan did. Price then filled his cupped hands with water from the sink and extended his hands toward Bryan in an eerie form of communion. "Drink."

Bryan drank, almost gratefully.

"Now I'm going to take you upstairs, where you can lie down a bit, and I want you to do two things for me. Don't think about everything you've done wrong; we *all* fuck up. Think about what you want, how you really want people to perceive you, and nap on that. The other thing is, no crying. That stops now. Okay?"

Bryan nodded again, done with words that could not serve him.

"I think I got this one," Price said to Art as he helped Bryan up and slung a brotherly arm around the bigger man's shoulders. "You can take a piss now, if you want."

● ● ● When Art emerged from the bathroom, hands still damp, face rinsed as though to cleanse away the drama he'd just witnessed, a stranger lassoed him in a wobbly, buddy-buddy embrace just short of a headlock. It was a woman with a snake tattooed on the upper hemisphere of her capacious right breast, its body winding downward with serpent's promises.

"Babydoll, I want to go now, okay?" She looked around the living room like someone dismayed at a faulty fence on a gator pit. "I feel too much danger, and I want to go, and I don't know if you if you're ready yet, but—"

Michelle was standing in the alcove, arms folded, one brow

arched, her lips hinting at a private smile. "Back off, Maureen. You need to go cuddle up to Jeremiah before he starts masturbating in public over you. That's your mission. Now disengage from our friend, here."

Maureen cast her eyes down, submissively, and retreated into the throng.

"Had enough?" Michelle said to Art. "Please say no."

Art shook his head indecisively, almost the way Blitz would. "I haven't been to a party in a bit of a while."

"Well, come on, then." She offered her arm. "Head-on's always the best way."

Suzanne had been right about Michelle. Whenever she crossed a room, all eyes tended to follow her. Whom she was with. Whom she was talking to, or not. Price was not in the immediate vicinity, and a microscopic quadrant of Art's civilized mind asked him, *Just what the hell do you think you're doing?*

"That somewhat frazzled-looking young man at the main bar is Kyle."

Art's brow furrowed. "That bar wasn't there before."

"Oh, really? You sure you just didn't notice it?" Her eyes said she was deciding whether to tease him.

"The space is different." The bar was a Rat Pack wet dream of onyx surfaces and mirrored glass; it was almost impossible *not* to see.

"I forgot your calling. Anyway, you're right. It comes up out of the floor. The whole thing elevators up from an apartment that's the only room on the lower level. Good for catering because it has its own kitchen and doesn't clutter things up here." She cast her gaze about the room; people looked to see what she was looking for, trying to anticipate her, perhaps to grab a chance at pleasing her, or merely getting her to acknowledge them. "Now, that shorter woman dressed identically to Kyle—black shirt and pants, red bow tie—see her?"

"Yes." The woman was fussing over several sizzling dim sum platters whose aroma gradually thickened the air.

"Her name is Elpidia. Offhand, I'd say either Kyle got more than he bargained for during his break, or Elpidia met someone new."

"Maybe they were just napping," said Art. "Keeping this crowd lubricated would exhaust me."

"Ah, but look at them. She looks battened, fully fueled. Her eyes are dark and deep and you can just smell she had some kind of nourishing sex. He looks tapped, as though half his blood got drained. It was interesting to watch them circling each other last night, all the while doing their jobs. They're never less than professional. God knows where Price finds help like this."

Art imagined the two of them logging a full shift, then riding their Dean Martin-y lift down to paradise in some stuffy servants' quarters. He visualized the cocky Kyle yanking off his ridiculous, servile neck ornament and making his move on sweet little Elpidia . . . who then had nearly eaten him alive.

The main room, the interior of the turret Art had seen outside, was radiused into concentric descending circles, like steps, carpeted and arrayed with cushions. Flat surfaces of one-square-foot laminate were laid in every so often to serve as tables; most featured electronics mounted into the risers, including a series of small television monitors interspersed so that no matter where one was sitting, a screen was visible across the circle. The whole setup bellowed a crude Las Vegas anti-charm, which instantly reminded Art of a *Playboy* magazine passion pit.

"It is a bit much," Michelle said, apparently reading his mind. "But it came with the house."

112

An iron staircase curled up toward the mezzanine level, where the turret was fitted with an Industrial Revolution—style catwalk that covered three-quarters of the circumference. This was to access a library that no longer existed; Art saw the built-in shelves, but precious few books. Some guests sat up there, dangling their legs through the wrought interstices. Higher up, a ring of storm-glass windows, original to the structure, completed the lighthouse effect. The upper floor followed the L-shape of the two wings, with the elbow of the hallway opening into a railed balcony that over-looked the turret. Just seeing the clash of styles and motifs in this place made Art itch to redesign it. Apart from several backbreak-ingly huge abstracts hung on the main interior walls, there was very little actual decoration; the whole joint was a big, hollow tomb of lavish waste and gimmicked gimcrackery.

"This place looks like it was built by two different designers . . . who really *hated* each other."

That brought forth her sumptuous laugh again. "Don't worry about offending us; it's just a lease."

"Yeah, how do I say this? This place isn't you."

"Is it Price?"

"Him, neither. Tell me, Michelle, what does he do? For that mat-ter, what do you do?"

She pursed her lips. "Come on." She practically dragged him to the bar. "Kyle, honey, vodka rocks, use the distilled ice, one-quarter lime exactly, and fresh-cut it. And whatever Mr. Latimer wants." She looked Kyle in the eyes as though sobriety-testing him. "Rough night?"

"No, ma'am," said Kyle. "Trouble sleeping, is all."

Her eyes went big and motherly. "Aww."

"No worries." He made the drink smoothly, barely looking at the glass or ingredients.

"I hope that's not your two-word book report on last night. And Kyle, a favor? Don't call me *ma'am;* it makes me feel forty."

"Certainly, miss."

She cocked a thumb at Art. "And call him *sir* if you know what's good for you."

Kyle turned to Art. "Sir?"

"Don't call me *sir,*" said Art. "It makes me feel the way I feel when I'm pulled over by a cop younger than me—you know, the sort of guy you would have bitch-slapped in high school."

"We would have pantsed him, painted his ass with whitewash, and made him run naked through the girls' locker room," said Kyle, with a knowing grin—overly knowing. His expressions changed like slides in a projector, *clunk,* next.

"I'll just have a club soda." To Michelle, he added, "How did you know my last name?"

"Oh, that's easy—it's on your business card."

About then the deck doors seemed to burst inward, bringing rain and cold and razor-blade wind. At the head of this minor-league tornado was a bedraggled, bowlegged man wearing a wet suit, a nylon windbreaker with a hood, and whisper-thin rubber water-sport slippers. His gear was a riot of brand names in Day-Glo colors, and he dropped his hood and shook water off himself like a dog. "*Whooooo,* DAMN, it's *cold* outside, brothers and sisters!"

"That's Solomon," said Michelle.

Solomon possessed the pan-blackened suntan and bleached-out hair and eyes of a beach rat, the square-headed type whose chin and forehead seemed eternally to be reaching for each other. So much of his life was spent in the water that the sea had begun to reshape him to its needs; his bowlegged stance made him appear froggy. He was obviously a party animal and spent a bit of time playing to his instant audience, stomping around and getting people wet.

114

"Solomon wants the waves to get up to hurricane strength so he can try surfing them," she said. "He does push-ups and burns incense and waits like a monk. He figures tonight or tomorrow will be the only moment he's alive."

"You didn't answer my question," Art said, testing her limits . . . and wondering how Michelle had seen his business card.

"Oh, the boring shit; what-do-YOU-do." She pulled half the vodka at a swallow with no grimacing or drinker's theatrics. "Well, Price is determined to stay a mystery, so the most I'll tell you is that he's a sort of freelancer. Troubleshooter. Consultant type. We met in Rome, where I was busy being a model. Not trying; being. Now we're superheroes, and we fly around fighting crime and defending the helpless." Her eyes were all champagne and seduction.

"You were a model?"

"How do you think we got all these amazingly attractive women here?" She dared him to doubt her superpowers.

"Yeah, I did notice there were precious few plain-looking people around. I'm afraid I stand out in the wrong way."

"Nonsense." She made a point of pretending to look him over, scalp to soles. "I'd say you were within five years of Price. You don't wear contacts and I haven't seen you put on glasses. I'd guess you keep your hair that way because most men your age have lost theirs."

"That way?" Art could not help feeling self-conscious under her scrutiny. The last time he'd bothered with a haircut had been over a year ago.

"Shaggy. It's makes you look rumpled, but it's kind of sexy and natural." She knew how to stroke his vanity. She probably never turned her charm full off.

"At least I shaved," he said, adding a smile to defang whatever caveats she might have in store for him. Michelle's inviting manner was another brand of weapon, and if Art asked prickly questions, she would use it to deflect them. For now, he played along, wondering where she really wanted to take him.

"Used a dab of cologne, too—about a drop. So on some level you knew you were going to be socializing today."

Guilty, Art thought.

What did he look like to these people? Good days, or bad, were usually determined by what he saw in his own mirror. But what did Price see? What did Michelle see? A contemporary, perhaps, on the cusp of middle age, good eyesight, full head of hair. Five-nine, clean-shaven, reasonably fit, well nourished. Brown-gray eyes, wide set and expressive, what one old girlfriend had once called "St. Bernard eyes." Dark brown hair (frequently mistaken for black) with slivers of silver. Brows thick but not hirsute. He'd always thought he had a weak jaw and a bit too much forehead, but nobody had ever stated this to him outright in his lifetime. Average body, average hands, a big moby overdose of average. All this added up to . . . what? Ephemera. Statistics. Lorelle had argued that statistics never meant anything, because they could be interpreted to support any side of an argument.

"My, that's an introspective look," said Michelle.

"Sorry."

"Listen, you fit in as well as any of the other deviates here. Indulge me, and I'll tell you what I see, and you tell me how far off I am."

Art blushed. She was reading him as though his doubts were scrawled on his forehead in block letters.

"You've been married once or twice but aren't now. Definitely a college graduate, probably with more than one degree. You've tasted most recreational drugs but now you stick to the legal ones, excepting the occasional rare dabble. You're an ex-smoker. You're a professional. You're comfortably well off, but rarely extravagant."

Art felt his skin was on inside out. "Whoa, this is starting to sound like a horoscope."

"Don't interrupt. You have a dog—that's an easy one. I already know you're an architect, but you pursue it more like a painter. You're smarter than most of the people you deal with on a day-to-day, and that's frustrating; it's caused you to withdraw. You're not quite a misanthrope yet, but one or two more major tragedies ought to do it."

"Well, this is getting uncomfortable," he tried to joke, maintaining eye contact almost defensively, thinking of X-ray Spex, the kind that advertised the ability to see people naked. "A century ago, they'd've burned you at the stake for this."

"Nope, my obligation as hostess is to see to your comfort. You keep asking about this party, and I'm trying to frame an explanation for you. People are rarely the same as the image they project—just look at all the people here. We see surfaces; all Price wants to do is peel those envelopes back a bit. Hang around and you might find it educational."

"Price wanted that big guy in the bathroom to dissolve into a puddle of tears?"

"Not specifically. That's just how another side of Bryan's personality happened to express itself today. You saw Price; he didn't abuse that guy."

"No, he treated him like an altar boy, then fed him dope."

"See, you're not comfortable with the idea, yet." Michelle was beginning to sound proselytic. "Watch and learn. Circulate."

He was already thinking about leaving. "I've got to find Suzanne, or Dina, before I do anything else."

"Everyone awaits." She indicated the living room. "Stairs are over there; turn left, and climb. I'll see you in a bit, yes?"

He nodded, finished his soft drink, and angled his way toward the stairs in that odd way that would resemble an interpretive dance, were he not packed among other bodies. A bearded roughneck, his hands laden with skull rings, was abusing an unplugged Fender Strat more or less in time to the guitarless music. A tight knot of admirers egged on his silent solo. A red-eyed dude with a buzz cut like tire tread held his palms against the cold window glass and vibrated, making Art think of a tweaker on too much speed. If Art spotted a barefoot chick doing a stoned Grateful Dead veil dance, he knew he'd bolt.

As he ascended the stairs he looked directly up the skirt of a woman leaning from the balcony to survey the atrium of the turret. There was no underwear to be seen. She lifted her glass in a mocking little toast that told him she could see his thoughts just as clearly.

The upper corridor was a gauntlet of closed doors. There was a large guest bathroom at the far north end, and Art decided to work his way toward it from the opposite terminus. He tapped on the first door, not nearly declarative enough, or so he thought until a lugubrious voice answered him from within.

"Yay-esss?"

"Uh—excuse me, is either Dina or Suzanne in there?"

"Couldn't say," said the voice, airing out the syllables. "Come on in."

Art opened the door to a smallish, nine-by-nine room with barely enough leeway for the queen-size bed it contained. A scarf on a lamp diffused the light to a sodium-colored batik pattern on the wall. Three people were on the bed. The two men were naked. The woman between them was on her hands and knees, with her

dress rucked onto her back as she engorged them from both directions. The men were facing each other, as if over an end table, their
hands clasped, vising her, thrusting toward each other. Art recognized the woman as Estelle-Leigh, late of the floor show atop Price's
big speaker.

"Are you Phil?" said the man stuck on the half that eats.

"No."

"Well, there's one more hole here you can *phill*, if you want,
because neither Joey nor me like pussy very much."

"Will you two fags *shut up* and *fuck* me?" snarled Estelle-Leigh.

"Sorry," said Art, quickly closing the door. He heard them all
laughing.

Great. A quick one-eighty toward the nearest exit was probably
a grand idea, rather than Xeroxing his humiliation at Door Number
Two, or Three, or beyond. Maybe there was aspirin to be found in
the bathroom at the end of this puzzle maze. Maybe Suzanne was
behind the next door.

No such luck. The door opened before he could touch it, and a
very angry black man raged out, sweat-speckled, bare-chested
except for his shoulder holster.

"Outta the way, *bitch*," he said, not even looking at Art. The
sclera of his eyes were jaundiced, and he had the sickly skin pop of
a man cresting on too much blow. Art spotted the earring dangling
from his left ear, the Eye of Ra.

"Hey, slow down, Luther. It's Luther, right?"

The man's whole body stiffened, and he turned back slowly, like
a gun turret sighting and calibrating, then struck so fast that he
defied normal time-space. He grabbed Art's Adam's apple in a textbook finger pinch, to cut off his wind, lifting and bulldogging him
into the wall. Art knew his own feet were off the floor, and he could
feel a gun muzzle kissing his ribs, rooting up into his chest cavity.

"Who the fuck told you that! I don't fuckin know you!"

Art couldn't speak, couldn't breathe, was starting to see violet spheres colliding in the air.

"Luther." Somewhere down the hall another door closed. "Knock that shit off. This is my guest." It was Price's voice, never raised in anger, or threat, or any of the fiery, reactionary conceits. It did, however, firm up: "*Luther*. Abuse my guests and I'll abuse you."

Art saw Luther's eyes track over, then back. He was slowly lowered. Gently. Luther was hyperventilating. Through clenched teeth, he said, "Sorry, I thought you was maybe somebody else."

Price stood dominating the hallway, arms crossed, his interest up, but his face maintaining the same clinical flatness Art had noticed before, the manner of a virologist checking rats for tumors, one by one. "Now hand over your gun, Luther."

Art was still trying to catch up on his breathing. Luther had a hell of a crab-claw grip.

"Say what?"

Price smiled, looked down, rubbed his nose with the tip of his finger. The deferential host. "Oh, god, I'm sorry—I probably slurred my words or something; hell, even *I* couldn't understand me." He laughed, and Luther nervously laughed along. "Please let me repeat: Hand. Over. Your gun. *Now.*"

Luther's jollity curdled instantaneously, and Art could see the war for capitulation wage in his eyes. He licked his lips, swallowed hard and audibly, and extended the pistol to Price, butt first, upside down, so Price could see he was only holding the barrel.

"Not to *me*, stupid." Price's eyes indicated Art.

The weight of the blue-steeled automatic settled into Art's hand.

"That's great," said Price. "You don't get to eat shit that often, do you, Luther, my man?"

Luther stepped back a pace, unsure of whether to watch the gun, or Price. "Sure don't."

"Okay, now, Art? You okay?"

Art massaged his throat, keeping the muzzle of the gun angled away from any available human targets. "Just a misunderstanding. No worries."

"Glad to hear it. Go ahead and shoot Luther in the chest. That is, I mean, if you feel like it. If you want to."

Luther's jaw unhinged. *"What the fuck—?"* He had already started to move, but Price's voice froze him in midstride.

"Luther, put your ass on hold right where it is."

Art saw, in his own hand, an AMT Hardballer. From its weight he guessed it was packing a full magazine, seven fat .45-caliber slugs, plus one in the pipe. Any one of these cartridges could blow an arm off at the shoulder. The thumb safety was off and the hammer at full cock. He popped the clip, snapped back the slide to jack the spare round, and returned the gun to Luther, decocked and with the safety on.

"Don't carry a monster like this cocked if it's not locked," he said, as though they were two buddies swapping lore.

Luther blinked very fast, several times, and sniffed as though drawing clean oxygen. "Yeah." He shook his head. Silly, wasn't it? "Sorry. That was majorly dumb." He reinstalled the magazine and slotted the gun into his shoulder rig as Art retrieved the stray cartridge from the floor.

"That's a Shark, isn't it?" said Art, meaning the holster.

"Huh? Oh, yeah. It's adjustable for the slide."

"I've got a couple, myself."

"See?" said Price, walking forward and grabbing their shoulders like a priest reassuring two members of his flock. "I knew you two would like each other right away. Art—knock first, okay? And Luther—you really don't need that firepower in my house, at my party, so do what Art says and leave the fucking safety on. Please?" Price obviously knew better than to ask Luther to disarm.

"Yeah, right. Price, listen, I'm sorry about—"

"Will you stop apologizing to everybody, because I know you, and when you say *I'm sorry* it means *fuck you*."

Luther reined it back. "Whatever." To Art he added: "I owe you one, what's your name . . . Art?"

"*That's* more like it. Be sure you do Art a favor that matters, because you *do* owe him. He could've blasted your ass out the window and the storm would've picked you up and blown you away, and nobody would give a shit, and nobody would come looking. I would've said, 'Luther? I don't know any Luther.' Remember it. I'm downstairs." Price moved past them and down toward the living room.

Luther offered Art his hand. "That was nuts. I'm a little jumpy today." He was clearly impressed with how Art had handled the weapon.

"Just remember me as 'Art, the guy you're not supposed to shoot,' and I'll be happy." They shook on it.

Luther shook his head. "Well, okay, that's not the weirdest thing that's happened to me tonight. I don't know what it is, man, I been wired ever since I walked into this place. I'm having weird thoughts, like stuff I've known since I was tiny, but it all never bugged me so much before; it's like I got itching powder on my brain." He seemed honestly perplexed.

"I know how you feel," said Art. "Listen, let's start this over again. We'll have a drink or something downstairs and talk about our mutual passions."

"Yeah, sort of reset the whole tape. Good idea."

"But not right this minute, because I've got to find somebody."

Luther nodded, indicating no further explanation was needed. "Whoever he or she is, he or she ain't in there." He jabbed a thumb over his shoulder at the door through which he had exited. "What's in there is an *it*. I think I'll go rinse off my face, splash some disinfectant on my dick."

Luther lumbered around the crook of the hallway, and Art stifled the urge to ask him to look for aspirin in the bathroom.

Door Number Three was the one from which Price had appeared. That meant Bryan the Bry-Guy was probably in there, convalescing. Thrashing through a nightmare of guilt, more like. The room seemed silent; the crack beneath the jamb was dark.

Did this Lady-or-Tiger obstacle course keep getting more phantasmagoric as it progressed? When Art knocked on the final door in the corridor, would he find Zeus, Allah, and the Christian Satan in a cross-legged circle jerk, kidding one another about bringing back dinosaurs, or perhaps the plague, just for a hoot?

He rounded the turn and briefly looked down into the circular main room just as a nail-splitting catfight erupted between two women. One was blocky, with a brush cut, wearing a bolero vest and pants with conchos and thongs; her nemesis had a sterile Aryan look, blond over blue, dressed in black trousers and a billowing white dress shirt. Conchita tossed a cocktail in Hamlet's face, obviously thinking this an imperious rejoinder. Hamlet punched Conchita right in the kisser, ejecting a tooth, and as soon as they tussled, other people were yanking them apart. They swung and yammered; Hamlet had a good six inches of reach over Conchita, and managed to bash her one more time.

Art did not applaud. He turned his back on the show and contin-

123

ued down the upstairs hall, toward the bathroom. Luther passed him headed in the opposite direction, still contrite. "Later, Art." He danced easily down the stairs without touching the rail.

The fourth room of five seemed the largest. In Art's home, it would have been an office. Yellow light streamed from a separate bathroom, forming hot trapezoids of reflection on a big window that normally boasted a sea view, but now was a wash of pelting rain flying from a roiling gray limbo. At the deep end of the room was a large showy bed, possibly circular, apparently strewn with clothing and coats. When Art squinted he could make out an inestimable number of people sprawled there as well. Fewer than ten. Nobody moved. The air was thick and atonic with the odor of powdered latex and pheromones, water-based lubricants, alcohol, and perspiration. It was a sedentary, hanging miasma that reminded Art of peepshow booths, not that he had devoted much time to Tenderloin field trips. Somebody groaned, and the whole dog pile rearranged itself like a many-tentacled space creature in midslither. Art thought of the way Blitz's paws twitched, in the realm of canine dreams. He felt no need to gently disturb a crowd.

A woman's voice answered the moment he tapped on the fifth door.

"Go away."

It was embarrassing, the way Art's body automatically moved to do what it was told. He persisted. "Suzanne?"

"She's not here. Just leave."

He cracked the door. Five minutes ago he'd had a gun in his face; how much more stressful could this be? The music from downstairs hummed up through the floor, having changed gears to bass-mechanic hip-hop.

"Oh, fuck, doesn't anybody *listen?*"

124

"Sorry. I don't want to bother you. But I need to find Suzanne, if you know where she is."

His eyes adjusted to the light and tracked a glowing cigarette coal, near the bed, rising, flaring, descending. The single occupant sat, legs hugged to chest, outlined against a white stack of pillows. Art saw the glint of dark eyes wet with grief, luminous enough to catch the poor lamplight from the opposite nightstand. He pushed the door quietly shut behind him.

"You want Suzanne, Price took her. Away. And I can't fuck you, whoever you are, so please leave." The cigarette killed itself in an ashtray, scattering orange embers. A plastic butane lighter flicked to ignite another, and in that moment Art saw the long legs clad in leather pants—barefoot, now—the amethyst choker, the sharp jewelry.

"You're Dina, Suzanne's friend," he said. "The one who brought her here."

"No, I'm nobody, and I don't have any fucking friends." She puffed too fast and caught a cough. "I can't believe Price picked her. He walked right in here, right in front of me, and picked her."

"Price is downstairs. I saw him in the hall just a second ago."

"No, Price has got Suzanne's heels against the fucking ceiling and he's ramming her just to make me feel like shit." She blew her nose. A roll of toilet paper sat near the ashtray, and she dropped her sodden wad on the floor. "I thought she was my fucking *friend,* how could somebody who says they're your friend pull crap like that?"

"She is your friend, as far as I know. She spoke very highly of you." Art had been permitted to come deeper into the room; at least Dina hadn't started screaming or throwing things.

"Yeah, well, that's all probably bullshit, too. I mean, look at Suzanne—she's dumpy, her hair's washed out, big pillowy mammaries. Look at me—I'm tall, goddammit, I've got great bones, I've been in goddamn *magazines*. Yeah, if I was Price, I'd pick her, because all guys care about is hooters."

"That's not true." Art was trying to pass for native on a planet where the language was a mystery; once again he was treading a negotiative tightrope on the verge of unraveling. One look at Dina told him that her relationship with Suzanne was one of those classic hot-dog-and-hamburger combos. Dina was long, thin, and angular, like a French model. Her jawline and cheekbones bespoke pedigree and her jet-black hair (no dye job, there) was machined into a perfect Louise Brooks bob. Her waistline was twenty-two inches, tops, while Art estimated her inseam at a stunning thirty-six, or better. The expensive shoes discarded on the floor had four-inch heels. She and Suzanne would make the perfect party pair; between them they possessed most of the attributes needed to allow them to pick and choose. What didn't work for one was compensated for by the other, and the buried resentment that conditioned such a dynamic had to be potent and toxic.

Dina was used to acquiring any partner she wanted. Apparently she wanted Price, who was beyond acquisition.

Art angled toward a love seat near the window. When he sat down—slowly, easily—he felt like a mountain climber gaining a critical foothold. "Besides, isn't Price with Michelle?"

"That *cunt*," said Dina. "I'm better than her. She's his fucking arm doily. He's blowing her off so he can stick his root into Suzanne, right now, I bet. Fucking bitch betrayed me; you can't trust *anybody*." She sniffed and dabbed at her face. She would not want anyone to see her without prep or makeup. "You didn't bring anything to drink, did you? You another one of Price's toys?"

"Let me get you something."

Another sniffle. Art was aware of leading her onto familiar turf, the puppet show where men brought any damned thing Dina might think of to request. He was not obligated, nor trapped, but suffused with endless curiosity, not only about her, right now, but about all the people he was encountering in this uncharted landscape. Dina's eyes were light brown, shot through with spikes of green and amber, which made them slightly chatoyant; the kind of eyes you could easily lose yourself in. Too easily.

"A glass of water would be nice," she admitted. "A double Black Jack on the rocks, and make sure that faggot Kyle doesn't put any fruit in it."

"I can do that." He rose carefully. Sometimes cornered animals might still attack for no reason at all.

"Hey, who are you supposed to be, anyway?"

"Call me Art."

Her jaw stalled. "Not *the* Art?"

"I don't understand."

She freed a plume of gray smoke. "Oh, holy shit, this toilet's backing up for sure. You're *Art?* Suzanne says you raped her. You *that* Art?"

"I didn't rape anybody." His heartbeat kicked into triple time.

"Suzanne says she went to your house to ask to use the phone to call me, and you fucking raped her. Last night. Said you came on to her, all sleazy—*take off your clothes, use my dryer, here, sleep in my bed*—and you were all over her."

"That's not what happened." Art felt his bowels plunge. This was his payback for sex that came too easily, the punchline that made him a mark, a sucker to be fleeced, another gob of meat for the grinder. Where had his caution been last night? Had he reinvented his memory to the point where yesterday's glorious, cleansing liberation was just white noise, a story he had cooked up to mask the foul truth?

127

Was this the check he now had to pick up for cheating on Lorelle, if only in principle?

A brand-new headache sank in and nested, half hangover, half migraine. He struggled with the hindbrain urge to bolt. "Dina, listen to me. We spent some time together, but it wasn't like that."

"Man, that's fucking *cold*," she said, already brewing up invective for the sort of man she knew he really was. "That's like saying Charlie Manson 'spent some time with celebrities.'"

"Suzanne was upset last night—"

"Not half as upset as when I saw her half an hour ago," Dina said, in a tone that implied she disliked interruption or disagreement. "When she was telling me about calling the cops on you for fucking a minor."

Another railroad spike of pain split Art's head. On top of that, an illogical irritation, because Art knew from his reading that Manson had never actually killed anybody, so Dina's simile was for shit. He tried to breathe in some patience while his eyes were throbbing.

"I didn't rape anybody, goddammit!"

Her gaze brightened. "Wow, I was wondering what it'd take to get a rise out of you." At least she wasn't crying, now. "Like I care, if she's going to cut in on Price. She fucking raped *me* by doing that shit. So I don't care." She said it again, *she didn't care*, as if rehearsing, or feeling out the line for watertightness.

Art was already backing away. *Those faint of heart, or who might be appalled by the inmates of the asylum, feel free to run screaming out the EXIT door . . . if you can find it.* "I'll just stop bothering you now," he said, hoping she was bright enough to catch his corrosive tone, stinging her as good as she gave.

"Wait."

"No, Dina, you wait, on whatever psychosis is bubbling away in your brain right now. I've hit my limit."

128

"Please."

Art wanted to start flinging wild blows. Was she still trying to manipulate him? He kept his distance. "What?"

Dina stood up, and my god, was she tall and gorgeous, even raccooned in smeared mascara. A tear hung pendant from the point of her chin. "Am I pretty?"

Art looked around to see if she was addressing someone else in the room, some new intruder, some rapist. "*What?*"

"Stop saying *what*. It's an easy question. Do you think I'm pretty?" She hung her index finger in the loop of her choker. Posing.

He did not have to look her up and down, but did anyway. "Yes, Dina, you're pretty," he tried to say firmly. "You're probably too goddamned pretty, which I'm sure is the source of most of your problems, and the reason you're crying your face off, up here, alone in the dark, when at any other party you'd play queen bee."

She dabbed at her face with another spiral of tissue.

"I have no idea what your current stress is. I just delivered Suzanne back here the way she asked me to. From what I can see, nearly everybody at this so-called party is having a miserable, schizophrenic time, that is, whenever they're not banging total strangers or otherwise proving how radical they are by bathing in each other's flesh."

"Everybody's fucked up anyway," she said.

"Regardless, you don't need me to reassure you how attractive you are, and I know you know that."

"I'm ugly," she said, her voice small and recalcitrant. "I feel *so* ugly."

"It'll pass." He sounded more frigid than he'd intended. He was supposed to protest, and feed her some more, which was how people like Dina battened on the souls they consumed. He owed her nothing, and resented the obligation being forced on him. He was expected to ply her, to aspire to her pampered beauty, the DNA leash around his cock and balls said so . . . but he just felt angry and put-upon.

Yeah, because you just got laid, and can afford to be this nasty, now.

"I could still use that drink," she said. Still playing him.

"I'm sure Kyle would be happy to be of service. I think I'm leaving." He left it at that, without appending more of the barbs lining up in his head, without offering her more material to leverage. She was in midsentence as he shut the door behind him, thinking, *jee-sus.*

The upstairs bathroom was a wonderland of spotless hexagonal tile, the kind New Yorkers found comforting. A claw-foot bathtub that could effortlessly seat four occupied most of the space, enameled white on the inside, black without, to match the tile. An oval mirror cut across the western wall like a huge dinosaur eye, making Art think of the tattoo on the back of Derek's hand. He idly wondered if there was a camera hidden behind it; if Price was clandestinely taping all that transpired on his upper floors for some yet-unguessed psychological gameplay.

There was an unflushed cigarette butt in the john, and hair on the floor. Art looked down and saw he was standing in a drift of human hair, a whole head's worth, apparently shaved off and left where it dropped. Medium-length black hair with a few threads of gray; genderless, wavy, upsetting because it appeared to have simply disconnected, and fallen, and nobody had bothered to clean it up. With his foot he scooted it into a little pile, wondering why he was afraid to touch it.

He splashed water on his face from a beveled rectangular sink of metal, aware of several people moving about the hallway, loitering, wandering, or going room to room, sampling a kind of berserk sensual smorgasbord. An antique, windowed surgeon's cabinet held a

130

generous assortment of recognizable commercial palliatives. Art gulped four Excedrin and swallowed tap water from his cupped hands, remembering how Price had done it when feeding drugs to the very conflicted Bry-Guy. He did not notice any of the odd black-and-white capsules among the stuff crowding the cabinet.

The door was pushed open and Suzanne walked halfway in, now wearing her shoes, clunky, squared-off heels with fat rubber soles. Her expression contracted upon recognizing Art and her mouth shrank to a tiny puncture of surprise.

"*Oh* . . . shit." She began to back away.

"Suzanne, wait up a minute." Art moved toward her and quickly saw this was a rotten idea. Her hands moved up in defense and her eyes glinted at him in warning.

"You stay the fuck away from me!"

"Hold on. I need you to tell me what the hell—"

"Price!" she yelled, waxing toward panic. "*Price!* Get your ass up here, Price! And *you* just . . . stay right there."

Their host must have been within earshot, even past the din of the music, because Art saw him loping up the stairs two at a time. When he saw there was no immediate bloodshed or weapons involved, his mien relaxed. Art, meanwhile, tried to configure new sentences, new ways of asking what in blazes was going on. None made it past the first few syllables. Suzanne was wild-eyed, hair-triggered; he could see in her eyes that she was on the verge of smashing crockery.

"You just back the fuck off, or I'll gouge your eyes out. I'll do it!"

"Oh, I doubt that," said Price. "But I want to watch, if you try it. Art?"

"I don't know what's wrong with her, Price, I just—"

"That asshole raped me!" Suzanne interrupted, moving to position Price between her and Art.

"I didn't rape anybody," said Art.

"Rape is a highly fluid term," said Price. "Art, did you rape our Suzanne?" She was clutching at his arm.

"No." Now was the time to be succinct. Later Art could unreel his more verbose explorations. The situation—whatever it was—needed defusing in the moment, and Price was aware of this.

"Suzanne, did my new friend Art rape you?"

"He took advantage of me!"

"Just now?"

Doubt or confusion clouded her rage. "No! Last night! Got me drunk and was all over me!"

Two beers and a pint of club soda did not, in Art's most remote recognition, classify as drunk. Staring at Price, he merely shook his head no.

"Price, he did! I was trapped there!"

Price turned; maybe he just inclined his head, but the move was a study in economy of motion. His fingertip homed directly to Suzanne's lips, and he spoke quite evenly. "Suzanne. Shut up." Her mouth still moved but her voice failed her. When Art made to jump into the sonic gap, Price shushed him, too.

Once Art had bumped into a woman on the BART train, a woman who smelled like laundry, wore too much damp tweed, and was bindled to a well-worn nylon backpack. She had begun hollering that Art had tried to steal her "purse," and a transit cop hustled forth to intercede. It was the only time Art had ever seen a member of the enforcement arm of mass transit actually riding the train, and though he was completely innocent, he paled, broke a freshet of cold sweat, and began trembling. He felt the same way now.

"I don't scope Art as the raping type," said Price. "But what the hell, the night is young. Didja fuck her, Art? Never mind. Your expression says you did. Now, Suzanne—did you fuck him?"

Her expression faltered. Art saw her attitude, her poise, click from offense to defense, and she did not like it. "Took advantage of me," she said again.

"Please. Next you're going to say someone *had his way with you,* and I'm going to start laughing. Either make me believe you or be quiet."

"I just asked to use his phone and got, like, attacked."

"That true, Art? Did you, how you say, force your affections on her? Let's try to clarify this: Did you put anything of yours inside anything of hers against her will?"

"That's really nobody's business," said Art.

Reflections in Price's eyes sought Art, now, like sunlight winking off fighter jets at high altitude. "Take a look around you, new fish. Everything here is my business."

Art was startled by the way this man could command. He rallied enough to say, "I'll just be leaving you to that business, then, whatever it is."

Price's hand shot out, open. "Not so fast. That's not like you, Art. Cut and run? Escape? That makes you look guilty." He sniffed hard to catch fresh air for the jury in his head. "Here's what I think: I think you two had a little ooh-la-la, and now Suzanne is trying to excuse what may or may not have been a hasty choice of sex partners. An ill-considered, spur-of-the-moment deal. Art, on the other hand, is embarrassed at acting like some horny sophomore." He turned back to Suzanne. "Were you hurt? I mean damaged."

"My arms are all bruised."

Art remembered clamping her upper arms when he orgasmed. Too hard.

Price checked, and saw her light parallel contusions. "*Oww,* two points for Suzanne's argument."

Art felt hopeless again. Suzanne brightened. Then Price changed channels on them both, again.

"But, as evidence of rape, less than shit. You wouldn't have allowed yourself to be chauffeured back here, you would've screamed about this the second you rolled in the door. Nope, this rape was invented long after the actual fucking went down, so here's what I suggest: Suzanne, go visit the cabana or stay up here with Bryan or Dina for at least an hour. Art, you come downstairs with me. Everybody calm down and see what you think in an hour."

"No, I think it's definitely time for me to leave," said Art.

"Come on, Art, it's a misunderstanding. Don't make me get all stern. It's a misunderstanding, *right*, Suzanne?"

"I'll stay up here," she said, and retreated to the third bedroom, nearly stumbling, slamming the door.

Price transfixed Art with a dour stare, then snickered. "You've never raped anybody. She probably begged you for it."

Art felt the irrational urge to defend her. "I don't buy that. Nobody 'begs' to be assaulted, no matter how they're dressed, or how they behave."

"You saying you assaulted her?"

"No, I just—I don't—this is all too much for me, Price. She was friendly when we came here. You saw it. Now . . ."

"She flipped on you," he said. "Became sort of the opposite of what she was before." It was as reasoned an answer as any.

"Price, what the hell is going on here? At this party? I see people feeding people drugs and everybody's suddenly acting mental."

"But you don't know any of these people. They could be this way all the time." Price started walking him toward the stairs.

"Yeah," said Art. "But I get the feeling they're not."

Price nodded as though Art had confirmed some suspicion. He seemed mildly pleased. "Stick around, and you'll find out. You seem pretty smart."

"No, I think I've got to go home." Right now, Art missed the solitude of his home very much.

"C'mon, one beer won't kill you. Who knows? You might get laid." He laughed.

Art recalled the first time he had watched a football game, utterly unaware of the rules. The motions and objectives had all seemed baffling then, too. Now he felt a jolt of competitive macho; he wanted to return Price's hard serves in a fashion that said he was not a child, that he could be a worthy contender, even an opponent.

"Dina says you were screwing Suzanne. She's all upset because she thinks you don't want her."

It was good enough to interrupt Price's stride. "*Dina* said that? Wow." He shook his head in the manner of someone who expects bad news, but is prepared for it. "I'm surprised that chick was able to get her head out of her own ass long enough to consider the world outside the envelope of her ego. She wants to fuck me?"

"That's the general impression."

"Hm. I don't think I will. I already know how it would go."

"She's upset because of you and Suzanne. She said."

"Nah, I didn't do Suzanne either. She's nice—like a Wally Wood cartoon come to life—but I don't need the grief. Some of these women crave the attention victims get; they think their lives are more interesting if they come to you in peril, so you can rescue them. But it's all a setup, because you then must become the new peril from which they'll require someone else to rescue them, in order to continuously demonstrate their idea of worth, which is

135

based on some imaginary profile of a person so attractive or interesting that they are constantly victimized."

"Somebody seems to have shaved their head in your upstairs bathroom. There's hair all over the floor."

"Is it black?" Price nodded. "That'd be Malcolm. He wants to write meaningful novels that only get reviewed in the free papers. He's constantly worried he's not rad enough, punk rawk enough, edge enough. He's probably out in the cabana getting his ear pierced with a hot ice pick, right now. Wonder where he got the razor?"

The main open space downstairs branched off in two directions from the turret, forming an area which, in an architectural show-and-tell, would be called the hot space. Together Art and Price descended back into this warren of morphing activity, part green room, part Bedlam. Art noticed there were no clocks, and the TV screens in the circular pit of the turret were obviously broadcasting prerecorded material. Price surveyed what he had wrought with the air of a minor god choosing his next mortal folly. "So, Dina's nursing a secret lust for me?" he said again, as though the idea was unexpected, yet obliquely pleasing.

"Like I said."

Michelle spotted them and snaked past bodies without upsetting any drinks. "We've got a couple more MIAs, not in the cabana. I think they went outside."

Price looked toward the picture windows, bowing now and again with the force of the wind and rain. "Solomon?"

"Not Solomon, he came in. Unless a few just went home."

"Nonsense, it's too early to go home, right, Art?"

"I should be," Art said. "Soon, anyway."

"You should cruise the cabana," said Price. "Find out where your limits are, maybe redefine a couple."

Art stopped Price from moving into the fray by placing his hand on one arm. "Price, you've got to understand about Suzanne. I don't know why she threw that fit upstairs. It surprised me. Earlier, she was the way you saw her when we came in. Now . . . I just don't know what's going on."

"Like she acted in a completely unpredictable way?"

"*Very* unpredictable."

"Might have something to do with the fact she's been baby-sitting her ex-boyfriend upstairs—a guy whom she despises and fears. I'm sure she told you."

Art was honestly perplexed. "Why?"

"Because she tells everybody the Bryan story."

"No, I mean why go back to him?"

"Who knows? Revenge, maybe." Price's kung fu skill at deflecting queries was undeniable.

"C'mon, allow me to drag you away, sweetheart," said Michelle, taking Art's hand.

As soon as Price disengaged, Michelle had him. Her sway was persuasive, but he stuck to his plan of sane escape. "Drag me back toward the kitchen, because I've really got to go home and feed my dog."

"The cabana doesn't strike me as your scene," she said. "Unless you'd enjoy having your asshole widened by a domme with wildly mismatched skin illustrations covering more than eighty percent of her body."

"It's not that," said Art as they interleaved partygoers. "People can scar or burn or pierce or ink themselves however they want. It's just that it's become assimilated; tattoos are now what van art was to the seventies." He liked making Michelle laugh.

"God, I'd disagree, except I've seen some really stupid ones. You sure you want to take off?" She was gauging what to offer as an incentive for him to linger.

"I can't ignore the storm," he said. "But tell me something, Michelle. This whole party is a bipolar mood swing personified as a crowd. It seems like a big round of musical chairs. People scurry around a selection of different personalities and flop down on whichever one they can grab, and it all changes again at a moment's notice."

"Musical chairs is an elimination game."

"The odd man would be whoever freaks out in the bathroom next."

"I see the point, but this isn't that."

"No, the real point is that Price seems to know this, like he's responsible for it, somehow. He talked about getting people together here like some sort of social experiment, a big Skinner box full of volatile ingredients, a petri dish for emotional stress testing."

She regarded his thumbnail with frank admiration. "That's Price. Just celebrating somebody's birthday with a cake would be a drag."

"But, Michelle . . . if it's on purpose, doesn't it all seem a bit *cruel?*"

She lowered her eyes. "Sometimes yes, I suppose."

"Michelle, have you seen Tobias anywhere?" It was Shinya, the Asian woman Art had originally met in the kitchen. "I was scanning the room for that big blue shirt he was wearing, and"—she held up the shirt—"I found it on the couch, but he wasn't in it."

"You check upstairs?" Michelle said.

Shinya shook her head. "He had this kind of mad fit, you know, like when you suddenly just have to get out of a room? He said if he took off his glasses, he could see how ugly everybody was and it was starting to bug him." Shinya was fidgeting. Her hands did not know where to land; they got pocketed and withdrawn, moved to compulsively twirl strands of hair, then toyed with her broad belt, yanking out the leather tongue, then slotting it back. She might have actually been trembling.

"Hang on," said Michelle. She press-ganged a partygoer from just outside the kitchen arch, a tall woman in a pencil skirt and vintage forties lingerie, whose face read as male, pancaked in too much makeup, as though in preparation for a silent-movie shoot. "Chantelle, darling, go ask Kyle and Elpidia if they've got a twenty on Tobias, and see if you can spot him yourself. He might have pulled a costume change on us."

While Michelle was occupied with Chantelle, Shinya moved very close to Art and took both of his hands in hers, furtively glancing back to ensure her hostess would not overhear.

"You've got the right idea," she said in a low voice, to Art. Whispering was impossible here. "Get out. Before you get hurt." Then she quickly kissed his gathered hands, and retreated.

"Okay, doll," Michelle said to Shinya as she returned. "Our girl Chantelle is on it, and if she doesn't turn him up, you and I will do a search of the closets and storage areas."

Shinya nodded, her obsidian gaze welling with tears she regarded with surprise, as though she had no idea why she was running off at the eyes.

Art collected his slickers, his bomber jacket, and the coat he had loaned Suzanne from the peg near the door. Michelle stopped him before he could get rainproofed.

"You have to promise me you'll come back, or I'll come looking for you," she said, turning his head with one hand and kissing his cheek. "Don't panic. I'm not attracted to you in *that* way, at least not yet. More of a kindred spirit thing. We have a lot in common. You and me together could overlord this entire party."

"What would Price say?"

"Price won't mind. Promise me."

Art didn't want another semantic battle. He wanted to get out into the storm, which was at least something he thought he could deal with. He settled for: "I'll see you again."

Michelle vanished back into her party, and Art made it through the door. The storm on the outside had grown ten times worse than the one on the inside. Or was it the other way around? He could not decide.

● ● ● The dash clock in the Jeep read 7 P.M. Price's house, and the menagerie it contained, seemed to collapse time; Art might have sworn he'd only been there an hour or so. Among the vehicles parked outside, the wind was threatening to tear the ragtop off a Caddy convertible and the newer, smaller cars were visibly rocking with each gust. A yacht-size black Buick Riviera held its ground, determined as a squatting cockroach.

Foliage had taken wing from the hills and debris scooted across the road like tumbleweeds, in the narrow brilliance of the high beams and the Jeep's bonus rack of halogen floods in shock-mounted titanium. Sheets of water unfolded themselves across the driving surface as Art engaged the four-wheel drive and managed a steady thirty-per, leery of booby traps, alert for a washout. He wanted to hole up in his sanctuary, fix a hamburger, and empty his head of the cacophony of the party. He had not partaken of any of the edibles at Price's; he now admitted to himself it was because he backhandedly feared the food was drugged. Half the people he'd encountered had seemed dangerously high. Paradoxically, a part of him wanted to go home and plug down Dixie Double Hexes until he lapsed into sleep, but he promised himself he'd be good tonight.

He wanted to know the hidden linkages that would bring the

whole story into light. Price was adept at talking around the truth, and Michelle was his creature, so anything they revealed indicated a concurrent action list of facts in partial shadow. They seemed to be ringmastering the whole circus; they *knew* why Suzanne's personality had fishtailed on him, but Art was not permitted to know because he was an outsider.

Forget it, he told himself. Cut your losses, don't try to figure it out, and just drive. Leave it behind and it becomes the past. It's not like you had any make on Suzanne's personality—whatever it was, for real.

He thought of his own isolation, his self-imposed exile from the vertiginous soap opera represented in microcosm by Price's party. For every upside to dealing with people, there was a downside; for every benefit, an emotional bill to be paid. Somehow Price had seized the more jagged emotions of each of his guests and propelled them to the fore; he unburied fears and needs and denuded them, right on the surface, where they were unshielded enough to strike sparks against all the other fears and needs distilled from every other partygoer. Price could be a sadistic child in a room full of windup robots, setting them all in motion, heedless of how they collided or fell over. What remained hidden to Art was the benefit derived by Price himself, a guy who acted like he always had an angle hardwired to an agenda . . . unless it was to simply humiliate and embarrass everyone enough to give him some kind of future leverage.

Michelle seemed to know what was going on, too, but her only reaction, apparently, was bemusement at the demolition derby. She was luminescently attractive; another kind of armor. Art could not deny that his glands surged whenever she touched him or made eye contact, and she was pointedly aware of this, and the best defense he could muster was a passing-fair stone face. If you permitted yourself to be seduced by the song of the Sirens, you crashed your longboat on the reef—that was the entire purpose of the transfixing tune. Venus flytraps looked like flowers. Mosquitoes anesthetized their puncture points so you didn't know your blood had been sucked until they were gone. Legend said cobras mesmerized their prey. After the seduction, Art wondered, what sort of feeding took place?

Suzanne remained an enigma. Art felt the need to see her one more time, to talk with the version of her that had engaged him from a safe distance, before the roller-coaster free-for-all that had transpired in the bedroom. Pulling against this was the voice in his head that advised him to just let it go. It was what it was, and the story had ended. The End. Next page.

Dina disturbed him. He felt a conflicting desire to reach out to her, to engage her seeming manic depression, because past her perimeter of Bouncing Betty mines and razor wire there was a human being in considerable pain. He felt like a kid who had been warned not to touch something hot. The burn might teach him something he desperately needed to learn and know, the shape of which might only be clear after he'd taken the risk. Or it might merely scald and scar him, proving that reaching out was foolish.

All of them, the hosts and partygoers, were from a world Art had forsaken and did not miss. He could bail and leave them to their damnation and self-destruction. He owed the world nothing, and the world did not care about his grief. It wasn't living, but it was a life.

What happened next, happened fast.

First impression: A zebra sprang across the Jeep's path just as something shattered the right front windscreen.

It was too late to brake, but Art stomped the pedal in pure reflex, his entire body contracting as though electroshocked. The

Jeep brodied off the rainswept road, tires hydroplaning, then vaulted a wet dune as though kicked in the ass. Sandgrass divided like hair ripped by a comb. The Jeep was airborne for a quarter of a second. It crunched down hard on its right front fender and tipped over, mostly because the front wheels were turned. It made a heavy woodblock impression as it settled into the sand on its passenger side.

Art's brain lurched like an egg in a dropped jar of vinegar as the world took a forty-five-degree tilt and his harness pushed the air out of his lungs. Touchdown punched him in the face, and his extremities blunted into remote, as though his hands and feet were sending signals from far away. His head banged the padded underside of the roll bar as all the loose junk inside the cab pelted him. The engine revved wildly, a keening noise that strained upward; the sound of a prehistoric beast in pain. He tried to force his arm to stretch, to cut the ignition, and his right shoulder hollered. The headlamps carved a triangular spray of featureless sand and slanted needles of rain. The motor chugged and expired, leaving the hiss of falling water and the echoes of the last five seconds inside Art's swimming cognizance. Cold air pierced the cab. His legs seemed nailed into a pretzel configuration and the rest of him was strung aloft by the bondage of the driving harness like a parachutist hung up in an apple tree. Gravity insisted he go down. He undogged the latches and collapsed into a cramped astronaut crouch, feeling the door handle bruise his back, the gearshift jabbing his balls. Sharp things poked into his kidneys and he was able to draw two deep, raw breaths of air before he thought: *A zebra?!*

Maybe just someone in a patterned coat. Faux fur.

The Jeep gave a creak and cubes of shattered safety glass blizzarded down from the driver's-side window like crushed ice. Cold air lashed through the exposed cabin, bringing hostile raindrops. It was incentive enough. He wanted to lapse into unconsciousness, a blissful reprieve. Instead he keyed his own uncooperative, broken-robot body toward the task of climbing out of the upended Jeep, using his elbows for leverage.

Maybe just his imagination. Faux monster.

When he was upright, he pounded the glove box with his fist, one, two, three times, before the goddamned door popped and jettisoned its contents—manuals, maps, old Life Savers, brown paper towels, flashlight. The rain slicker was still constricting his movements like a spiderweb. He hoped there wasn't any glass in his eyes.

Somebody was shouting in the distance. To Art it was all unintelligible rigmarole, like the voodoo bullshit assigned to black natives in serial thrillers, back when no one gave a damn about political correctitude. Art tried clumsily to dismount the Jeep and fell on his ass in the sand. Even as he contracted into a squat, the wind kept up its mission to knock him over again.

Flickering light was visible inside the Spilsbury house. Art realized he had gone off the road thirty yards shy of the driveway. Oddly, he felt very warm even though the wind and rain were frigid and unrelenting.

What to do first?

Somewhere inside the disorder of the Jeep was one of his guns—a Heckler & Koch USP compact, he remembered. A hammerless Glock knockoff packing a ten-round, nine-millimeter mag. Normally it was stashed inside a fake Day Runner in the glove box. You could purchase these things out of any firearms periodical, and they usually featured a concealed, lockable back flap that concealed storage snugs "sized to your weapon" plus room for an extra clip. Why had he stashed a gun in the Jeep? Or had he misremembered this as well, which was why there was no gun to be found, and no attendant security to be had from tucking it against the small of his back (an "SOB carry," in gun argot).

The plastic flashlight was inadequate as a weapon. He blinked it several times in the direction from which he thought he had heard voices. No response, incomprehensible or otherwise.

Art flopped his hood into place and began to plod. It was time at last to check out the Spilsbury house, close up.

● ● ● Art knew exactly nothing about his nearest so-called neighbors, the Spilsburys. Were there more than one? Wet sand sucked at his boots. There were small ponds everywhere, even this far from the beach. More than once, the storm tried to bowl him over.

The highway side of the two-story house was dark, but as Art rounded to the south he saw light flickering downstairs, dully orange and wavering. Firelight. If the wooden structure was burning, the interior would eat itself flagrantly until the doors and windows imploded and the blaze introduced itself to the abundance of rain. That would leave a gutted shell, unless the struts and supporting walls collapsed; then the pitched roof would cave in like a circus tent with the central pole removed. Bye-bye, vacation retreat.

One of the table-size board-ups securing the oceanside bow windows had been liberated. Thin curtains had blown themselves to rags on the edges of broken glass. Apparently someone had pried off the plywood and hurled it through the window as a battering ram. Possibly more than one person, since the ledges were up past Art's head height. He imagined invaders standing on one another's shoulders, breaching the battlements with Viet Cong stealth. Smoke was steadily feeding from the top of the window frame and disintegrating like cotton candy on the wind.

Before he could locate some way to climb, he saw the front door was wide open. He eased toward the entrance and at the threshold clicked on his light. The beam cut the yellowish smoke.

The Spilsbury living room had been tarted out in New England nautical chic: rockers, furniture with fake antique veneer, carved wooden gewgaws. Model sailing ships on the mantel. A metal-gridded, porthole-style window that had been framed by a ship's wheel. The wheel was gone, but Art was close enough to see the pattern of dust and sun-fade it had left behind. It had been smashed, along with one of the rockers and some of the sea-chest tables, for firewood. An ungainly pile burned fitfully in the red-brick fireplace. The more porous woods had kindled faster, and the pile had spilled across the hearth, where it had already set a woven rug to smoldering.

Cold air lashed Art from behind and he thought he felt the house sway gently. The fire horripilated and rearranged itself, spitting glowering embers onto the floor, which was mostly waxed hard-wood. There was probably an extinguisher in the kitchen.

The layout was traditional, even classic. Art moved past the main stairwell and saw the expected risers in velvet-finish white against polished wood treads, the banisters and newel post both lathed into overdetail. Brass rods secured a carpet runner. Dominating the dining room was a large, scalloped brown table and high-backed chairs with cockleshelled, cabriole legs. A poster from the Burt Lancaster movie *The Crimson Pirate* hung framed on the north wall. A buffet cabinet had toppled, to dog-pile the liquor bottles within; several had ruptured, and the air was redolent with the sharp tang of alcohol. He saw a phone and delicately lifted the receiver, noticing it was a Bakelite oldie with a rotary dial. No tone. He jiggled the cradle the way people do in Forties films when they can't get an operator. It never worked then and it didn't work now.

Something fell in the living room and Art twisted, light up. Just the wind. He wished he had his gun, *a* gun, any gun.

He clicked the first wall switch he found. No power. There was no fire extinguisher in the kitchen, but he saw a molded plastic sink liner he could use as a bucket to douse the fire. It would be a two-handed job, and he did not want to relinquish his only reliable source of light.

Fast, metered thumping, trailing away, from above. Whoever was here was upstairs, hurrying down the hallway to the landing. Art clicked off his light and sprang back into the dining room, landing in a crouch, hoping the firelight was sufficient for ambush . . . and waited. His heart was doing a mad, jivey finger-snap inside his rib cage. He was the miscreant here, the uninvited trespasser.

What if he had run down a *person* in the road back there? That would make him a murderer, like Derek . . . assuming Derek's story had not been another serving of high-floating delusional bushwah.

More thumping, more lively. One set of feet, more likely two, now traversing the hall in the opposite direction.

Art angled back toward the far end of the living room, keeping the stairs in sight. Maybe he'd already been made by his unseen opponents, and they were holing up, afraid he was packing. Maybe they'd spotted him and run back to arm themselves . . . or arm themselves *better.*

He ghosted past an archway and was momentarily startled to feel rough hair brush his face. After another moment in the dark, with no further sounds but those caused by the storm, he gambled a spot of light, blindered by his own fingers over the lens. He had bumped into a tusked snout, dusty fur, his light mirrored in two dead eyes of black glass. The den; every home like this had one.

The room was about ten by ten with the desk of a high-school principal and club chairs in red leather. Festooning the walls was a zoology of taxidermied kills—caribou, stag, wapati, bobcat, a wolf, game fish mounted on plaques, even a large bat. A display shelf had been swept of small preserved snakes and birds, and several elongated rodental skulls littered the floor in shards and scattered teeth. Art had brushed past the head of a boar. The room had been ransacked but he perceived, with relief, a locked gun cabinet, empty. Had there been a stock of weapons, the glass would have been smashed. Above the fireplace there were pegs for some showpiece, maybe an elephant gun or a huge spear. A blank spot before the hearth attested to where some pelt had lain. There was more than one vacant space on the floor.

He held his position for nearly twenty minutes more, to no new ruckus. His teeth unclenched and he relaxed, just a notch, enough to pick a cautious path back to the kitchen, where he filled the plastic basin and splashed the remnants of the fire, which had pretty much petered out on its own.

Perhaps the unseen interlopers had cleared out, thinking Art was the owner. They could have spotted him and escaped from an upstairs window. Maybe they had passed out. Maybe they were waiting for him to calm down, so they could strike.

The stairs did not beckon; they warned. To ascend would leave him exposed to whatever might lunge from the blackness that enshrouded the landing. Art realized he was afraid of going up there. Scared. What business of his was this? In the city, such a smash-and-grab would be laughed off and forgotten as "paying the crime tax." He had a bigger headache waiting for him outside. Though lunatic, it seemed at least practical; the stairs were unknown territory, promising new risks.

Disgust washed through his system. How far did he have to go to demonstrate he wasn't a coward? Shouldn't he be tending to his

148

own house? What if this damage and vandalism had been wrought by a clique of hard partiers from Price's place? What if they, spaced-out on some designer shit that left them violent and stupid, had exhausted their fun possibilities here and had decamped to seek further nuttiness?

Like at Art's own house, for example.

That technically decided him, though his own feet were already pacing carefully backward toward the front door. Downbeach, waves were already slapping in twenty feet beyond the tide line, breaking upward in waterfall froth, the ocean trying to take to the air. The storm had commenced a low, grumbling noise, similar to Art's memory of apartment dwelling in the city, on the days the behemoths of municipal garbage trucks literally shook the ground with their passage. His ears clogged as the air pressure changed around him, cutting the audible noise in half. The fire was out, the threat apparently evaporated, if not avoided. He had to get moving.

● ● ● There was a swatch of hide stuck in the front grille of the Jeep, like a shred of meat in the teeth of a predator. Art's vehicle was now in the middle of a pond trying to grow into a small lake.

Art waded in and checked the wheels. All good. He turned the scrap of hide over in his light. Zebra, all right—but dyed, fake.

He scanned about as best as the storm would permit. No bush-whack, no concealed predators, no aggression, apart from the Wind, which desired only to carry him away.

Ultimately, three meager saplings, already tormented into stooping by the storm, got uprooted by Art's efforts to winch his Jeep back to a standing position. He was able to loop cable geomet-rically in order to use the vehicle's own weight to tip it upright, but there was not much near the road dunes to employ as an anchor.

Had he wrecked on the other side of the road, there would have been actual trees, but he was confounded by the length of his winch cable. He wished for gloves; handling the braid of wire with wet hands quickly abraded his palms raw.

The Jeep started on the first try. Art was grateful for the hard-shell roof even though both he and the cabin were completely soaked. The driver's-side window was only a memory, and the breach admitted more of the storm, but it was a tiny price. Two of the halogens were dead, along with the left headlight. Mirrors and trim had been sanded off the port side. As soon as Art navigated the vehicle back onto the washed-out roadway, he realized that the alignment was shot. It was like having to constantly jog a shopping cart with a cocked wheel. The front axle was dinged out of true and was probably dangerously fragile. At least the tires had not burst. After this latest side trip into craziness, Art appreciated the comedy value of being forced to change a flat in a hurricane, a biting mundanity intruding upon the phantasmagorical. The Wind had seemingly spared him, so far.

Hard turns were more difficult. Art could feel the vibration of tread grinding against the dislocated front fender as he negotiated his own undulant driveway. At the corners of his dwelling, the emergency floods were on, and he could already hear the alarm siren.

New problems.

He forwent the dashboard key combination that would open the garage door, fire the interior lights, and otherwise announce his arrival. The funride of adrenaline was leaving him nauseous and weary, and a new spike flooded through him to break a thin sweat in spite of the chill. He felt jabbed in the ass by demons with pitchforks, prodded forward. He dismounted and checked his flashlight. *Here we go again.*

Now the storm favored him, covering his progress and masking his noise. He left the Jeep door hanging open and warily circled the perimeter of the house, starting with the fenced yard and working counterclockwise, ducking his own extra-long-life floodlights, which glared down in pairs from motion sensors mounted high on each corner, caged in all-weather shields. The leeward side of his kitchen appeared untouched and dark except for the counter night-light he knew to be there.

Rain piled across the outside deck in inch-deep waves, fauceting from the edges in a steady stream. Art had stowed his patio furniture, but had forgotten the row of wind chimes on the deck. All twelve sets were gone. Inside, Blitz spotted him creeping around and began dealing out harsh, sharp warning barks, evenly spaced, utterly aggressive. The dog cleared the sofa in an easy leap and locked onto his movements, slamming into the window with both front paws. Good boy. If anyone had found a way in, Blitz would still have them occupied.

The southernmost panel of Plexi was scored and pitted, waist to chest height, presuming someone standing on the deck and trying to raze the barrier with a pointed tool. Directional scrapes hinted that the tool might have splintered in the process. The window might give against the push of the sea blow, but was more than adequate to some burglar, whacking away.

Blitz tracked Art the length of the deck, deploying more dog-macho and speckling the window with saliva. It would do no good to try calming him down from outside. Art hung the corner to the north face, sweeping with his torch. All clear. The only footprints were his own, and they began to melt as soon as he stepped out of them. The rain was worsening, coming down more fiercely than a mere half hour before. Just the sound of it assaulting Art's poncho hood sounded like thousands of marbles hitting a stone floor, fed by an endless treadmill.

If anyone had been around, they were gone now. Unless they were inside, and Art trusted Blitz's behavior enough to stake odds on a clean entry.

He parked the Jeep in the garage and threw the interior bolts to completely secure the door. The Jeep was battered and leaking fluid. It might not start again, and if it did, it might not move. Art removed his poncho one-handed, hulling himself, and left it on the hood. As for keeping his clothing dry, he might as well have just strolled out of a swimming pool. His shearling jacket was ten pounds heavier, with water, and as he wrestled out of it he suddenly thought that he, too, had been wearing an animal skin. He raked his hair back and rubbed his face roughly, allowing himself a beat to savor the relative quiet, and sanctuary from the elements.

He started speaking to the garage-kitchen door as he unlocked it, so Blitz could begin to register the sound of his voice and not kill him. He had never seen the dog this worked up before. Perhaps maturity had seasoned his deadlier instincts to the point where Blitz was actually *capable* of killing, as opposed to disabling, nullifying, or threatening. Art and his dog had both grown older.

He cracked the door and let the dog recognize him before giving him room. Then Blitz began bouncing up and down, a clown on a pogo stick, his barking louder but in altered timbre, his greeting nearly bowling Art over. Art hunkered down and ruffled Blitz's head, getting slobber on his hands for his effort.

"Some killer," he said, instantly reassessing his pet's capacity for dealing death. He could barely hear himself over the alarm.

The status display indicated no other section of the house had been breached, and the motion lights told him that no sectors had been compromised by trespassers, at least not by anything bigger than the dog. The LED button for the big windows was blinking red. Art tapped in his password and the air horn cut out.

He let Blitz walk point as he checked out each room, methodically, just in case. Nothing was amiss except for the few items scattered near the windows by the dog leaping around. Blitz had not been dozing on his defense watch. All the phones were dead.

If a group of party animals from Price's had sacked the Spilsbury house, then attempted entry at Art's and failed, they would have enough grief dealing with the storm outside.

Art's muscles felt drawn on a rack, and he was ravenous. His hands were shaking as he pulled a packet of sliced ham out of the fridge and chomped a mouth-filling bite out of the slab. He chugged one of his juice slams and fed another gob of ham to the dog. After a moment he felt steady enough to seek painkillers and a decongestant for his head, after which he might devote actual time and labor toward constructing a civilized sandwich.

In the living room, he flipped the cover from the security module and depressed the orange button. Relays thunked inside the walls, and the metal shutters ratcheted slowly down to shield the slanted windows. Each one featured a pillbox-style viewing slit. Art leaned on the wall until each shutter locked into position with a reassuring double click.

That was it: He was fortressed in, his drawbridge up.

The power went out at 11:32 P.M., by the kitchen clock. The ambient, almost subaural presence of all of Art's machines and devices was dunked into silence. The refrigerator quieted and the heating ducts began to click as they cooled. Afterimages of light temporarily blinded him until the battery floods snapped on. These were not so numerous or obtrusive as the exterior lights, and were blended into the wall plan in a way that kept the lines clean—one for the back hallway, one for the living room, one for the kitchen. His design of the house had assured that terminating power from the outside was impossible—unless one brought bolt cutters and a backhoe—which indicated electricity had failed for the entire area. He cut the floods to conserve battery life and dug out candles and a pair of oil lamps.

He used the contents of the water heater while still hot, showering by lantern light to thump the cold from his bonework. Then he fell asleep, sprawled across his bed, still robed and damp, his gun on standby next to the water carafe. Blitz circled in a holding pattern for a few revolutions, then dropped into a lay-down near the foot of the bed.

According to the learned monks of New Skete, who have graduated generations of scrupulously trained German shepherds from their monastery in upstate New York, dogs can generate a deep respect for the privilege of being permitted to sleep in their master's den. They pick their own spot and enjoy a silent, uncomplicated interaction with their human, a time when no demands are necessitated by either being. For dogs, bedrooms contain the most concentrated scents—clothing, carpeting, bedding—which amplify an essential bond. Trust is fortified, and as the master or mistress relaxes, the dog learns to relax in parallel.

Head on paws, Blitz watched the open bedroom door for at least half an hour after Art had begun the soft, metered respiration of deep sleep.

SATURDAY

The generator in the garage was an industrial rig that could produce seventy-five hundred watts continuously for eight hours on just over three gallons of gas. It was housed in a wall bay resembling a refrigerator turned on its side, with rubber-insulated double doors to prevent carbon monoxide leakage, and vented to the outside world by air intakes Art had designed after the horns he'd seen on the forecastle of a hovercraft. The gennie's tubular frame reminded him of a Harley chassis. It could power up via battery-fed push button, or, if that failed, a lawn-mower-style cable pull. The exhaust was mufflered, and the heavy doors reduced the noise rating of its chugging operation to nothing. There were two twenty-gallon military fuel drums in reserve, not counting what could be unstrapped or siphoned from the Jeep if things got tight.

Art hit transfer switches to feed fire to selected sectors of the house. His satellite dish was incapacitated, probably stolen by the Wind, but he needed to check his computers, which had been set to stack stormwatch updates from the National Oceanic and Atmospheric Administration until the signals got compromised; there would be a backlog of listings. He could conserve use of his lights and alternate with candles and lanterns. Anything with a motor pulled more power, such as the heating system or the refrigerator, so once his interior doors were all closed or braced, he really only needed to heat one room at a time. The fridge could be turned to maximum cold, opened only when necessary, and spelled according to the timeshare needs of his available power. Except for the rollers for the window shutters (which could be cranked manually), the house's security system was on its own independent circuit, juiced by a car battery. He regretted that the solar panel array had not yet been enabled; the cells would have stored more than a day's worth of extra power already. He checklisted himself around the house, unplugging everything that was nonessential.

The last online bulletin from the NOAA had specified gale-force winds in excess of eighty miles per hour, then the DSL line had ceased to function. The range of the weather service radio in the garage was only about forty miles, but past the crackle Art learned the hurricane specs had jumped from "watch" to "warning," which meant that people who lived inland had probably evacuated already. The danger of flash floods was stressed by a public advisory from the National Hurricane Center. No one wasted time talking about how rare such a combination of conditions was in the Pacific Northwest, but Art knew the coastal population had increased dramatically at other points along the line . . . and few of these people had ever experienced the kind of storm this had already become. Some of them lived in mobile homes, for god's sake. If they hadn't cleared out, Art hoped they were used to flying.

Coffeed and dressed, holding his own against the fury outside, he felt three steps closer to civilized. Blitz refused to do his doggie business outdoors, and under these conditions, Art couldn't blame him. He provided a spread of newspaper in the garage and cleaned up after his buddy, flashing back to the puppy period, and the endless regimen of housebreaking. Then he decided to fill some of the haunted air in the kitchen with music from a boombox formerly shelved in the office. Something by Holst or Mahler; something cosmically weighty.

Only the gods, seated around their breakfast plinth in Olympus, knew how Price's party was handling the storm this morning.

It seemed a week since he had actually eaten, even though his steak blowout was still in transit through his GI tract. He assembled a ham and cheese sandwich on whole wheat, not accustomed to eating this early in the day. It seemed tasteless, mere fuel, and chewing it was a chore. Time was blurring. The bloc of processed ham still had a mouth-size chunk bitten out of it. Art regarded it as if some stranger had done it. It was messy. He finally sliced away the section to square the stack. Better. He took care not to wolf his snack. Blitz's expression said etiquette did not faze him. He was rewarded with a skinny strip of 98 percent fat-free meat with a bite out of it.

Art could not help wondering at the current status of all the people he had just met. Twenty-four hours ago, none of it had happened, except for Derek's visit, followed by Suzanne's. Was Dina still holed up in suicidal despondency? Was Suzanne's maniac boyfriend turning a new leaf, even as Suzanne herself was schizzing out? Were there Zebra People aprowl somewhere on the beach right now, as oblivious to the weather as Green Berets, or *cliqua* on crack? Was Shinya, the little Japanese girl, still on the lookout for her lost date-that-wasn't-a-date? She had seemed so young and open that the thought of her being manipulated by Price caused Art's heart to ache. This was the sort of drama Art had tried to subtract from his life.

He sipped his extra-strong coffee and let one hand float down to rub Blitz's skull. The dog was sticking close by while the storm was afoot, unsure of the elemental chaos, looking to Art for solace and normalcy. There was an abundance of same-old in this house; Art disliked change. Perhaps that was a problem.

He considered the world beyond his walls, specifically Price's party, since it was the freshest input. Predators and prey, all in display or retreat, bridging the gulf between what had been "normal" forty years ago and the modern incarnation of *Homo psychopathicus*. People fed one another the same lines and suffered the same malfunctions, and Art had witnessed banality and exoticism in equal measure, a jostling crowd brandishing edginess and attitude in order to hide their self-doubts. Images were being shot down, then propped up, then disqualified, as Price deconstructed his guests. It was a passion play repellent in its nakedness, the kind of thing that had forced Art to lock himself into his fortress and ignore his phone, shred his documents, and find more simple humanity in his dog.

The people at the party house wanted to be nomads, rootless hunter-gatherers. Responsibility was the tough part; it was the thing that had helped Art and Lorelle to marry in a world that had decreed wedlock outmoded. When two people decided to become a couple, the responsibilities piled on. On Derek's one-through-ten scale, a couple had to deal with six, seven, eight, the lovely commitment of "in sickness and health" advising that, eventually, one partner would have to tend to the death of the other. The willingness to accept this responsibility, Art thought, was a good way to perceive who was special, and who was transient. Another clue was the sensation that you just weren't whole without your partner; you became literally incomplete, and the landscape became a bleaker place to survey. For people to meld in this fashion required time and tolerance, but when such an essential part was removed, the loss was not to be ignored or glossed over. When devices lost critical parts, they ceased to function, so the heartbreak that had incapacitated Art was not so strange. It was easy for people to leave, and often safer—no obligations, no commitment, wipe the slate, back to one. It was wrenching enough, when you left them. It was intolerable when they were torn out of you.

The swing of the weather did not become important until you stuck in one place.

It occurred to Art that he was just elaborately restating the tenets of the note he had discovered on the beach. *I feel torn between the things I feel I should do,* it read, *versus the things I know I must do.* The inadequate nourishment in his gut did a queasy Immelmann turn as the identity of the note's long-lost author suggested itself. Art had paper of this grade in the office. All manner of inks, pens, nibs. *I'd say beware of all the ways in which love can become a lie.* Wasn't that was a good, all-purpose warning against the things that had happened once he had dared to leave his home and take a chance on Price's party?

He tried to pace his breathing, not ready to admit that *he* might have written this, and tossed it into the sea. A page of his makeup, torn out and discarded, relegated to the elements; a cunning edit of his own personality, shunned . . . but determined to come back to him all the same, therefore, undeniable. True fact overwhelmed willful ignorance the way paper wrapped stone in rock-paper-scissors.

In an extreme structural crisis, the vent network on top of Art's house could be louvered to deflect the wind dynamically so as to actually hold the building down rather than batter against it. That was another backstop advantage of his basic plan, not yet required, because everything seemed to be nominal. When he peered out through one of the horizontal shutter slits, all he could see was rain blur against the Plexiglas, which pulsed subtly to accommodate the morphing flow of pressure. His revolutionary triangular pane design caused the emplacement to function like a snake's shifting, overlapping scalework. Presumably the superstructure would coast through an earthquake just as adroitly; Art wondered if and when that test might come.

Nice, in a tilted way, it would be to have the high-strung presence of that guy Luther around, if just to shoot the shit about guns and have another voice to react to. Art had done more talking to strangers in the last day than he had spent across the previous month.

He had slept with a loaded gun on his night table—the one he had been positive was in the Jeep, but turned out to be in the gun safe all along. Now it seemed paranoid and stupid. Unbidden, the joke rose—the one about the sleepyhead who keeps a revolver next to his bedside phone. When the phone rings, he picks up the gun and blows his brains out. Hello? *Bang.*

Sitting on the bed, he thought about unloading the weapon and checking it unnecessarily. Pointless busywork, that—another practice to fuel the mechanism of denial. When he spotted Lorelle's Egyptian box nearby, he remembered the capsule inside, the drug variously referenced as "party favors" (by Suzanne) and "house mix" (by Price). He dissected it on the granite countertop in the kitchen.

He suspected the white, plastery powder to be coke, but his palate did not recognize the sting. It contained black flecks, like pepper polluting salt, at a ratio of about one to twenty. The particles were not greasy, like hashish, or clotted like dark heroin. They were inscrutably enigmatic. If Art pondered them long enough, he'd feel mocked. Or he could just swallow it and see what happened. What harm? Most of the people at the party had downed them, according to Price's manner about the dose he'd termed a "mild accelerator." On the other hand, Suzanne had taken them, and Art still could not figure out what had gone wrong with her yesterday.

Art decided he could probably use a mild accelerator today.

Impulsively, he scooped the grains together and dumped them into his mouth, where they lay on his tongue like sea salt, mildly acidic. He washed them down with coffee and they burned all the way to his stomach.

"What the fuck," he told Blitz. "If I get obnoxious, you have permission to bite me." He felt a cheesy thrill, as though he was a teenager preparing crash space for an acid trip. "It's not like we have anything else to do right now."

There was no rush, no metabolic shift, no plunging vertigo, no impact jolt at all. Just a fulminating undertow that made him thirsty and sent him to the fridge for seltzer. His vision and balance were fine. He realized that the grandest gag of all would have been for Price to supply a talked-up placebo to his suggestible guests—something that would excuse them from the responsibility of being even more suggestible, when Price started talking. Art sat for several minutes watching the clock, letting his blood cycle. Nothing strange happened.

On calm days it was possible to walk far out on the jetty of tombstones, near the Sundial dish, and peer into the deeper parts of the ocean. The jetty terminated about where the sand shelf began to drop away beneath the water; under the right conditions, land creatures could stand dry and look down into a murky world of sea life. Presumably, the life-forms down there peered up at you at the same time, enjoying the inverted fishbowl effect. The microwave dish always loomed solid, its immobile tonnage like some Aztec relic, never moving when you looked at it, though you always had the sense it was abuzz with data, sending and receiving, coordinating satellites or tracking missile platforms or zeroing in on some space station. Then, when you were distracted, and looked back after looking away, you'd find the dish had tilted, sometimes so indistinctly that the sight nagged at you, insisted you were seeing things. From this vantage, on clear nights, you could watch the clarion lights of approaching planes, northbound, stacking up for landing patterns at San Francisco International. The days were often calm but rarely clear. Too moist, this far north.

The burn had nested in Art's stomach, reminiscent of a double shot of liquor. Apart from craving an antacid, he noticed no change in the room, the walls, the colors, *or the spider-headed little men coming out of the walls*—just kidding.

He still had his eye on the sweep of the clock's second hand when Blitz started barking. It was ten-fifteen in the morning.

"Oh, what is it?" He teased the dog. "You're gonna get all jiggy now? You think you hear something? You're just seeing a doggie mirage. You're seeing a gigantic Monster Dog approaching out of the ocean. Dog-zilla is coming, and boy, is he pissed."

It stopped being fun. This was Blitz's intruder bark, for certain, and Art's hand sought his pistol while his ears tried to pierce the cacophony of the storm.

You are completely in control, he told himself. You are ready for anything. That was the whole point, wasn't it?

Then the alarms tripped as somebody drove a car through his locked garage door, making the day more interesting in a big rush. The battering-ram impact shook the whole house.

● ● ● It was logical, in a skewed, Bizarro-World way. Art had protected himself with dead bolts, alarms, shutters, fail-safe systems, armament, supplies, and a floor plan intended to defy the fury outside. He was inside, not coming out. Anything that happened *had* to come to him. At first crash, his assumption was that the northeast corner of the house had collapsed due to the storm, but standing in the kitchen, the garage a single secure door away, above and past the hellish buffet of wind and bulleting rain, he could hear a big-block car engine strain to reach high revs, then die all at once.

Art had bypassed the house's few security cameras to save the batteries, and the little screen matrix for observing zones in sequence was powered down anyway. Screw it; he had a backup—a wide-angle peephole port in the garage door. The glare of the lights in there was harsh, and something black and hugely indistinct was shoved near enough to the obverse of the door to cause a large cataract of black on the lower left of the field. Art could perceive everything else with clarity.

The prow of a large black car was jutting through the lower right side of the garage door. The strutted metal of the door was peeled back like foil. Miraculously, the heavy-duty door track and horizon-tally shot bolts had withstood getting rammed; Art guessed an impact speed of twenty-five miles an hour, practically pokey. Factoring in a stranger not used to the convolutions of the drive, the slick surface, and the current conditions, twenty-five per was probably about the best that could be mustered. Automobile industry impact tests were carried out at that speed. Baby seats and airbags and seat mounts were approved for hitting cinderblock walls at that speed. The velocity had been good enough to punch a corner out of the garage door and rear-end the Jeep, shoving it diagonally to scrape the Jag's dusty finish, jostling the fancier car into the mobile tool rack, scattering the tools, its right headlamp denting the doors for the generator mount. The panoramic peephole view was par-tially blocked by the broadside of the Jeep. When Art squinted to figure out what was what, he saw the pilot-side door of the intruder car open. A large man rose from the car. The door was so long that it chocked with a squeal against the garage frame and the man was forced to step over it. The window had burst from the collision and pieces of it glittered like quartz in the hot light from the floods. The man had a baseball bat.

No worries, as Art had said once or twice before. The house door had a cross-braced aluminum core, like a webwork of little girders, and the hinges were on the inside of the sandwich. The frame into which it was mounted was completely unbreachable. The only way anything was coming through that door would be if Art opened it. The instant he saw the ballbat, and perceived the intended threat, Art opened the garage door.

Because: He was calm. The person who had just landed was not. He was seething with violent intent and brandishing a club, ready to yell and bash. Art already had a gun in his hand, feeling that if this was more blowback from Price's party, what was about to happen lacked even the thrill of a new experience. He could clip this one if he misbehaved. Art opened the door because he was utterly, almost uncannily at ease with whatever the storm decided to toss at him today. He wanted to unplug the Little Leaguer in the garage before the guy realized there were useful tools sitting right in front of him, or perhaps damaged the generator with his Louisville Slugger. He was similarly expecting to power his way into the house. Art had surprise and distance to his advantage. Reach out and touch someone, hard enough to knock them down. That's what guns were for. That's what he had always been told.

He didn't say a word. Banging back was sufficient to catch the attention of the intruder. The large man in the water-speckled leather jacket cut loose a long, vowel-rich howl and tried to charge with the bat, but the Jeep blocked his trajectory. Art sniffed, and squeezed off rock steady. The hardball round caught the man in the right biceps and spun him as if he'd run full speed into a fence post. He dropped the bat and jackknifed across the hood of his own car.

He slid, then stuck halfway to the floor, dangling. As Art picked his way across the garage, he could hear the man making tiny gasping noises, hyperventilating.

There—Art had just shot another human being with a gun. Rubicon crossed. Lorelle's arguments decomposed to hash. The difference between talking and doing, demonstrated. A threat handily abated. No need for a pump-up of anger, a trade of insults, or a stairstep series of escalating warnings. Just open the door and shoot the guy. Hello? *Bang.* Done deal. At last.

Art's heart was thudding triple time and his neck felt hot and prickly. His hands were sweating.

The car was the black Buick Riviera Art had noticed parked at Price's. The driver was Bryan, the Bry-Guy. A nasty triangular curl of sundered metal from the garage door had impaled one of his sculpted pecs, and he hung bleeding like a hooked fish. The gunshot had caused plaster dust to sift down from the ceiling. There was no need for another round; Bryan's hitting arm was thoroughly wrecked.

As unexpectedly as love at first sight, Art's anger grew a full hard-on. "You dumb piece of shit," he said, grabbing Bryan's good arm to flip him over. The spear of metal ripped free and Bryan howled again, this time for real, as his prospects turned to cowflop and he fell, gracelessly, onto his face.

"Suhn . . . ofa . . . bitch . . ."

Kick him in the stomach to shut him up, Art's feverish new attitude suggested. That worked pretty well, too.

Bryan woofed and curled, trying to go down fighting, failing. What was with this egregious, machismo programming? This strut and preen, these bad-motherfucker muscles and hairy-armpit jerkoff had been obsolete a thousand years ago, and counted for nothing when one was beaten without a fight.

Helpless before Art was a caricature of every clichéd masculine trait he loathed. Bryan attempted to hoist himself using his left arm. Art pegged him in the ribs with another kick and dumped him onto his back. Bryan tried to contract, then swooned.

This felt sort of . . . good.

When Bryan's pain yoked him back to consciousness, his head dipped as though he was fighting off a serious nod. He gradually registered the duct tape securing his wrists to a bolt-anchored rack. When he perceived the plastic sheeting spread around and beneath him, panic zipped to and fro in his eyes, and Art was glad to see it.

"Pretty embarrassing, isn't it, tough guy?"

There was blood on Bryan's mouth, from where he'd bitten through his tongue. "My arm," he managed, through clenched teeth.

"What about my *garage?*" said Art, leaning in, placing the muzzle of the Heckler-Koch between Bryan's eyebrows. "You know what a rolling door like that *costs?* No, of course you wouldn't. You ever have to pay for *anything,* you fucking imbecile?"

During Bryan's unscheduled nap, Art had backed out the Buick and whanged the garage door with a rubber mallet until the lower bolt could be roughhoused into the slot. If the bolt was drawn, the door edge would explode loose like a catapult. The car was crippled, the radiator trash-compacted into the engine and frothing coolant; after wheezing six feet in reverse, the motor chuddered, died, and would not restart. Then, methodically, Art had returned to the house, reloaded his gun to full capacity with 124-grain Federal Hydra-Shok hollow points, trussed Bry-Guy to the rack, finished his sandwich, calmed Blitz down, and donned a fur-ridged weatherproof parka.

"Please," said Bryan. His teeth were starting to chatter.

In Bryan's pocket Art had found a fang-bladed Kaiser lock-back knife with a serrated tip, which he used to slice away Bryan's jacket, making sure the Bry-Guy could see and recognize it, as it calved thousands of dollars' worth of buttery leather with razor-blade ease. Sure enough, Bryan had one of those idiotic barbed-wire tattoos around his right biceps. The rattlesnake in Art's chest was fully awake now, hot-eyed, pissed off and buzzing. He pegged Bryan's skull with the gun, mostly because of the tattoo. The bullet puncture was still exsanguinating freely. Bryan could not see most of the damage, but if he lived, his arm would be useless for half a year from bone frags and trauma. Gore slicked his bare shoulder and glued flat leather to his back. The corrugated lip of the garage door had sliced a diagonal flap from his chest, straight through one nipple. Art assessed the wounds, then stepped back and laughed. "Wow—get a load of *you.*"

"Cold." Worse, when you were splayed out cruciform, with no way to hug yourself.

"Sure is. Guess you better start talking, to stay warm."

"I can't—breathe—" His movements were weak and vague. Frigid blades of air sneaked past the rents in the door in regular gusts. Bryan felt every degree. For every breath he gulped, vapor twinned from his nostrils and was snatched away by the moving air.

"I got a blowtorch over there that'll heat your sorry ass up doublequick if you don't stop whining."

"What . . . do you want me to . . . ?"

Art backhanded him, whiplashing his neck and bringing new blood from his tongue. "Don't waste my time, fuckstick. You came over here in a goddamned hurricane just to drive your car through my house. Am I wearing a fucking Pirates uniform? You think I was gonna pitch you a few lowballs, easy hitters?" He picked up the unused baseball bat. "This could come in very handy."

Bryan said, "Suzanne."

"Speak up, Bruno, I don't think I caught that."

"You took her away . . ."

It was too easy, too stupid, too reactionary, too goddamned male. Bryan had got all het up and thought all he needed to wield dominance were his car keys, a ballbat, an address, and his bulgy macho self.

Bryan's head clunked against the aluminum rail. Keeping it aloft was too draining. He was blacking out again.

Art prodded him. "Where's Suzanne?"

"Left her," Bryan croaked, his eyes indicating the garage door, meaning *out there*. Outside, somewhere. Probably dragged by the hair.

Art still had other things that would be exciting to say. Things like: *Then you get to stay here and bleed.* Or: *You're really too dumb to live, aren't you?* Instead, he checked the restraints, pocketed the single spent cartridge from the floor (*always recycle your brass*), then marched back to his kitchen for a beer, since it was getting a bit chilly in the garage.

He chugged a Dixie Double Hex and fed Blitz the rest of the ham a chomp at a time while he sorted through the junk he had stripped from Bryan's pockets. Besides the wicked knife, there was a slim wallet holding $1,500 in cash and a full house of platinum cards. His driver's-license photo resembled a Polaroid mug shot, the colors muddy, his eyes glinting like mineral chips. No business cards; Suzanne had said Bryan never did anything that could be mistaken for work. There was a flat plastic backup key for the Buick, and a couple of broker's cards bearing San Francisco contacts. Scrawled on the backs of these in various inks was an assortment of names and phone numbers—new women, dope dealers, opportunities for fun awaiting. His trousers—a twenty-nine-inch waist, Art noticed—yielded up a two-gram coke vial attached to a silver chain fob, and a Zippo lighter featuring an enameled red devil girl Art recognized as a Coop special. Bryan had left his own keys in the ignition of the Buick. A burnished pillbox held five or six of Price's special capsules in dividered grape felt. One of them had fallen apart, spattering the rest. It was a different mix; black particles to white in almost equal ratio.

In the bedroom Art dug into the gun safe and wired a Shark shoulder holster around himself, for the pistol. He mufflered his face and found a pair of clear goggles, the kind of eye protection normally used for metalwork or sanding. With the parka and boots, he looked geared up for an arctic expedition. After cutting the power and putting the alarms on standby, he posted Blitz in the garage to stand watch over the unconscious Bry-Guy.

"Wenn er sich bewegt, machst du in kalt," he said, liking the sound of that, wondering where he'd picked it up. *Kill him if he moves.*

He popped one of Bryan's black-and-white pill stash. If he was going to forge a one-man expedition into the storm, a "mild accelerator" was practically a must.

Suzanne was probably dying of exposure, somewhere between his house and Price's. Dumb bitch. Art wasn't precisely sure where the urge to search for her came from. Rescue? He felt like yelling at her, maybe cuffing her face back and forth until some common sense dribbled into her brainpan. Payback? He wanted to countermand the image of himself as a talker. Time to get proactive.

The parka increased his mass and gave the storm more to push against. Walking compelled him to incline sixty degrees versus resistance that felt corporeal, like giant hands that chased him in a circular pattern, trying to collect and lift him. Most of the shove was east to west. From the head of his driveway he could see the feebly glowing taillights of a car, and he worked his way north on the feeder road to marry up with it.

It was a pathetic Volkswagen bug—the one he'd seen on the road yesterday—tipped onto its starboard side, its nose trenched into sand, the windscreen spiderwebbed by a huge sycamore limb that had seemingly dropped out of orbit. No occupants. Apparently some of Price's guests had gotten evacuation into their minds a tot late, and when the carapace of this vehicle proved inadequate, they'd bared themselves to the elements. Art could not make out any bodies in the immediate area; there was a good chance the Bug's passengers were huddled uphill, stuck to trees like slugs, praying to gods they didn't believe in, hoping nothing else fell on them as they froze to death.

Bryan would not have doubled back, so Art proceeded south along the shoulder. Rain worked him over, then sprayed off his coat to the east without touching the ground, to updraft and soar around to strafe him anew. Just moving through the air had become a lot like trodding snowpack, with the same frustrating measure of retardation. He had to wipe down his goggles once every fifteen seconds; his own exertion was fogging the plastic.

There was an excellent likelihood that Suzanne had crawled onto the beach and her own grave had blown over her. Had Bryan jettisoned her conscious or unconscious? Was she already dead, killed for some unfathomable betrayal? Unless she was close to the road, she might be no more than another pathetic missing-person statistic.

After bulling against the storm for several interminable minutes more, he spotted her hair, spin-cycling in the blow like a dandelion hoarding its fibers in a wind tunnel. He found her clinging to an uprooted pine trunk four feet in diameter. She was naked from the waist down, knees skinned, legs streaked with mud. Her left eye was swollen shut and purple, cheekbone thickly confused. Her teeth were intact, maybe loosened in front, and she had a fat lip. She had crawled about thirty yards before giving up, but was still breathing.

Stupid little party cooze, he thought. *What have we learned?* He pried her loose and turned her over. Her functional eye flinched as the rain slashed it. Maybe if he just left her here, her tiny mind might be soiled by the passage of an actual thought.

It was too goddamned cold for ratiocination, anyway.

At best, visibility held at a fast boil of twilight. Dense pewter clouds shrouded the sky and the downpour was darkly claustrophobic. He hefted Suzanne into a fireman's carry, mostly because if he abandoned her, that would make him exactly like Bryan, his opponent, his enemy. She wasn't that big overall, but lifting her was unexpectedly difficult for Art, who faulted the conditions and his own lack of meaningful exercise. She groaned as she was rearranged, and grip and gravity redistributed her aches.

"Shut up," Art muttered.

The storm thrashed around like a wounded reptile, mindlessly stinging and biting Art's legs and face. His goggles made the road blurry, an iron-colored swatch of runny paste. He had to stop every few yards and fight to siphon breath from the wind, his parka a bulky, movement-restricting spacesuit as he tried to freight the limp burden of her weight, which actually helped him lean against the air masses intent on pushing him back. His heart was still ramming along at ninety per. Stop, breathe, check to see if she's alive, press onward. Finding her had taken fifteen minutes. Dragging her home consumed another hour.

Blitz had devoted himself to his guard post admirably, breaking his nine-foot perimeter only to take a modest dump on the entertainment section of Friday's *Examiner.* Bryan was still as unconscious as a minimum-wage watchman, respiration thin and wisping up from the cavity of his muscle-bound stomach. Blood was congealed to a shiny spray-paint layer on his arm and shoulder, the wound garish but manageable. Once, Art had swallowed more of his own blood than Bryan had lost in the last hour. Fucking wimp.

He resisted the urge to smash Blitz's fastidious turd into Bryan's face. It was a funny thought, though. Unlike the regular Art.

The temperature in the house had dropped twenty degrees during his absence. He powered up the heat, thankful that Bryan's destructive entrance hadn't taken out the generator.

Suzanne made a few incoherent noises as Art deposited her in the guest tub and left her to simmer in hot water that quickly turned pink. He sliced off the remnants of her clothing with Bryan's knife. Her tits were as cold as iced fruit. He balled her crap into a plastic garbage bag. She'd lost her purse again.

In the kitchen Art poured two more beers down his neck, leaving the empties alongside the first. He was as parched as a mummy, and knew alcohol would not quench his thirst. Like he gave a shit.

His two guests just irritated him. They weren't worth the linen, the towels, the time or the hassle.

When Suzanne woke up, she began sobbing in deep, husking hitches of air. The hot water hurt. Every inch of her was edged in different volumes of pain. She sloshed around clumsily, her arms and legs incorrectly interpreting her brain's instruction. Art thought of a schizophrenic, suddenly waking to find herself neck-deep in a therapy basin, to ask *what, where, how?* He didn't want an interview, and felt fed up and spiky. He grabbed her hair and fixed her head so she would see nothing but him.

"Hey. Listen to me. Fart around and your ass gets ejected. Do you understand me?"

"Nuhh," she said, her eyes rolled up and stayed there.

His mind lunged against propriety like a leashed bobcat. It took hardcore effort to keep from punching her face until she died.

Instead, he stored her under comforters in the guest room. Pain in the butt; if he didn't restrain her, he'd have to keep checking. He wished he owned handcuffs. She did not move or make a sound when he gathered her out of the tub. Bruises all over her body had bulged and ripened to a sooty violet with coronas of poisonous ocher. Burst blood vessels had caused impact patterns to surface on her skin in serious crimson. Bad idea, to feed her painkillers in such a state. Her lower lip was swollen, split, and crusting. Her eye was congealed into a slit as tight as the line between two knuckles in a fist. If she woke up, she'd cause trouble. Half an hour after he had put her down, he looked in, mostly out of irrational fear. The covers were still pulled up to her chin and her position had not changed; her breathing was slow and steady, congested into a soft snore.

In the last half hour his racing heart had calmed and his blood had stopped percolating.

Another beer. He could do society a favor and put one more bullet, just one, into the center of Bryan's brain. Leave him ditched on the roadside in his Buick. Maybe stuff him in the trunk and lose the car altogether. Or dump it into the drink, Bry-Guy and all, several miles north at the cliff provided by the Point Pitt Overlook. Or tape the corpse up in the plastic sheet—neatness counts—and deep-six him off the jetty in the middle of the night, when the weather relaxed. Then what? Every time Art stared into those formerly mystic depths, Bryan would be staring right back at him. He was thinking like a murderer.

"Fuck!" He hurled the empty bottle across the kitchen. It bounced off the fridge door, leaving a crescent moon dent, and shattered on the floor. Lorelle had always been so neat in "her" kitchen; it was spiteful fun to slob things up, for once. Blitz jolted, unsure of what to do. "Sit your ugly ass back down," Art told the dog. "*Platz! Aber sofort jetzt, du Scheissköter!*"

How could Lorelle have been so inconsiderate as to just subtract herself from his life? Love was supposed to transcend everything; if she was dead, why no ghostly visitations or signals from beyond? Art did not feel aggrieved so much as abandoned and unloved. What about *his* fucking needs, the deal they'd made for their life together? Lorelle had died bravely. Maybe that was because escaping him, even through death, was enough to make her happy. She had bailed right out of the world, leaving Art to fend for himself and clean up after her memory. Why, if she was here, right now . . .

"Bitch," he mumbled, uncapping another beer. How dare she leave him like this?

Suzanne, however, had come back. Art's temples pulsed—maybe this was payment for gulping those salt-and-pepper capsules. He felt unmoored and confused, not exactly certain of the focus of his anger. He was mad, but at whom, precisely? And how had he come to be *this* enraged? Was he finally boiling over?

Was this the "harmless" effect worked by Price's house mix?

The storm might bring others. This house was the only secure location, excepting perhaps the bunker of missile-silo-grade concrete that held up the Sundial dish, which was inaccessible. Other people might try to get into where Art was. They'd see what he'd done to Bryan, in the garage. He needed a plan. Or he could pile up bullet-holed trespassers in the carport until he ran out of ammo. He tried to dope out a plan over a few more beers . . .

Sure enough, pounding on the front door woke him up. Blitz commenced his *achtung* bark.

Art's eyes bleared open. He was sprawled on the sofa in the living room and his neck felt permanently sprung to the left. His nerve endings were effervescent and tender, snapping like Pop Rocks; when he moved his body, it felt distant and alien, a robot remote-controlled by a novice on the stick. The heat was still on, pulsing from the vents, and had swaddled him into a sleeping delirium. He had to thump the wall panel twice before his knuckle hit the comm button.

"What?" He waved the dog back. "Shut up a minute, kiddo."

The speaker crackled with wind distortion. "My name is Captain Willowmore; could we please have a word with whoever is in there? It's colder than Eskimo Hell out here."

Panic flooded through Art's vascular system like acid. "Police?"

"U.S. Navy—*please?*"

Art switched the alarms to standby, got a grab on Blitz's collar, and unbolted the metal door. Two figures stood in the porch foyer, sealed up in insulated rain suits, goggles on their foreheads. The weather needled around them and tried to enter the house, like iron filings pulled by magnetism. The lead man had to speak over the harsh blow.

"Man!" Cold had thickened his speech; it sounded to Art like he had said *mom*. He touched the bill of his cap. "Captain Willowmore. This is Corporal Brookman." He jerked his thumb over his shoulder. "We came here for the dish but we ran into a problem, and yours is the only light for about a mile. Please tell me that dog doesn't bite."

"Only when he eats," said Art, lying already. He pulled Blitz back and gave the bulky men room to enter.

"Frankly, we're amazed that you're still here," said Willowmore.

Brookman shucked his hood and vised his forehead as though he was suffering a tension spike. "*Jesus*, it's cold," he said mostly to himself.

The abrupt entry into heat caused Willowmore's eyes to water. He was a clean-cut, close-cropped officer with the carriage of a

Bantu tribal leader; his eyes were wide set and never missed anything. Art sensed there would be trouble if he started snooping. His subordinate, Brookman, was a functionary, a driver, an assistant. He reminded Art of Solomon, the surfer dude at Price's, but with a Bourbon County accent.

"I bet you guys could use something hot," said Art.

"Only if you want us to be grateful to you for the rest of our lives," said Willowmore. "You mind if we get out of these jackets?" He had to speak past Blitz's renewed barking.

Art hung up their weather gear. "Pull your gloves and let him get a whiff of you, then you'll be okay." It was oddly pleasurable, to give orders to military guys. "Blitz—*Das sind Freunde; komm, beschnuppere sie und dann sei ruhig!*"

"Wow," said Brookman, when the dog dutifully sniffed them, then stood down.

They skinned out of their coats. Art saw uniforms and sidearms.

"Excuse me if I say we're surprised to find you still out here," said Willowmore.

Art realized he was going to have to concoct a briefer and more definitive version of his story if he was going to keep encountering strangers in his own house. While he told the men the immediate essentials, he caught them exchanging sidelong looks of doubt.

The pair gratefully accepted paper cups of instant soup, but never stopped glancing around the house like policemen. Willowmore related that their assignment had to do with manually adjusting the dish tracking for the Sundial, since remote control had been pushed to failure by the raging storm. They had arrived in a wide, flat Humvee to discover the bunker entryway submerged and the tunnel access, farther upbeach, obscured by rockfall. Mission aborted. Art told them the nature of the small avalanche—broken tombstones—and offered in trade his own story of how he had stayed to monitor the progress of his house's revolutionary design. Willowmore nodded, as though he accepted this but had further questions.

"I'm sorry," said Willowmore. "You *did* say your name was Art, right?" His tone was just patronizing enough to suggest that Art's entire story was casting long shadows of doubt.

"That's right," said Art.

"Excuse me?" said Brookman. "Do you mind if I—?"

Art realized Brookman was speaking to him.

"Rest room?" he clarified.

Art pointed the way. "How can you guys just waltz back out into that?" he said, meaning the storm, wishing they would leave already.

Willowmore ran his hands back through his close-cropped hair. "The Humvee is pretty good protection. It's almost a half-track, with double rear tires. Run-flats. Armored windows. The electronics are sealed. Fording kit lets it cruise through several feet of water, and it's not likely to flip because it weighs a couple of tons. Low center of gravity, high clearance. We rolled over or around nearly everything in the road. Can't say that for a lot of travelers whose cars we saw, usually tipped over. Nobody in any of them. We could crawl back north, but the base is in worse shape than this neck of the woods. No rush there."

Did that mean they intended to hang around? Art feared that Bryan would regain consciousness and start flailing, which would cause Blitz to bark, and split open a whole rancid carcass of black possibility. He was fairly certain that these men lacked the authority to snoop around his home, but he surely did not want to contest them, let alone get into some three-way drawdown.

"You're officially in what's called the 'eyewall' of a hurricane," Willowmore continued. "If the eye of the storm passes south, it'll get real calm for a moment, then the winds will reverse direction with equal force and hit you again. Just so you're ready for that, if you're determined to stay."

Brookman returned, massaging his hands, which he had thawed out in hot water. "You got a sister here, too?"

It startled Art more than it should have. "Sister?"

"Yeah, she peeked out of the bedroom." Brookman was pointedly circumspect about how he expressed his next thought. "She looked, uh, a little banged up." The blackhanded accusation of his tone was still too clear.

"My wife," said Art, and the men swapped another dubious glance. "We had a little trouble battening down," said Art. To hesitate was to perforate his own lie. "You probably saw how the garage door got all bent out of shape. The edge flew up and nailed her. I asked her not to stay for this, but—" He shrugged. "She got a shiner."

"We can get her to a hospital," said Willowmore.

"No, she took a sleeping pill. She'll be okay. I might get a little banged up myself, before the night's done with us."

"You have a gun on the kitchen counter for a reason?" said Willowmore.

"Call me overzealous." Art worked up a placating smile that took effort to sustain. "You never know who'll come pounding on your door in the middle of something like this. That it was you guys just proves I don't really have much to worry about, apart from Mother Nature kicking my butt."

"What happened to the window?" Brookman was inspecting the gouges from the inside of the Plexiglas.

"Pine-tree branch," said Art. "Flew out of nowhere and splintered apart before I could get the shutters down."

"Think it's a good idea to be drinking so much?" said Willowmore, who had not missed the crowd of beer bottles on the kitchen counter.

"Those are mostly out of the recycling bin," said Art. "Better stacked up in here than flying around out there, right? But I'll confess one or two of those dead boys is mine; I needed to calm down a bit when the storm really started to bite." He hoped this minor admission might shield some of the bigger falsehoods.

Willowmore's gaze moved to the longneck bottles, gathered like a crowd at a traffic accident. His expression remained maddeningly neutral. "There's broken glass on the floor and a dent in the refrigerator door like somebody threw one of those bottles at it. Aren't you afraid your dog will get hurt?"

"I was just cleaning that up when you knocked."

A crash from the garage turned all their heads. Brookman's hand flew down to his holstered .45.

"Let me make sure my generator's not about to fly away," said Art, already moving.

Willowmore rose. "You need a hand?"

"Just sit tight. I've got coffee in two minutes."

Luckily, the men did not tailgate him into the kitchen. His shoes crunched slivers of glass as he cracked the garage door for a look-see. Bryan was still taped to the rack, as left. Wind stirred loose paper and caused the plastic sheet beneath him to flap. The dented portion of the outer door had sprung loose from the position into which Art had locked it. It would have to wait.

"Good thing you've got a generator going," said Brookman, staring at the dark fireplace. "That wind would blow a wood fire right into your face; come landsliding right down your chimney."

"Yeah, the flue has got a compression seal on it so it can't be blown open." Art's heartbeat was redlining. If they checked the garage, it was adios. If they walked outside and peered through the resprung door, ditto. The wind lashing in through the breach was fearful enough. What if it revived Bryan?

He detoured down the hall and checked the guest bedroom. Suzanne was not in it. His heart pistoned, straining like the transmission of a car whose accelerator and brake are both floored.

"Problem?" said Willowmore's voice.

Just leave. Just die, Art thought, hurrying past the bathroom and checking his own bedroom. *Just stop bugging me.* Suzanne had awakened and plodded, zombiatically, to the bigger bed, where she was now curled up, unmoving. She had become upright exactly long enough for Brookman to spot her.

"No," Art said, teeth clenched. "Just checking on my honey." Fleeting thought: He could bring his nosy good-cop, bad-cop guests their coffee, and shoot one in the back of the head while the other was mulling over cream or sugar. Problem solved. He imagined blotting blood spray off the tabletop; out of the carpet nap. Willowmore first. Get the smug prick while he was on the upswing of another prying, accusatory question. Brookman would hesitate at the sight of his ranking superior getting unplugged. That delay would cost him his future, because Art's weapon could speak again while Brookman's was still holstered. It could all be over in fewer than five seconds. But for the bodies, everything would be back to normal.

Except that, "normally," Art still had bodies to deal with, not dead ones, not yet.

Brookman blew on his coffee mug; Willowmore took a mouthful of the scalding fresh liquid without changing expression. Some guys liked it really hot.

"That's good," said Willowmore, taking another gulp fast on the wake of the first. "You sure you're not in some kind of trouble here?"

Art's pleasant expression felt as petrified as a pasted-on papier-mâché masque. "Not unless my house can't take the storm, which would be a disaster for me in another direction. Can't say the same if anybody stayed in those houses to the south. If anybody's there, by now, they're hurting. Me, I'm sort of obligated to stay."

Willowmore did not rise to Art's bait, but Brookman did. "Sir? Maybe we should check them other houses?"

"Not in our purview," said the captain. "We're only here because this is right next to our jetty." He sighed heavily and massaged his knees with his hands. "So, you two are . . . married, am I correct?"

"Very observant, Captain," said Art.

Willowmore nodded as though an entire questionnaire had been filled out in his brain. "And both of you choose to stay here for the duration of the storm?"

"Yes. For the house. It can take it."

"Then you won't mind if the lady in the other room tells us that for herself, would you?"

Brookman interjected, "They don't need a ride out, maybe somebody down there still does." He turned to Art. "How far?"

"Two more places, a half mile and about a quarter mile down-beach. I don't think there's anyone there; they've been dark since before the storm." His brain was warning him not to embellish too much—too many separate lies to keep track of. But if he mentioned any of the occupants, there would come a fresh salvo of questions.

"Perhaps *you* want to stay for this show," said Willowmore, as though Art had left the room. Obviously the captain had run the figures in his head and the magic words *wife abuser* had plopped out of his calculator.

Which was stupid. These men weren't police. Their affiliation regardless, they did not have the right to come into Art's house and start enforcing orders . . . unless they suspected bad shit, and Willowmore was wearing a face that said things had begun to stink, just a bit. Art realized his own reaction to these men was as primitive as any knee-jerk macho-tude Bryan could have frothed forth. Combat imperatives were blinding him. He had invited these guys in; now he had to invite them to leave.

"Sweetie . . . ?"

Suzanne was peering from the corner of the hallway, smothered in Art's big terry bathrobe, barefoot, a clean washrag held to the injured side of her face. Her good eye squinted against the light. Art's heart nearly speed-stopped.

Brookman bolted to his feet in atavistic politeness, or fright, or something. "Missus."

"Ma'am." Willowmore eyeballed her carefully.

"I'm Suzanne," she said thickly, with a slight lisp imparted by her inflated lip and jarred dentition.

"You shouldn't be up," said Art, rising to meet her.

"I heard all this talking. Honey, I need a pain pill." She chose her words delicately, aware they might be mangled on the way out. "Did Art tell you how the damned door jumped up and kissed me? Ow." She tried a smile; made it halfway before the pain canceled it. "Seen my watch anywhere?"

The watch was on the nightstand, a bulky skin-diver-style chronometer. Art had stripped it off her wrist before he dunked her.

"Just a minute, guys," Art said as he guided Suzanne back to the bedroom. Blitz looked up from his sleeping place near the foot of the bed. He'd been with Suzanne all along. Sitting sentry, something the dog had never done when strangers were on the premises . . .

with a single lifetime exception. If Lorelle had been in the bedroom, the dog would have stayed with her. The dog was acting as though Suzanne had, in one day, earned a rank equivalent to his departed mistress. When Art and Suzanne came in together, Blitz responded as if to a telepathic command, and automatically loped back to the living room to plop down near the windows and play interim host. Hello.

Art pushed the bedroom door mostly shut. "How long have you been with us?"

"Please, later." When Art heard her say this, he saw how much she had dressed up her voice for the guests. Despite all recent craziness, he felt a surge of protective sympathy for her. Talking hurt. Speaking coherently hurt more. She had to take frequent short breaths to push the words out. "Later. All later. Right now I need some Percodans. I feel like my head's been ripped off."

She was able to tip back a couple of Vicodin and draw enough water for two swallows with a straw. She said, "later," one more time, then put her head back on the pillows, every movement an effort, every effort a minor agony.

"Thanks, Art." It was distant, feeble; he might have only imagined her saying that. It sounded like *thang-sard.*

When he returned to the living room he saw Willowmore with his eye to the kitchen-door peephole, leaning forward with his hands clasped behind his back as though in aesthetic appreciation of some impenetrable artwork. Terror jarred Art's bones. He froze in place, blanching, and tried not to collapse to his knees. His tongue inflated spitlessly, and it was suddenly hard to breathe.

Blitz had posted himself exactly between the two men, his gaze sweeping left to right, his stance rigid.

"That the garage?" said Willowmore, not looking at Art.

The Heckler-Koch was still on the kitchen counter right behind the captain. For a fast reach, it might as well have been on top of Mount Diablo, which was out past the Berkeley Hills, and could be seen from San Francisco on a clear day. Part of Art's conscience backhanded him for not murdering the two navy men when he had the drop on them. Now the option had evaporated, and Art envisioned his immediate destiny as an ugly tell-all or a pointless physical struggle, or both.

Uh—what was the question?

"Yes." Art tried to tamp down his own capering panic.

"So, your generator is out there?"

"Yes." Art had to clear his throat. Something was not right.

"Runs off gas?" Willowmore finally looked at him.

"Yes. If there's no juice, it can buy me a day."

"How much one of those things cost, if you don't mind my asking?"

"You can get different efficiencies and different capacities. Starting at a couple hundred." The closer Art got to Willowmore, babbling, the better chance he had at the gun.

"Nice thing to have."

Art nodded.

"Coffee sure is good," said Brookman from the sofa. Blitz shifted position to move nearer the corporal as Art got closer to Willowmore.

"Thanks."

"I hate to sound like a broken record," said Willowmore, "but are you *sure* there's nothing we can help you with? You seem a little . . . I can't really find the word . . ."

"Stressed-out," Brookman chimed in, as though cued.

"I mean, apart from the obvious—the storm and all?" Willowmore's voice had gone folksy but he had this really off-putting way of not blinking when he was firing off a direct inquiry.

You mean, apart from the hostage in my garage? Art put his eye to the peephole. *Maybe the tarp blew over the Bry-Guy. Maybe, if he was no longer squirming, he was indistinct in the glass of the security viewport. Maybe he had crawled under the Jeep to croak. Maybe . . .*

"Nothing else wrong, except I'm worried about the storm." The dog's alert attitude was starting to annoy him. Squirrely behavior might lose the game, not that Art was excelling in the poker-face department today, either. He ordered Blitz to sit in German, too sharply. The dog cast a narrowed glance at Art, as if to ask, *Are you sure?*

"You're sure about that, now?" It was Willowmore, not the dog, who had spoken. Art's gut plunged. Was somebody reading his mind?

"Why do you ask?"

Willowmore half shrugged. "Because when you came back out from talking to your partner, there—your wife—you looked kind of like you'd just seen a booger."

Every time the storm lashed the house and rattled some extremity, Blitz's ears came up. Then he'd raise his head, nervously. Then he'd plunk it back down in defeat. He hated bad weather. It was un-doggish.

Art was trying to think of something else useless to say, another line that would buy him a breath of time, as he checked the peephole himself.

Bryan was no longer strapped to the utility rack in the garage. He was absent from the view at all angles. Even the shreds of duct tape that had held him were in plain sight and clear focus. The tarp on which he had bled had been folded double by the wind and stuffed up against one side of the Jeep. He had either wormed between the cars, or was on the far side of the Jaguar, or—

"Uh . . . booger?" said Art.

—or, if he was still in the garage, in order to be out of sight of the peephole he had to be curled up right underneath the kitchen door.

Brookman clarified. "Booger bear. Sir."

Willowmore drifted from the kitchen to the hallway, with Blitz tailing him. The dog finally gave up trying to comprehend this opaque standoff of humans, and returned to resume his picket duty in the bedroom. Willowmore made a point of inspecting the display of family photos in the hall, geometrically framed and trued into an abstract scatter pattern favoring the diagonal plane across the east wall, next to the door for the guest bathroom. He hinged forward, as he had in the kitchen, to peer like a dunk-bird in uniform. "I recognize you in this picture, but is this your wife? What did you say her name was?"

"I don't think I said," said Art.

"Suzanne," said Brookman.

"This photo doesn't look much like her," said Willowmore with a calculated scowl.

A rabid rat was running feverish circles in Art's brain, pausing only to urinate in the fissures, gnaw on his higher functions, and scratch away his composure with filthy clotted claws. "Well, she's not at her best right now, and that shot was taken five years ago. She's a bit . . . you know, heavier."

"Um-hm. So how come this picture says her name is Lorelei?"

"Lorelle. That's her middle name. Her family called her that. I call her Suzanne." Spacing out the words to specify his irritation was a bad tactic, but Art could not stop the rat in his head, the rattler in his chest.

Art's interior viper noticed the frantic rat, struck with a full-venom bite, and began to swallow. The rat was gone, the snake occupied, Art could win this game.

Willowmore decided to back off—mercifully so, thought Art, since to add one more untruth to the pile in his own skull might cause an avalanche of black lies to come cascading out his ears.

"Tell you what," the ranking officer said evenly. "The corporal and I will sortie down the road; see if there are any stragglers to evac. I think it would be a good idea to stop here again on the way back north. The road might become impassable. Some of the others, if there are others, might be injured. We all might need shelter more than escape, and so far your fancy design seems to be holding back Mother Nature pretty good here . . . Art." It seemed as thought Willowmore had to force himself to recall the name.

"Thanks," Art said.

Willowmore's gaze clouded, his eyes as minatory as the sky outside. He stopped blinking again. "Whatever you're up to here that you don't want us to see, you settle it before we get back. Do I make myself clear?"

Art held up his hands in an unthinking gesture of surrender. "I'm sorry, guys. It's just that my wife got hurt—"

"Your *wife*," said Willowmore, as if giving Art one final chance to prove or deny it.

"Yes. And I don't know what's going to happen moment to moment, your showing up was a complete surprise, and now I feel like I'm being interrogated. If I had something to hide, I never would've opened the door."

"So why did you open it?"

"Because I'm not going to leave anybody out in *that*." Art lied yet again. "I'm sorry you think I'm acting weird. Wouldn't you?"

Willowmore sniffed brusquely. "No need to apologize. Come on,

Corporal." He spared Art the white heat of his gaze at last. Art thought of gun turrets muzzled in canvas covers.

It took the men five minutes just to get redressed against the storm, yanking zippers and sealing Velcro flaps. Blitz emerged from the bedroom to apply his rapt interest to their every movement, far too late. *Some accomplice,* thought Art. He needed to keep his fear and anger at bay so he could decide what to do next. The dog had kept an eye on Suzanne; that was more important than unnecessarily playing Costello to Art's Abbott for the sake of the navy. Suzanne had played along, for reasons of her own. And the navy was leaving.

Grabbing the pistol before escorting his latest guests to their ride was out of the question, but Art knew he had to go outside with them. If the much-abused Bryan, or any part of him, was visibly lingering, bloodied and obviously in desperate need of assistance such as Willowmore was eager to provide, Art needed to apply bias. On a blueprint, you could force uneven lines to marry up; you could defy strict mathematics and mandate symmetry where the horizontals and verticals refused to agree. In a relationship, you could tint the shades until opposites equalized. And in a disaster, such as this weekend had already become, you could write your own history, depending on how picky your witnesses were. If the navy men insisted on knowing everything, or if Bryan inconveniently betrayed him, Art would have to add victims to the storm's body count. Simply.

Rain shone whitely in the triangle of light spilling from the rent in the garage door; Art thought of reel scratches on spooled film. Wind pushed his hair into his face. The blow was strong enough to loft wet sand from the beach, dry it enough to make it airborne, and hurl it in the spaces between raindrops, which were already brutally large—to stand out here for any length of time was like getting sandblasted. Bryan's body was not sprawled on the front walkway. So far so good.

Captain Willowmore tapped his sleeved wrist, to indicate time. "It's fifteen-twenty hours now," he said, focusing his voice toward Art with a cupped hand. "I'm hoping this check is a milk run. No complications. We should be back here by sixteen-thirty, estimate."

"Four-thirty," Brookman clarified.

"I want to be out of here before night drops on our head. It's bad enough already. You batten this place down and be here when we get back."

"Yes, sir," Art said, distantly amused. His spirits were buoyed by the fact that the Bry-Guy didn't seem to be around at all. Magic.

The military Humvee backed into a two-point turn. Its lamps were not even clear of the first crick in the driveway before Art dashed back into the house, to arm himself and make a complete circuit of the grounds, gun in one hand, high-beam flashlight in the other. The still-moist blood skids on the garage floor suggested that Bryan had scuttled outside. Scraps of his flesh clung to the burst duct tape. You had to be strong and desperate to rip yourself free that way, like a coyote chewing off a leg to escape an iron-jawed trap. Art had rushed, too hurried, too sloppy; he'd noticed Bryan's workout muscle, yet not trussed him more firmly. He should have mummified the guy's damned arms to the cross beams; should have used the whole fucking roll of tape.

Clouds of moisture hung low and swirled, similar to the thick, ground-hugging smoke of a forest fire. The fierce wind reshaped them, but they remained airbrushed to the sky, blocking out the feeble sun, limiting vision to less than twenty feet, impermeable. If Bryan had left a trail, the storm had erased it already.

If Bryan had escaped. If Bryan had ever actually been here at all. An icicle of pain calved his left eye, and it felt as though his sinuses were packed with rusty steel wool. He had plenty of evidence this time—the Buick, the ballbat, the bloodied tarp. Evidence wasn't his problem, this time. Now he was absorbed in thoughts more immediate and practical than worrying about his sanity. He could no longer fritter time in speculation about whether people had actually existed, or events transpired. Now he had to focus on covering his ass; what stories to tell which people. Which *real* people. Maybe he should start snapping Polaroids.

Blitz waited at the door, unwilling to play outside. Art locked up and did a quick survey of the beach through the slits in the westward shutters. He saw nothing and nobody.

What about the damned soldiers? nagged the serpent squeezing his heart, still digesting the rat of panic, *Sailors. Whatever.* Willowmore and Brookman—both fanciful, sylvan names. A black man in command of a white Southerner; another wish fulfillment. Authority figures who materialized out of the height of the storm to push every guilt button in Art's hardwiring, from his culpability for gun-shooting and hostage-holding, to his inherited baggage of Suzanne's damning injuries, making him suffer the incisive humiliation of a chess novice beaten by a computer. Willowmore had seen right through the husband-wife sham but had chosen to bypass it, for unknown reasons. For every move, no matter how considered, Art won the complication of a new wrinkle that threatened to end his illusion of control. He had felt like the storm was an isolated pocket of suspended time, in which he could try out unpredictably hazardous new emotions. Now, with every minute, he was becoming aware that once the storm of nature ended, a fresh tempest of consequences was going to touch down on his life's ground zero. Willowmore and Brookman could very well have been an externalization of his accountability, and pondering such subtle insanities could only drive him deeper into self-doubt about everything he saw and experienced.

Then again, they could have been real . . . in which case Art had manfully outfoxed them and bought himself a caesura in the middle of a raging storm.

Suzanne was drugged and logy in the master bedroom, her good eye cracked open, half in, half out of some unfathomable other-zone. Mostly in. Technically she was asleep.

"Art? Need to tell you." Her voice was turbid and conflicted, distant behind layers of disorientation, bullied under the noise of the storm outside. Hasty, perhaps, to have given her painkillers so readily; Art had not considered which other drugs might already be freestyling through her metabolism, or maybe he just had not cared at the time he had pretended to be a pharmacist.

He sat, said nothing, squeezed her hand, made sure she knew he was right there.

"Sorry," she said, in a way that caused the snake in his chest to constrict. "Not my fault."

Was she trying to apologize, or aver blame?

"What are you talking about?" he said.

"I gotta tell you I'm sorry. I need something for my head."

"We already did that. No more pills. Sorry about what?"

"Price. His idea. I didn't want to, really—" Her hand drifted up to touch her *own* face, as if touching a stranger's physiognomy in a dark room. She found her features rearranged.

"What was Price's idea?"

A long, depleted sigh leaked out of her. "Fucking with you."

This was too touchy, fraught with bobby traps. Did she mean

Price, the marionette master, had decreed that Suzanne wind up naked in Art's bed? Or was the scenario more cloaked, indicating a deeper and more sinister blueprint, making Art a game piece, and teaching him the *real* meaning of getting fucked?

"I said no but he—"

Her fragments were maddening. Each one forced ugly possibilities nearer, hidden flaws in the grand blueprint, with Art as their target.

"He wouldn't . . . I couldn't . . . you can't say no to him."

Yes, the snake was wide-awake now, warming, hungry, malign, fed but wanting more. Tears glistened in Suzanne's good eye and leaked in reluctant drops from her ruined one. The best strategists played vulnerability as a lure; show 'em a weakness, then reel 'em in. Stick your face out into the world and predators perked up, desirous of snatching fresh meat. When you considered the totally impersonal hazards out there, a hermit's existence did not seem so unreasonable, or deviant.

"I'm just . . . sorry."

Or was she throwing herself on his mercy, seeking forgiveness for damage done because it seemed like a good idea at the time? Art himself was utterly conflicted. Did he want some sort of savage biblical retribution, an eye for an eye . . . plus an arm and a leg, and two pints of fresh blood? This hurricane fever dream had all begun with Suzanne. Now she seemed to be apologizing. Was this real, or part of the next phase, leading to fresh torments?

And what was up with his damned dog? Blitz seemed to be treating her like a member of the family, and Blitz had never done that. Well, almost never; he had taken a doggie shine to Derek, too. Was the dog just skipping grooves like everyone else around here? Art looked toward him, because he needed somewhere else to look.

Blitz's eyes were open and alert, two dots of onyx in the dim light of the bedroom. He emitted a grunt; the sound of an old man settling into an easy chair. The air was enriched by the oily overcast of a dog fart.

"Oh, for christ sake," muttered Art. He should never have fed the beast so much processed ham.

The power died at exactly 5:10 P.M. by the nightstand clock, the old-fashioned flip-over digits freezing in place while Art sat on the rim of the bed trying to figure Suzanne out. The deadness of the three-second delay on the emergency lights was especially unnerving. For several heartbeats there was total darkness, and nothing else in the universe but the assault of the hurricane. Then the floods tripped, and just like that atmosphere was acrackle with danger again, more problems to solve, new threats incoming.

"Sorry," Suzanne said, oblivious to this world.

● ● ● Art rounded up the rest of his weapons and stuck them inside the gun safe, stopping short of locking the door. He kept the Heckler-Koch with him for the sake (the excuse) of confidence.

Just what did he think he was doing?

Did he really have the gristle to shoot another living, breathing, walking, talking person? Bryan, still missing in action, almost did not count. That had been easy, simple, one-way; Art had put him down without thinking. Wasn't that the way it was supposed to go? Instinct, reflex, *bang,* the threat is neutralized. Now it seemed inadmissible because his opponent had not been armed, too. A turkey shoot, fish-in-a-barrel time. Too easy, to plug somebody who wasn't shooting back. And what had it changed? Zero. Bryan had escaped despite the end-all solution of Art's weaponry.

The only thing Art knew for certain was that he had fired the pistol. He still had the spent brass in his pocket to prove that. The rest was subject to conjecture. His wish fulfillment might have been egged on by the startling effects of Price's party drug.

Also too easy. Almost desirable, as a story.

He held the gun ready and stuck a rubber-gripped baton flashlight into his armpit. He eased up on the kitchen door to the garage, with Blitz providing silent backup.

If he farts again, it'll be silent-but-DEADLY backup. Art thought, his senses lunatic, his perceptions so acute that he felt as if he were constantly plunging forward, trying to arrest the dark and divest it of any more surprises. He was a fool trying to grab ghosts and tie them in knots, recognizable configurations. Even the air seemed acrid and charged; the smell of burning psyche.

He looked through the peephole in the kitchen door just as the bank of emergency floods in the garage was destroyed in a messy scatter of broken glass. The white pop in the magnified confines of the viewport left Art seeing dancing flashbulb globes, just as Blitz started barking his heart out; forelegs braced, ruff hackled, the compleat Monster Fighter. Art heard more civil unrest within the garage—the tool cart overturned, the autos taking dents, and, under the rollick of the wind and rain, a voice in primordial agony, almost howling, buying each destructive hit with a overdose of pain and effort.

Art's own heart ramped up as he prepared to storm. The next intruder noise nearly launched him out of his shoes: three gunshots, grouped so tight they could have been one. The funnel acoustics made them loud as cannon fire. The howler ceased competing with the weather and the abrupt termination of his noisemaking was somehow scarier than all the portents of his mysterious attack.

"*Art! Art!* You in there, man?! Oww, *fuck!*" This last epithet was

194

followed by another crash—somebody falling over something in the dark. The voice, familiar. Not "oddly" familiar. A friendly.

Flat-handed pounding now, on the door. "Art! Come on, *Art!* Open up, chief! I hadda shoot this asshole out here and I'm freezing my tits off! Art! It's Luther, man, right?! You know, *Luther!*"

The bottom seemed to drop out of Art's gut, leaving a direct tunnel from his mouth to his asshole; as the saying goes, you could see daylight. "Holy shit," he mumbled, his hands quickly depositing his hardware on the counter and moving for the bolts. "Blitz, shut up! *Halt's Maul! Hör' auf!*"

Blitz backed up half a dog-step. Stop what he was doing? *I thought we were partners.*

Luther practically fell into the kitchen, bringing his own storm with him. He was bundled into a thin three-quarter leather coat as saturated as a bath sponge, collar up. His Eye of Ra earring dangled over the collar and his eyes were so wild they'd gone yellow. He rammed right into Art's embrace, knees sagging, the AMT Hardballer in his right fist banging Art's shoulder, muzzle indifferently directed at the ceiling, then his ear, then the living room. Art caught him gun-first.

"Jesus *fuck* it's a shitty night!" Luther panted. "Super-hostile; *damn!*" As soon as he spoke, Blitz cut loose more barks in a cannonade.

Art ordered the dog back to the bedroom: "Blitz! *In's Schlafzimmer! Sofort!*"

Luther was shivering, trying to husk out his passwords, his rationale, anything that might buy him a tiny bit of shelter. "I knew you'd be here. Knew it. Christ, it's fuckin unbelievable out there. Trees are flying, boss. The sand is fuckin *alive.* Driven everybody bugfuck, it's like one muthafuck of a horror movie, like that Living Dead shit. The ocean is hungry, like Moby Dick. Counted on you being here, man. I knew it, figured ole Art's hanging tight against all the bullshit of the outside world, right? *Knew* it!"

"Whoa, Luther—slow down, stow the piece, okay?"

He gulped air as though it was being rationed by a miser. "Yeah, whatever, right?" He abandoned his beloved pistol on the counter so casually it was almost comedic.

Art was still hanging on to him. "Calm down. You straight?"

"Fuckin A. Caught that cocksucker dead center, triple-tap, end of story."

"In the garage? Who?"

"That fucker Bryan, man—all taped up, raving like a crazy person. I think you can smooch your generator bye-bye. He butt-fucked it with a crowbar. I came in through the bust in your door, the one that looks like he drove through it? I sighted him just as he swung at the floodlight. Clearly hostile intent, so I collected him." A bitter little smile divided his face as he made a rubber-stamping motion. "Bam-bam-bam; paid in full. We're even for that favor I owe ya."

"I guess so," Art said.

"Shit, not truly. It was a pleasure to plug that asshole directly, tell ya the truth. Man, I sure am glad you're here. Emergency station. Safe house. Fuck, I woulda been blown out to sea and the minnows would be chomping my butt about now. *Damn* it's cold out there, like the fuckin Arctic or something; Ice Station My-Ass."

Art felt as though he was in a control tower, talking down an inexperienced pilot. He kept command, put a mug of coffee between Luther's shaking hands, left his coat in a pool on the floor, wrapped him in a blanket, and checked out the garage while Luther sat trying to fight his way back to zero.

Bryan—the Bry-Guy—was spread across the hood of the Jaguar like flung laundry, an amazing amount of blood collecting in the bevels of trim and funneling away to drip across the chrome grille, mirroring itself with a candy-flake shimmer. By flashlight Art could see that when Bryan had freed himself, at considerable cost of his own shredded skin, he had used the duct tape to immobilize his malfunctioning arm and seal the gunshot wound he'd won earlier. It was an expenditure of energy and sheer will that Art would normally credit to a man out of his head on PCP, so many steps requiring stamina and endurance that Art doubted he could achieve the escape, let alone the survival, if he were similarly hobbled. The guy had grit, no lie. Grievously wounded, he had put all his gym time to work and torn himself free only to crab out into the broiling hell of the full-bore hurricane, perhaps holing up like an Inuit in a snow shelter as the storm tried to sandblast his face off. Not dying. Then crawling back and wreaking vengeance upon the garage where Art had held him prisoner, swinging with his good arm.

The Jag's paint job was scored with gouges across the driver's-side flank, its even dust disturbed by runnels of water that lent it a berserk, abstract quality, like marbled paper. One headlight was smashed out. The generator was history, useful now only as scrap or a really big paperweight. The batteries charging the emergency system would fade soon enough. Bryan had come back long enough to run one of Art's own crowbars right through the heart of the house. Then Luther had blown in just in time to go bam-bam-bam. It was too much like good chess.

No, Art thought. *You were a twitch away from shooting him yourself. You would have. You already had. He'd be just as dead, probably in the same time frame . . . only you didn't have to do it.* Not that those navy boys would buy any of this for an eyeblink of time; any lie Art could fabricate now would just be lame.

"Anybody else make it?" said Luther, when Art had resecured

the sundered garage door and locked up. He was a straggler, a for-saken point man asking for mission stats.

"Suzanne, from the party," said Art. "She's in the bedroom. She's pretty messed up."

"Suzanne, huh. Another chick. Don't know her."

Neither do I, thought Art. "What happened at Price's?"

Luther stretched his neck back against the sofa and Art heard three audible vertebra pops. "Storm kicked up full and Price kicked most everybody out. Coupla carloads headed for Half Moon Bay. I stayed long enough to watch half the house come down. Windows blew in. Most of that turret thing collapsed with some people on it. Cabana outside completely blew away like it was headed for Oz; when we checked on it, it was just *gone,* chief. The outside deck peeled up like piano keys. Coupla people took to their cars; they're mostly decorating the roadside now. Not that there's much road left. I took a tumble on the stairs and rolled, you know, but I lost a piece of time there. Hit my head. Woke up and most of the furniture was flying around. You said you was up here and I kinda force-marched it on the road. Saw a fuckin funnel cloud, man, that was scary as shit, close up. Was light when I started; don't know how long that took, but . . . fuck." He rubbed the tight crop of his skull, imagining a concussion lying in wait to mess him up. "I think I mighta passed out between here and there."

"You feel like you need a hospital?" Art decided to partake of the coffee himself.

"Naw, no hospital. I'm good. Kinda pointless, anyway—who can get to a hospital? I've never depended on them."

"Well, about an hour ago some guys from the navy showed up here in a Hummer that looked like a landing craft. They were going to check on the houses downbeach and then come back, in case anybody needed a lift back to civilization."

Luther's expression darkened. With the rain wiped from his face and head, perspiration beaded in its place as stress voided through his pores. He could not stop continually probing the back of his head. "You mean you *stayed* here, like, on purpose?"

"I'm an architect. I designed this house to stand up to a hurricane. Here's a hurricane. So this is the acid test. If it passes, I win a lot of contracts."

"Nice shutters," said Luther, observing the corrugated metal that shielded the windows. "Like a fortress. I thought maybe you stayed because of, you know, that woman."

"Suzanne."

"Yeah, right, Suzanne."

"I only met her yesterday."

Luther's eyebrows went up, then down; no big deal. "That ain't right. It's too weird."

Art watched Luther's gaze focus on the intangible, doping through evidence, working it out in his head, seeing if the story held water. He zapped over the topic of Suzanne easy as a speedbump and zeroed-in on the stuff that interested him.

"Navy wouldn't send guys out in this kinda storm for any reason," Luther said. "What'd they say they were here for?"

"There's a huge microwave dish out on the end of the jetty north of here," said Art. "They said their remotes were down and they couldn't adjust the dish, and were nervous about the storm."

"Ahh, bullshit." Luther waved his hand, dismissing that plotline. "No reason to check something like that until the storm goes down. Stupid to check it in the *middle* of the storm, man, think about it. They anchor those things in pilings that go down fifty feet. You couldn't break into it; I couldn't. It's just a big relay dish. Anything they tell you about having to get in there in the *middle* of a goddamned storm, somebody's jackin you."

As paranoia, it was tempting. "They had uniforms. They acted like military guys. They were driving a military vehicle." Art leapfrogged to the most important question: "If they're not for real, why did they come here? Why me?"

Luther stared into the depths of his coffee mug. Coffee always provided answers. "M'kay. If they're for real, they're incredibly stupid, reckless, or acting against orders. If they're not for real, then what? Ratpackers, maybe, pretending to be some sort of authority so they can case houses, knock them off using the storm as cover? Unlikely. The score'd have to be small and portable—cash, jewelry, something like that—and it'd have to be worth the risk. The uniforms would be like those bank robbers who wear suits and ties, right? All the witnesses remember is the suit and tie."

"So I'd remember the uniforms and not the faces?" said Art. "If so, that failed miserably. I could sketch both these guys."

"Was that Humvee a military one, or one of the civilian knockoffs?" Luther was racking up angles of attack like any decent strategist.

"Big, dark, you tell me. It was a Hummer, that's all I know."

"Hummers are civilian. Humvees are military. Can't get the civilian ones in military green, or camo, or desert tan, anymore. Military ones don't have amenities like leather seats. Or air-conditioning, except for the ambulances. Best way to check: Sit in the driver's seat. If there's no PARK setting on the transmission, it's military; don't know why. The military ones have really wimpy horns, like, who needs it, right?"

"A civilian one could be tricked out to fake a military one, though?"

"I guess. Some people have been able to buy decommissioned ones and spruce them up. I know a producer guy in Malibu who leases a couple from the government for a buck a year—you know, because he makes the military look so good in his movies."

Jesus, thought Art, did *everybody* know somebody in Hollywood?

Luther bulled ahead. "Anyway, whoever they are, if they're coming back here, we need to clean house, right?"

They just looked at each other.

● ● ● Art's loaner jacket was ridiculously tight on Luther, where Suzanne had vanished into it, despite what a smartass would call her substantial front porch. Cowled in ponchos, zipped up and weather-snapped secure, the two men leaned against the storm to accomplish their work.

The final resting place of the late Bryan Simonsen, the former Bry-Guy, turned out to be thirty yards up the slope of the hill on the far side of the coast road. His bier was a wheelbarrow; his shroud, the bloodstained plastic tarp from the garage. The two men—judge and executioner, torturer and assassin—discovered an uprooted sycamore tree, roots dangling, ripped free like a rotten molar. It had upended a gouge nearly three feet deep, which the men spaded out to waist depth by the light from a pair of nine-volt lanterns. The wind kept knocking the lanterns over. The focused twin sprays of lamplight made the evening look like a projection of severely damaged nitrate-black film. Blowing rain bowed the two men, both of whom had done violence with gunfire to the stiffening body they had wrestled and cursed all the way up the hill. It sheeted the mud from their plastic cloaks as they interred him without obsequies. It was too noisy outside to make themselves heard, anyway. To keep themselves from cartwheeling down the slope on the return hike, they literally had to hold hands, sealing this compact, this vow of silence between two murderers. Both men knew the circumstances and justifications, yet the entire process seemed, to Art, to be tainted with guilt. They did the best they could.

Only one murderer, truly, Art thought. What did that make him? An accessory *before* the fact?

Back at the house, with Blitz calmed down anew, Luther held another mug of coffee to thaw his frozen fingers and ran details like someone who was used to this kind of hasslement.

"Okay. We didn't have time to dig for slugs, so I'd suggest you make that gun disappear. You have others?"

"Yes." Art had changed into doubled dry sweatshirts. Suzanne was still dead to the world. His eyes kept checking the emergency floods, which he swore he could see dimming already.

"You got specific ammo for it, I'd ditch that, too. Unless you have spare barrels, and you can switch those out and keep the gun. No? Shame to lose it."

Art was already running the tab in his head. A couple grand for the generator and attachments, two more for the pistol, plus damage to the Jaguar and the garage in general. Another bill Bryan would never pick up. Compared to attorney fees for a trial, this killing was still a bargain. He wondered what Derek's hotshot lawyer, that Cutler Jr. guy, would make of such an account.

"So where are the so-called navy dudes? Aren't they supposed to be back by now? Maybe you got lucky and the storm ate them." Luther delicately tested the back of his skull again, hoping the news was better this time.

Art shrugged. "Does your head hurt? You want something for—?"

"Naw, better to be straight. Too many toxins at Price's. I needed the exercise, outside, and the adrenaline to flush my system. You know, if those guys in the Humvee are for real, we can't get rid of Bryan's car. It'd look suspicious. Have to dump it eventually, though."

"What about the toxins at Price's?" Art tried to make it sound concerned and innocent, and fumbled the emotion.

"Shit, you saw me at the party. I was out of control."

"Seemed like you were a little too *in* control. So sharp it hurt. I figured speed; some kind of upper."

Luther laughed. It was harsh, like a smoker's cough. "Fucking Price and his party favors, man. He slip you any of that shit?"

Art was glad to be occupied in the kitchen, and not seeing Luther's eyes directly as he lied. "What shit?"

"Those capsules. These capsules." He dig into his pants pocket and produced a prescription bottle with the label torn off. He spilled several of the home-dipped black-and-white capsules onto the glass of the coffee table for inspection.

"Do you know what they are?"

Luther pursed his lips dourly and shook his head. "I heard Michelle call them Mr. Hyde. They flip you. Flip you for real."

"What, you mean they uninhibit you? Hell, all drugs do that— change your personality."

"Naw, it's different. It's like they locate your opposite self and bring it right up to the surface. Or they find what you do your best to suppress and spotlight it. Maybe put you face-to-face with what you don't want people to see, ever. All I know is I took one, and I ain't never hit a woman before in my life, until I had that girl Katha rolled over—you should pardon my Frog. I just started slapping her, and it made me hard as a spear. Right after that was when you met me in the hallway."

Art remembered Bryan weeping in Price's bathroom. Suzanne's one-eighty mood swings, just like Jekyll and Hyde. The way he'd savaged Bryan in the garage after ingesting the drug. He had not felt possessed or spacey, just angry, collecting his due. Perhaps that was the most sinister quality of Price's concoction—you didn't feel any different. As Luther said, you just . . . flipped. Almost instantly.

"I figured there was some high-end coke in here, but I'm not a pharmacist," said Luther as he snapped open a Buck knife from yet another pocket. He unscrewed one of the capsules and dumped it onto the glass, using the knife tip to browse the granules.

Art saw that the contents of this capsule were almost all black. The difference between this and the dosage he'd swallowed was like the contrast between a graphite sketch on white paper and scratchboard. Scratchboard was black; you made images on it with white lines. He could swallow one of these now, and become the guy who could rape Suzanne and leave her for dead, the guy who could shoot Bryan and think about frying his nipples with a blowtorch, the guy who could defeat all comers in the middle of this god-damned hurricane.

"It looks like ground pepper," Art said, heart thudding.

"Little more kick than that," Luther said with a grin. "It was a horror show, all right, with Price playing super-dad and feeding these to his flock and watching them flip. Didn't bother him no more than some wacko artist, picking colors for a painting—you know, one of them masterpieces that looks like throwup? But you know what? I never saw Price take one."

"That's when you decided to leave?"

"Well, the house coming apart had something to do with it, but yeah, the party was pretty much over for me."

"Excuse me for saying so, Luther, and tell me I'm out of line, but what does a guy like you owe a guy like Price, that he'd do that to you?"

"Wasn't like that. Price was my friend. Got me a high-end lawyer once when I needed it. Regular customer for, you know—" Luther mimicked a pistol with his thumb and forefinger. "I figured Price's little get-togethers are always good for new customers. Hell, I met you, didn't I?"

"But what about him doping you?"

"Wasn't like that, neither. I take shit or don't take shit of my own free will. I was just taste-tasting the latest. Decided I didn't like it. So, keep these if you want." Next to the sinister mound of black powder, four of the capsules were getting ready to roll off the table. Luther scooped them back into the bottle he'd brought and casually tossed them to Art, who caught the pitch one-handed. The house seemed to lurch again but it was an illusion; both men felt the press of moving air bulldozing against the exterior. Luther looked up toward heaven. "Damn."

"Did you really hit that woman?" Art felt like his own ventriloquist's dummy, his arm up his own ass, wiggling his jaw and making him say things to deter notice from all the aberrant things he'd done in the past few hours.

"Katha? Oh, man." Luther drained his coffee but his voice stayed parched. "She's this corporate ice princess from the city. Real standoffish. So naturally I come in looking like her worst nightmare. No business card, no lunch there."

"You weren't appropriate dating material?"

"Huh! You tell me." Luther presented himself as though the conclusion was obvious to anyone with a brain. "Till later last night, when she got a look at my gun, grabbed my crotch, and asked me to fuck her. With the gun. Never asked my name. She drops her clothes and wants me to put a rubber on my gun, wants the barrel up her ass with a round in the chamber and the trigger cocked."

"Jesus. She must have dropped one of Price's little party favors."

"Maybe. I didn't see her do it. But by the time I was butt-naked

205

with her trying to ride me like a horsey, I sure had, and she found herself on top of a different guy. You know what? I think Price had cameras in all them rooms upstairs. Why not? It'd be his style."

"Like, for blackmail?"

Luther shrugged. "For whatever. What are you going to do with whatsername, Susan, in there? She's part of this, too."

"I don't know. I don't even know if I know what she's like in reality."

"Yeah, but you banged her anyway, didn't you?"

Art's expression seemed to crack. He felt lame.

"My point," said Luther. "Man, you got any water? I'm dry as kindling."

Art desperately craved another beer, but forwent the urge. Blitz trotted back in, looking for an excuse for recess. The three of them went to the garage. While Blitz peed, humiliated at having an audience, the two men cleaned up whatever evidence of Bryan they could locate. A little Windex, some scouring powder, a squirt of lime dissolver to remove the smell. Art had some of that silicon-based abrasive for cleaning scuffs off the Jag while matching the paint tone. Luther poured some salt on blood spatters on the concrete floor and pulled most of it up. He frowned at an indistinct, stubborn stain and dribbled a dollop of motor oil on the spot, smearing it around, then mopping up. "This way, not even a police dog could sniff it out," he said, and Blitz wandered over to make sure.

Art stripped the tatters of duct tape from the metal frame, and wedged a brace against the ruptured portion of the garage door so it wouldn't blow open again. They swept up a pound or two of broken glass. The generator, hanging half out of its special compartment, was totaled; Bryan might as well have used a sledgehammer. The Jeep was bleeding transmission fluid onto the floor.

Luther returned Art's grin. They had beaten the return of the navy guys, whether they existed or not.

Blitz began to look toward the ceiling, sniffing air that had some sort of new message for him, and Luther put his hand out in a cautionary mode. *Freeze.*

Art pantomimed his response: *What?*

"Listen," Luther whispered, his eyes now tracking around identically to the dog's.

Art said *what?* again, his hands open, his breath barely exhaling the word. He heard himself do this. More importantly, Luther heard it, too.

"The storm," said Luther. "It's stopped."

● ● ● Art thought of Neil Armstrong, of spacewalks, of being the first human to set foot on Mars. That was how he felt when he stepped out his own front door, with Luther and Blitz handling the rearguard action.

The quiet was unnerving, an atmospheric presence that leaned against their eardrums with its lack of input, bringing tinnitus, the roar of silence, phantom ringing, aural anomalies. The gentler air now feeling them up was heavily ionized and tasted like electricity. Gray clouds peeled upward in the distance. The sense of moving air masses, far above them. The denizens of Atlantis must have experienced all these weird sensations just before they sank for good.

"Is that it?" said Luther, touching the back of his head and feeling static. "Holy shit—look at that!"

The air had regained enough lateral visibility for both men to clearly see the funnel cloud that was tearing things up downbeach. South, about where the Spilsbury house would be. It was hundreds of feet high, its scorpion tail tearing up the ground and anchoring the black dervish to the earth. The top of the funnel modulated as though hungry for more. All the way up its corrugated length, airborne debris was embedded in the loops and twists of its fury.

And the ocean was now more than halfway to the house. Fifty yards of the beach Art had been accustomed to seeing every day were underwater. The tip of the jetty was submerged, but the Sundial was still there, pointed at a forty-five-degree angle to the horizon. It had several feet to go before the lip of the dish tasted the ocean.

"Ten minutes ago the wind was a hundred and twenty miles per hour," said Art, unable to take his gaze off the tornado raping the shoreline just inside the half-mile mark from his home. "This is nuts."

Art looked straight up, and for five seconds imagined he could actually see the evening sky.

"Look at that thing," said Luther, equally transfixed by the funnel. "Bet there's people flying around inside it."

Maybe Price, thought Art. One could always hope.

"I can't tell if it's headed for us or away from us," said Luther. Blitz barked a couple of times but the tornado ignored him.

Art was holding his head. His sinuses had impacted at race-car speed. "What did he call it?"

"Who?"

"Willowmore. The navy guy. The eyewall. He said that if the eye of the storm passed south, it would . . . that tornado is inside the eyewall of the storm."

"We're in the eye of a hurricane?"

"Which is moving south, which means the other side of the eyewall is coming right at us from the north. The wind is going to change direction any minute now, and we'll get hit again." Behind them, in the direction of the jetty, the sky had assumed an ultraviolet hue. When Art saw the clouds moving, he thought of cream in coffee.

"How much time?" said Luther, just as a thunderstrike shook the ground. That was plenty for Blitz, who indicated that he would await them inside, thank you very much.

"I don't know!" Art shouted, frustrated at having no data, no hookups, no advisories, and no rescue. "We need to check the perimeter—around the house—superfast. That water could come another hundred yards or so inland. It's called storm surge—the storm combines with the high tide."

Luther did not want this duty, but was prepared to execute it. He was already three paces toward the yard where Art had done his shooting practice. The wooden fence was gone, airlifted away forever. "What am I looking for?!"

"Damage to the outer structure, pieces of the roof down, any debris, any weakness we might have to patch up." Art moved past the exterior wall of the guest room. "Hurry."

The two men could feel the Wind changing its mind, prickling their flesh. Tasting them.

Art met up with Luther near the huge aerodynamic stanchion that secured the beachward foundation. The exterior deck had buckled in the middle, but held, almost as if a passing dinosaur had decided not to trust it with his full weight. The air around them was darkening by the second, and the sea was marshaling for a fresh siege.

"Guess we batten down the hatches again," said Art.

"Did you vacuum?" said Luther.

Art's whole body needed to retreat to the house, but the question was so goofy it immobilized him. Had Luther just lost his mind, too? "Say what?"

Luther pointed downbeach, toward what was left of the ravaged Spilsbury house. "Because we've got company coming, and I don't need glasses."

Art followed Luther's direction. Several figures were visible in the haze and twilight, and it seemed obvious that they were going for broke, trying to reach Art's house before the leeward end of the eyewall got to them. The envelope of calm was rushing south, providing a window for their end run. At least one of them was wearing what looked like a zebra skin.

● ● ● Without a word, Luther worked the action on his gun to put a slug in the pipe, then dropped the magazine and slammed in a spare from the sleeves riveted to his shoulder holster. He was now racked hot, with a full house.

He slapped Art on the shoulder and pointed, indicating a retreat path. Another gesture to indicate they had not necessarily been seen. All nonverbal information Art could comprehend instantly. They pulled back, hugging the walls.

Art wanted to waste time gaping at the stragglers in the distance, not willing to believe his home was their target. He felt the same way whenever he saw a movie special effect that did not quite convince. What he was witnessing was unrealistic, improbable. He could waste even more time by protesting. *This can't be happening.* Or he could stop fretting over what was real and what was not, and deal with the story as it changed in front of him.

He made Luther pay attention to the cross bolts on the front door, pointing them out so Luther could see that they shot two up, two down, two on each side, in the manner of a vault lock. Off electrics, they could be seated manually by cranking a little wheel.

For emergency exits, the window shutters were designed to un-dog from inside; same deal.

Once he secured the front door, Art's eyes sought his own gun. The Heckler-Koch was still on the kitchen counter.

"Your alarms on a battery backup?" said Luther, all biz. He had his focus back.

"Yeah." Art double-checked the status panel anyway.

"Cameras?"

"Not as dependable without the generator," Art said. To demonstrate, he clicked on the monitor covering the front walk. The image was discernible—if you already knew what it was—and the lens suffered intermittent blur from the water blowing across it, leaving a shimmering and halated point of view. "How aliens from outer space see us." Art shrugged.

"Got any forty-five ammo?"

"That's affirmative." He knew it was in the gun safe, next to the racked Desert Eagle. Luther would snicker if Art produced a piece like that. It was a showoff gun, a bigass movie gun.

"Wait up. Not yet. All those shutters down?"

"Yeah. I think it was them that tried to get in before."

"And?"

"Held secure." That was something to be proud of.

"Okay. They might just try again and give up again. But just in case, you know, right?" Luther was ducking in and out of doorways, checking rooms.

"What are you looking for?"

"This hallway right here," said Luther, pointing. "Walls against walls. Layers. In case they have something mightier than pointed sticks, right?"

Smart, thought Art. In case they can penetrate one wall, but not two. The outsiders had access to a lot of windows, but the hallway gave Art and Luther the archer's advantage from the castle keep. His family was in that space, framed on the wall in safety—Lorelle, his parents, hers, some siblings, a shortform of a past life in pictures.

"Lemme see your piece," said Luther. Art handed him the Heckler-Koch from the counter. Luther sprang the mag and jacked the round in the chamber, checking the barrel. "Nice. I'd prefer the Mark 23, the civvie version of the Special Ops." He peered at the ejected bullet and thumbed it back into the clip, assuming a precious expression. "Don't you know that hollow points are *illegal* in the great state of California?" Luther shook his head and grinned. "Got anything with more beef?"

"Shotgun," said Art. "Twelve gauge."

"Save that for if they get in. Make sure it's loaded and get me those forty-fives now. Go, while we got time. And kill the lights in here. Save the outside ones for when we need them."

When Art had turned off the battery floods, he went back to the bedroom with his baton flashlight and a small, flickering candle in a votive holder, to check Suzanne and ensure she was still alive. Her position had not changed and her pulse was feeble.

"Hafta go to the bathroom," she said, bleary.

"Power's out," he said of the darkness.

He helped her up, leery of possibly broken bones, another checklist item he'd neglected to think of when it was important. He left the door partway open in case she toppled and dashed her brains out on the shower ledge. As he slotted seven rounds into the Benelli riot gun he heard the aerosol sound of pissing, a distinctly feminine noise, strangely intimate.

Here he was, ramming ammo into a shotgun, girding for an assault on his turf. His life had morphed into an action movie, and he was supposed to save her, or protect her, or something. His blood was high, and his nerves were singing, and he realized, with electroshock abruptness, that he *wanted* all this to happen. His life in the house after the loss of Lorelle had become a robotic succession of chores and expert denial. No matter how well he kept the place up, no matter what strides he made, Lorelle was never coming back, and he had been hanging on, waiting for ghosts to show up to take him backward in time, to what "used to be," when he had at least *thought* he was happy. That life had ceased to exist, years ago, and he had sunk into a living-dead simulacrum of living, boozing into a coma, holing up to refute the world beyond his driveway. And it had turned out that he could not keep the world away; now it had come looking for him.

Come ahead on, he thought, snapping the safety near the Benelli's pistol grip and leaning it against the wall, out of sight, when he heard the toilet flush. At least the waterlines were intact. He credited the specifications on his plumbing plan.

Inside his own head, he was straight, he was good, he was even a tiny smidge righteous. Except for the fact that his every new move made him a mad dog, in the outside world. He had kept Bryan's ball-bat, as a sort of caveman trophy. It was in the kitchen, leaning against the wall behind the fridge.

"What day is it?" said Suzanne as she allowed herself to be led back to bed.

"Saturday night. Suzanne, there might be some trouble outside. I want you to stay put in here no matter what you hear." He left the votive near his own bedside clock, to provide that one small point of light in the darkness about which he'd always read, but never genuinely appreciated.

" 'Kay." Her arm sought a pillow to hug as her head depressed another. She said, "Candle's romantic," and was out again.

Art brought the shotgun into the living room along with a box of shells for Luther's Hardballer—jacketed Hornady hollow points that could deliver nearly a thousand foot-pounds of velocity from the muzzle. He swore he could hear Luther mumbling to himself.

"Now, if the bad guys come round thataway, your job is to let us know, okay? That good for you? Okay, deal."

Luther was squatting down, elbows on thighs, as if for story-telling time. Art got into view just in time to see Blitz raise his paw for a shake, in the glow from a single candle affixed in wax to an ashtray on the coffee table.

"What the hell's going on here?" said Art, affecting a stricken grimace.

"The team's now three," said Luther. "We came to an arrangement. We made a deal. Right?" The dog lifted his head, tongue hanging out, panting in agreement.

"How'd you do that?"

"Easy. I have secret power." Luther held up the packet of jerky Art had bought at the Toot 'N Moo. It had Blitz's complete concentration as Luther moved it to and fro, hypnotist-style.

"Traitor," Art said to the dog. Who did not care. "Some watchdog. He's all show. If the bad guys get in here, he'll roll over."

"Will you roll over?" Luther said to Blitz. "Roll over!"

Blitz flopped and rolled. It was a disgusting display. Obviously his damned dog had been picking up some bad English . . . somewhere.

"How's the roof on this place?"

Art placed the shotgun on the counter. "I guess you could smash up the solar panel array and kick through, but you'd probably need tools, and I don't think anybody is going to climb on the roof in the middle of the storm. Hear that?"

Outside, the wind was torquing up again. The house creaked and groaned in accommodation as the candle hurled spooky shadows around.

214

"What about under? Any way to come up from under?"

Art shook his head. "They'll never find it." More credit to his design, thank you.

"You keep those big ole ears open or I'll tie 'em in a knot," said Luther to the dog, sealing his coercion with another shred of jerky, then chewing on some for himself. Blitz chose a post near the fireplace, at the window where the attackers had tried before, and plunked his butt down.

"That your family?" said Luther, of the pictures in the hallway.

"My wife died," Art said, and he tried to keep the saga short. The more he told the story, the better he was getting at making it concise. Just hit the high points. Emphasize the grief and loss. Season with adjectives to taste.

Luther took it in patiently, sipping bottled water, his gun holstered. "Once, in Seattle, I worked a surround crew—you know, bodyguarding? Some politician asshole. It was all slightly shady, but to make a hard target out of a soft one isn't necessarily a thing you can buy outta the Yellow Pages. They made us stealth into the city. I had to drive up in a VW bug with a disguise on. There was this lady on the squad, hard enough to job with a male crew, and I admired that right away, and she was easy to look at, too. And I asked her name and she said, 'I am Counselor Zero.' Shut me down in a heartbeat. Somebody took a shot at this clown we were guarding, and anybody could see it was a pro contract. We shared gunfire and nobody got killed. After that was twenty-four solid hours of doing the classic cover patterns, using decoys, all that shit. At the guy's hotel—he was booked into three different ones under three different names—we're above, below, and on each side. And this watch is amounting to nothing. I mentioned we were going to need high-capacity mags if ever the shooters figured out all our zigzags, right? Comes one A.M., there's a knock on my door and it's her, and she says, 'All this waiting is giving me a bitch of a headache.' I come on real cold and say, 'So?' and she grabs my head and kisses me, just like a fantasy. Man, that was some fucking kiss. Then she says, 'That's the only way I know of to get rid of the damned headaches, and by the way, you requested some magazines?' She's talking like some stewardess, right? And she hands over the hi-cap mags I'd mentioned, and acts like she's going to leave, and stops at the door and turns and says. 'Is there anything else you need, or would like to see?'

"So right away I'm thinking she's a mole, it's a trick, it's a fucking setup, but you know what? I did a radio check and everything was five-by; the relief crew was getting ready to stand us down. Mission accomplished. She was completely straight with me. Talk about falling in love. We were married like the way you talked about. For one night. It was that intense."

"What was her name?" said Art.

Luther leaned against the wall, watching the candleflame. "She never asked mine, and I never found out hers."

"Are you serious?"

"That's the way the biz goes. But she staked a claim to a place inside me, and not a day goes by that I don't think of her, always kindly, always with that little bit of regret that keeps that flame alive. Kind of like what you're doing."

"What about your little firefight?"

"It was in the papers the next day as a drive-by. Gangs." He snorted. "Sheeeit. People who watch the news don't see nothing."

Art looked around, trying to stay alert. "Nothing's happening."

"Relax," said Luther. "The waiting's the tough part."

The front door took a battering-ram hit, as though a caber had been slung into it by a crane. The impact shook the house. Yelling, from outside.

"Hit them floodlights," Luther said, keeping low, looking up.

Wham—the door was struck again. Whoever was out there sounded mightily pissed off. Simultaneously, another whoever began banging on the deck shutters near the dining-area door.

Luther was already on the move, pointing quickly. At his direction, Art took a position that allowed him to monitor both doors, front entry and garage. As Luther passed the kitchen he caught sight of the shotgun. "Is this hot?"

Art gave him a thumbs-up.

"Any way I can get out through the garage, catch that sucker from behind?"

Can-opening the door was out (too noisy), but if Art knew one thing well, it was the specs for his fortress. "There's a little window, ten feet back from the door along the front walk. It's shuttered. You ease open the shutter—quietly—and the exterior lights are in your favor. It's a perfect bushwhack. You can bag them from behind and drop the shutter before anybody notices."

"Good idea." Luther holstered his pistol and racked the debut round on the riot gun. "Here's a better idea." .

Art held firm as Blitz started barking, full tilt, doing his bit. An instant later the deck door was hit hard enough to partially break the glass behind the shutter. *Note: Next time, use Plexi in all seaward door glass as well as the windows.*

"Hold it," said Art.

"What is it?"

"If they had guns they'd be shooting them at the house by now. They don't sound like paragons of self-restraint."

"So?"

"Just hold off a second."

Luther treated himself to a spare deep breath, almost a sigh. Bad for the glands, to rocket-fuel himself for action and then do nothing. To fill the gap he said, "What's a paragon?"

Art looked comically taken aback. "Umm . . . a good example. Like an expert or a perfect expression."

Luther chewed on this for a beat. "Why didn't you just say they was all too squirrely not to shoot?"

"Right."

"Shit, man, nobody talks normal human anymore."

"Sorry."

"Stop apologizing. I don't need nobody watching my back who only has apologies to whip out."

"Right. Would you like to go shoot someone, so you'll get off my back?"

Luther grinned big and wide, pointing at Art. "You should see your face. Now, *that's* the face I need at my back."

The front door took another jarring hit. A nick-dent sprang across the inner facing for the first time.

"That gonna hold?" said Luther.

"Not if he hits it for half a goddamned hour."

"I'm gonna go around to that little window in the garage."

Another slam of wind silenced the activity outside for a moment. After a few more desultory (but no less startling) whacks and bangs from outside, the attack seemed to stop, or pause. Coffee break, perhaps.

"You're sweating like a steambath, man," Luther said. "Drink some water when you get a minute." Art was astonished by the guy's cool under fire.

The perspiration on Art's palms was hot and slick against the custom rubber Pachmayr grips on the Heckler-Koch. Luther probably thought Art was the world's biggest gun poseur. Expensive guns, fancy add-ons, target practice. All that roundy-round with Lorelle about morals versus ballistics. Luther had scratched the Bry-Guy outside with less deliberation than Art would have applied to scratching a fleabite. He envied Luther's attitude. It was practical, pragmatic, unstinting. Art realized that since Luther had pegged one intruder already, now Art was expected to ante up in an equal-share kind of blood bond. Art was transfixed near the kitchen, jerking at every sound, clutching one of his overpriced firearms, wondering if he would have to look in another person's eyes and shoot them. And, if Luther's tale held true, remember a stranger's face for the rest of his life. His pal Derek had said the same thing about the guy he supposedly shot.

Art's face grew warm and he knew he was blushing. What was next—panic farts?

The window shutter above the kitchen sink took a couple of test hits before Art heard another destructive sound, repeated banging, like metalwork, higher up. The outsiders were trying to take out the lights. Doing a good job of it, too, from the racket. The banks covering the north face of the house, from the corners, ceased to exist in a cascade of ruptured glass and broken sensors. Art knew the sounds.

If these were illusions, why not take fierce control of them? It did not matter what was real or what was not. This wasn't some abstract, theoretical situation in which he was locked and loaded, testy and nerve-racked. Very Western thinking, that, with rigid rules and structures. You should, he thought, access the head that inspires you to transform a shopping mall into a translucent glass cathedral. Apply your skill to your actual life. See what happens.

Another weighty thud, from the front door. Apparently the

assailant had given up tool use and was now running against the barrier. Or maybe Luther had taken the guy out. But Art had heard no roaring report of the shotgun, talking dirty.

Luther was back in the kitchen. "I can't get the little window crank-thing to work. Can't see to shoot."

Art motioned him over. Luther squatted close, for confab.

"How about we don't do any shooting at all?"

Luther gulped in surprise. "Say what?"

"How about," said Art, "we just open the door?"

Luther rocked back on his heels, then wiped his brow, then split another huge grin, brightening. "Now, *that* requires balls. I like it. We'd make a great comedy team, you and me. Do road pictures. Yep, I'm for it." He motioned toward the door. "You go low, I'll stay high and cover you. Your house, your rules."

Keeping the pistol right-handed, Art quietly pulled the big bolts on the door. Blitz was still barking.

Time sped up to fast-forward as Art yanked the door. It stuck on the first try. He put one foot against the frame and almost dislocated his shoulder hurling the door wide open, getting his gun up to eye level, shouting into the incoming storm so loudly that his throat hurt.

"Don't you fucking move, you piece of—!"

The person standing outside sprang so quickly, and was in Art's face so fast, that he seemed to scoot around real time. Art's gun went spinning across the floor and the next thing he knew, he was being swarmed by a mad savage painted up like a psychedelic Indian.

Who went limp on top of him when Luther reversed the shotgun and cracked him on the back of the head, a skillful, well-aimed, smart tap that negated all the incoming fury in an instant. He stepped over both of them to slam and relock the door.

"You got an ax stuck in your front door," Luther said as he

stepped over the two of them to resecure the entrance. Art fought not to black out.

● ● ● "Lookit this guy," said Luther, rolling over the prostrate form of the invader, who was, in fact, clad in a zebra skin. The front door had a frightening amount of exterior damage but was now resecured, the only clue on the inside face being the tiny impact blister Art had seen to appear on the otherwise smooth surface. The ax he and Luther had pried out of the door was the sort of thing woodsmen used to split rails, and Art had a pretty good estimate of where it had come from.

It's like those wild West serial adventures, Art thought. *Take out the leader and the whole tribe of savages backs off.* Apparently the other outsiders had given up, or gone to beat on the immutable monument of the radar dish, or blown out to sea. Who really knew?

The guy piled in the entryway like dropped laundry was definitely a man, definitely wearing no other clothing apart from neon-logoed running shoes, no socks. He was bald and still had fresh cuts healing on his head, which was newly and indifferently shaven. Black paste raccooned his eyes and his face was striped in red paint that looked queerly familiar. Braided thongs and elephant-hide wristlet. He was wearing a coyote skull on a piece of lamp cord tied around his neck. When Luther thumbed back the guy's eyelids, Art saw brown eyes and pupils contracted to saltshaker pinpricks like spatters of ink.

"This looks like ole Malcolm," Luther said, shaking his head.

"Spilsbury's," said Art, nearly simultaneously. He related the story of the break-in, downbeach, and the near calamity that had almost finished off his Jeep.

"Maybe he's pissed off you almost ran over him."

221

The feeling hit Art again, the gnawing constancy of being forced to pay for everything that happened to him. All at once.

Luther peered at the coyote skull (*alas, poor Yorick*), and stripped it away. "So he took all this stuff from that other house, that Pillsbury? Man, I don't know how they stayed standing in this shitstorm. That wind through the door, just now? Tried to peel my eyelids off."

"I think they had some high-octane encouragement," said Art. "Price's tiny time pills."

"Oh, yeah. Fuck. Not counting what other shit there was to suck up. They probably didn't even feel the cold."

Blitz had left his post near the windows to sniff the unmoving form of Malcolm (or whoever this really was), then did a patrol turn of the house, then resumed his original spot.

Art considered his home's latest uninvited guest. "He's not dead, is he?"

"Naw." Luther checked the pulse at the wrist and throat. "I think we should wake him up, though. Maybe tie him up, *then* wake him up."

"What about his buddies outside?"

"You hear 'em banging? I say we don't worry about them until we hear 'em banging. If they were still hanging around, all them windows in a row on your beach side are too good to resist."

Somehow, the authority in Art's realm had surreptitiously settled on Luther's shoulders. But he was right, and Art suspected that Price's idea of chemical recreation did not allow for a great deal of linear logic. Art and Luther had been smart, but they had been lucky, too. It might not occur to the marauders to come back for another try.

Luther reached over and smacked Art on the shoulder. "Hey. You here or not?"

"Yeah, yeah. I'm here." His entire body felt flushed and warm.

"Don't you fuckin go all girly on me now. We got him." Luther wiped away his own stress sweat. "Fuckin' *zebra*."

"It's not real," said Art. "Spilsbury's had a lot of decor in early Great White Hunter."

"So these dudes got too high and instituted their own back-to-nature movement, right here on the beach?"

"Maybe he can tell us. Somehow I don't think the story will really matter."

Luther rose, kneecaps cracking audibly, and checked the garage. "They sprung the damned door again."

Art stood up, shaking less now, his movements more controllable. "I'll see if I can get it to stay shut. Where's the dog?"

Luther shielded his eyes with his palm against the glare from the hallway emergency lights. "Looks like he's sleeping on duty. Near the window. Listen, you want me to bend that door back, y'know, give it a little more gorilla power?"

"No, take five while you've got it. I'll fix it."

"Your house. Fair enough." Luther cracked a plastic bottle of water from the deactivated fridge and began to chug it down.

It took fifteen seconds, give or take, for Art to work his way over to the triangular rent in the garage door. The whole thing would have to be replaced. The spit-and-baling-wire method was not even working, right now. This was the thought in his head when he heard the shotgun go off, inside the house.

For a fraction of a moment, it was louder than the storm.

Then, suddenly, it wasn't noisy *enough*.

Art sprang back into the house, skidding on the floor and seeing a hole in the kitchen wall the size of half a dinner plate, like a big bite edged with fresh blood. Luther was splayed atop the intruder—Malcolm?—his wide-legged fall dumping him half out of the kitchen.

Art thought of World War II movies, of guys throwing themselves on top of live grenades. Blitz was barking, braced, holding back, snarling wetly for added threat.

Luther emitted a horrible braying sound, that of an animal in the iron jaws of a trap, tearing loose one of its own limbs to get free. He lolled over and grabbed the hole in the wall, trying to upright himself, using just his upper-body leverage. The rest of him was not working. Art was still standing eight feet away with his mouth hanging open. The crotch of Luther's pants was shredded and oily with dark blood that had been inside of him, just a second ago.

"Mother *fucker*," he gasped. "Foxed me."

Malcolm (or whoever it turned out to be for real) had rolled, captured the Benelli, which had been left leaning against the foyer wall, and pulled the trigger once as Luther tried to stop him. Now the man in fake zebra hide was on his back, his face distended in a frozen wax scream, eyes bugged, wearing the last expression he would ever display. No breathing, no pulse, not anymore. Luther had managed to break his neck while most of his own left thigh was being vaporized by double-ought buckshot.

It no longer mattered who Malcolm really was.

Art tried to tend his new ally, but the white towels from the kitchen drawer turned sodden crimson too quickly.

"Ya can't put pressure," Luther said between clenched, shallow breaths. "I think that cocksucker got my artery down there. Shit!"

Art grabbed his phone, the response of a person who has finally acknowledged the situation has gotten out of hand. Nothing. Cellular, ditto. Emergency evacuation by the navy, no way.

"Suzanne!" Art screamed toward the back of the house. "Get your ass out here and help me!"

No movement from the bedroom.

Luther went *gauuuu* and wrenched upward in an excruciating spasm. "I can't feel my hands." He was sitting in an enormous pool of blood that Art could see spreading, even in the dark. He was shaking now, vibrating with shock trauma. "Art?"

"I'm right here." He yelled for Suzanne again. No good.

"It ain't working," said Luther. "I'm sorry." Now his teeth were outlined in blood.

"You did everything right. No apologies. I don't want anybody at my back that just has apologies to whip out."

Luther almost smiled at that, but could not force it past the pain, and his imminent system shutdown. "No, I mean . . . I'm sorry about Price. I never shoulda listened to his bullshit, played along, you know?"

"To hell with him," said Art. "What can I do?"

"Can't do nothin." He coughed up a phlegmy rattle from deep in his chest, unable to keep his head up. "This is gonna sound . . . stupid."

"Anything."

Luther was able to roll one eye to meet Art's gaze. "I want you to kiss me," he said. "Kiss me and send me on my way."

Another grenade, another shotgun blast, erupted inside Art's brain. Say *WHAT*?!

"Hurry. You ain't all that bad-lookin, y'know?"

Luther convulsed again, hard enough to lift his nerve-dead legs, then slap them down on the red-moist floor. Art was certain that was it. But Luther's eye still transfixed him.

It was probably very simple. Luther was delirious. Luther was gay. Luther was flashing back to his combat ladylove. What difference did it make, as he died?

Art tilted Luther's chin up and kissed him as gently as he could. He

225

caught Luther's final exhale into his own mouth. Dead man's breath. He was still holding his friend's hand when it no longer mattered.

Blitz was growling. The sound, ominously constant, gradually trickled through to Art's perception. Art blotted his forehead with his biceps. He felt a dot of Luther's blood on his lower lip. The stench of blood all around was palpable, sickening.

This is no time to be jealous, you dumb hairbag. Art tried to invent something reassuring and only a dry click issued from his throat. What was the command in German?

The dog came for Art at a charge, launching off the floor. All Art saw was a crowd of onrushing teeth.

His eyeblink of hesitation almost cost him his face. He caught Blitz on his forearm and felt the teeth nest deeply into his flesh. They teakettled backward into the kitchen.

No command in any language could deactivate Blitz.

The dog was all over Art like a gang of muggers, fast enough to score high marks on any K-9 test. Peculiar and interesting, yes, but not when Art was the attack dummy. He clopped Blitz on the snout hard enough to break the clamp of his jaws and get his chewed arm free. He tried to grab the dog by the ears. Blitz feinted and snapped, practically rabid, and tore another furrow along the heel of his master's right hand. There were no guns around; hell, there weren't even any blunt objects.

Art slung the dog around and fell back, putting both feet against Blitz's chest, the place where he most liked to be rubbed, in another life. He kicked and Blitz somersaulted backward into the garage through the still-open door. He banged against the grille of the Jeep, scrabbling for equilibrium, paws already accelerating on the concrete floor for another charge. Art slammed the door on Blitz's nose. The dog yelped and withdrew, leaving brackets of Art's blood on the frame as the door seated with a declarative click.

He slumped against the counter, leaning heavily on his thighs, panting. "Damn it, *dammit!*" His own fucking *dog.*

Reason kept his head from subdividing on the spot, like an amoeba. Luther had fed Blitz jerky. Luther had dissected the mystery pill on the living-room table. Blitz had sampled the powder, which no doubt had retained the tang of Luther's jerky-greased fingers. Blitz had Hyded out and become the perfect attack canine, payback for his shortcomings as a wannabe cop.

"You guys sure make a lot of *noise,*" said Suzanne, causing Art's heart to nearly catapult from his throat. Someone pulled the ejector-seat ring on his rib cage.

"Jesus christ, Suzanne, fuck!"

She was holding the votive candle and wearing an old, thick UCSB sweatshirt with fabric pills on the shoulders. "Jesus christ, yourself! You're all bloody. Is the war over? Did you win?"

Blitz was frothing and thudding against the door.

"It's bad," Art said, his lungs still trying to find air. How did you boil the evening's events down to a one-liner? *All hell broke loose. Shit happened. My life changed forever and ever.* "Don't walk out here." He gestured feebly. "Broken glass."

"Oh, I found shoes, I figured that." She pointed. Somewhere in the closet she'd unearthed Lorelle's old canvas deck shoes.

"Don't come out anyway."

"Don't be stupid, I mean, look at you."

The anger rose in him unbidden. He was pressed rudely against the fabric of his own sanity and could hear rips and tears widening. There was a corpse in the foyer, Luther was gone, and the air reeked of madness and death. The house was punctured, pierced, trashed, nearly powerless. His dog had gone insane.

"Suzanne, go back into the bedroom," he said, gutturally, eyes squeezed shut. He was on the verge of losing it, flipping out. Plus, he was hurt and bleeding. Now was not the time to try walking Suzanne's tightrope. "Do it now."

"You need help. Look at you."

True enough. But he did not think she would be eager to help him stack bodies in the garage. A persistent burn had settled into the corners of Art's eyes, damage that hurt when he blinked, and felt caustic, as though solvent had been rubbed into the tender flesh there. The candle in Suzanne's hand stung his eyes.

"What's wrong with the dog?" Blitz was barking, ragged and wild, behind the closed door two feet away.

Hot acid jetted into Art's throat from his stomach. He swallowed it back down, thirsty and depleted. "He got hurt. He's a little crazy. I had to lock him out."

"Come on in here and lie down, just for a moment. You look like death."

"Can't." It felt like the wall was the only thing holding him up as he spoke. The starch was leaching out of his bones.

"You've got to. Please?" She was still looking him up and down with the candle, assessing his damage.

"Can't." Disharmony furrowed his brow. "*Got to*—why?"

"I don't know," she said, turning the hand that held the candle to show him she was wearing her diver's watch, the one that it was so important to her not to lose track of earlier. "Because it's almost nine?"

That didn't make any sense.

"Come on," she said. "Don't make me force you."

That made even less sense. He looked at her, nude from the waist down, abused and hanging on like a castaway.

She smiled, face pulling up oddly on one side due to her shiner. Her other hand came into the small circle of light to reveal his own Beretta, semiauto, from the open gun safe, hammer back. "Daddy had guns," she said. The muzzle idled in his direction, not exactly a threat, not yet. "I made sure I grabbed this when all the commotion started."

"Put that away," he said, just annoyed. "Give it to me."

She shook her head, backing up a step in case he wanted to try a grab. "I said, it's nearly nine, so it's time for you to. Sit. Down."

He should have smacked away the pistol with the heel of his hand and grabbed Suzanne by the throat, but he had already missed the moment. They had Luther between them and she was stepping back from the tide of blood oozing toward her feet. The fine hairs on the back of Art's neck scared up. The rattler in his chest was looped into a defensive fallback position above his lungs, cornered, its weight making breathing a chore. He felt too depleted, as though a dump vent on his will had been tripped. Blitz was still schizzing out, oblivious to his own doggie damage. A nasty slipstream of wet, cold air was keening from another opening, somewhere yet unmanned, and seeking passage through the destroyed kitchen door, thence to chase back out into the night and return again. It was like the output of a big commercial freezer. He was cut and bitten, bleeding and beaten, and he could not summon his hand to strike.

Sometime during the calamitous events in the living room, she had calmly strolled to the safe, withdrawn the pistol, and thought, *Yeah, this'll do.* Then she waited, through gunfire and violence, destruction and death, maybe flinching a little if a shot was fired out where she could not monitor the action, but with a frightening detachment, no more afraid than if she had been tapping her foot for a pizza delivery.

He pushed off from the counter.

"Easy," she said, the gun now pointed at him, its threat now definitely meant for him. She pointed out features of the Beretta.

"See? Safety off. Hammer cocked. Round in the chamber. The bullet will come out here. I know how to use this thing; don't think I don't."

He tried to give her his calmest, most paternal manner . . . in order to fox her, snatch the gun, and maybe beat the shit out of her on general principles. "Suzanne, I know it's been a little nuts, but please don't point that at me." He combined the succor with his move forward, lying his ass off. "I have to turn the lights back on. This is no time for this."

She quickly placed the candle on a bureau near the door and used both hands to grip the gun. "Stay right there."

The snake was abuzz, calculating strike reach, brimming with venom and gushing new energy into his beleaguered body. He had to nail her now, before she got farther back, toward the bedroom.

"Ah, my favorite party favor." It was Price's voice, near the foyer.

Art tried to come around the dividing wall from the kitchen in a surprise move, but the fat prongs of a Viper stun baton caught him hard in the left tit. The hit was textbook, and Art began to dance.

● ● ● Once, Art had a dream in which he knew he was going to die. In the dream, he booked a lot of flights and did a sort of tour around the country, dropping in and thanking people for things they had done. He wore a good suit and was extremely pleasant. Some of the people he contacted were people he had not seen for years; decades, even. Ex-lovers, old friends, colleagues, enough of them for him to develop a lead line in his head: *Once, you did me a kindness, or once, I did you a wrong. Whether it was unearned or frivolous or just unthinking, I wanted to say I've never forgotten. And know that I've always been grateful; or know that I've always been sorry.* Some were shaded with regret, like a woman to whom he had been unaccountably cruel, because someone better had come along. Others boiled down to things and events which, taken baldly, were essentially quite simple—a friend who had gone way out on a limb on his behalf, for no reason or recompense apart from being a friend, because that's what friends were really for (as he had explained, patiently, to Art), or another who stayed on call when Art's emotions threatened to spiral into despair. Behind Art, in the past, was a network of unrelated people who had unselfishly helped him to perceive little glimpses of light as he groped through the dark room of his life. In his travels back along his own timeline, he made sure to be pleasant and caring, and did not lumber his sometimes surprised targets with any of his own baggage. He needed to acknowledge them. He shook hands, clasped shoulders, dispensed hugs, and dwelt on his own kindnesses or transgressions only insofar as they related to evening the score with those on his list. He wanted to bring the chart of his existence back to double zero, true north; to "square the box," as they said in his trade, and bring all spiritual debts to the equilateral. Equations and formulae were a kind of poetry he could now appreciate, and arriving at this ethos had run up a karmic tab that he was determined to settle. He found the people from his past happy to see him, even if they had not thought of him in years. Most of them said, *how sweet,* or *you didn't have to do that,* or *that was a long time ago, and I'm not that person anymore.* By and large they were people who had oth-erwise become peripheral: A hotelier who had defied company pol-icy to ensure his comfort. A lover who had loved him without any agenda whatsoever. A reviewer who had quietly championed his work. A waiter who always had a smile for him, and automatically whipped up his to-go coffee without a word of reminder. A woman who, quite against cliché, had lent her mobile phone and moral support to his car breakdown on a remote back road. People he did not know at all who had given up airline seats, or thrown in to help with an overload of boxes at some shipping dock, or fixed his persnickety computer with a bemused shake of the head and no charge. Art never forgot them, and needed them to know that. And with each person he saw, he felt a vast relief and release, cumulating to a buoyancy that lifted him to meet the universe. He felt the chains of the past drop away as old guilts were expunged and old debts repaid. In sum, he had not been as rotten a fucker as he thought himself daily. He maxed his plastic and murdered his accounts, and doled the money out freely, in person. He made time for those who had given him theirs. He returned love. And he did not elicit their sympathy, nor did he reveal anything about his impending demise.

And he suddenly realized what a grandiose, hollow gesture it all was. He was biasing the curve. He wanted all these people to note how swell he was after he had died. It was selfish and manipulative, naked in its intent. He had done everything in his life this way, and he hated it, but he could not stop.

Lorelle was not in the dream. Neither was Derek, or any of his new buddies from the party downbeach.

In the dream, Art kept on boarding the flights and making the whistle-stops. His people list was long and amorphous. He enjoyed the enclosed microcosm of travel. He kept going, because he realized that when he had finally made enough reparations, his plane would simply crash and that would be the end. Provided one could ever make enough reparations.

● ● ● ". . . no, she could even be touching me and there's no danger of getting zapped. It's called shock-back. Not like the movies."

Voices. Everything was black.

"It converts all your blood sugar into lactic acid in, like, a micro-second. You literally don't have any energy to make your muscles do anything, and the signals are all scrambled."

"How powerful is that thing?" Female voice, not Suzanne.

"Six hundred fifty thousand volts."

"Holy shit. That's Frankenstein time." Different female voice, still not Suzanne.

Price, talking: "Not really. It's kind of interesting. Voltage doesn't kill you. Amperage does. One amp will kill you. You take twenty-five thousand volts every time you shuffle your feet across a carpet and feel static."

"That blood sugar stuff doesn't make any sense. I mean, you don't knock someone out by lowering their blood sugar . . ." That was Suzanne, meaning Michelle—Price's lady—was probably one of the others. "Do you?"

"Sure you can, babe, if you max it out. What you do is dump all the energy into the muscles, at a pulse frequency that tells those muscles to do a shitload of work, all at once. The neuromuscular system is literally overwhelmed. Balance goes, muscle control goes, you get a car wreck's worth of confusion, disorientation, all without a bruise."

Flink. Someone lit a cigarette.

"What if he goes into cardiac arrest?"

Price again: "Can't happen."

The mystery female voice: "How come you don't have to haul your own generator around behind you?"

"Power source for this thing is a nine-volt battery."

"That's not for real." Michelle, now a 90 percent certainty.

"Absolutely. Nicad, pretty much like a wristwatch battery."

"Just another fabulous product of human development, right?" Michelle, *definitely.*

As definitive as the harsh slap to the cheek, jarring.

"Hey? You with us? Speak to me. Wake up. We're at your floor, ma'am. Strap-ons and linens. Hello? Come on, don't play this stupid game where you pretend to be asleep."

"People waking up from operations do that," said the third woman.

Price, impatient: "Oh, don't make me use the *name* anymore." Beat. "Okay . . . *Art!* Mail call!"

Art cracked his eyes open. Tear tracks ran back into his ears on both sides of his head, which felt stomped on. The wind screamed and moaned, making its haunted house noises, seemingly blowing right through his skull like a pitch pipe. Hot points of pain on his shins, his arms, his dog-bitten hand.

Suzanne snickered. "*You've* got mail!"

Several of Art's kerosene-fed lanterns were grouped on the uprights of the coffee table. The glass top was sprinkled all over the floor in a billion shards, each winking back pinpoints of wavering light. The figure seated on the couch across from Art was a black-hole silhouette of a person; indistinguishable. Another figure crossed behind it, arms folded in contemplation, but with an unmistakable air of supervision or command. That would be Price.

"Can you do anything about these lights?"

Art's head was pointed toward one of the double banks of emergency floods, now fired, but ebbing. He tried to say: *Those batteries have the half-life of a melting candy bar,* but nothing came out.

"Ask her does she have a special radio in here, or something?" Art knew this voice, but could not place it, nor could he see past his own desire to squint back toward sleep.

No good. Storm killed everything. Even a ham key won't work.

His body knew he was sitting on his own sofa—one of the trio of

234

them in the living room. The leather cushions sought to suck him in, to drown his body pore by pore.

"You've got blood all over your shirt, Suze."

"That's okay—it's not mine."

Art tried to push himself up but could not get his arms and legs to cooperate.

"You are currently enjoying the afterburn of a mild tranquilizer," said Price in a facetious tour-guide voice. "Your arms and legs will be like floppy toys for a while. It was either that or, you know, tie you up. The vomit you smell on your shirtfront is an unfortunate side effect. Once you puke, though, it's pretty mellow."

Art could see Price's face, leaning in closer, an Expressionist caricature of deep upthrown shadows, complexion etched by exposure to the elements outside. "You may notice the odd sensation of being naked. If you get feeling back in your extremities and don't tell us, well, it's like a psychological advantage. It was either that or tie you up in your own house. You're less likely to run around playing action heroine with your tits hanging out."

"Do we have to do this?" Michelle said. "I mean, do it *this* way? It's demeaning. It's not necessary." She was trying to damp-dry her hair with one of Art's towels.

"What the hell do you want?" Art managed. His tongue was framed in stomach bile.

"Well, our own little shindig got compromised, so we thought we'd bring the party to you. You don't mind, right?"

"Make yourself at home."

Price grinned, but it was a pasted-on expression; inappropriate, like the malevolent upturn on the mouth of a puff adder. "Most of our guests you already know. That's Michelle."

Michelle had a cut on her forehead. She kept trying to maneuver the towel around it. "Sorry about all this," she said.

"You already know Suzanne, ah, intimately, as they say."

Suzanne toasted him with a bottle of Dixie Double Hex from his own fridge.

"Bachelorette Number Three, that's Dina, the one who looks like that waterlogged pussycat from the Pepe Le Pew cartoons."

"Price," she said. "I don't see why we have to stay here. Why not do what Michelle says, leave well enough alone." Dina had been the one lighting the cigarette, with a Zippo, from the sound.

"Please shut the fuck up, Dina. You recall Dina, right, Art? You met her in the middle of one of her daily nervous breakdowns."

Art could not see her, but the lazy tracer arc of her cigarette coal told him she was near the kitchen, chain-smoking the night away.

"God, Dina, why don't you just get on your knees, stick your tongue as far out as it'll go, and see if you can find the asshole by touch . . . and get all that *stress* out of your system?" Suzanne's voice, from the hallway. "You need to relax."

"Fuck you," Dina returned.

"Ladies, ladies," said Price. "Please save it. Everybody gets to fuck anybody they want, so retract the damned claws, because it's boring. That's all the place settings. I'm afraid we're a couple of guys short of a perfectly balanced porn film."

"What happened to . . ." Art lost track. "Everybody?"

Price snorted. "Got lost in the storm, like nearly everybody else—at least, everybody that didn't get killed in *your* house."

"Guys came to evacuate them." Getting the words out was a labor.

"Hey, I am not responsible for what adults decide to do on their own," said Price. "The earlybirds chickened out to Half Moon Bay, like that was any safer. You were right about the windows in that dump. Boom, crash, panic, all gone. Last time I saw—hey, whatser-name, Shinya?" Price turned back to consult Michelle, who nodded.

"Little Shinya was headed for the group grope in the cabana; then the cabana blew away. I guess somewhere on the beach there's little clots of naked frozen people, still stuck together like dogs on the lawn. Get the hose."

Suzanne laughed, short, sharp, not a pleasant sound.

"You remember Solomon, the mad surfer? Apparently he disappeared into a monster wave. Can't you just see him, eating his own board while the big whitecap eats him? *Duuuuuuude!*"

To Art, they were still little more than talking heads, floating like errant moons in the lamp flicker and sickly backlight of the floods, which were dying prematurely and inexplicably. Some glitch; some faulty connection or short circuit was draining the batteries.

"Let's see, who else? Luther's fate, you know about. I'll miss that guy. Bryan's car is still outside—parts of it, anyway—and you should probably fill me in on what happened to *that* macho dick. I presume he paid for whatever he bought."

"Luther got him." Art found it difficult to clear his throat.

"That's poetic, I guess. Now, Malcolm, our aspiring novelist, he took an interesting turn. He fomented a mini-grass-roots movement to find his inner Neanderthal. Back to nature. You may recall him as the, uh, corpse in your foyer? You hit him with your Jeep?"

"He attacked me."

"Oh, poor baby. Self-defense, and all that, right?"

"She ran over Malcolm?" said Suzanne. "I missed that part."

"Civilized murderers always have the best excuses," said Price. "Malcolm's dead, either way. Exposure would've nailed him. But he lived long enough for his buddies to drag him back to base, where he told some interesting stories about you, roaming around in the middle of a storm. Not quite the modest tale of a quiet architect, is it? You seem to have undergone a few dramatic character shifts of your own."

"They were all high."

"Yep, and from the looks of it, his impromptu tribe came after you, looking for payback, which just happened to be Luther's big wet-dream fantasy come to life. Combat flashbacks, and all that. So did Luther take them all out, or did you help? I really need to know."

"They tried to get in." Art's fingertips were tingling, as though he had slept on them wrong.

"That house between yours and mine? It caught fire. Burned on the inside, then blew away on the outside. There's nothing left but the foundation and a lot of garbage. I think Malcolm and his neo-hunter-gatherers tried to barbecue some animal in the living room and it kind of went haywire."

"Tobias was one of those morons," said Dina, practically without moving her lips. She had moved closer to the circle of light. Art could see her hair drenched and plastered to her scalp by strong rain. Water was probably still running down her neck. That meant Art had not been unconscious for long.

Tobias was the MIA boyfriend of Shinya, the Asian girl Art now remembered. He could have been any one of the tribal contingent. The vandals had all been indistinguishable apart from the patterns on their fake animal skins.

"Maybe ole Tobias stuck that fireman's ax in the front door," said Price. "Actualizing his fantasy of being a get-it-done kind of guy. At least that's more interesting than his usual boring rant about spiking stocks on the internet. Jesus—most of these dudes watch too many guy movies, don't you think, dear?"

"They weren't in their right mind," said Art. "You gave them that drug."

Price was never less than cagey. "Now wait just a minute. I didn't force anybody to ingest anything. What you saw was all free will in flower."

"You didn't tell them what would happen."

"Hey, I'm not a mystic seer, okay? Someone wants to plug down mystery drugs at my party, they're responsible for their own actions."

"But you supplied the mystery drugs."

"True. But so what?"

What Art wanted to do was sleep for a week. What he did not want to do was play semantic Ping-Pong with Price, who might not get to his point before next New Year's. "I saw what your pills did to that guy Bryan. And Suzanne. And Dina. And even Luther. You're responsible for all this."

Price's voice went flat, into the threat register Art recalled from the party. "Reconsider the burdens of responsibility, before you start flinging accusations around."

"I don't know what you're talking about."

Price returned his gaze directly, eye to eye. "I mean, I want to know what kind of chemical cocktail *you're* on. I'd love to try it."

"I was minding my own business."

Price sat closer to Art and squeezed his bare knee, though Art could not yet feel anything down there. "You know why I doled out my free party mix? Because, my new friend, I wanted to see what all those losers would do. Just like I wanted to see what *you* would do, given a bit of shake-up."

"I don't even know you," said Art. His brain sloshed in his head and a wave of nausea nearly brought more vomit. The dimly lit room in front of him was oozing in and out of focus.

"What-hell, *you* don't even know you. You think this was easy, all of us girding our loins and calling you *sir*, pretending you're some widowed rich guy in his super-house, hermited in with his dog and his gun collection, boom-boom-boom every fucking day on the beach, no human contact except with ole Rocko at the

239

Toot 'N Moo. Like a lab rat just begging for a tumor shot. I couldn't resist you."

This was really beginning to pain Art's consciousness. "Price . . . I don't understand any of this."

Suzanne handed Price a Dixie Double Hex. Price took a long swig and smacked his lips. "Okay, let's try another angle: I've been in that house down the beach for, say, a month. House between—Spilsbury's—is all boarded up for the off-season, nobody home. But here's this person, this presence, *you* in all your wonderfulness, next to the jetty. We're your closest human contact, and we never see you, not even once by chance. You don't even stop by to make neighborly introductions, borrow a cup of whatever. That's cool; privacy is a precious thing. But now I'm curious. So I surveilled you out. Watched you do target practice, watched you walk your dog. It gave me an excuse to get all camouflaged and stealth around on the beach. Your routine is completely locked, man, and I began to wonder what you were up to, what you were about. So Michelle and I waited until you went to get supplies at the store, and came a little closer. First thing we see is a house crammed to the rafters with security, more than a goddamn bank. So I took a look at your mail, which comes like clockwork every Thursday. You scoop it up when you toddle out of your fortress to dump the trash, so I had a window of about an hour between the time the mail got to the box, versus when it got to you. Your bank statements indicate that you are comfortably well-off, but not rich; in fact, you're looking for some new gig. But it turns out your happy hubby didn't die. He left you."

"My wife," said Art. "Lorelle died. Two years ago."

"No way," said Price. "Your goddamned *husband* lives in New York City with some lady journalist—don't you read the fucking *letters?*"

It was suddenly impossible to draw breath. The storm was sucking the air right out of Art. Spots blossomed in his vision. He felt doped or delirious. The ferocity of the weather began to tilt the house, or maybe that was an illusion, too. His heart began to thud so hard in his chest that it constricted his throat. Somewhere between heartbeats, midnight came and went, unnoticed.

SUNDAY

Her extremities were beginning to announce pain. More pain, new pain; every time she opened her eyes it was to a revised catalog of hurts and wounds. She deduced she was still nude, still sitting on the sofa. Price had been right about psychologically unmanning her.

"Look in the mirror and tell me what you see." Price's voice again, hectoring.

Her captors were bulked out in sweaters and coats, holding forth from the only secure shelter for miles. It was almost logical . . . but for the body count and mayhem damage, let alone the sadistic craziness capering around in Price's head. At the height of the storm she would have opened her door to any of them. In fact, she had, to most of them, at least once already.

Price, she'd never invited inside.

" '*I know you are confused and hurt and angry and lost.*' " Price was reading the note from the bottle found on the beach. "*And it pains me,* yadda-yadda, et cetera, and so on . . . *the things I feel I should do, versus the things I know I must do.*" Sound of the page riffling. "Well, it's a little purple, but it sounds like it was from the heart."

"Just stop it." Michelle, speaking from somewhere else in the room. "This isn't funny anymore."

"Come on. Look in the mirror. Tell me what you see."

It was a trick, a joke, a dodge using one of the framed photos of Lorelle from the hallway.

Until the image of Lorelle blinked when the naked woman on the couch blinked, and felt her pain at the same time.

Your ballroom days are over, baby.

"So, *now* who's delusional?"

Supremely satisfied with himself, Price rose to stretch and take a turn around the room. En route he pulled the cigarette out of Dina's mouth, took a lordly puff, and stuck it back where he found it. "Man, I wish I could've been a fly on the wall when those navy yahoos showed up. That must've been choice. Bet you acted like a serial killer with a cellarful of half-eaten schoolkids."

"They assumed we were, you know, gay," said Suzanne. "You could see the expression on that Suthrin guy's face, like, yikes— *dykes!*"

"And all you really had up your bum at that moment was ole Bryan, the Bry-Guy. Shit, Lorelle, why didn't you just tell the story the way it was, as in: *This nutcase drove through my garage door and tried to tenderize me with a ballbat?*"

It was an excellent question, but forcing words out still felt to Lorelle as though a barbell was resting on her chest, bowing her ribs.

"Okay, I'll admit I dropped little Suze on you like a bomb," Price said. "And telling Luther to call you 'Art' and act like you were a guy was a bit of a stretch, but I also told him he would win a whole bunch of pretty guns when we were through. But the navy guys, they were a wild card. At least they brought us a sturdy vehicle."

Now she realized just how Price had evacked his coterie of intimates.

"So who needs the reality check here, Lorelle, I mean, *really?*"

The more important question was, what would have changed?

Probably nothing. Price still would have come, on time and on target. She would still be sitting here, a prisoner in her own house, doped on the sofa with cold air stinging her bare butt.

And tears coursing down her face. Luther had helped her, but he had been in on the lie. In the end all he wanted was a kiss as he died. So many people had been hurt. Price was a maker, one of those sinister malefactors who pulled you into his orbit and stirred the ingredients out of perversity, what the older writers once called a usurer. Lorelle hated people who seemed to have everything figured out. It made it that much tougher on everybody else in the world.

"You used everybody," she managed to say, almost choking.

"*Excuse-moi,*" said Price. "I'm not the one who told the navy guys Suzanne was my *wife.* And you just caught that fly and ran with it, didn't you? I'm the guy who wound her up and sent her out. *Oh, please, 'Art,' give a cute woman a safe harbor from all this madness* . . . Darling, I'm the only guy you can trust."

Suzanne did a sort of clumsy curtsy, smiling at Price. Lorelle thought of Suzanne pretending to be more disabled than she had been, feigning drugged sleep, popping black capsules and doing educated inventory on the contents of the gun safe while she and Luther tried to keep the savages from the battlements.

"Oh, get over yourself, Suzanne," Dina said from the bar, snubbing her smoke and instantly firing up a new one. She had to cup her hand to keep the drafts from snuffing the flame.

It was Price's idea, Suzanne had said, between acts. *Fucking with you. I said no, but . . . you can't say no to him.*

Echoes of their lovemaking scuffed her memory. Lorelle had become her own husband, then cheated on herself.

"What did you do to her?" she said.

"Our Suzanne?" Price wrapped an arm around her and she

244

● ● ●D A V I D   J.   S C H O W

rubbed against him like a cat. Her black eye, her split lip were still real. "I gave her what she wanted. I do that for practically everybody, haven't you noticed?" He kissed the bruised orbit of her eye, the edge of her mouth, demarcated in dried blood. "Suzanne wants to be an actress, more than anything, right, sweetie?"

She purred and squeezed his groin.

"Please, spare us," Dina said, blowing smoke with disgust.

"You see before you the classic actress-model dynamic in play here," said Price. "I could have picked Dina to throw at you, but that was dicier. I saved her for backup. When you didn't come on to her in the upstairs bedroom, back at the party, I knew I was dealing with—you should pardon the expression—a man of substance. Nobody else could have said no to Dina when she turns on the waterworks." Price scrunched his pitted face into an alarming parody of grief. "Sniff, sniff . . . am I *pretty?*"

"Shut up, Price." Dina was annoyed by the instant replay.

"So you're all like a traveling mime troupe," said Lorelle. "If I give you spare change, will you go away?"

Price lit up. "That's *funny!* Humor in the midst of travail. Honey, you're truly a special person. I mean that sincerely. Yep, we're all just mimes, walking against the wind. Tonight, especially."

"I want you to get out of my house," said Lorelle.

"Hey, action bulletin: You're not in charge anymore. You think you have the balls to force me, why, then point that mirror at your crotch. Besides, I haven't told you the best part yet." He was clearly reveling in his own schemata.

All the prep, her planning and hoarding, had come to nothing. Threat had strolled right into her fortress and put a gun to her head, if only figuratively. Real security was a social illusion, a nonverbal contract. If Luther's story was to be believed, he had watched a spectral assassin try to pluck a guy buried in more personal security

245

than Lorelle had ever imagined. Everything was just a matter of deception, the spin of the story told. Lorelle had been living her own lie until Price had come along to puncture it, like some obscene civil servant. People buried their pain in lies when they could not handle the truth. But people wanted to buy into fantasy; Lorelle had anted up when she'd first let Suzanne into the house, and believed *her* story.

"You saw all those people at the house," said Price. "Full up with their own hipness. So edge they could cut a turd into single servings like a Tootsie Roll, fresh from the sphincter."

"Gross," said Suzanne, scowling.

"Everybody wants to project the image of what they want to be. Nobody is happy being what they are. Except for you, the hermit up the beach. You were so fresh and pure, compared to all the other basket cases, that I couldn't stop thinking about you. I had to rattle your cage, this neat bubble you've sealed yourself into. Because messing with the entry-level humans at the party was totally predictable; bound to get dull. Look at you now. This is all pretty thrilling, right? Sex, drugs, adventure, risk. What was all your target practice for, if you never wondered what you'd do in a crisis? I'm your fucking angel, lady. You're my masterpiece. Are you excited?"

"Have to use the bathroom," Lorelle said.

"I think I have to throw up," Dina added, by way of critique on Price's speechifying.

"How's the can?" Price asked Suzanne.

"Clean. I scoped it out before you got here."

"Yeah, but a lot's happened since then, and I want to make sure a stray firearm didn't find its way under the washcloths." Price folded his arms.

"I bagged all the bullets in a pillowcase," said Suzanne. "Guns, too. The gun safe is empty."

246

"Good girl. What about Luther's piece?"

"Got it. Accounted for."

"Suze? Were the guns in the safe loaded?"

"Not anymore," she returned. "I cleaned them out, clips and chambers. Luther's, too." Daddy had apparently taught little Suzanne quite a lot about firearms.

Price *tch*'ed at Lorelle. "*All* loaded? Anybody that didn't know you better might think that was a touch paranoid."

Lorelle's eyes tried to see into the dark corners of the room. *They hadn't mentioned the shotgun.*

"What about weapons at Spilsbury's?" said Michelle.

Price shook his head. "Just crap they used to make spears and shit out of. Curtain rods and bamboo poles and shit."

The Benelli riot gun had to have a round or two left, but where was it hiding? It had hit the floor and skidded away in the dark when Luther died. She tried to calculate possible trajectories and realized she was most likely sitting right on top of it. If they hadn't found it, it had to be under the middle sofa of the three-group.

The house heaved again, holding itself down against the storm and the force of the moving masses of air trying to tear it free of the earth. Price whistled in awe.

"So tell me about Malcolm, dear. How did that go down?"

Lorelle just returned Price's glare, dully. How was she supposed to casually check beneath the sofa for the shotgun?

"You know—Malcolm. Shaved his head, wearing a little skull he liberated? I can drag his carcass back in here if you need reminding."

"He was on the road home."

"Managed to mess up your Jeep, too, from the story his little tribal brothers told. They dragged him in out of the storm, played spy-spy on you while you were stalking around downstairs at that house that isn't there, much, anymore."

A thick, deadly pain was sliding around the occipital cup of Lorelle's skull like quick-dry cement, petrifying her neck muscles. It was as though Art's imagined rattlesnake had slithered up into her head to coil around her brain, suffocating it with constriction, holding its venom in reserve for later.

"I didn't know it was Malcolm," said Lorelle. "I didn't know Malcolm."

"Sure you did," said Price. "You were standing in his hair in my bathroom. You need to know a little more about some of the people you've helped to kill." He moved closer and hunkered down. "Now, Malcolm made a lot of noise about writing the great American punk chronicle, but never managed to produce any copy. In other words, a total amateur, one of those, you know"—Price affected the *duhh* manner of a chimp fathoming a calculator, tapping his temple—"those *I've got this swell idea* guys, the guys that never seem to get the swell idea out of their creative little heads? What Malcolm actually was, was the world's longest-running temp worker. His whole life was made of leftovers, so he invented this fantasy about being a brilliant writer the world just wasn't cool enough to understand, which is a lot more romantic and interesting, and probably got him laid once in a while. But he wasn't up to it. Never was. Total amateur."

Malcolm's story was another unfinished book, like the novel Lorelle had begun decanting from her own head, the fragment that still resided in a box in the back room, never to be completed.

"Tobias was his war chief, in the New World Order on this here beach. When Malcolm went into your house, but didn't come out, I think Tobias nominated himself as tribal leader, and after a bit of squabbling and a few head wounds, he probably took charge. Quite different from loitering at Starbucks with a laptop, hoping someone will ask what you're doing. Proactive, as they say. Tobias—I think he

248

wore the fake leopard skin—was an account yuppie for a firm called Bryanstone Partners. They'll have to call for a temp, come Monday. Too bad Malcolm's not available. There was another one, too, called Ricou, I think. He was in a band called Pinch, which will most likely be needing a new drummer after tonight."

"I didn't have anything to do with the others. I didn't even see them." She still perceived things through a turbid fog, and her head ached with the slightest nudge. It was exactly like the epic hangovers she had felt, during the time when she drank to anesthetize memory.

"Where is the dog?" She felt low, having not thought of Blitz, who might be dead by now. Another victim of Price's "truths."

"Still in the garage," said Price. "We opened that door a crack and it filled up with snarly doggy, all snapping and fangs, so we figured on keeping that one shut and going for Door Number Two. That dog was literally foaming at the mouth."

"Don't hurt him."

Price looked offended. "That would be low, to hurt an animal, man. Unless it tried to bite you. Which, I suppose, explains Malcolm."

"He tried to get in." The surging pain was melding with the amoebic light plus whatever drugs Price had put into her, all oozing toward a critical mass that felt like thumbs pressed hard against her eyeballs. It was tough to force whole sentences out.

"All they had to do was knock, right? See, they were no longer civilized. We are, and we walked right in. Door was open for us, in fact. There's a lesson there, somewhere." Price shrugged. "No matter. Before Malcolm and his crew came your way, they decided to storm the cabana," said Price. "Just burst in and started raping and pillaging. Very Visigoth, all hard-ons and bloodlust. So you got this fuck-chamber full of inked-and-pierced ne'er-do-wells, all lolling through their idea of Extreme Sex . . . and they screamed and ran away into the storm like kindergartners, the ones that weren't tied or cuffed, anyway. God, I wish I could have seen their faces."

"I thought you said the cabana blew away."

"It did, shortly after that. By then I think Malcolm's crew had repaired to the house with the trophies, probably to plot their renewed assault on you."

She was defenseless, handicapped and half-frozen, but she still could not get the missing shotgun out of her mind. "I'm cold."

"Christ, Price, give the girl a fucking break, will you?" Michelle was the only woman in the room who would deign to give a direct order to the like of Price. She had brought Lorelle's house clothes out of the bedroom, and dropped them on the sofa next to her. "Like I said, I'm sorry," she told Lorelle. "I didn't want this. We'll be out of your hair soon, I promise."

Price swigged, let it happen without comment.

Then he resumed a seat that kept him center stage in Lorelle's field of view, but with a light behind him. It was a trick executives used during meetings: sit against a big window flooded in daylight, so the illuminated subject—you—has to address a vague silhouette behind a desk. Lorelle thought of office design, of the intimidation of corporate feng shui. Execs always sat in hard, straight chairs while inviting you to take a place on a sofa—and you sank into quicksand cushions while the person in charge kept his head higher than yours, forcing you to look up.

Price toyed with his stun baton. It looked like a nasty black sex device. "All weekend, you know what I haven't had? An intelligent conversation. You'll excuse me for making the most of this little drama, won't you, Lorelle? Like the lady says, we're sorry."

"Then why the fuck are we still here, when we've got a god-damned tank out there to drive away in?" Dina slammed her empty beer bottle down on the kitchen counter; it made a distressing glass *clink,* but did not fracture.

"We wait till there's no storm," said Price. "Don't act stupid—it hurts the perceived image of all models, you know. There's no place else to hole up, right now. At least, no place with amenities." He snapped his fingers and extended an open hand in her direction; Dina placed a fresh beer in his grasp and he took a long pull, spelling himself. "Cigarette me, love." She lit one of her slender 100s and delivered it after one puff.

"Then how long is this going to take?" she said, just a bit petulantly. She probably had a hair appointment she did not want canceled on account of catastrophe and killing.

"Would you rather sit in that tank, D, out in the storm, or enjoy Lorelle's accoutrements?" said Price. "You should spend more time appreciating this place. It was Art's Sistine Chapel ceiling . . . and it's roomier than the Humvee."

Mention of Art's name still had the power to physically coldcock Lorelle, to freeze her in place like a house pet subsumed in terror. Like a limping bunny in the meadow. Art. Art. People had called her that, played along. Others had called her that, not knowing or caring, in a whatever-world where gender was no longer assigned to many names.

Price had said "conversation," but he seemed more focused on monologue. "Over and over, the question that recurs to you is *why?*" He had obviously prepared for this topic. "And because I respect you, I'll let you in on a little secret. I've always wanted to achieve a delusional state as pure as yours. An altered reality that is unforced, and comes with its own checks and balances. It becomes the dominant urge, and so rearranges the world around it until everything suits. It's survival-oriented in an intellectual sense—it saves your mind from going off the cliff. But you can't control every-

251

thing, and you can't keep the world out. I'm the goddamned world and look how easily I just walked in."

Price's voice was becoming an insectile drone in Lorelle's pained head. "Okay, Price," she said. "You win. You got me. You've flayed my psyche down to a raw nub. What's next? When is this idiotic game over?"

When Price replied, "I don't know," Lorelle got a scary glimpse of the man's devilishly contracted pupils. Price was redlining. "I'd hoped that maybe I could retreat into *your* little world of make-believe."

"That's not the only thing you wish you were inside," said Michelle.

Price grabbed his chest, near his heart. "Owww, stung by the matriarchy! You want to play balls versus slots?"

"You'd lose."

"Not necessarily. I may be outnumbered but I'm not outclassed. And I've still got the dog on my side, gender-wise. Come to think of it, I've got Lorelle, too." Before Lorelle could protest, he turned back to her. "Tell me: Did you go through all that egregiously moony shit about not being able to survive being torn apart? Typical bifurcated rationalization. Whatever you can't bear, you assign to your, ahem, better half. Now you can accomplish murder without guilt. Now you are suited and predisposed to violent action. Now you can get away with it . . . you just can't be sure of which person you are. Overall, I wouldn't worry; you've got the important stuff locked."

Suzanne had repaired to the master bathroom, presumably to work some cosmetic miracle. Dina had probably taken up a post on the bed, readying another dose of self-hatred. Michelle tended to stay in Price's vicinity, sometimes as far away as the back of the kitchen, sometimes as just a ghostly presence behind the sofa, always in nervous motion like an errant satellite.

"What happened to Luther?" said Lorelle.

"We cleaned up while you were sleeping," said Price. "You're a gal who likes things neat. If this storm *ever* stops, they'll be scooping bodies out of the beach for a week."

Translation: No one was accountable.

Suzanne headed for the kitchen to advantage food or drink or both, pausing long enough to say, "Bathroom's clear. You still need to pee?"

Codicil: Price was going to make Lorelle wriggle a bit before allowing her to relieve herself in that bathroom.

"Tell me something," said Price. "What did you think of those people you saw at the party?"

"All lost, or all losers," she said. "Makes me wonder why you'd have anything to do with them; what they could possibly offer someone like you."

Price grinned, all snaky. "You're being way too kind. Most of those dazzled idiots had nothing to offer me except closure. I'd except Luther, and Michelle. But you smelled the talent of the room. Most of them were the sort of arrested adolescents who are still looking for a free ride at twenty-five. Beautiful people who are only beautiful when they're on a junk nod. So they stick holes in themselves and ink up their flesh like a rest-room wall, and bead until they look like iguanas, and when that stops exciting their dead nerves and deader emotions, they go back to jamming shit inside themselves, because the biggest thing they fear isn't the storm, or loss of love, or their own shallowness—it's the fear they might actually make it to age thirty or forty or fifty, and realize they've still got a fucking life-size squirrel tattooed on the back of their head. Like you said: lost and losers. Talk about your self-renewing state of denial. Better they should perish in a storm, an act of God if you will, than in the ignominious way most of them will burn out anyway."

"You're saying all those people were junkies?" said Lorelle. "That doesn't seem possible."

"Yeah, I know, to look at them you'd think otherwise. If they weren't humping one kind of dope, it was another. Crack, black tar, yayo, speed, diet pills, M&M's, money—what's the difference? Goddammit, I hate junkies. They waste my oxygen and their bodies are so polluted they don't even make good fertilizer. They were all losers, and I felt the urge to jettison them. Hence, closure. Before you throw something away, you always check one last time to see if the item has any residual worth. Voilà, party time."

"So you solved this big problem by giving them *more* drugs?" Lorelle tried to will her legs to cross and got one to twitch, bonelessly. That jive about a fifteen-minute recovery period from a stun gun was obviously sell-copy from some brochure.

"I made them honest," said Price, leaning forward so Lorelle could see his eyes in the wavering lamplight. "A lot of them, for the first time ever."

"You just . . . threw them all away."

"Very empowering. You should learn that lesson, my dear, about trash. Garbage. The things you throw away." In the absence of an ashtray, Price flicked his ashes on the floor. Drafts caught most and swirled them.

"I couldn't do that to somebody I really cared about," said Lorelle.

Price snorted. "Neither could I, love.

"Once, I was working on this piece," he went on. "Call it a story. There were all these pages. It just kind of poured out of me onto paper like I was channeling it. And I started thinking it was important enough to type up. So I typed from the pages, adding stuff as I went, changing stuff, deleting stuff; I'm sure you know how it goes."

And Lorelle did. Becoming Art had mandated the development of some sort of design aesthetic, if for no better reason than it would make her story more convincing.

"As drafts came and went, the notes got used and went into the trash with all the other spent paper. The trash went into a Dumpster out back of this place I had in Walnut Creek. Well, come trash day, I cut across my alley and what do I see but my pages, my notes, dead drafts, all spread up and down the street like lost homework for anybody to just pick up. It wasn't finished, it wasn't ready, it wasn't right that anybody should see that stuff that way. After that, I shredded everything. Burned the shreddings. Do you know how many people just *throw away* their junk mail? You might as well print up flyers with your credit info, your Social, all your numbers, and just hand it out on the street. More to the point, Ms. Lorelle Latimer, you should really be more careful about what you dump in your trash can."

● ● ● The Thursday ritual: Collect the mail shipped in from the nice Japanese lady in San Francisco. Sort it at the trash bin and jettison most of the junk.

Anybody with half a brain could outfox the locks on the mailbox, the trash bins.

Derek, Art's visiting best friend of three days prior, forever ago, probably would have liked the Lorelle backstory better if it had been more sordid. Playing the death card was an expeditious way to keep people—everyone—from asking too many of the questions that hurt even now. Questions about how you failed, or how you lost, or why.

Denial was something failures, and losers, indulged in every waking moment.

One morning she rolled over and said, "I think we need to see other people," Derek had said. *She hung around most of the day but it was clear all she wanted to do was run.*

Had Lorelle retrofitted her personal disaster to come out of Derek's possibly-imaginary mouth, with the proper degree of flamboyance added?

The only thing Art had *not* left behind was a lame note. Too soap operatic. He left his clothes, his bathroom stuff, his family pictures, his plans and drawings and sketches, all ahang, with no end to their story, either. Whenever Lorelle thought about all the particles of Art still lingering in the house—skin flakes, strands of hair behind the sideboard, molecules—she tended to crack, and cry.

He had strolled out of her life like someone leaving a dull movie before the credit roll.

Lorelle had never actuated the divorce process. The waivers would need Art's signature, and thus, painful contact; the no-fault statements she had typed up were entombed in a file in the office deceptively labeled FINANCE. Given the choice between gangrene and amputation, most sane people opt for slow decay, buying time on credit, hoping some external event will relieve them of the burden of responsibility. You had to suffer the slow rot, the stench of your own parts betraying you, to learn the value of the quicker alternative. Most people did not learn, or resisted the lesson anyway.

Derek, again: *Her whole life had been smash-and-grab, chase-and-run, trade on her looks, slip through the cracks, and as soon as she stabilized and got a tiny bit of security, of permanence, I think it scared the shit out of her.*

Lorelle had set about finalizing the herculean task of their dream house like a woman on a quest. The house was an achievement, bedrock in an impermanent world. It would have left Art free to do whatever he wanted, and that freedom had become a cage to him. Cages require escape, and Art had eventually discovered another way out. According to a tilt on their original plan, he found other things to do, new things.

Back to one, as Derek might have said.

True, that maybe love *was* based on banal things. Romance was the attraction. Magnetism yields magic. With the attraction satiated, the romance, the pull, was bound to diffuse a bit, since its job was done. It got replaced by other important things, more reliable things. But people don't permit you to get under their skin and root around through what you find, if you're going to reject them.

Art had been so angry that many of his newer designs had been lumbered, misunderstood, or rejected, by an outside world, which wanted things simplistically easy and unimaginative. Which, in turn, was a rejection of his whole life, from which Lorelle could not rescue him. Art, who had never done violence to a person other than himself, extracted himself. It had been like pulling away the fundamental support in a house. Sometime in the middle of the night, it all just caves in at once.

Lorelle stayed, as though manning an outpost. She drank and drugged, nearly flushing her life. The only way up out of the pit was to make that Lorelle dead. In her head, the murder was easy. Bricking up the crypt she had built for herself was even easier. Easier still, to commence memorializing her in the most glowing terms possible, as the guy who would know. Art was very creative. He had trophies to prove it.

Somewhere along the line, the house had become her cage, too. Her existence, and Art's, had become one of theoretical toughness. But all the prep and armor on Earth cannot save you when a person decides to leave you behind.

Normal people did this every day. Normal people wanted others to think the best of them. You played to your strengths. If you were good at it, you could write your own version of history.

You told stories.

● ● ● Sitting on the toilet like an invalid, Lorelle forced a few drops of urine that smelled vile, loaded with poisons decanted from her system. The door was cracked. If her captor, and his complicitors, thought she was moving her bowels, they might not watch her so avidly.

Luther's vial of Price's special all-black capsules was on the rack above the hand towels, feigning complete innocence, hiding behind a pharmacy label for sinus medication. Lorelle watched them and thought: The solution to my problem is right at hand.

Pop one or two of those babies and she would Hyde out, become reckless again, heedless of personal safety, blind to risk, coldly uncaring, and ruthless enough to engage these damned predators on their own emotional terms. The pills would make her more like them; they could swivel the advantage, and it would be ironic indeed to turn Price's own chemicals against him. The Bry-Guy had certainly learned a rude lesson about payback. Under the influence of the drug, Lorelle had screamed in his face, bashed him about, hurt him even more when he was tied up and helpless . . . and had done it all without hesitation or misgivings. Price wanted to wind up Lorelle, to see what she would do. Well, she thought, why not show the son of a bitch for real? The pills were the edge she needed, and the prompt to act. Swallow them, and you donned cape and boots and became capable of super-deeds.

Lorelle made her decision.

She stood up, wobbly but under her own power, and flushed the toilet, ignoring the pills. Dina and Michelle marched her back into the living room, slinging an arm each.

"Where's your fearless leader?" Lorelle said, trying to peer beneath the sofa as she was eased down, still seeing nothing.

"He's back in the Blue Room giving Suzanne her reward," Dina said.

Lorelle immediately sought Michelle's expression, her reaction to this. Michelle refused to be read.

"You don't completely understand about Price," Michelle said, weighing her words as though testing them for her own reasons. "Once he noticed you, learned about you, you became a part of him whether you wanted to or not."

Lorelle let her next words go just as carefully, honing for impact, intending to goad for reaction. "So, he's like a pimp, then?"

Dina actually cut loose a monosyllabic laugh.

Michelle just smiled. "Or a God complex. You can't make me angry at him. He saved my life. He just saved yours, tonight, although I'm sure you don't see it that way."

Lorelle tried to even her breathing. Appear to settle in for another story. Buy time to marshal the returning ability in her limbs.

"I met him in New York," said Michelle. "Art, I mean."

Lorelle realized she was sitting in her own home less than a foot away from the woman for whom her husband had walked out the door. Their shiny, almost unbreachable, stainless-steel front door. The whole west face of the house seemed to give a couple of inches as it was slammed. A stray huff of chilly air extinguished the candle someone had added to the remains of the coffee table; its flame jerked hard left as though slapped.

Memories of the party (only yesterday?) flooded back in a blast wave. Michelle saying *So relax and tell me a little about yourself,* when she already knew. Saying, *It's nice to get a look at you at last, strange as that may sound.* Now Lorelle knew what she had meant. Saying, *I'm not attracted to you in THAT way, at least not yet. More of a kindred spirit thing. We have a lot in common.*

Lorelle's eyes had gone wide, white, bright with new tears. Her heart felt like a chunk of rust.

"He really put you on a pedestal," Michelle said, in the here and now. "By his own reckoning, he could never do better than you. He was satisfied and you weren't. So you had an affair with his closest friend."

The swashbuckling Derek had never come to the house. Not then, not more recently. That had been their ground rule: never in the house.

"Art met me." Michelle shrugged. "Then I met Price, because Art couldn't let go of you. He really did love you, not that that's something anyone values anymore. Everybody ignores love in favor of focusing on Doing Better."

Derek's gritty tale—about grabbing gun in hand and duly unplugging his own rival—was a fiction. In it, Lorelle recognized elements of her own wish fulfillment, the staircase wit of wanting to do something branding-iron hot and deliciously appropriate, too late.

"From what Price gathered, Art tried to contact you and you tossed his first letter into the ocean, a separate bottle for each page. He could have tried a suicide note, one of those cry-for-help things, but knew you wouldn't rise to that. He could have just slipped into a black hole, changed his identity, but he didn't. You knew what was best for him. You spoke when people called, and Art was covered. Since he didn't care about erasing himself, you took his life. Literally. You took his life along with the house and the dog. But he *left* that gap, for you to fill."

Art had been inside this woman, more recently than Lorelle.

Today, Art was off happily penetrating some lady journalist, as Price had divulged.

The world could not collapse any further. It had hit rock bottom and was tasting Jurassic sediment.

At the party, Lorelle had asked, *But, Michelle, if it's on purpose, doesn't it all seem a bit cruel?* And Michelle had said, *sometimes, yes, I suppose.*

There seemed to be a tennis ball blocking Lorelle's throat. "I need to check on Blitz. He's hurt."

"Sorry, hon, we're not opening that door."

"Can I at least have some water?"

Dina rousted up another bottle in the kitchen and put it in Lorelle's hand, already open. She also had a Dixie Double Hex with the bottle cap still on. Derek would have said, *Never trust a beer that unscrews.* She did not open it. She held it by the long neck and swung it right into Michelle's head, the heel of glass hitting next door to her left eye. Lorelle could hear Michelle's neckbones crack as her face (and expression of total surprise) snapped to starboard for a close-up. Michelle fell across Lorelle's lap, still conscious, until Dina bonked her again on the back of the skull, hard enough to make her still-damp hair jump.

"That's enough of *that,*" Dina said, having not uttered a syllable during Michelle's entire discourse. She took the church key she had held in her other hand all along and opened her beer. It foamed over but she drew a long swallow anyway.

Drinking the beer helped allay Lorelle's unavoidable thought that perhaps she was next for a bludgeoning. Michelle was facedown in her lap. It was highly unlikely that Dina was going to suggest building a campfire and singing songs.

"We don't have much time," she said. "Can you move?"

Lorelle held one arm straight one and flexed her fingers. Then she hoisted the inert Michelle away to hang limply, half off the couch, terrible for the posture. One raven eye was slitted and gleaming in the lamplight but she was not seeing anything. They waited until they were sure they could see her breathing, faintly.

Lorelle rummaged around beneath the sofa. Sure enough, the shotgun was there. When she held it up, Dina nodded.

"I'll be right back," Dina said, and headed for the bedroom.

● ● ● "Blitz!"

The dog's nose was instantly in her face, slurping. Blitz's bloodied breath was worse than maggoty pork, but his doggie contrition caused an ache in Lorelle that nearly brought another downpour of tears.

All she could hear from the bedroom was a yelp of surprise, and a lower, more basso protest from Price, words she could not interpret. Outside, the Wind insisted on taking them all away, jolting the barricades of the house and rendering all other sounds secondary, adulterated. Dina did not reemerge right away, and Lorelle thought, *trap.*

Another trick out of Price's sorcery bag was coming, surely, to take her between the eyes.

Lorelle held fast in the kitchen, low against the counter, shotgun ready, one arm wrapped around Blitz. "I'm not letting you go, buddy." Michelle remained non compos mentis in the living room.

Behind the fast fright boiling in her veins, which threatened to begin shaking her uncontrollably, was a jolly elf who opined that a nap would be a really grand idea right about now. Or a nice downward swoon into oblivion, like a lady of breeding in a Victorian potboiler. But Art's rattler was still alive in her chest. *Don't pass out,* it nagged. *You've spent too much time sleeping. Avoiding. Dreaming. You've used up your allotment. You can't dodge any more.*

It got ridiculous, this waiting.

"Dina?" Her voice stayed small, and she pushed to make it bigger. "Dina, you coming out? Because if you're not—"

Dina responded from the bedroom door. "It's okay, just a minute."

"That's not the answer I was looking for." All the guns in the house were still back there in the bedroom.

Dina was acting like someone interrupted in the midst of an important phone call, subdividing her attention, talking in one direction and doing something else, invisibly, in another. "I got 'em both with that shocker thing. They can't move any more than Michelle."

"So . . . come out."

"I can't, until—"

Even Blitz thought this sounded like hooey. Lorelle overrode. "Dina, listen to me. I'm coming in if you're not coming out. Period."

"Just a—oh, all right, dammit, I can't . . ." She must have realized it sounded lame, or that Lorelle had a point. "Okay, *shit!*"

Dina appeared, holding Price's stun baton in one hand. She was half-undressed.

"Please lower that thing," said Lorelle. "In fact, put it on the floor."

Dina registered the baton as though it had just astral-projected into her grasp from another dimension. Her eyes widened with comprehension. "Oh. *Oh!* Right, sorry."

"Dina, what the fuck are you doing?" Lorelle indicated she should precede back into the bedroom, where a single candle flickered on the nightstand.

Price was nude, spread-eagled on his back across the bed, electroshock having seriously compromised his ability to pass a drunk test. He was still wearing his socks. Suzanne, equally insensate, had been rolled off onto the floor like a dirty quilt.

And Dina stood there, her expensive blouse open, her leather pants undone, shoes off. Her choker caught the fingertip of illumination from the candle and rendered it violet. Her breasts were so excellent that even Lorelle had to admire them—a graceful, modest swell, perfect contour, and dark nipples of zero-defect symmetry.

(Art would have liked them, too. Might have.)

Dina folded her arms, where normally she'd dive for another cigarette. She sighed as though exhaling smoke anyhow. Finally, she said, "You understand?"

"Yeah," said Lorelle.

Blitz watched her back while she rummaged through Price's clothing for high-caliber death dealers, or pointy sticks, for that matter. She collected the pillowcase into which Suzanne had gathered the small arms and searched up the pistol Suzanne had been pointing at her head, just a little while ago. Lorelle locked everything into the gun safe, holding back the nine-millimeter for herself, jamming it into her waistband in what Art had told her was known as a "Mexican carry."

"I'm taking this, too," Lorelle said of the stun baton. "You need a hand, call out. Just don't take too long."

Dina nodded. There were tears on her face, too, but they were hydrodynamically flawless, coming from those compelling eyes of green/amber. She left the door most of the way open.

Suzanne had had Price, and Dina felt betrayed. Michelle had had Price, and Lorelle had learned Dina's opinion on that pairing, back at the party. Now Dina was going to have Price, one way, if not another.

It took her about twenty minutes, give or take.

Lorelle finally rediscovered the painkillers in the kitchen, and swallowed a combination designed to ease her braincase but keep her alert. She put away another bottle of water, remembering what Luther had told her about stress.

"You need an aspirin, kiddo?" she said to the dog, unsure as to whether feeding one to an animal was recommended. Blitz's teeth were severely chipped on one side of his jaw; two were blackly cracked and oozing, and would soon fester into an impacted compound toothache. He lapped water gratefully from a big steel bowl in the wrecked kitchen. Animals rarely complained about their lot in the world.

Something smashed into the roof with enough force to suggest a large meteorite, shaking the entire house. Blitz wigged out and began barking.

"Christ." She had to grab back a skipped breath, and remind herself not to ask how it could all get worse.

Michelle stirred with a groan, but gravity kept her in her original position. A line of drool had escaped from her slack mouth. Her arms and neck were scared into gooseflesh. Good—if she revived, the cold would slow her down, too. Whatever had crash-landed on the roof was not obvious from inside the house. Maybe a chunk of the storm-dissected Spilsbury place. Maybe the corpse of Tobias. Maybe a fingernail from some pissed-off lesser god.

Hard spray assaulted the entire structure from the west. The sea was determined to make it all the way to the deck, and eat it. Blitz fretted in canine circles, now wary of sitting down.

It was half-past eleven, out in the world where time mattered. A minute or two later, Dina emerged from the bedroom. "He's all yours," she said.

That seemed chilling enough for Lorelle to ask, "Is he—?"

Dina's expression said, *Jeez, who do you think I am, some kind of murderer?*

Lorelle imagined Dina zapping Price in the gonads with the baton, and winced.

"But we might have a problem with our dear Suzanne. She managed to scuttle into the bathroom and lock the door."

Lorelle did not tarry to invent some kind of response to a question as thorny and perforated with loopholes as *Who do you think I am?* Up until today it had been a more innocent question, rhetorical.

● ● ● The door to the master bathroom was shut, and indistinct candlelight shone from the jamb's floor crack.

"Suzanne? It's Lorelle. Come on out."

It had gone exactly this way when Art had announced his intention to leave, no preamble, no conflict, no argument—just the Wind, ghosting him to more fulfilling ports. It wasn't that he didn't love her. In an oddly convex way, it had almost nothing to do with her. They had tried talk, and Lorelle had tried tears, and nothing would deter Art's resolve, and at some point where communication just vaporlocked and they had run out of words, she had sought sanctuary in the bathroom, door closed, as if that was all the point that needed to be made. Her chosen person, her partner, her mate, had decided that their exclusive deal was off, reneging on all the promises of love and one-and-only, the silly, dangerous words that people like Lorelle had the ill humor to take at face value, and seriously. Art had been a kind of predator, too, frustrated that she could not seem to perceive the clean sense of his honesty. What was she, stupid?

Flash-forward through the storm and madness of the last three days, and here she was, facing the same closed door again, with much the same sense of dread. In parallel to Derek's saga of make-believe, Lorelle had arrived at an unpredictable destination via violence, gunfire, and the worst convolutions of human nature. To tell this story would bring the easy accusation that it was all made up; heroic braggadocio designed to make her look good, and counter the shame of having lost her husband to the Wind.

"Don't hurt her," Dina said, resolving out of the darkness behind Lorelle with her ever-present cigarette, like the Roman slave whose purpose was to utter *sic transit gloria*. "Don't hurt Michelle, either, okay? I mean, any more than I did." She had not asked *What about me?* or *What the hell am I going to do?* or *Am I pretty?* She had asked Lorelle not to hurt them. That was her price for their pact.

Suzanne had evidently bypassed that deal memo. "I've got a gun," she said from within the bathroom. "Go away."

Art had also simply *gone away*, meaning, can't we just pretend this whole partnership thing was a mistake, and we're old college cafeteria buddies, and can't you just turn loose of the *love* thing and let me go, because I've got to move on? It was easy for him, to alter the blueprint and delete the essentials. He was still out there, a coast apart, changing things around to suit his immediate wants, while Lorelle had been struggling to keep things the same, working more and more maintenance on a stasis that was impossible.

It was no longer time to be waving guns around, and Lorelle hoped this psychic resolve would leak through the door, and infect Suzanne's train of thought . . . if she really did have a weapon, and wasn't bluffing outrageously from behind a closed door.

"You don't have a gun, Suzanne," Lorelle said. "Nobody has a gun." Dina's expression, her face also close to the door, advised that this might not be a ploy. She and Lorelle waited for the next answer (but they kept away from the center of the door, ruefully) while Lorelle battled the toxic brim of bad memory.

One night stood out in particular.

Art had slept on the sectional, leaving Blitz in uncomprehending dog conflict, forced to divide his watchdog time between the master in the living room and the mistress in the bedroom. It was not a scenario that accommodated easy slumber for any of them. Sometime during that endless night, Lorelle had thought of going to the (open) gun safe, choosing a weapon, and putting it to Art's head while he was in dreamland. It was important to note that she never progressed to the second stage of this fancy, which involved killing herself once the topic of Art was rendered moot by a gunshot. She could not bring herself to keep him, at least not that way.

Behind the barrier of the door, they could hear Suzanne weeping. Probably sitting on the toilet, head in hands, more or less the original way Lorelle had found Dina. On the bed, Price had all of Blitz's concentration. Price was still a floppy toy, but the dog was hurting, angry, and in no mood to cut slack for troublemakers.

"Suzanne, babe, we've got to go. Party's over." Dina, talking.

"It's not over," Suzanne said from inside. "Price promised. He fucking promised me."

"That's your version of the story, not his," said Dina. "He talked about how he was going to do both of us, but only on his terms, to get the things he wanted. That makes any deal null and void. No fun warranty. He would have beat me up, same as you, to get himself what he wanted."

Price had split Suzanne's lip, blackened her eye, battered her, dumped her on the roadside in the storm, and sacrificed her to the Bry-Guy . . . merely to bait the trap for Lorelle. Suzanne had let him do all this, afloat with dreams of a sort of commitment and bond that could transcend anything Price could get from the perfect Michelle, or the only-slightly-less-perfect Dina, or any of the other candidates at the party house. Suzanne viewed each blow and injury as affirmed love, and now she was being cheated.

Whatever Price had done to her, it could no longer be perfumed as *making love,* and she was understandably defensive, for all the wrong reasons.

"It's all fucked up," said Suzanne between sniffles. "Just let me go."

Lorelle spoke while advising Dina with her eyes in the cone of illumination from the flashlight. "That's exactly what Dina's going to do. She can get you out. Thanks to Dina, everyone will be safe from the storm."

"*No,* I don't believe you. I want Price to tell me."

"He doesn't give a damn about you," said Dina.

"You're just saying that because you want him for yourself," said Suzanne. "Fucking *cunt;* you're supposed to be my friend."

"Oh great, she's five," said Dina, lighting up what was apparently her last cigarette.

"Price has left the building," Lorelle said carefully. "Remember how you said it yourself—Michelle always wins. She's more important to him than you are—before, after, now. It's just us, now, and Dina wants to take you out of here."

In a breath of smoke, Dina said, "She's right, Suzanne; Price used us both. Neither one of us is good enough for him. We always knew that. Nobody will ever be enough for Price. Michelle will run out of gas herself, someday. I'd like to be there when it happens, just to watch her flame out. Can't we just get out of here? We can go home."

"We're not going to grab you, or blind you with the flashlight, or hurt you, Suzanne. We just want you to come out. Both of us."

Price went *ung* and tried to move. His bones lacked starch, and commanding them was a miserable failure because he had supplied—typically—one of the most powerful stun guns on the market. Having experienced its bite personally, Lorelle was aware of her own window for decision and action. Price's blood sugar parameters were the same as any other human's, but his metabolism was a question mark. For now, the fight was out of him, having abandoned ship.

"Talk to her." Lorelle spoke to the cherry of Dina's cigarette in the dark, the way she had when they first met. She needed to check on Michelle.

Bandage her head. On the way out she got a better look at Price, and saw glints of fresh blood on his chest.

Where Dina had carved her initials. Shallowly, but painfully; blood was pooled in his navel. Lorelle recalled Suzanne's mention of a knife in Dina's belt. Dina had gotten naked, slid around on top of Price to whatever oblique purpose she kept a secret, and then marked him. End of story.

Michelle's temple had colored with subdermal bleeding. Her pupils were shrunken, cowed. Her nostrils dilated in slow and unthinking breaths. Lorelle applied antibiotics and gauze by lamplight. This was Price's partner, his second, his familiar. The queen bee.

You and me together could overlord this entire party, she had told Lorelle . . . after she had had her go-round with Lorelle's husband. Her jolly secret.

Everybody has relationship problems, Lorelle thought. Even exotic creatures like Price and Michelle.

From the bedroom, Dina's voice assumed the register of steady, calm patter. She had been painted into a corner of circumstance like all of them. She needed to deploy her wiles to charm Suzanne out of the bathroom and end this awkward stalemate. Back in the world, this scenario might have been trivial, part of the day-to-day psychodrama all of Price's guests held as essential as nourishment, to make their existence important. Now it really *was* important, and Lorelle had left Dina to unlock the impasse. Not fair.

Whose house was this, anyway? If there were problems here, Lorelle had to take care of them.

She watched the unmoving, softly breathing form of Michelle. She short-listed her own hurts, thinking *excuses, excuses*. Then she bent to set Michelle upright, and do what she had to do. Since this was her house; *hers*, dammit.

● ● ● You try to dope out a syllabus for your life, thinking that fiction is better than reality, then what actually happens to you is so absurd that it wouldn't even make a coherent story. Nobody would buy it. Too many holes. No character arc. An absence of sympathetic players. That was why people read stories, watched movies, and lied to themselves a million times a day—they not only preferred the unreal, they craved it, needed it to replace the dreams they grew incapable of manufacturing in slumber. Dreams ended. Life just . . . stopped, one day.

Lorelle well and truly felt that she had *earned* this day of living, like a proto-woman scoring a kill and shelter in the wild. The hostile, uncaring cosmos-at-large was represented by the fulminating storm, ever closer, ever louder, a malignant giant that threatened the house with every breath. Players had come and gone, been protected and brutalized. Battle had been enacted. Her faithful canine companion stood by, on guard. That was the primal version of the whole story.

Dina and Suzanne appeared in the hallway. Suzanne looked

chastened and diminished, defeat rounding her shoulders. After an uncomfortable static moment she said, "Is the dog okay?"

Blitz stuck his snout into her hand. "Oh, sweetie, you're all bloody," she said. "You're a mess." Her eyes sought the fireplace, recalling the haven she had seen on her first visit. Home and hearth, dog and fire, warm clothes and sympathy.

"You really need to have a doctor look at you," Dina said.

"You *hate* me," Suzanne returned.

"No. We both said some nasty things, and I'm sorry. The truth is that Price doesn't deserve either of us. He gave everybody drugs that fucked up their heads. He just let the storm sweep into that house and didn't care what happened to anybody. You should have heard him— we were all disposable to him. Expendable, just for laughs. He talked about all of us like garbage. People *died* over there, Suze. And Price scooted away clean, like he always does, bailing out just in time."

"You want to send us away," Suzanne said to Lorelle. "Into that fucking storm."

"Because this house might collapse or get hit by a Force Ten wave any minute," said Lorelle. "Thanks to Price, it's not safe here anymore. I don't know what might happen."

"So then why aren't you coming with us?"

"I explained that before. It's my house. I have to stay."

Now Lorelle needed Dina to make a personal plea having to do with her own insanity. She moved to the kitchen and Blitz followed. The dog was wobbly and needed a vet, and the only need that superseded that was Lorelle's imperative to get everyone out, until it was just her and the dog, as it had been in the beginning. *Back to one,* as Derek would have said.

Dina leaned closer and spoke to Suzanne in a hushed whisper that Lorelle dearly wished to overhear, but she already knew the gist: *This chick is nuts, she wants to stay here and get killed by the*

*storm, she's out of her mind, and can we please get the hell out
of here?*

Suzanne took Dina's hand and Lorelle heard her say, "I'm sorry,"
one of her favorite expressions. Everybody was just sorry as fuck. It
was a sorry world. *Sorry* was the big emotional Band-Aid supposed
to fix all the hurts, when it merely covered them up. Art had been so
sorry. *Sorry* had not stopped him from driving Lorelle's whole life
off a cliff. Sorry, shrug, move on to tastier fields. It occurred to
Lorelle that Art had a few things in common with Price. *I can't
change what I feel; sorry.* Responsibility, commitment, obligation;
sorry beat them all in the grand game.

When Lorelle felt her status as a madwoman had been con-
cretized, she drifted closer to their circle of light.

"We'll need coats," said Dina.

"What about them?" Suzanne indicated their former host and
hostess.

"Michelle goes," said Lorelle. "Price stays. He's mine, now. And I
only need him for a couple of minutes."

"God, I let him *hit* me, I wanted him so bad . . ." Suzanne's voice
trailed away, out of ammo.

Dina took a position at a sisterly distance. "I wanted him the
same way. Look at us now."

"Yeah. Okay." She could somehow comprehend that everybody
was entitled to a shot at Price.

"That Humvee has a hard shell and weighs a couple of tons," said
Lorelle. "If you hit a snag in the road, just sit tight." It was the only
ride that could have brought them during the height of the storm;
just the walk to the driveway would be like groping through oil.

The air bludgeoned in, stinking of the sea. Michelle's perceptions were that of a drunk stuck in a revolving door; no fight there.
Lorelle and Dina got her installed and seat-belted.

Lorelle pulled Dina close enough to get her lips next to her ear inside the fluttering fur of the parka she had given her. "You did good. Thanks."

"Yeah. Good luck," Dina said, not really meaning it.

Nobody hugged anybody.

It took Dina a moment to wheel the big vehicle around in the crowded turnout of the driveway. A windblown tree had water-falled out of the sky to smash the roof of Bryan's Riviera into a vee. The Humvee's Industrial Revolution roar was barely audible above the storm. The taillights dwindled into the spume at a steady five miles per as the armored car commenced its slow trek back toward civilization. Lorelle was forced to fall back to the garage to watch; the lashing of the hurricane was just too brutal.

Lorelle tried to massage warmth back into her hands. "It's just you and me now, big guy," she said as she secured the garage door. It was almost midnight.

● ● ● "When I was in the eighth grade, I had the most gorgeous complexion. Fair; feminine, almost. Then, wham, hormones, zit apocalypse, and I might as well have used Spackle to seal the pits. I used to have this friend named Tito. He boiled everything in the world down to two opinions: *'That sucks,'* he'd say, or *'That's pretty cool.'*"

Price rambled like a boring inebriate at a party, eyes closed or drawn to dark corners of the room, seeing only the monsters that cats can see. His whole attitude had been slapped out of focus; he acted vaguely strung-out, jittery, nervous, keeping up patter against the noisy violence of the storm outside.

"You don't want to mess with me, bitch meat; you don't know

half the shit I've done." It was like he was doing different character voices.

His threat bore no danger. Price was naked on the sofa, turned toward the room on his left side like a beached dolphin, in roughly the same state as Lorelle had been after receiving a full-charge blast from the Viper stun baton. His bare feet felt as though they were freezing in the next county. He could not feel his arms. Nor his wrists, which were zip-stripped together with plastic so durable it would take a tow truck to snap them apart. The strips had been among the scattered tools in the garage. They would have been useful on the late Bryan.

"Tell me how you feel," Lorelle said, seated a safe distance away, drinking half a cup of instant soup. She let Blitz finish off the rest.

"I feel like ripping off your head and shoving it up your ass until you can see out your own neck while I stump-fuck you in the eyehole."

The snake in Lorelle's chest (*Art's* snake), sensed the presence of another of its own kind, assumed the S-curve for striking, and began to buzz.

"Michelle warned me I should stop playing with you," said Price. "Said I needed to get the people at the party out. When did that hoity-toity gash scrape together a conscience? Said get the numb fucks outta the cabana. Cabana blew away already, stupid. And now she doesn't want to play, because of you. Like she felt sorry for you or something, and the goddamn roof caves in, and she fucking *betrays* me right at the climax of our exciting episode. So, Art— Lorelle, I mean . . . did you at least get a piece of that action?"

She held firm and level. "No."

"You must be really disappointed. You know you were having a humid little fuck fantasy the minute you saw her. And that would've

275

been like, I don't know. Getting a fuck-telegram from your idiot husband. What a fucking tool *that* guy is. But you did make do with leftovers from my pussy drawer, didn't you? Low class."

Lorelle rather enjoyed Price in this mood. At least it was honest.

"That was some shit with that fucking dog. You think I don't know German? You're an imbecile, too." He craned his neck to shout at Blitz, his voice raw: "Blitz! *Fass, und reiss' ihm den Arsch auf!*"

Price had just ordered Lorelle's own dog to rip her ass open. Lorelle overrode: *"Nein! Tu das nicht! Vergiss es!"*

The dog got up, then sat back down, as though manipulated by an inept puppeteer. He snorted in disgust, opting to go with what he smelled rather than the nonsense he heard.

"I had this dog," said Price, still cresting between worlds. "I wouldn't talk to this bitch at school, Marlena, so she poisoned him. I found his body right in front of her house. I thought, *I'll do the lugs on her car so the wheels drop off.* Then I got pissed and slashed the tires. Pretty soon I was so mad that I just torched the fucker right there; lit a rag in the gas tank and *kaboom.* I did juvie time and I did grownup time, so don't think *you* can do anything to me."

The lanterns flickered and the storm outside stopped howling and started screaming. The house seemed to undulate against its rage. Lorelle sat across from her captive, unsure of how to proceed. Part of her just wanted to observe while Price thrashed about, raving. It was the same impulse that makes people stare at dangerous animals in captivity. Already maturing in Lorelle's head was the idea that no simple punishment would be suitable for Price, and who was she to be meting out justice, anyway? This warred with the demon that wanted to close Price's face by filling it with the shotgun barrel. The conflicting stew of emotions held at a volatile rolling boil.

Price had learned a lot about being accountable since the fiery indiscretions of his youth. He had not beaten anybody up, except

Suzanne, who gave her permission. He had not attacked Lorelle or her house; merely walked in an open door. He had not shot anyone. He had probably directed Suzanne and Michelle to strip Lorelle just to see her naked. *I didn't force anybody to ingest anything,* he had said. *I am not responsible for what adults decide to do on their own.* Except for his penchant for aiming people at one another and letting their worst self-interests wreak havoc, Price was unimpeachable. That was his talent. It would be evil unless it was compared to Lorelle's own recent hit list of conditional crimes, situational sins.

Damn it all, Lorelle was supposed to have the upper hand here, but Price had succeeded in making her feel guilty.

"People like you *need* people like me," said Price, almost whiny now.

"Really? The marks of the world need con men?"

"Ouch, that's harsh. C'mon, untie me and let's make up."

"I'm not available for dating, right now."

"So where does that leave us? C'mon, you're pretty smart . . . for a *girl.*"

She shook her head, not caring whether Price could see the gesture in the dark. Thus far she had kept the demon safely back, knowing Price was trying to piss her off, make her do something rash.

"Your wiring got crossed in the factory," said Lorelle. "You think anything's acceptable as long as you spin it to make your victims thankful that they didn't get burned *more.*"

"My victims? Oh, ho, ho, ho—excuse me, Supergirl, I'm not the gun nut running around holding people *hostage.*"

"You ruined my sofa. I might as well trash what's left, since you're lying on it."

Lorelle saw unexpected fear arc across the cockiness shining from Price's eyes, something that surprised Price as well. "You're not going to blow me away, Lorelle. You don't function like that."

277

"Maybe I've learned some new tricks from you."

"Doesn't turn you into a maniac. You just defended your turf. Look at me—I'm not a threat."

Look at me was what Price said whenever he was engaging his odd process of mesmerization. Using her name in that fake-intimate way. She let the tip of the stun gun drift within sniffing distance of Price's nose. "Yeah, you're right. Hope this doesn't go off *accidentally.*"

Price's grin was patently bogus, the fine print of his doubletalk as apparent as his exposed butt. "Just trying to see what you're made of, man."

"Remember when you were pontificating about how you were the real world?" said Lorelle, holding firm. She needed this sociopath to acknowledge her point of view. "You were right. You're the world— you're everything that's wrong with it, one of those parasites that always slips through the cracks and gestates inside the decay. You thrive when people are at their worst. You eat the lives you destroy and only get stronger."

"Wooo, I'd applaud if you'd untie my hands."

"Haven't you wondered, yet, about why you feel so disoriented—or do you normally cultivate suckers by babbling about your fucking dog and your madcap high-school days. What, is that supposed to make you appear more human?"

"What the fuck are you talking about? Baby, you're high."

"No, *you* are."

It was especially pleasing to watch the way the blood drained from Price's superior expression. His next utterance was low, deadly, too controlled—the old, recognizable version of Classic Price. "What?"

"When Bryan showed up here he had a snap case of your special little capsules," said Lorelle. "Luther had more in a prescription bottle I stashed in the bathroom. We took one apart. It was almost all black crystals—the shit you'd been feeding to your guests. And while you were dishragged, just now, I fed them to you, one at a time. All of them. Taste your own tongue and tell me I'm lying."

Guardedly, Price ventured, "You're fucking with me, right?"

"Nope. But in a minute, *you're* going to be fucking with you. What did Michelle call it—Mr. Hyde? What's the Hyde version of you, Price? What happens when your normal personality gets squashed underneath the things you don't want anyone to see? Did you product-test your party mix on yourself, or did you just sit back and observe?"

"That's not even remotely humorous, Lorelle."

It was fun to watch raw fear swell inside Price, for a change. "It's not meant to be funny, Price, my new best pal. I'm done amusing you. All I want is my due: I want you to get the fuck out of my house."

"You're kidding. Out in that? Stop it."

"You might say that *I want to see what you'll do,* but you know what? I don't even care. My responsibility for you ends where my door begins. And you know what else?"

Price shut his trap and watched her as she touched the stun baton to his buttock. He arched galvanically, biting his tongue.

"I can do this, is what else."

She dumped Price off the couch at a dead drag, by the wrists. It was not that far to haul him toward the deck door on the seaward side of the house.

"You ought to regain enough juice in your legs to run around like a naked idiot in the storm, but as I said, by that stage I don't care."

Blitz brought up the rear as Lorelle released Price to flop side-wise near the remains of the dining-room table, three feet from where Luther had died. She began to crank up the shutter manually, and frigid air careened in through broken door glass.

Price formulated inchoate objection; he could barely speak. The man had iron in him, for certain. "Don't do . . ." he croaked. "Want me to beg, I will . . ." He was crying. As Dina had cried, as Suzanne had, as Lorelle herself had when Art had abandoned her. Lorelle had swallowed too much instruction, lately, on the uselessness of weeping.

The ocean was gobbling the beach in a feeding frenzy, within sight of the partially collapsed deck now, far too damned close for any design specs or zoning slack. The breakers seemed ninety feet high, and Lorelle imagined the intrepid Solomon atop the biggest one, surfing his heart out. *Duuuude.*

"Please," Price mumbled, not even sounding like Price anymore. "Why . . . ?"

"Because I *can*. I learned this very valuable lesson from someone who lectured me about garbage." Lorelle had to yell against the storm, which stung and bit at her exposed face like a swarm of wasps; god knew how it felt on Price's flesh. "Before you throw something away, you always check one last time to see if the item has any residual worth. See you around, Price."

She hoisted him upright the way she might unfold a lawn chair, his face pressed to the jamb by her hand on the back of his neck.

His lips formed a bubble around the word *don't*. Wind shear popped it.

"Party time," Lorelle said. She let gravity take him. For personal reasons, she put a foot into his ass to help propel him off the deck. When she looked up, she could see a monster wave swelling toward the house, luminescent in the swirling chaos of night, like some radioactive mountain on the move, tipping over. Avalanche. She had to hurry to crank the door shutters back down, and skinned a knuckle in her haste. The shield was six inches from the floor when incoming storm surge plastered what was left of the beach like Godzilla stomping on a pagoda. The whole house shook when it hit. Seawater gushed through the breach and bowled her over. Blitz whimpered and went low, ears flat, as the house buckled and rocked.

It held, at least until the next wave.

"Come on, kiddo," Lorelle said to the dog. They pulled back to the hallway—walls within walls, per Luther's counsel. Walls which might not stop certain bullets, but which Art Latimer had designed specifically according to stress distribution criteria. In the guest bathroom, in the medicine cabinet, were Bryan's fancy little pillbox and Luther's prescription bottle. Both were still fully stocked.

MONDAY MORNING

The thing that had crash-landed on the roof in the middle of the night had been the hood from a cherry-red classic Cadillac, a '59, from the look of the contour. Lorelle never spotted the rest of any such car up-beach, down, floating in the sea, or hamstrung in the trees. The hood had destroyed the heart of the solar panel array and remained jutting upward like a shark fin. The last time Lorelle looked at her fortified beach home, the final thing she saw was the sparkling wedge of red hood, as clean as though polished by the rain.

Now Lorelle watched the drowned world, and its denizens: big, lazily moving tropicals in lurid, attenuated colors. Unreal, like dreamland creatures someone had made up. For all their beauty they appeared stunned or drugged; oblivious to the limits of their world, the way Price's intimates had seemed. The aquarium was their whole universe.

"Ms. Latimer? Find those cigarettes?" It was a nice young blue-smocked man whose tag advised his name might be René.

Lorelle turned her abstracted gaze from the huge display tank—a window to that otherworld—and tried to recalibrate to the here and now. "Oh, yeah—two doors down at the Kwik-Stop". She had somehow made her return trip—twenty feet on the sidewalk, easy—

last a whole smoke, a 100. She appreciated the concept of "a cigarette's worth of time."

"Dr. Coulter says to come on back."

The bloated, gasping fish in the aquarium ignored Lorelle's intrusive god-like judgment and continued paddling about, perhaps thinking of predating on one another.

Blitz was sitting up attentively on the stainless-steel exam table, his hindquarters splayed to one side as though he was lounging.

"Tried to catch something that caught you instead, eh, boy?" said Dr. Coulter, ruffing Blitz's chest. Coulter was a barrel-shaped man with huge, callused hands and a fatherly sort of handlebar mustache. He wore very modest bifocals that were overwhelmed by the size of his head, wire frames that had the effect of lightly pinching a melon in midsection.

"This guy needs what's called a vital pulpotomy on that lower first molar; that's fancy talk for the prelude to a possible root canal. I just cleaned out all the junk and spackled it up with temporary fillings. That fourth premolar will have to go, and in a couple of days, too, before it impacts. We're not equipped here for proper endodontic procedures, so you'll have to see my guy in the city right away. Posthaste. Pronto. Because otherwise, this big faker is going to be in a world of hurt."

"*Du bist halt mein Bester Hund,*" Lorelle said, letting Blitz get a good snort of her hand. "*Guter Hund.*" To the doc she said, "Faker?"

"Yes. Animals prefer to suffer in silence if they're hurt. They rarely let on to the degree of hurt unless it's unbearable. I need you to call up my recommended specialist; his name's Dr. Beschorner. He can diagnose oral pathology and perform a proper dental prophylaxis. This guy is going to lose at least two teeth. But Dr. B can do proper X rays, use a laser for dental surgery, do proper restoration on the damaged teeth, and bond the loose ones up with dental acrylic, proper." Dr. Coulter used the word *proper* a lot; it was a comforting, specific, on-target word for him. He cocked one eyebrow and his expression was comically similar to that of a cartoon dog. "You're staring at me like the next thing you're going to say is, *christ, how much is this going to cost me?!*"

"I don't care what it costs," said Lorelle. "It'll get done, and within a day, if I can help it along." She had her petty cash, and plastic—plenty.

"I won't lie," said Coulter. "It can be pricey. Figure a couple grand to do it right. If they have to put him under, make sure they have isoflurane gas anesthesia. Some places use acupuncture to ease pain during surgery."

"*Dog* acupuncture?"

"Sure, why not? Canine dentistry is a wider-spread specialty than it was, say, twenty years ago. You have to take your dog to a separate facility, but it's more focused. Proper."

Coulter showed Lorelle a couple of different medications, already labeled for Blitz. More pills in bottles, meant to change things. "Now, first, remember that those temporaries will only last a day or two. Dogs can't help biting hard on things, even when it hurts. He's lucky his jaw's not broken. Keep an eye on those carninasal molars."

Now it was Lorelle who made the confused dog-face. Coulter clarified: "The broken teeth. Don't feed him anything crunchy or hard. He'll be in some pain, but like a headache."

"Can I give him an aspirin?"

"Bad idea. His system's not set up to handle it. Keep giving him the antibiotics; it's important not to miss a dose. You look like you've been through a little adventure yourself."

She grimaced. Her homemade bandages needed changing. "The hurricane," she said.

"Up north? Jeez, that was a bitch of a bear up there. You see it?"

"I was right in the middle of it."

"You're lucky to be standing here, then. It was all over the news."

As Luther had said, *People who watch the news don't see nothing.* TV screens were another form of inside-out aquarium. All anyone would care about is that a storm had whipped through the Pacific Northwest, and all anyone would pay any attention to was whether any damage had been done to San Francisco. The aftermath had been tough to describe; the closest Lorelle could get was her impression that the ocean and the land had tried to swap places, and failed catastrophically. Even the inland highway had been backed up and strewn with dead animals, car parts, trees, and swatches of buildings or their component material. Helicopters hovered, videotaping powerline flashes. The twisted rootwork of exposed gas and water pipes offered their pretzel configurations to the cameras. Scything winds had left Half Moon Bay resembling Dresden after the firebombing. Enough salt water had blown past town to start killing much of the flora that decorated the bedroom community sections closer to the ocean. Rumor held that even the pumpkin harvest had been jeopardized. The anomalies of the storm's body count and devastation totals in the millions would be tilted against the believe-it-or-don't statistics of who or what had survived against odds that would keep medics and storm chasers marveling for weeks.

Lorelle could have been vacuumed away to oblivion any of the times she had sortied out into the blackness and blow. She remembered reading the story of Baby Aleah, an infant who had been sucked up into the funnel cloud of a killer tornado in Oklahoma in 1999, snatched from the arms of her grandmother, only to be discovered unharmed in the woods. The grandmother had been crushed. As an observer at the scene had noted at the time, "Some of the most vulnerable survived."

Which meant that Price had as good a chance at life as anybody else in the catastrophe. File closed.

While escaping Point Pitt, Lorelle had not been able to resist cruising the party house. The white modernist structure was gone, as if teleported from the earth by a wizard. Rather, it had been reconfigured. Puzzle pieces of it were strewn everywhere. Nobody was there, picking through the meager remnants. Zero partygoers.

"What was it like up there?" said Dr. Coulter. "Were you there for the whole thing?"

"Yes."

What had it been like? How could she enumerate the things that had happened without stumbling over the loose ends that had piled up to ambush her, including death, drugs, and madness? Impossible. To replay the storm in terms of numbers? Futile. This natural disaster had been nowhere near as apocalyptic as the "super outbreak"— a massive chain of 148 interlocked tornadoes that had laid waste in a two-thousand-mile swath from Alabama to Canada in 1974. Hundreds of people were trapped beneath the remnants of their own homes. Lorelle's home had acted as a different kind of trap.

Better to deflect Coulter's question altogether: "I wouldn't be talking to you now if it weren't for my dog saving my ass."

"Well, he'll live." Coulter kept stroking Blitz's back and flanks as he spoke, his tone working to calm the animal. Sleight of sound. Vets could disburse this talent at will, like mild hypnosis—all the good vets could, anyway, thought Lorelle.

Blitz had been quaking with exhaustion and weakness when she had cradled him out to the Jaguar's backseat—inadequate for humans, perfectly sized to a prone, sleepy, injured dog. Lorelle could guess how her buddy, *das Wuschelchen,* felt: Blown out, used up, rubbed raw, cut and sundered by stress, tapped to fumes, damaged and leaking, ready to quit now. The havoc wreaked on the Jag by the Bry-Guy turned out superficial; dents and scores. Wild hits. The worst handicaps were the busted headlamp, the web-starred windshield. The challenge was clearing the garage, clearing the drive, and navigating on the obstacle-course roadways out of Point Pitt in a low-slung sports car.

Add six hours to the trip, minimum. A lot of beeping heavy machinery conflicted the roads with their dinosauric clearance of junk. Orange flags, hazard cones, restriction tape, delays.

Lorelle witnessed the leavings of the storm through the surreal quartzite perspective of smashed safety glass. The world she saw was a puppet's shadow box of disaster, enclosed by the borders of her windshield. The tilted cup of the Sundial dish was abrim with jetsam, but the structure had stood fast. It was practically the only fabrication on the whole beach that was still upright, or occupying its original space.

"Could I trouble you for the use of your phone?" said Lorelle. "I've gotta call ahead." Coulter directed her and René assisted, with his impermeable smile. Lorelle had left her cell phone, dead battery and all, behind.

Wading through normal, everyday shit was proving to be more difficult than she had anticipated. Having a mundane, chitchat conversation with the veterinary staff or simply entering a number for a phone call had become tasks abruptly beyond her competence. When your existence ceased being a matter of the next heartbeat, or which way a gun was pointed, it was tough to summon the next dull numeral in a sequence or beckon the next boring, workaday phrase. She remembered the easy banter she had shared with Rocko, back at the Toot 'N Moo, a long, long time ago. To where had that version of Lorelle been abducted?

By contrast, locating Art Latimer in New York City had been a snap. A relief, when she had made the first call and spoken to a voice she knew, having dreaded the contact for so long, on top of a new phobia that the first voice she would hear would be Price— resurrected, back for the sequel, having outfoxed the world again.

Her ex sounded happy to hear from her. She had to explain what had happened to the house. She let him down easy, terming it a failure of contract, instead of design. A write-off as R&D, another demolishment of the storm's fury.

She left out the part about the jerry cans of gasoline she had liberally sprinkled around, like charcoal starter. She had ignited a single weatherproof match (*strike anywhere*). With the alarms and dousing systems disabled and turned off, the fire burned until the ocean had put it out.

With Blitz reinstalled in the backseat, convalescing, Lorelle continued to pick her way eastward, the roads bettering as she went. She'd pass Las Vegas next. Where waited the fabled Dr. B, for Blitz.

In New York, Art awaited her, whatever that was going to ultimately mean. Pulling against this was the voice in her head that advised her to just let it all go. There was no hidden meaning or shady subtext. Just as she had thought in the Jeep, driving away from Price's party house a lifetime ago, *It was what it was, and the story had ended. The End. Next page.* All of us are all the sum total of the stories we tell, and the stories told about us. Sometimes the stories we tell about ourselves are the worst lie.

End of story, Lorelle thought, keeping a steady course and trying to concentrate on what was to be. *The End. Next page.*

t h a n k - y o u s . .

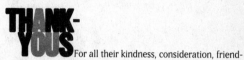

THANK-YOUS For all their kindness, consideration, friend-
ship, inspiration, and outright, hardcore help, I'd like to thank and acknowledge my
Aussie paladins—Alex Proyas, Andrew Mason, Topher Dow, Matthew Dabner and Lizzie
Bryant; Mr. Michael Boatman; the stalwart and always reliable Klaus Beschorner (for the
dog talk); Anthony Bourdain; Frank Darabont; editress Sarah Durand; the Dust Brothers
(Michael Simpson and John King); John and Peter Farris; David Fincher; Kerry Fitzmau-
rice (in memory of the long-lost Leon); Virginia Guilford and Thomas Moylan; Paula
Guran; Melissa Mia Hall; Shen Chuan (martial science); master Joe Lansdale; Lydia
Marano and Arthur Cover of Babbage Press; Chuck Palahniuk; gun guru Bret Paul (who
posited the whole "limping bunny in the meadow" thing); Kaz Prapuolenis and Linda
Marotta; the Mad Scots of Noblesgate—Andrew Abbott, Russell Leven, Mark Kermode &
Co; Darren McKeeman of *Gothic.net*; Keith Rainville; Mark Rance and the wily bunch at
Three-Legged Cat; Jeff Rovin; William Schafer and the too live crew at Subterranean
Press; the Schows—John, Eloisa, Tina, Elizabeth, and James, and in memory of my dad,
the Good Major (who died in 2001 at age eighty); John Scoleri, webmaster supreme; my
mutant brother Lew Shiner; go-get-'em reps John Silbersack and Scott Miller of Trident
Media Group; Peter Straub (for badgering me to write another novel), and Susan Straub
(for the home away from home); Tony Taylor, Bill Fraker, and the late Conrad Hall for
the wild *Incubus* weekend; ace finance wizard Douglas Venturelli; Mehitobel J. Wilson
(for hours and hours); Douglas and Lynne Winter; Bernie Wrightson, for all the midnight
runs; Boaz Yakin; Jane Yolen, for writing *The Girl Who Loved the Wind* . . . and everyone else who helped me make it through a rather traumatic change of calendar.

289